Rejoice Evermore
in the
Presence of the Lord

Rejoice Evermore
in the
Presence of the Lord

C. Thambi Simon

ISPCK
2019

Rejoice Evermore in the Presence of the Lord — published by the Rev. Dr. Ashish Amos of the Indian Society for Promoting Christian Knowledge (ISPCK), Post Box 1585, Kashmere Gate, Delhi-110006.

ISBN: 978-93-88945-31-8

Laser typeset by

ISPCK, Post Box 1585, 1654, Madarsa Road, Kashmere Gate, Delhi-110006
• *Tel:* 23866323

e-mail: ashish@ispck.org.in • ella@ispck.org.in
website: www.ispck.org.in

Why must I weep when others sing?

'To test the deeps of suffering.'

Why must I work while others rest?

'To spend my strength at God's request.'

Why must I loose while others gain?

'To understand defeat's sharp pain.'

Why must this lot of life be mine

When that which fairer seems is Yours?

'Because God knows what plans for me

Shall blossom better in darkness;

Just to feel Your hand and follow You.'

-- An Unknown Poet

Contents

Abbreviations ... xi

Introduction ... xiii

Chapter 1
Unleash My Insight Vision ... 1

Chapter 2
Primary Steps to Enter In ... 21

Chapter 3
Tuning to Insightful Intuition ... 46

Chapter 4
The Power of *Rhema* ... 52

Chapter 5
Practicing Quiet Time ... 61

Chapter 6
Vision in Prayer Lives ... 75

Chapter 7
Biblical Patterns for Approaching God ... 100

Chapter 8
How Can I Know for Sure it is God's Voice? ... 125

Chapter 9
More Thoughts on Prayer ... 136

Chapter 10
The Accuser and the Comforter ... 147

Chapter 11
Incubating only Christ and Striving to Grow Spirituality ... 165

Chapter 12
Seeing God in the Past ... 173

Chapter 13
From Fear to Faith ... 179

Chapter 14
From Guilt to Hope ... 187

Chapter 15
From Anger to Love ... 196

Chapter 16
From Inferiority to Identity ... 206

Chapter 17
From Depression to Joy ... 216

Chapter 18
Victory through Death and Resurrection ... 228

Chapter 19
Seeing God in All ... 235

Chapter 20
Living Tuned to the Lord ... 248

Chapter 21
Joy and Pain of Suffering ... 256

Appendix ... 263

Abbreviations

NASB   New American Standard Bible, by The Lockman Foundation: 1995 ed.

KJV   King James Version, by Thomas Nelson Inc.

NKJV   New King James Version, by Thomas Nelson Inc. 1982 ed.

NIV   New International Version, by Tyndale House Publishers Inc. & Zondervan Publishing House

Amp. Bible   The Amplified Bible, Expanded Edition 1987, by Zondervan Corporation & The Lockman Foundation.

Gen	Genesis	Matt	Matthew
Ex	Exodus	Mk	Mark
Num	Numbers	Lk	Luke
Deut	Deuteronomy	Jn	John
Josh	Joshua	Rom	Romans
Jud	Judges	1 Cor	First Corinthians
1 Sam	First Samuel	2 Cor	Second Corinthians
2 Sam	Second Samuel	Gal	Galatians

1 Chro	First Chronicles	Eph	Ephesians
2 Chro	Second Chronicles	Phil	Philippians
Ps	Psalms	Col	Colossians
Prov	Proverbs	1 Thess	First Thessalonians
Isa	Isaiah	2 Thess	Second Thessalonians
Jer	Jeremiah	1 Tim	First Timothy
Ezek	Ezekiel	2 Tim	Second Timothy
Dan	Daniel	Heb	Hebrews
Mic	Micah	Jas	James
Hab	Habakkuk	1 Pet	First Peter
Zech	Zechariah	2 Pet	Second Peter
Mal	Malachi	1 Jn	First John
		Rev	Revelation

Introduction

J oy is the flower of love, the very loveliness of love. A joyless Christian is a contradiction of terms. Christ pledged himself to impart joy, His own untainted joy: *"My joy may be in you, and that your joy may be made full"* (Jn. 15:11). Such a divine joy springs from a realization of forgiveness which comes as a result of abiding in Christ. Divine joy is contentment and satisfaction with God and with His dealings.

Joy is intensely personal and impressively corporate. It is dynamic and serene, explosive and gentle, manifesting itself in blazing glory or profound contemplation. Very often we are caught in paradoxes when speaking of the essence of joy.

Joy is not divorced from sorrow and pain, and therefore it is not artificial and not superficial, but springs up from the passion and glory of Jesus. It can only be experienced and communicated in its profound depth and high ecstasy when painted upon a larger canvas of the totality of human existence. The light and glory of joy is seen in all its beauty only when the darker shades and tones of sorrow and suffering are contained within the canvas. Joy is more accessible, when the story of pain and sorrow are told alongside it. The empty tomb takes away our empty gloom. We have an Easter morning to celebrate our faith, and that means there is always a reason to rejoice. Those who can sing in the face of death can sing in the face of everything.

St. Irenaeus, martyred at Lyons around CE 200, wrote: "The glory of God is man fully alive, for man's true life is the vision of God." Irenaeus exemplified the gospel in his life and thus encountered joy. And that joy encompasses the whole of human life, the totality of human experience, with all its problems and pain, with all its loveliness and ecstasies. Even martyrdom could be counted all joy! To be fully alive is the experience of joy, and such an experience culminates in the vision of God.

Dr: William Barclay claimed that joy is the distinctive atmosphere of Christian life. "Whatever the ingredients of Christian experience," he said, "and in whatever proportions they are mixed together, joy is one of them." Joy is always present in the heart of a true Christian. It may not always be felt or recognized, but it is always there. And eventually it will break through to the surface, no matter what our situation or our circumstances.

We can better understand the supernatural joy if we distinguish it from the pleasures of life with which it is sometimes confused. Divine joy is quite different from pleasure or happiness. Other faith believers can experience pleasure and happiness, but cannot experience supernatural joy. Indeed, worldly people often pride themselves on knowing how to experience pleasure. Yet pleasure and Christian joy are different. Pleasure depends on circumstances. Christian joy, however, is completely independent of circumstances. It has no relationship to the transient settings of the life, and therefore it is not a victim of the passing day. It is there in the believer even when strength and health and friends are gone – when circumstances are not only unkind but savage. Out of all miracles I have witnessed in my life, none is more wonderful than seeing Christ's exuberant joy burst forth in those who are caught up in pain or persecution. That joy can prove triumphant is not just a theory but a glorious fact.

The only joy that can be communicated is that which is real, which is experienced. The reason why there is so much perplexity when real problems of suffering, sickness and bereavement overtake Christians is that they have tended to confuse emotional excitement and natural enthusiasm with the joy of which Jesus speaks. I am not saying that emotion is not part of religion or that enthusiasm is not part of

Christian life. My own human and Christian life have suffered both. But I have had to learn, through some bitter experiences of loneliness, darkness and pain that the roots of joy are in God and that such joy can be known alone, in those dark places of human desolation. I do not promise you a new set of circumstances in the future if you follow Christ in true sense. Indeed, you may experience many difficulties and disappointments, perhaps even a greater deal of pain. But I can promise you, if you keep your eyes on Jesus, and make him the main focus of your attention, and then whatever happens, the Holy Spirit will help you rise above your circumstances and reflect Christ's characteristics – the characteristics that shone out from him when he was here on earth with flesh and blood: love, peace, joy, and gentleness.

This earths the experience of joy within creation itself, giving priority to life, light and love which are at the heart of the created life. The cosmos is alive and dancing, and that movement, rhythm, pattern and design are the gifts of God's continual creation as he communicates in the material world.

When I first turned my mind to write about joy in Christian life and experience, I turned to the Bible, this being the source where our own experiential thinking is clarified, corrected and given new dimensions of experimentation. And I was embarrassed by the riches of joy, exhilaration and sheer vitality found in both the Old and New Testaments.

But another fact about bringing one's thoughts and experience to the scrutiny of Scripture is that it imparts objectivity to one's thinking that is salutary. It is an easy matter to select quotations, themes and stories of joy, assurance and creative vitality to sustain the argument that joy is inherent in the created order. But through the Scriptures we may be faced with pain and sorrow, with complaint and anger, with disappointment, sickness, and death. There are Psalms which groan and cry to God because of the frailty of human nature, the prosperity of the wicked and the seeming negligence of God and his indifference to the tragic human situation. And these I could not ignore. They are equally part of our human experience, and it is not possible to consider on the themes of joy and glory without a clear recognition of the sorrows and misery of humankind.

God himself was suffering with grief and pain of the world. The heart of God *always* suffered, the tears of God *always* fell, and the blood of God was *eternally* shed for the sins and the sorrows of the world.

But there is another side to it. Looking back on the path that Jesus trod, the theology of the Epistle to the Hebrews portrays him as entering the joy of the redeemed even as he descended into the abyss of darkness and death. He not only endured the cross but glorified it (Heb. 12:2). This was no superficial or transient joy for the Man of Sorrows who was acquainted with grief. But it was the joy of consummation.

The very word redemption was used of the buying back of the life of a slave in the market place, and one can imagine the sheer joy of redemption in the experience of a slave thus liberated. The redeeming power of the cross was born out of suffering.

If that was true, then the compassion of God overflowed in love towards suffering humanity, and it was expressed primarily in the incarnate life of our Lord Jesus Christ, for as gospel of Matthew says about healing ministry of Jesus, quoting the prophet Isaiah:

"He himself took our infirmities and carried away our diseases" (Matt. 8:17).

In his life, death, and resurrection, Jesus made himself available to human need in all its manifestations. It meant that we can come to him in all our human vulnerability, receiving his healing and compassion, and become a channel of his healing power to other lives also.

There is immense joy in the assurance of sins forgiven and reconciliation with God through the redeeming work of our Lord Jesus Christ. And there is immense joy in the experienced awareness of God in all the beauty, harmony and balance of the created world. Yet our salvation is not yet complete – fullness of joy is not yet, and one of the marks of a redeemed humanity in its present state is the sense of incompleteness and yearning for full redemption. We feel this most when offering praise and adoration to the Almighty God for the beauty of creation and redemption.

The compassion of God is at work from the very beginning of this world. The source of all joy is the triune love of God. Love is beautifully expressed in the penitential psalm *Miserere* (Psa. 51:10-12). When we affirm the inheritance of our humanity, in the depths of its pain and the height of its joy, we become aware of spiritual vitality in our experience. The risen Christ promised the gift of the Holy Spirit to the Pentecostal Church, and on the day of Pentecost the promise was fulfilled in the outpouring of power, love and joy. Such was the effect of the mighty rushing wind and tongues of flame symbolising the Spirit's power, that the disciples were full of rejoicing and proclamation. Such was their spiritual inebriation that the onlookers and critics thought they were full of sweet wine.

Wherever the Holy Spirit was in evidence there was power, liberty, love, and joy. Spiritual joy is not only one of the Pentecostal gifts but is also a fruit of the Spirit's indwelling (Rom. 14:17). And while writing to the Roman Christians Paul says: *"May the God of hope fill you with all joy and peace in believing, so that you will abound in hope by the power of the Holy Spirit"* (Rom. 15:13).

The charismatic gifts in the early church were manifestations of this Pentecostal Spirit, and wherever the gifts abounded, there joy abounded too. In tongues and prophecy, in healing and discernment, in all the graces of the Spirit's manifestations there was joy and gladness of heart. These are the gifts which continue in Christ's church today, and wherever there are loving, Spirit-filled Christians, they communicate infectious joy, contagious enthusiasm and radiant gladness of heart. Human joy, which is rooted in righteousness and compassion, and often overflows in an infusion of spiritual inebriation, finds God as its very source. Joy is the upsurge and overflow of the divine life in nature and in human experience.

If any believer is indwelt by the Holy Spirit and if he is constantly under his guidance, he will be filled with joy, and those around him will become aware of God's living presence. It is a divine gift and comes only from the union with God in Christ. As such it can abide, even in days of darkness and difficulty, giving cheerful courage in the face of disappointment, and an inward serenity and confidence in sickness and suffering. Those who possess it can be content, for Christ's sake, with weakness, contempt, persecution, hardship and frustration; for when they are weak, the joy of God's strength is made known.

Let me again emphasise that the primary requirement of experiencing fullness of divine joy in human life is to keep close communion with the Lord Jesus Christ in everyday life. To be guided by him every day, every hour, and every minute we must be able to build up a two-way communication and be counselled by him.

We often live in a box of rationalism we have built for ourselves. Our Christian life has been always governed by rules and principles for successful living that we have understood through our study of the Scriptures. Our prayers are monologues, never managing to break through to "the other side of silence," to a spiritual world of *two-way communication* with the Lord Jesus Christ. But I always believed that Christians should be able *to generate a communication channel* directly with the Creator. We have the privilege of being aware of his presence and of being called to reciprocate it; that is, we are called to be present to God as God is present to us.

God's presence is realised by a prayerful life and constant communion with the Lord. Jesus clearly stated that *"My sheep hear my voice."* Yet no matter how hard I tried; I never could hear that *voice* speaking to me. I read books of eminent authors. I studied the word. My searching seemed to be in vain. It seemed to come so easily and normally to those who knew the voice of God within them.

But the Lord had seen the desire of my heart to know his voice, a desire that could not be crushed even by repeated failures and disappointments. He gradually led me to the right resources to teach me the skills I needed: inner stillness; spontaneity; and vision. When all the pieces were in place, I realized that I had received much more than I expected. I was *looking for a voice*; I *found a Person*. I was *looking for guidance*; I *found a Shepherd*. I was *looking for the will of God*; I *found a relationship* with the Son of God.

Since I have been able to discern the voice of the Lord in my heart, I have moved into a life of sweet fellowship with Jesus. I no longer live under human-made *precepts*, for now I am governed by *love*. Rules have given way to relationship.

Permit me to draw your attention to St: Paul's second letter to Corinthians, chapter three, wherein he discusses that unconverted Jews, who rest their spiritual hope on keeping the law rather than on the grace of God manifested in Jesus Christ, have a veil over their minds. However, when anyone turns to Christ this veil is automatically removed. We can then stand before the Saviour with no obstruction between us and him, and thus reflect like mirrors the glory of the Lord. The Amplified Bible words 2 Cor. 3:18 like this,

> "And all of us, as with unveiled face, continue to behold as in a mirror the glory of the Lord, are constantly being transfigured into His very own image in ever increasing splendour and from one degree of glory to another; this comes from the Lord Who is the Spirit."

In the new dispensation of grace, God gives us more than a piece of chiselled stone (the Ten Commandments); he gives us his presence, and the law is written on our hearts. Eugene Peterson paraphrases 2 Cor. 3:18 in this way:

> "...when God is personally present, a living Spirit, that old, constricting legislation is recognized as obsolete. We are free of it! All of us! Nothing between us and God, our faces shinning with brightness of his face."

The relationship between law and grace is puzzling to many Christians. Often, I have been asked, "Is the law of God still binding on a Christian?" The answer is, "Yes and No." "No" in the sense that our acceptance by

God does not depend on us keeping the law, and "Yes" in the sense that we are expected to live by the law. A Christian has *"died to the Law"* (Gal. 2:19). Does this mean that the believer is at liberty to break the Ten Commandments as he wants? No, he lives a holy life, not through the fear of the law, but out of love to the One who died for him. Christians who desire to be under the Old Testament books of the law (Genesis through Deuteronomy) as a pattern of behaviour cannot touch the law in one point without being responsible to keep it completely. Pharisaical legalism was not the keeping of all details of the law, but the hollow sham of keeping laws externally, to gain merit before God, while breaking them inwardly. It was following the letter of the law while ignoring its spirit. The Old Testament law is a unit; submission to it cannot be selective. If anybody is seeking to be justified by keeping the law, then he is severed from Christ as his only possible hope of righteousness; he has *"fallen from grace."* (Gal. 5:4). The only way we can *"live to God"* is by being dead to the law. The law could never produce a holy life; God never intended that it should. Let me put it this way: obedience to the law does not lead to salvation, but salvation leads to obedience to the law. Those who have trusted Christ does not observe law as a means of obtaining salvation, but because he loves his Saviour. C. F. Hogg and W. E. Vine express it clearly in their *Epistle of Paul the Apostle to the Galatians:* "Christ must be everything or nothing to a man; no limited trust or divided allegiance is acceptable to him. The man who is justified by the grace of the Lord Jesus Christ is a Christian; the man who seeks to be justified by the works of the law is not." God's way of holiness is explained by St. Paul in his epistle to Galatians:

> *"I* [Paul] *have been crucified with Christ* [in him I have shared his crucifixion]; *it is no longer I who live, but Christ* (the Messiah) *lives in me; and the life I now live in the body I live by faith in* (by adherence to and reliance on and complete trust in) *the Son of God, Who loved me and gave Himself up for me."* (2:20, Amp. Bible).

The believer is identified *"with Christ"* in His death. Not only was he crucified on Calvary's cross, I [the believer] was *"crucified"* there as well

– in him. This means the end of me seeking to merit or earn salvation by my own efforts and no more am I a sinner in the sight of God. God's blessing has never been earned but has always been freely given. This is true as to my standing before God; but it should be true as to my behaviour. The Saviour did not die for me in order that I might go on living my life as I choose. He died for me so that from now on he might be able to live his life in me. *"The life I now live in the body I live by faith in* (by adherence to and reliance on and complete trust in) Jesus Christ. Christian character is produced by the Holy Spirit, not by the mere moral discipline of trying to live by the law. The indwelling Holy Spirit produces Christian virtues in a believer's life. A Christian lives by continued dependence on Christ, by yielding to him, by allowing Christ to live his life in him. Living by the promptings and power of the Holy Spirit is the key to conquering sinful desires. Thus, believer's rule of life is Christ and not the law. He lives a holy life, not out of fear of punishment but out of love to *"the Son of God, who loved"* him *"and gave Himself up for"* him.

The law says in effect, "Do this and live" (Gal. 3:12). Faith tells us, "Believe in Christ, and live" (Gal. 3:11). The motive has changed – and that is where the difference lies.

John Stott raises the point that perhaps one of the reasons why the gospel is not appreciated in the way it should be is because there is not enough emphasis on why God gave the law in the first place. He comments, "Not until the law has arrested and imprisoned us will we pine for Christ to set us free. Not until the law has condemned and killed us will we call upon Christ for our justification and life. Not until the law has driven us to despair of ourselves will we ever believe in Jesus. Not until the law has humbled us will we turn to the gospel to raise us to heaven." He further warns: "When Christianity is turned into a bondage to rules and regulations, its victims are inevitably in subjection, tied to the apron strings of their teachers."

Since the time I am in immediate contact with my Lord, my whole life has changed. My personality, my family and my meagre ministry have all been altered by the wisdom and compassion of Jesus now available to me. My heart has been convinced of the love God has for me and I will never be the same.

The deep love God expressed for his children and his great desire to communicate with each one compelled me to write down the blessing I was showered upon. I wish to share the love of the Lord that every Christian would enjoy and the blessed communion with him that I am blessed with. I began to find enjoyment in sharing with others what I knew, how to hear God's voice in the heart of the believer and breakthrough in a two-way communication with him. Let many more joyfully enter this new way of living.

The Church must abundantly seek to hear God's voice and see God's vision in all her activities. The time for mourning has passed. The moment of renaissance and restoration is upon us. The prophets calling for repentance have done their part of work. The Church must awaken to her responsibilities and her kingdom authority. The kingdom of this world shall indeed become the kingdom of our Lord and of his Christ. He shall reign through us in every aspect of life on this earth.

When the impairment of our souls cries out for help, what a blessing it is to turn to our Wonderful Counsellor (Isa. 9:6)! When our lives are crippled by the bondages of fear and doubt, thank God for our Wonderful Counsellor! When the world can only point to our past as a reason for the brokenness of our present, we yet have hope in our Wonderful Counsellor! Our heavenly Father does not expect us to live our lives on our own. He has graciously placed us within a body, a family, of like believers. He commands us to exhort, encourage, love and nurture one another. But no human can provide the grace to overcome faulty or sinful habits. No human can pour the balm of Gilead into a broken soul. Counsellors who truly bring lasting change and deep healing are those who know how to lead the suffering one to the feet of Jesus where his touch makes all things new.

This small book does not contain the solutions to all your problems. It does not provide a formula for healing. It does not give fool proof methods of restoration. This is truly a large canvas, and though I am unable to deal adequately with it, I have glimpsed enough of it to set me alight with joy and with pain, and if I can share some of my glimpses, it will establish both the writer and the reader in the fullness of divine joy which is here and in eternity.

Right living results from right thinking. If a person's thought-life is pure then his life will be pure. On the other hand, if a person's mind is a fountain of corruption, then you can be sure that the stream that issues from it will be filthy also. And we should always remember that if a person thinks an evil thought long enough, he will eventually do it.

What this little book suggests is that the root cause of the majority of difficulties in our lives is losing sight of God and His working in our lives. Jesus said, *"Blessed are the pure in heart, for they shall see God"* (Matt. 5:8). Conversely, it may be assumed that contamination of the heart prevents us from seeing God and that seeing God purifies and heals the heart. Therefore, the message of this book is encouragement to you to meet with the Wonderful Counsellor, experience his touch of compassion, and be made whole. It is only through divine encounter that our lives are changed forever.

It is my prayer that the Lord will anoint this book, using it to bring people like me into a new dimension of Christianity, a place of two-way communion with the Lord and counselled by him in everyday life. I pray that the love and acceptance you receive from the Lord may heal you of all fears and inadequacies and transform your life. I pray that God's vision may be birthed within you, that you may discover your place in the kingdom of God. I pray that you may find life, as you talk with God *"face-to-face, as a man talks with his friend."*

If you are satisfied with your life and feel no need for any help outside yourself, this book is not for you. Most of us feel this need either because of some problem for which we have no answer or because of a nagging consciousness that we should be getting more out of life or putting more into it. Surely our half-somnolent existence is not living as it was meant to be! We must yearn for something more.

This book, then, is the story of a pilgrimage. The end has not yet been written. In a sense, you and I will be doing that in the days and years ahead. What I have written here is for anyone who longs for something more and who wants to be a part of the quest.

Chapter 1

Unleash My Insight Vision

Our Lord Jesus Christ, called the word (in Greek, *Logos*), is a distinct Person from God the Father, and yet most intimately and ineffably united to Him, -- and that he is the Creator of all things. God the Son is the source of all spiritual life and light (Jn. 1:1-18). The Holy Spirit is he who at the creation moved and brooded over the face of the deep, and as the Lord and life-giver breathed the life of God into the whole created order. The Bible says in the book of Genesis 1:1, 2;

> *"In the beginning God created the heavens and the earth. The earth was formless and void, and darkness was over the surface of the deep, and the Spirit of God was moving over the surface of the waters."*

> Also, in the same book 2:7 says: *"Then the Lord God formed man of dust from the ground and breathed into his nostrils the breath of life; and man became a living being."*

By the power of the Holy Spirit cosmos was produced out of chaos and by the ever present and active power of the same Spirit in the processes of nature cosmos is maintained. The union of the Triune God is doubtless one of the greatest mysteries of the Christianity. It is just one of those great truths which are not meant to be curiously pried into, but to be reverently believed.

To those who walk in the Spirit, all creation is seen to be of God. No man can find God through nature, but every man may find nature through God. Or otherwise if man begin with nature, he cannot climb from it to God; but if he begins with God, he may enter the mystic region, wherein lies true appreciation of the glories and beauties of nature.

Prophet Isaiah says: "*... the whole earth is full of His glory*" (Isa. 6:3). A marvellous declaration of the fact of the presence of God in all nature is to be found also in the great theophany of the book of Job (Job 41, 42).

No lower form of life knows God. In every flower which decks the surface of the ground, there is present the touch of God, but no flower knows it. In all life there are present the power and energy of God. All things live and move and have their being in him, but apart from humans, none are conscious of it.

Humanity was created to look back into the face of God, and to know him, to understand in some measure the mystery of his being and to keep intimate relationship with him. Humanity entered the perfect environment of the Garden, knew it, appreciated it, and discovered God in it, because there had been in breathed to him the breath of lives.

The ministry of the Holy Spirit in the present age is by no means confined within the limits of the Church. We read in the book of Acts 2:17-18, Simon Peter quoting the prophet Joel:

> "'And it shall be in the last days,' God says, 'that I will pour forth of My Spirit on all mankind; and your sons and your daughters shall prophecy, and your young men shall see visions, and your old men shall dream dreams; even on My bond slaves, both men and women, I will in those days pour forth of My Spirit and they shall prophecy.'"

The "*last days*" can refer to the future generally, but usually in the Bible, it seems to have in view the Messianic era. In a real sense the last days began with the first coming of Christ (Heb. 1:2) and will be fulfilled at his second coming and is another way of saying "from now on." The Holy Spirit was poured upon *all humankind,* so that the whole human race was thereby brought into a new relationship with him as a result of the work of the Lord Jesus Christ. The Holy Spirit was poured not merely upon the company of disciples, but also upon *all humankind*. This is the larger outlook upon the mission of the Holy Spirit. There is, however, a distinct difference between the relationship that the Holy Spirit bears to the believer and to the unbeliever. The Holy Spirit by indwelling in the believer is keeping him in union with the Lord Jesus Christ. However, although every Christian has the Holy Spirit, he does not have every Christian in the sense that Holy Spirit is not allowed to fill every part of their lives. Similarly, even though the Holy Spirit always strives the unbeliever as a Spirit of conviction, of reasoning, wooing him in patience to the way of God and persuade him of the fact that without Christ his eternal future will be one of gloom and despair. The difference is most marked, yet the ministry of the Holy Spirit is a ministry which touches all human beings.

All true believers are indwelt and inspired by the Holy Trinity, and as the Father, Son and Holy Spirit interpenetrate and mutually indwell one another in the mystery and unity of the Godhead. Wonderful and awesome though it may be to have the Spirit with us, there can be no radical change in our lives until the Holy Spirit moves within us. So, humanity is called to share in the creative and redemptive life of God. God is reaching out to touch the hearts of his children. He wants to join their spirits with his, to breathe upon them the renewing life of his Holy Spirit.

This means that there is no human being who is completely forsaken by God, for the very air that we breathe is a physical manifestation of the divine *ruach Yahweh*, the breath of God. The image of God in humans may be distorted, damaged and perverted beyond the aid of people to regenerate, but it is not destroyed. There are traces of God within the world and within our humanity.

There is in every man and woman a longing for God, that the ache which earth cannot satisfy can be satisfied by God, the Creator and that all feel it, though not all understand it. Some theologians use the term *'nostalgia'* to describe this longing in our spirit for God. The word *'nostalgia'* comes from two Greek words: *'nostos'* meaning 'return home,' and *'algos'* meaning 'pain.' Every human spirit is in pain when it tries to function outside of relationship with God and, as the psychologist Freud said, the main preoccupation of every human being is to "minimise pain and maximise pleasure." As Augustine said in his *Confessions,* "O Lord, you have made us for yourself, and our hearts are restless till they rest in you."

For any true believer to enjoy life in the presence of the Lord, he must be *"filled with the Spirit"* (Eph. 5:18). This blessing of unspeakable divine joy is the one that we can experience now, in this world itself. However, since the verb is in the passive voice, being filled with the Spirit is not something a Christian achieves through his own efforts but is something that is done for him and to which he submits. Hence, the Scriptures depict a theocentric view of the Holy Spirit's filling, in which the higher reaches down to gather up the lower into ultimate communion. Clarity on the point dismisses the criticism or misunderstanding of some who seem to see this experience as something merely conjured up by human suggestion, proposition, or excitement.

Although the Holy Spirit has been *'with'* you in order to bring you to Christ and is now *'in'* you through the work of regeneration, the question remains: Have you experienced your own personal Pentecost and you know the Spirit clothing you, enduring you with divine energy and power? Whatever your view of the Holy Spirit, it is essential that you ask: Is he a dynamic or merely a doctrine?

When we think of divine joy as the inheritance of our humanity, however, that joy is not intended to relieve us of all our troubles; rather, the joy that comes from fellowship with Christ and from the hope we have of future glory strengthens us in life's struggles. St. Paul writes in Romans 8:23,

> "...we ourselves groan within ourselves, waiting eagerly for our adoption as sons ..."

This tension between joy and an inward groan is one with whichChristians live daily – joy at receiving the gift of eternal life and a groan because of our knowledge that we live in a world adrift from God. The experience of groaning, which is mentioned in the verse above, is something that several preachers try to help us avoid. The gospel of health and wealth, for example, ignores the fact that we are called to suffer. The aim of those who teach it is not to help us learn how to face legitimate and unavoidable suffering, but rather how to rearrange our circumstances in order to enjoy greater comfort.

Joy is a bye-product of love. The term 'joy' is used in the present context that it is only divine joy and a fruit of Spirit. No one can deny that from time to time each of us has to face suffering. However, a Christian possesses a subterranean spring of joy that will, if we allow it, burst upwards even in times of suffering.

I am aware of thinking not solely in Christian terms. There is universal experience of God and it means that the divine presence is universal and excludes no-one who seeks for God in love, honesty and truth. Certainly, the presence of the cosmic Christ, the universal word can be recognized in all that is true, good, and beautiful in every culture.

In the past the Church has been guilty of destroying human cultures, languages and traditions, and even of taking the Gospel of Christ (or our version of it) with cannon and sword. It is right and good to seek to share the riches of Christ throughout the world, but how much better it would have been if we had carried the love of Christ to other peoples, intent at the same time on discovering the hidden God already dwelling in their cultures and traditions.

In the Sermon on the Mount our Lord taught, *"Blessed are the pure in heart, for they shall see God"* (Matt. 5:8). The Holy God, who is 'of purer eyes than to behold iniquity,' calls here for purity of heart, and he promises a glorious and beautiful vision of himself: *'they shall see God.'* In biblical language the word *'heart'* means, the centre of the human spirit, from which spring emotions, thought, motivations, courage and action – *"the springs of life"* (Prov. 4:23). Purity is a thing called for in Scripture: *"You shall be holy, for I am holy"* (1 Pet. 1:16). Purity is the end of our election and redemption:

> *"He chose us in him before the foundation of the world, that we would be holy and blameless before him"* (Eph. 1:4).

> Not *for* holiness, but *to* holiness. *"Whom he foreknew, he also predestined to become conformed to the image of his Son"* (Rom. 8:29).

God predestines us to Christ's image, which image consists *"in righteousness and holiness"* (Eph. 4:24). Christ *"gave himself for us to redeem us from every lawless deed, and to purify for himself a people for his own possession"* (Titus 2:14).

He shed his blood to wash off our filth. The cross was both an altar and a laver. Jesus died not only to save us from wrath (1 Thess. 1:10), but to save us from sin (Matt. 1:21).

The heart must especially be kept pure, because the heart is the chief seat or place of God's residence. God dwells in the heart. He takes up the heart for his own lodging (Isa. 57:15; Eph. 3:17), therefore it must be pure and holy.

"Blessed are the pure in heart," healed are their spirits, free are they to laugh and dance their way through life, enjoying God and the fullness of his creation. Free are they to love the brethren. Free are they to love themselves. If having a pure, healthy, and liberated heart involves seeing God, then what does it mean to do so? Where can I look to find him? Where might I see him? The Bible offers an astounding array of answers to these questions.

In a Vision

One morning, the prophet Elisha was awakened by his servant with the frightening news, "A great army of horses and chariots has surrounded us during the night. The enemy knows where we are and surely, we will not escape. Alas, what shall we do?" What a great way to start the day! Alas, indeed! Do you know that this would be an easy morning to wonder where God is? It would be understandable if Elisha did not see God in these circumstances. But what was the prophet's response?

> "'O Lord, I pray, open his eyes that he may see.' And the Lord opened the servant's eyes, and he saw; and behold, the mountain was full of horses and chariots of fire all around Elisha" (2 Kings 6:17).

In a moment the servant's perspective was changed. In a moment fear became faith, doubt became hope, and depression became excitement. Why? Because he saw God!

Imagine for a moment the beloved apostle, advanced in years and in exile on the isle of Patmos. Jesus had promised that he would return, but years had passed with no deliverance. John had given his life to follow his Master, and in return he was alone, far from home and friends, in exile. In the same circumstances, don't you think you might wonder what was happening? Would you begin to doubt that God was really in control? But what was John's reaction?

> "After these things I looked, and behold, a door standing open in heaven and the first voice which I had heard, like the sound of a trumpet speaking with me, said, 'Come up here, and I will show you what must take place after these things.' Immediately I was in the Spirit; and behold, a throne was standing in heaven and One sitting on the throne" (Rev. 4:1, 2).

When John *looked*, he saw God on the throne, still ruling, still in control, even during imprisonment, exile, and loneliness.

No doubt there were people sitting nearby who did not see God. No doubt other prisoners and guards saw only the chains and the thick prison walls. Why was John able to see when others weren't? Part of the answer is found in the words, *"I looked."* If we are going to be a people who see God, one thing we must do is *look* with the eyes of our heart, in faith expecting to see him and his movement in our lives and circumstances.

Stephen was another disciple who could have become angry with God. Stephen had also given his life for Christ and the service of his body. What did he get in return? Execution by stoning. He could have looked at the "disaster" which had come upon him and shaken his fist in anger at God. He could have given in to doubt and despair. God couldn't be ruling, or this wouldn't be happening to him. Instead, Stephen kept his heart *pure,* and,

> *"being full of the Holy Spirit, he gazed intently into heaven and saw the glory of God, and Jesus standing at the right hand of God; and he said, 'Behold, I see the heavens opened and the Son of Man standing at the right hand of God'"* (Acts 7:55, 56).

God was still in control. Jesus still loved him and was awaiting his arrival into glory. Every vision of Christ granted to the believers has been the result of the presence in that believer of the Holy Spirit, who alone gives grace to say in the new realms of life, in new vistas of outlook, that Jesus is Lord.

One of the Old Testament words for prophet was "seer," or *ro'eh* (roh-ay) in Hebrew, since prophets frequently received messages from God through visions or they had blessing to see into the spirit world. However, the word *nabi'* (spokesman) is the preferred Hebrew word for prophet. Christ has opened the veil that in the New Covenant we may all see what only a few caught a glimpse of it in the past. We can also see beyond what is obvious to our fleshly eyes to what is equally obvious in the spirit world. We can see beyond the physical reality to the deeper spiritual reality which underlies it all, if we are willing to train ourselves with the guidance of the Holy Spirit. But some people, even believers, may ask, "How is it possible to go on living in intimate relationship with God when evil seems to triumph in the world?"

How we need to constantly pray: "O Lord, open our eyes that we may see!" Living in a visible world, we are to fear and bondage because of all our eyes can see. Invisible satanic foes surround us, often causing us to feel that we have no way of escape from evil powers. The consciousness, however, that God's chariots are surrounding us delivers us from panic and despair and maintains our hearts in courage and in confidence. We, too, come to endure by seeing him who is invisible. Such a faith is the assurance that invisible things are clearly seen by those who constantly pray: "Open my eyes that I may see!"

In His Creation

Not only can we see God in the spirit world, we can also see him clearly in the world which he has created (Rom. 1:20). The glory of God is revealed in the sunshine and the rain, in the trees and clouds, in the grass and flowers, in summer and winter. One may look out at the pouring rain and grumble, "I wanted the sun to shine today. Why did this have to happen? I hate the rain!" To another the sunshine is too hot and only adds to the burden of his labour. Yet to those who look, to those who want to see God, *"His invisible attributes, his eternal power and divine nature"* can be seen in all that he has created. Prophet Isaiah says:

> *"Lift up your eyes on high and see who has created these stars, ... because of the greatness of his might and the strength of his power, not one of them is missing"* (Isa. 40:26).

This is not pantheism, but a contemplative understanding of the doctrine of the immanence of God taught by patriarchs, prophets and psalmist. If pantheism teaches that God is the sum of all created things, and that created order exhausts the being of God, then that is not what I am affirming here. God is the ever-present One. He does not change, does not 'come' and 'go' from one place to another, for as the psalmist cries:

> *"Where can I go from your Spirit? Or where can I flee from your presence? If I ascend to heaven, you are there; if I make my bed in Sheol, behold, you are there. If I take the wings of the dawn, if I dwell in the remotest part of the sea, even there Your hand will lead me, and Your right hand will lay hold of me"* (Psa. 139:7-10).

This is not only an expression of a contemplative attitude towards the created order, but also a comforting doctrine in days of darkness and pain. But the doctrines of the omniscience and omnipresence of God, at least as portrayed in Psalm 139, are doctrines which are born out of the living experience of divine holiness and love. Because the psalmist writes out of direct and living experience of God, he cries out in adoration and praise. Joy mingles with wonder as he allows his soul to be exposed to the blazing scrutiny of the divine mystery and love:

> *"Search me, O God, and know my heart; try me and know my anxious thoughts; and see if there be any hurtful way in me and lead me in the everlasting way"* (Psa. 139:23, 24).

There is perpetual need for rigorous self-examination as to whether those professing loyalty are still in the faith. By disloyalty to God, the minds might have been blinded to the correct perception of the work of the Holy Spirit and without intending it; there may be hostility or resistance to his work.

In All Matter

Going a step further, not only can God be seen in the beauty and power of nature, he can be seen in every molecule of all matter. *"In him all things hold together"* (Col. 1:17). Even matter is alive, infused with the power and life of Almighty God. He is the force which holds all the molecules together. There is no place where God is not – he is inescapable. As Pascal said, "His centre is everywhere; his circumference is nowhere." Not only did God create the universe through Christ but that he is the One who holds it together. To use the words found in the Moffat translation, *"all coheres in him."* Christ is involved in his creation and takes a personal interest in every one of his creation. Because of this, every believer can experience the joy of God in creation mirrored in the depths of his own being. He is then able to recognize and affirm the biblical revelation of that creative joy reflected in the whole panorama of the biblical tradition. He is the Creator of all. But all of matter is *infused* with God. The psalmist says,

> *"Let the heavens be glad, and let the earth rejoice; let the sea roar, and all it contains; let the field exult, and all that is in it. Then all the trees of the forest will sing for joy before the Lord "* (Psa. 96:11-13).

Do you remember what Jesus said when the Pharisees tried to silence his disciples as he rode into Jerusalem? *"I tell you, if these become silent, the stones will cry out!"* (Lk. 19:40). Inanimate though they are, even the stones could be used to praise the King.

In Circumstances

When things are going your way, it's easy to see God's hand at work in your life. In the tragedies of life, can you still believe that Christ *"works all things after the counsel of his will"* (Eph. 1:11) and further, that he *"causes all things to work together for good"* (Rom. 8:28)?

We routinely hear broad day-light robbery, murder, kidnapping, looting, rape and other crimes with the support of influential class or with systematic intrusion of the political masters. Recently the area of darkness has been accentuated by frequent scams, swindles and various kinds of corruption at high profile places. Could any such circumstances possibly be worse to doubt, if God is working out all these for good? Could God still be caring for the nation that was his bride? Could he possibly causes such a situation to somehow work together for the good of his people?

"Yes," the prophet Jeremiah said. Yes, God's hand is still upon you. Submit to the enemy, for God will use all that comes upon you to purify and cleanse our nation. A remnant shall come forth and through that remnant shall come the salvation of the world. Though evil seems out of control, yet we must see God still on the throne.

Sometimes when we are suffering heartbreak, tragedy, disappointment, frustration, and bereavement, we wonder what good can come out of it (Rom. 8:28). But the following verse gives the answer: whatever God permits to come into our lives is designed to conform us to the image of his Son (v.29). Our lives are not controlled by impersonal forces such as chance, luck, or fate, but by our wonderful, personal Lord, who is "too loving to be unkind and too wise to err."

In Everything

"For in him we live, and move, and exist" (Acts 17:28). The pure in heart see God in the very breath that they breathe. They feel his strength in every muscle of their bodies.

God is always present with us. There is no time and no place in our daily life or occupations in which God is not present to us; there are not even certain times or occupations in which God is more present to us or less present to us. God is always the same, the Almighty, the Infinite, the Eternal. Everywhere and always he is, he is himself in his fullness; there is no sense in which he can be more 'here' or less 'there' since he is indivisible.

Creation is simply the communication of this presence, this mysterious life of God in himself. Everything that exists, every being that lives and thinks, does so by sharing in his Being, his divine life and self-awareness. It is from and through this very presence of God to himself that all creatures exist, that living creatures are born and grow, and finally becomes an individual being.

Because of his divine presence everywhere, the believer can experience the joy of God in creation mirrored in the depths of his own being. He is then able to recognize and affirm the biblical revelation of that creative joy reflected in the whole panorama of the biblical tradition. And then the believer can share personally and corporately that joy in all creative and redemptive experiences in which God's love is manifested. How deeply and powerfully do you experience God in your life? How aware are you of his presence, not as a theory but as a fact? Believe in me, God wants you to do more than take his presence by faith; he wants you to experience it also.

It is possible for us to enter in a divine-human partnership. Every Christian should be walking and working each day with a Senior Partner and walk arm in arm with him. Partnership with God does not mean that he dominates us; his purpose is to guide and not over-ride, as we read in Psalms 32:8;

"I will instruct you and teach you in the way which you should go; I will counsel you with my eye upon you."

He relates to us in a way that is helpful and supportive yet, at the same time, he takes care not to snuff out our initiative and creativity. Dr. Stanley Jones describes the divine–human partnership as follows: "God comes close to his children in a way that leaves them free to think and act, yet in a way that awakens the personality to aliveness and alertness of mind and spirit. His guidance is always sufficiently obvious to be found, but not so obvious that it does away with the necessity of thought and discriminating insight." Our loving God is no fair-weather companion, leaving us when the year grows dark and cold. He does not choose our days of prosperous festival, though not to be found in our days of impoverishment and defeat. He does not show himself only when we wear a garland and hide himself when we wear a crown of thorns. He is with us 'all the days' – the prosperous days and the days of adversity.

We learn from Scriptures that entering a relationship with God is not so much a matter of trying to find him as of letting him find us. No doubt, many people have an awareness of God's presence at times, but they can never experience the rich sense of his presence in their hearts until they invite him to come in and he resides within them. When we make ourselves available to Him, we will find that we have a deep and continuous sense of his presence.

No true believer in Christ is an orphan, and therefore not desolate. Jesus affirms this truth in John's gospel: *"I will not leave you as orphans; I will come to you"* (14:18). Orphanage is to cease; there is to be no desolateness. The sense of loneliness never comes to a person born of the Spirit and living in perpetual obedience to the Lord Jesus Christ. Divine peace and joy are his – peace which Jesus gives, through the ministry of a Person ever present. In the strength of that divine peace and joy believers become his witnesses, because they have a perpetual vision of the Lord.

Jesus told his disciples of the blessed assurance of God's presence with him (Jn. 16:32). This assurance should be ours as believers also. It is the blessed privilege of every follower of Christ to abide in loving union with him. We can rejoice, knowing that we have the joy of sharing heaven's companionship together. We have the promise of Heb. 13:5; *"I will never desert you, nor will I ever forsake you."* Those who trust in the Lord are as *"the apple of his eye"* (Zech. 2:8). Their names are engraved on the palms of his hands (Isa. 49:16). He hears them when they call and hasten to their assistance.

We have the company of the Father: *"My Father will love him, and we will come to him and make Our abode with him"* (Jn. 14:23). We have the fellowship with the Son: *"I am with you always, even to the end of the age"* (Matt. 28:20). We have the presence of the Holy Spirit: *"He may be with you forever"* (Jn. 14:16). With such a threefold companion, why should we be lonely or need other friendship? How expressive are the lines of S. Trevor Francis?

> My *yesterday* was Christ upon the tree,
>
> Who bore the condemnation due to me.
>
> *Today* I journey on and he shall lead,
>
> He knows my pathway, and he knows the need.
>
> *Tomorrow* is not; but his wisdom plans,
>
> I leave my future in his loving hands.

The most exciting fact about my life is not that I know God but that he knows me. Of course, I am excited that I know him, but I am more excited by the fact that he knows me. And why? Because my knowledge of him is based on his knowledge of me. If he didn't know me then I would never have come to know him.

But there is a difference between *affirming* the presence of God and *experiencing* the manifestation of that presence. Moses was certainly within the divine presence in the wilderness, though he was unaware of it until God manifested that presence from the glory of the bush which burned without being consumed.

Jacob was wandering in the wilderness, fleeing from his brother Esau, and seeking a pattern in his pilgrimage. He was not aware of the guiding providence of God, nor was he aware that God's living presence was everywhere about him. Weary, he took a stone for a pillow in a deserted place and went to sleep. Then came the dream – he saw a ladder of commerce between earth and heaven, with angelic beings ascending and descending, and the voice and revelation of God spoke to him from the midst of the mystery. Jacob's reaction when waking indicates the difference between the *presence* and the *manifestation* of the presence of God, when he said:

> *"Surely the Lord is in this place, and I did not know it."* And he was afraid, and said, *"How awesome is this place! This is none other than the house of God, and this is the gate of heaven."* (Gen. 28:16, 17).

Humankind alone among creatures has the privilege of being aware of his presence and of being called to reciprocate it. He is called to be present to God as God is present to him, in the way in which, within the Blessed Trinity, the Son of God is eternally present to the Father as the Father is present to him. Did not Jesus assure us that our relationship with him, and through him with the Father, is modelled on his own relationship with the Father?

> *"I know My own and My own know Me, even as the Father knows Me and I know the Father"* (Jn. 10:14, 15). *"... even as you, Father, are in me and I in you, that they also may be in us ... ...that they may be one, just as we are one; I in them and you in me, that they may be perfected in unity..."* (Jn. 17:21-23).

A life of prayer, a life of contemplation, is simply to realise God's presence in us. It is therefore not a special way of life reserved for those few individuals who are called to get away from the world and to dwell in isolation from the main stream. Both in the Old and New Testament we have specific records of guiding God's people by his *"still, small voice of calm."* Meditation and close communion with the Lord ought to be the very breath of every true believer of Christ.

But how can we see God in all these ways? When our heart is broken, our faith is shattered, our strength all gone, how can we see then? Only by revelation. Only by the grace of God can we see control during chaos, love during despair, and joy amid sorrow. We must come to him, empty of all our own efforts and pray that *"the eyes of"* our *"hearts may be enlightened so that"* we may *"know"* (Eph. 1:17, 18). This becomes our constant prayer, to see differently than the world or our flesh see, to see with the *eyes of our heart* the reality of the world of the Spirit.

David prayed, *"Open my eyes that I may behold..."* (Ps. 119:18). David's physical eyes were not blind. But his spiritual eyes were blinded by doubt or fear or sin. Only the power of the Spirit could cleanse his heart and open his spiritual eyes.

As two of the disciples walked the Emmaus road, life had lost all meaning (Lk. 24:13-35). Tragedy had struck. Jesus had been crucified, evil had triumphed, the healing love had ceased to flow, and life had become purposeless. No longer could they see God. They were separated from Christ, *"having no hope, and without God in this world"* (Eph. 2:12). As they walked the long road home, they discussed the terrible disaster which had befallen them. Perhaps they discussed their discouragement and disillusionment. After all, they thought the Messiah had come who would deliver them from oppression. They had left their homes and families to follow him. They thought it was going to be so wonderful, but instead it turned out awful. There was no Messiah, just empty wasted years following a wishful dream.

Suddenly *"Jesus himself approached and began travelling with them. But their eyes were prevented from recognizing him."* (Lk. 24:15, 16).

How often the same is true for us. Jesus is right beside us, longing to comfort and heal, but our eyes are blinded by the brokenness within. And Jesus said to the two disciples,

"What are these words that you are exchanging with one another as you are walking?" (Lk. 24:17).

Of course, Jesus knew what they were talking about. He knows all things. So why did he ask? Because he wanted to draw them out, to have them express the thoughts of their hearts. Often Jesus will do the same when we dialogue with him. He will ask us questions and we may want to respond, "But you know the answer to that. Why are you asking me?" But the beginning of our healing comes when we pour out our hearts to God. Don't be afraid or ashamed to let out all your questions and angers, doubts and fears. You will not shock or offend him. He wants you to bring every negative within your heart to him that he may touch them and turn them into glorious positives.

But the disciples did not recognize that it was Jesus Who asked them what they were talking about and they responded,

"Are you the only one visiting Jerusalem and unaware of the things which have happened here in these days?" (Lk. 24:18).

He was the only One Who really *knew* that had happened! Everyone else only saw what happened in the physical world, but Jesus knew how the physical realm intertwined with the spiritual, how events in one caused responses in the other. Only Jesus found cause for rejoicing in the "calamity" of his crucifixion. So, the disciples poured out their hearts to the stranger who responded by explaining how suffering gives way to glory and showing by illuminating Scriptures that God's purposes were being fulfilled, even during seeming tragedy.

How Jesus longs to do the same for us. He longs to open our eyes that we might recognize him in the dark moments of our lives. He wants to set our *"heart burning within"* us, exchanging our fear, guilt and anger for his glorious faith, hope and love.

Only God can transform hearts. Only by coming to him will this purifying take place. Only by doing what the Emmaus disciples did can we be healed. We must not only pour out our hearts to him but also listen to his response. When circumstances look bad and we wonder if things are out of control, He says, "Be at peace. I'm still on my throne." What seems like calamity to us is not to him. Calvary was not a disaster. It was not wicked men out of control, though it looked like that to the eyes of flesh. That's what is so marvellous about our God. He is big enough to take the wickedness of evil men and bring about his best purpose for us. He can accomplish his will for us no matter what we choose to do. We need not know how he does it; we only need to praise and worship him for that it is so.

Remember Joseph and the trials which plagued his footsteps, most brought on by the evil of men and woman around him? What was his evaluation of his life? *"You meant evil, but God meant it for good"* (Gen. 50:20). Joseph's brothers were motivated by wrath, anger, jealousy and bitterness, yet God used their wickedness to bring about his purposes. You see, God is Love. Love is ruling the universe. And love is more powerful than any weapon formed against it.

In Spiritual Growth

We tend to think that we are responsible for our spiritual growth. But God says:

> *"By his doing you are in Christ Jesus, who became to us wisdom from God, and righteousness, and sanctification, and redemption"* (I Cor. 1:30).

All we are and have come from him and that there is therefore no room for human glory. In ourselves we have nothing in the way of personal holiness, but in him we are positionally sanctified, and by his power we are transformed from one degree of sanctification to another. Finally, he is our redemption, when the Lord will come and take us home to be with him.

Spiritual growth involves increasing righteousness in our daily living and greater sanctification or setting apart of our lives from sin. We can try to do that by our own efforts, but it is only dead works, independent of Christ. True spiritual growth is the growth of Christ within us. We grow in righteousness by allowing him to be released through us. It is not our responsibility to sanctify ourselves, but rather our response to his ability to do so.

> *"Now may the God of peace himself sanctify you entirely and may your spirit and soul and body be preserved complete, without blame at the coming of our Lord Jesus Christ. Faithful is he who calls you, and he also will bring it to pass"* (1 Thess. 5:23, 24).

So even when we look at our own life, we can see our God at work.

The goodness of creation as it came from the hand of God is proclaimed in the book of Genesis before the story of the Fall. Humans were innocent before the fall. We should affirm the original basic goodness of the created order *before* we take cognizance of the fall and alienation which face us in the world. The way back to that original innocence in which the *imago Dei,* the image of God is to be restored is the way of redemption. It is to that fall and restoration through Christ that we now turn – from the original paradise, through paradise lost, to paradise regained. And as we take this path, we should recognize our own personal and corporate experience in the pilgrimage. We have glimpses of our original innocence, a sad awareness of our sinfulness and alienation, leading to the profound experience of joy in redemption.

Creation is the dance of joy, and what joy has been lost to us has been regained by the redeeming love of God in Christ. Therefore, the end of our redemption is restoration, the restoration of that immense joy of creation which is the inheritance of every child of Adam.

Summary
"Blessed are the pure in heart, for they shall see God." When we see God with the eyes of our heart, in nature, sustaining all matter, in our spiritual growth, in all our circumstances ("good" and "bad"), in short, in everything, our hearts are made pure and whole. But we can only see God by revelation.

Therefore, we must pray for the eyes of our hearts to be enlightened. We must pour out our hearts to him, and we must listen to his response. In the next chapter we will briefly review some key principles which can help us to discern his voice more clearly within our hearts.

Chapter 2

Primary Steps to Enter In

In the age in which we live, married so to rationalism and cognitive and analytical thought, it almost seems laughable to hear anyone claim that hearing God's voice is possible and desirable. Indeed, the world has stood by and mocked people of God who claimed to hear his voice, and for the most part, the Church has joined in their scepticism. Today, when alluring voices of the world are more insistent than ever, we need ears sensitive to the quiet whispers of the Spirit. How far we have come from the biblical norm, where to know God was to hear his voice! No wonder we have lost God's perspective and need the Wonderful Counsellor to set us free. We need ears alert to the cry of a lost world, desperately in need of God.

I said that in order to have a pure heart, in order to be counselled by God, we must be able to hear the voice of God, see the vision of God, and get his perspective on the situation. Even when we accept this as a worthy goal, it is often not an easy thing to do. In fact, for many years of my life as a Christian, I could not recognize the Lord's voice within my heart and I never saw one vision from him. My prayers were monologues, never managing to break through to "the other side of silence," to a place of two-way dialogue with the Lord Jesus Christ. I always believed that Christians should be able to hear God's voice. I knew he wanted to guide us continually and that one of the ways he guides are by his "still, small voice" apart from the Word of God given in the Scriptures.

How I was blessed

When I accepted the Lord as my personal Saviour, my immediate hunger was to learn God's Word or, as I liked to put it, to become a biblical man. This hunger was deep and insatiable. Practical, biblical, logical—those words have always appealed to me. Having grown up in a conservative, rural, orthodox Christian family, my approach to life had always been to make the Bible real, practical, and down-to-earth in my life. As I studied, I began to see that the voice of God, or the "Word of the Lord" as the prophets called it, was very real, and a continuous theme in Scripture. I noticed that from Genesis to Revelation, men and women heard God's voice speaking to them, and a hunger grew within me to hear God's voice in my own heart. A strong desire to become a spiritual man and to understand the ways of the Spirit began to burn as I recognized that I could only be a biblical man if I, too, could hear the voice of God.

So, I began searching for God's voice within my heart. I waited expectantly for the inner audible voice of God to speak to me. I imagined that he would have a deep bass voice, of course; maybe there would be lightning in the sky, the wind would blow, and the windows would shatter. I would then jump in instant obedience and do whatever he wanted me to do.

But nothing happened. I listened and listened, but I could not discern any "voice of God." All I heard were thoughts rummaging through my mind until I eventually wandered off in aimless day-dreams or, even worse, fell asleep.

It was extremely frustrating! Prayer simply didn't work for me and I couldn't understand why not. I thought that maybe if I study more of the Word it would help. Then I'd be able to hear God's voice, I reasoned. So, I tried to devour the Bible, but I still couldn't discern that quiet inner voice.

I read in Isaiah 58 that if we would fast with the right spirit, we could cry out to God and he would answer. We would hear him say, *"Here I am"* (Isa. 58:9). Jesus' teaching also indicated that fasting would increase our spiritual power and authority. So, I decided to try fasting and praying to see if it would make me more spiritually receptive. I fasted for days, but I still couldn't hear a voice within my heart.

I went back to the Scriptures to make sure that the people of God truly heard his voice. Yes, God unequivocally reaffirmed that in every covenant from Genesis to Revelation he had spoken to his children. Here are a few of the hundreds of verses of Scripture that confirmed this truth to my heart:

> *And they* [Adam and Eve] *heard the Lord God...* (Gen. 3:8).

> *Now the Lord said to Abram...* (Gen. 12:1).

> *The Lord said to Moses...* (Exo. 4:21).

> *Now the Lord said to Aaron...* (Exo. 4:27).

> *Now it shall come to pass, if you diligently obey the voice of the Lord your God...* (Deut. 28:1 NKJV).

> *The Lord spoke to Joshua...* (Josh. 1:1).

> *Then the Lord said to me* [Isaiah]*...* (Isa. 8:1).

> *The word that came to Jeremiah from the Lord, saying...* (Jer. 7:1).

> *The word of the Lord came...to Ezekiel* (Ezek. 1:3).

> *I* [Jesus] *can do nothing on My own initiative. As I hear, I judge...* (Jn. 5:30).

> *And the Spirit told me* [Peter] *to...* (Acts 11:12).

> [Paul] *having been forbidden by the Holy Spirit to...* (Acts 16:6).

> *But you have come to Mount Zion and to the city of the living God...and to Jesus, the mediator of a new covenant, ... See to it that you do not refuse him who is speaking* (Heb. 12:22, 24, 25).

I [John] was in the Spirit on the Lord's Day, and I heard behind me a loud voice like the sound of a trumpet, saying, "Write in a book what you see..." (Rev. 1:10, 11).

I just could not accept the premise that God would stop speaking in this dispensation of grace, especially when there was such a deep hunger within me to hear. That longing had to be placed there by God.

In total desperation, I examined the only remaining possibility I could think of: I checked to see if I was truly saved. It didn't take much contemplation to decide that I was. I had repented and confessed my sins. I had invited Christ in and asked him to become the Lord and Saviour of my life. I had been baptized in water when I was a little kid as per the norms of the Church. I believed the Bible to be the unerring Word of God and held to all the truths of evangelical theology.

Okay—I am saved. Well, what in the world was the problem? Maybe I was just trying too hard and being too practical about the whole thing. Maybe I was expecting too much of Christianity. Maybe I should just be content like so many other Christians seemed to be. I had the Bible—maybe I didn't need his inner voice after all. I was weary and at my wit's end. I tried everything I knew, and nothing worked. I listened as hard as I could and still had no inner voice in my heart. It just was not there. I was not going to enter deception and pretend it was there—if it wasn't there it wasn't there.

During this period of investigation and desperation, few Bible teachers have told me that hearing the "voice of God" is merely the subterranean rumblings of the spiritual mind. In other words, there is no such thing!

Part of me wanted to believe that. After all, it wouldn't be a weakness in my life not to have something that didn't exist, would it? But I knew that the hunger in my heart had not yet satisfied the relationship with Almighty God.

I thank God that even when I was unaware of a solution his hand was leading me. Through all my hunger and search he was leading me one small step at a time. Most of the steps were not even noticeable at the time, just seemingly insignificant events or fortunate circumstances. Yet today I can look back and see how the hand of God moved. Through all my failures and depression and confusion, he was always working all things out for my good.

While I was still struggling to find out the way to build-up a two-way communication channel with the Lord, I remembered having read few years back on the same topic written by Thomas A. Kempis, who lived in the fourteenth century. I was led by divine power to go through his writing once again, and I had to eagerly search through its pages.

The monk explains that we must convert ourselves with our whole heart to the Lord, prepare him a fit dwelling within us and permit Christ to enter within us. He further adds that "to know how to converse with Jesus is a great art; to know how to keep Jesus in our heart is the greatest prudence."

Finally grasping the significance of the moment, the Holy Spirit gave me the precious gift I had been seeking for so long and launched me into the calling that would become my passion for the rest of my life. He drew together all I had learned during a year of intensive study on prayer and hearing God's voice and showed me how it all fit together into four simple keys that were revealed in Habakkuk 2:1, 2.

Four Valuable Keys

I spent much of the next several months studying everything I could on prayer. I read few books and everything I could find in Scripture concerning prayer. I experimented with different kinds of prayer. To my surprise, I was divinely led to the Scripture portion found in Habakkuk 2:1 & 2, in which the prophet described what he did when he went before God to hear his voice, and in those verses, he showed me several revolutionary keys that I had never seen nor heard or taught before. Let me show them to you briefly now, and then I shall spend few chapters delving into each one individually, showing precisely how they can be developed and used in your prayer life.

*I will stand on my **guard post**...And I will keep **watch** and **see** what He will **speak** to me...Then the Lord...said, **Record** the vision....* (Hab. 2:1, 2 emphases added).

Obviously, Habakkuk could discern the sound of the Lord's voice in his heart when he very often says, *"Then the Lord said."* Also, throughout his writing, Habakkuk recorded what God spoke to him. Therefore, he knew the sound of God's voice. The *first key to hearing God's voice,* then, is learning *what his voice spoken within sounds like.* Rather than being an inner audible voice, I understood that God's voice in our hearts generally sounds like a flow of spontaneous thoughts. In fact, it is more likely an indication that I was too thick or too stubborn to get His message any other way! Like Paul on the road to Damascus, I had to be "hit upside the head" in order to hear what He had to say to me.

The Lord will take drastic measures if necessary, but he would rather teach us to learn and discern him speaking as spontaneous thoughts from within our hearts. I shall spend an entire chapter expounding on this idea, backing it up biblically and experientially, and then discussing the effect this truth has on our lives.

The *second key* found in Habakkuk is in the phrase, *"I will stand on my guard post."* Habakkuk knew how to go to a quiet place and quiet his own thoughts and emotions, so he could sense the spontaneous flow of God within. Most of us know we are supposed to quiet ourselves, but it is just so hard to do. Later, I shall present numerous biblical tools for quickly quieting our hearts and minds before God so that we can begin to sense the active flow of his Spirit within.

The *third key* is found in Habakkuk's phrase, *"I will keep watch to see."* I asked myself why he said it that way. Why didn't he say, "I will *listen* to hear what he will speak to me?" It makes more sense to me that one would listen to hear spoken words than watch to see them.

By the time this question was answered in my heart and mind, God had opened an entirely new revelation concerning the place of dream and vision in prayer. I had never even thought of looking for vision as I prayed. I had never considered presenting the eyes of my heart to God and asking him to fill them, looking to see what he wanted to show me. However, as I began to search the Scriptures, I found that *dream and vision* were a regular part of all the prophets' prayer lives. I shall try to unfold this revelation with Scriptural support and a careful examination of how dream and vision work in prayer.

Finally, the *fourth key* demonstrated in Habakkuk 2: Then the Lord said, *"Record the vision."* What an incredible idea—writing out my dialogue with God. And yet I soon saw that the whole book of Habakkuk is the story of a man who wrote down his prayers and the answers he received from God. And it was God who commanded him to write it down.

Even though recording dialogue with Almighty God is a part of this process, as beginners to enter the world of Spirit I personally would rather suggest that it is better to avoid in the initial stages to eliminate any possible negative effect. Mostly recording the visions were done by prophets and apostles. We find many examples of recording the visions in the book of prophets, and the entire book of Revelation.

Safeguards

Now, before we go any further, we need to discuss some safeguards for this journey into the world of Spirit impressions. When we talk about hearing the voice of the Spirit of Almighty God, people sometimes fear that they could get confused with the voice of Satan or the voice of their own hearts' desires. If that happened and they acted on it, it could bring real destruction into their lives, they fear. Too often, the solution they think best is not to seek the spiritual life at all—to simply live out of biblical law and ignore the possibility of hearing from God personally.

This is certainly one alternative, and many people have obviously taken this path, but it is clearly not the way of the abundant life Jesus promised us. Instead, God has given us several safeguards in Scripture that, if we will follow them, we can live as comfortable, confident and protected as much as we need to be and in the Father's care in both the spiritual and physical worlds.

The Scriptures

Probably the greatest protection we have in our spiritual journey is the Word of God. A good knowledge of the Scriptures can save us from many errors and heartaches. We require a certain level of biblical knowledge as a pre-requisite to this teaching on hearing God's voice. This is not to say, of course, that God does not speak to new Christians who have not yet completely read the Word. Of course, He does! But if they do not couple their prayer time with an intensive study of the Word and a relationship with a spiritual counsellor, they may quickly run into danger.

There are two basic ways in which the Scriptures can help and protect us. First, every revelation must be tested against the written Word of God. If the revelation violates either the letter of the Word or the spirit of the Word, it is to be rejected immediately. There is no place for rationalizing, twisting or explaining away the truth of the Bible. There can be no strange, personal interpretations of some obscure verse. The Word of the Lord will stand forever, and any word to us from God will be in total agreement with both the letter and spirit of the Eternal Word.

We must not only test God's voice in our hearts against the Bible, but see any revelation as built upon the Scriptures. The Lord told Joshua to meditate upon, confess, and act upon the law of God day and night so that he could give him success. If we have filled our minds and hearts with the Bible, the Holy Spirit will draw forth the precise verses, stories or principles we need in each situation. The spontaneous flow of illumined Scriptures will bring wisdom and insight far greater than our own mind could deliver if only we will pause and allow ourselves to be dependent on God.

We must turn our knowledge *about* God into knowledge *of* God. The process to do so is very demanding, but simple. We must turn each truth that we learn *about* God into matter for meditation *before* God. Unfortunately, now the process of meditation is an art lost among Christians.

Essence of Meditation

Meditation is an activity of calling to mind, and thinking over, and dwelling on, and applying to oneself the various truths that one knows about God's promises and ultimate purposes of the existence of individual who meditates on. It is an activity of holy thought, consciously performed under the divine guidance of the Holy Spirit. Its purpose is to clear one's mental and spiritual vision of God, and to let his truth make its impact on one's self. It is, indeed, often a matter of arguing with oneself, in the light of divine truths, leading into a clear apprehension of God's power and grace. Its effect is ever to humble us, as we contemplate God's greatness and glory, and our own sinfulness, but to encourage, re-assure, and comfort us, as we are enlightened upon the unsearchable riches of the divine mercy displayed in the Lord Jesus Christ.

The Body of Christ

The second important Scriptural safeguard from error and spiritual harm is a humble, teachable spirit. Jesus Christ had been the official teacher of his disciples while on earth. They called no man Rabbi except Jesus. They sat at no man's feet to learn their doctrines, but they had them direct from the lips of him. He promised them when he is gone, where shall they find the great infallible teacher. From John's gospel we learn:

> *"But when he, the Spirit of truth* [Gr. Paracletos], *comes, he will guide you into all the truth; ...he will speak; and he will disclose to you what is to come"* (Jn. 16:13).

He shall be the person who is to explain Scripture; he shall be the authoritative oracle of God, who shall make all dark things light, who shall unravel mysteries, who shall untwist all knots of revelation, and shall make you understand what you could not discover, had it not been for his influence. No man ever learns anything aright, unless he is taught of the Spirit.

So often the ones who claim to hear from the Lord are arrogant and self-righteous. Their attitude is, "God told me and that's all there is to it." But God resists the proud and gives grace to the humble. Such an arrogant spirit will eventually cause them to fall into deception.

All revelation should be tested. God does not speak to us so that we may lord it over anyone else. Rather, we ought to be known as the meekest of all .

We are a part of the Body of Christ. The full revelation of Jesus does not reside in us individually but only as we come together as a Body. We all need to be committed to a local expression of the Body of Christ, and anyone who wants to delve into the spiritual dimension of life should have a relationship with a spiritual counsellor they respect. We cannot survive if we try to walk alone. The Lord will show you with whom you are to establish an accountability relationship, if you ask him. This is a powerful protection for your life: *"In the multitude of counsellors there is safety"* (Prov. 11:14 NKJV).

Humility

There are other basic safeguards as well. God gives revelation only for the areas in which he has given authority and responsibility. Along with God-given authority comes God-given revelation to wisely exercise that authority. Therefore, you should expect revelation only in those areas for which you are legitimately responsible. Stay away from ego trips that seek revelation for areas in which you do not have authority. Don't look for a "word from the Lord" to the people in authority. Don't even look for a revelation for your employer or ordained person in the church, unless you are responsible to him as a close friend or counsellor. Revelation is often given only for the areas of authority to which you are directly responsibility.

Testing

Also, we should be sure that all revelation we receive is leading us towards greater wholeness and the ability to love and share God more perfectly. If at any time our attempts at dialoguing with God become destructive, we must stop at once and seek out our spiritual counsellor.

You may be frightened by such a warning, and even tempted to ignore the spiritual world altogether, rather than risk the dangers. But only those who think they can make it all alone, those with a "just Jesus and me" attitude, need be concerned. If you are applying safeguards such as those we have discussed and are sincerely seeking God's voice, you can confidently approach life in the Spirit.

Before continuing to read this book, I strongly encourage you to carefully examine your life to make sure these guardrails are intact. If they are not, please lay this book down, and take the time necessary to establish them in your life. Then come back, pick it up again, and go on.

The revelations the Lord gives us should be a great blessing to those who are walking righteously before God, but they could as well open the foolish man to Satan's wiles. A Christian who has placed God's safeguards around himself or herself need never fear deception, but all must be aware of our enemy, who *"prowls about like a roaring lion, seeking someone to devour"* (1 Pet. 5:8).

We must strictly learn to still our own mind and listen to the flow of God's inner spontaneous thoughts and open our heart to the flow of dream and vision that God places within.

We must first make sure that the safeguards are in place. We know the Word. We must be willing to submit all our inner revelation to the letter and the spirit of the Bible to walk in relationship with the Body of Christ and with the counsellor God had given to us. We must make sure that all revelations lead toward greater wholeness and the ability to love and share God more perfectly. Then we are ready to go on the greatest adventure of our life. Of course, we are peering into the unseen, spiritual realm where a great person and great forces are at work on our behalf.

The Desire of God's Heart

Why didn't God give up on me long ago? Why does he keep leading me to know his voice? And why is it that I want so desperately to hear his voice? In fact, why is this almost universal cry of Christians around the world and down through the ages?

Quite simply, it is because the deepest desire of God's heart is to have communion with his children. From the beginning of time his desire has remained the same. He calls us all gently, but persistently. He even lets us experience the dissatisfaction that life without him brings. Though our spirits are cluttered, and our minds confused, still we sense deep within us a longing for a special relationship, the special kind of love that will satisfy our hearts.

In the Garden

"Adam! Adam, where are you?" When we hear those words, we think of the sorrowful day when man's fellowship with God was broken. But let's think for a moment what it was like before that day. How many other days did the Father come to the garden in the cool of the day just to take a walk with the man and woman he loved so much? How often did He call, "Adam, Adam!" How many times did Adam respond joyfully, "Here I am, Lord!"

Can you see the three of them, perhaps hand in hand, slowly wandering through the lush flowers? That is communion. That is the sharing of love we were made to enjoy. Father wants us to come to him with our joys and successes. He wants us to share our laughter with him. And he wants to enjoy our pleasure in his creation. He wants to be our best friend, our companion, our lover.

How his heart rejoices when we take time to relax from our labours and devote ourselves wholly to conversing with him! It was for this that he created us. He longs for someone with whom he can share his love.

God is love, and as a song says, "Love isn't love until you give it away." God longs for us to come so that he may give that love to us. That is the purpose of creation and life.

He created us for the supreme purpose of sharing love with him. He created us with the capacity to love so we could return his love. We had lost sight of this somewhere in the hustle of life. We thought that producing *things* was more important than producing *love*.

His Chosen People

God has tried to restore the communion he enjoyed with Adam and Eve in the Garden of Eden. He established a covenant with the people of Israel in which he promised to be their God, and that they would be his people. At the mountain of God, he offered them his voice. He wanted desperately to talk with his children. After all, his whole purpose in creating them was so he could enjoy fellowship with them.

In Deuteronomy 5:22-31 Moses recounted what happened then. God offered his voice, but told the Israelites it came with fire, a common biblical symbol of purging and purification. Rather than embrace God's outstretched hand of love and fellowship, and endure the accompanying purging process, they came up with an alternative solution. Moses, the Israelites said,

> Why don't you *"go near and hear all that the Lord our God says; then speak to us all that the Lord our God will speak to you, and we will hear and do it"* (Deut. 5:27).

Rather than enjoying a face-to-face relationship with God as Moses did, they were content with a list of laws to live by (Deut. 5:31).

God has impressed deep within my heart that either I will accept living out of a relationship with him or I will live out of a list of laws. Having already tried to live out a list of New Testament laws, I concur with the Scripture: The end of the law is death. Trying to keep laws, no matter how good they are, ends up producing death processes of guilt, condemnation, depression, discouragement, and heaviness within me.

We are told in Paul's Epistle to Galatians: "

...if you are led by the Spirit, you are not under the Law" (5:18).

Those who are Spirit-led are not under the law. This verse might be understood in two ways. Led by the Spirit is a description of all Christians. Therefore, no Christians are under the law; they are not depending on self-effort. It is the Spirit who is resisting the motions of evil within them, not they themselves. Also, to be led by the Spirit means to be lifted above the flesh and to be occupied with the Lord. When one is so occupied, he is not thinking of the law or the flesh. The Spirit of God does not lead people to look to the law as a means of justification. Rather, he points them to the risen Christ as the only ground of acceptance before God.

Thus, finally began to dawn on me that if I am led by the Spirit, the veil of legalism and our intellectual hardness is removed, and we can talk with the Lord Jesus Christ face to face, as it were. If I will walk in fellowship with him, I will find myself spontaneously living the demands of the law. Life would be so much easier this way, don't you think? The burden of trying to keep a host of commandments would no longer be on us. We would be living out of a person, the person of Christ.

We must all come to the point where we can sense the Father's initiative within us and flow with it. We are to be moved from law to grace—continual, moment-by-moment grace.

David

God has continually offered communion and fellowship to his people, and they have continually broken his heart by refusing him and choosing instead to live under law. Still, occasionally down through the history of the Old Testament someone was not content to live under rules and sought instead the relationship for which he was created.

Probably the man who achieved the highest level of communion with God in the Old Testament was David. He was not one to keep his thoughts or feelings under wraps. When he heard Goliath challenging the armies of Israel and their God, he didn't care who knew what he thought about it or what the consequences were. When the Ark of the Covenant was returned to Jerusalem, David was not shy about expressing his joy, and he danced with so much excitement and exuberance that his wife was embarrassed.

David approached his relationship with God with the same fervour and emotional freedom. No matter what he felt, he went straight to the Lord and openly and passionately expressed his feelings. When the guilt of his sin was heavy upon him, David poured out his heart to God:

> *"Wash me thoroughly from my iniquity and cleanse me from my sin. For I know my transgressions, and my sin is ever before me. Against You, You only, I have sinned, and done what is evil in Your sight...Hide Your face from my sins and blot out all my iniquities...Deliver me from blood guiltiness, O God, Thou God of my salvation"* (Psa. 51:2-4, 9, 14).

When the danger of his situation overwhelmed him with fear, David cried out to his deliverer:

> *"I cry aloud with my voice to the Lord; I make supplication with my voice to the Lord. I pour out my complaint before him; I declare my trouble before him...I cried out to You, O Lord; I said, 'You are my refuge, my portion in the land of the living. Give heed to my cry, for I am brought very low; deliver me from my persecutors, for they are too strong for me'"* (Psa. 142:1, 2, 5, 6).

When the injustice of his enemies became more than he could endure, David very honestly and vehemently called out to the Judge of all for justice and vengeance:

> *"O God of my praise do not be silent! For they have opened the wicked and deceitful mouth against me; they have spoken against me with a lying tongue... Appoint a wicked man over him; and let an accuser stand at his right hand. When he is judged, let him come forth guilty; and let his prayer become sin. Let his days be few; let another take his office. Let his children be fatherless and his wife a widow"* (Psa. 109:1, 2, 6-9).

When joy and peace flooded David's soul, the earth could not contain his praise:

> *"Praise the Lord! Praise God in his sanctuary; praise him in his mighty expanse. Praise him for his mighty deeds; praise him according to his excellent greatness...Let everything that has breath praise the Lord. Praise the Lord!"* (Psa. 150:1, 2, 6).

How does our Father feel about such an unbridled relationship? Acts 13:22 make it clear: *"I have found David the son of Jesse, a man after My heart, who will do all My will."* To say that God was pleased with David would be an understatement! God delighted in their relationship as much as David did. This is the kind of open and honest communication he longs to have with each of us. He wants us to come to him with all our lives: the joys and sorrows, successes and failures, highs and lows.

As I pondered David's relationship with God, the Lord began showing me not to stuff my feelings down into my heart and cover them over with a simple thanksgiving *"Praise the Lord!"* He taught me to be totally open and honest with him. He wanted me to express all my fears and angers and hurts, to invite him into them, and to hear all he wanted to say to me about them.

The greatest change in a personality takes place when we move into a deeper relationship with God. And before we can move into a deeper relationship with God, we must understand the dynamics of repentance, for if there has been movement away from God there can be no return without repentance.

Thus, I learned to express myself fully and freely before God, then to quiet myself in his presence, and to hear what he spoke back. He replaced my anger with his love, my depression with his joy, my death with his life. As I listened, I truly discovered that he spoke words of life.

Jesus

Jesus told us a little of what his relationship with the Father was like. In his high priestly prayer, Jesus prayed that we may be one in him as he and his Father are one. He declared that he did not speak on his own initiative but on his Father's, who abided in him and accomplished all his works (Jn. 14:10). *"I speak the things which I have seen with My Father"* (Jn. 8:38). In fact, Jesus said he did *nothing* on his own initiative (Jn. 8:28). The unity and communion between Father and Son were so great that Jesus always responded according to the Father's promptings. He always knew his Father's will and he always obeyed. They were One.

Jesus prayed that we may be one with our Father also, that we may always hear and obey, that we may testify, "We do nothing on our own initiative, but as our Father speaks, his will is accomplished."

What an incredible way to live! Doing nothing on our own initiative— is such a lifestyle possible for man? Was Jesus demonstrating to us how we should live, or was he showing us how God would live in this world? It is interesting that the Lord ends every one of the seven messages to the churches recorded in the Book of Revelation with words which could be paraphrased like this: "Are you listening?" The problem is never that God is not speaking; rather, the problem is that we are not listening. There is a voice in the heart of every true Christian that calls us to the place that is reserved for us. The trouble is that we seldom hear that voice because we are too busy focussing on the things that are going on all around us.

I conclude from the *kenosis* passage in Philippians 2:5-8 that Jesus emptied himself and took the form of a bond servant so that he could be an example of how *we* should live in this world. Therefore, we should accept the challenge to seek to live as Christ lived. It is clear from John 5 and 8 that Jesus lived out of the Father's initiative, vision, and spoken word. Truly this is the fullness of what God has always desired.

However, this was so foreign to the way I lived that it looked like an almost impossible task. But I firmly believed: *"Is the Lord's power limited?"* (Num. 11:23). The human impossibility is an occasion for demonstrating the Lord's power. How quickly we forget the Lord's past mercies when circumstances close in around us! Could we come to a place where we did nothing on our own initiative; where we only spoke the words, we heard the Father speaking within; where we only did those things, we saw the Father doing? Could we really cultivate this kind of openness to God's voice and vision?

With the keys God was unfolding before me concerning prayer and from my attempts to hear his spoken voice to my heart; I was convinced it was possible to live by divine initiative as Jesus did. Therefore, I purposed to learn to be constantly tuned to God's voice and vision. I knew I was drawing away from my culture by seeking this way of life, but I believed that Christians are called to live as Jesus did, and I was willing to pay the price to change. It took a long year or more to begin to establish these fundamental changes in my life. These are not changes you decide in one day and find fully in place the next, especially if you're analytically inclined like I am. It has taken few years for Jesus to work this kind of alteration into my lifestyle, and it must continue to be a daily decision to maintain this way of life. I have found that God must take many of us through the same slow, painful breaking process he took me through. However, each of us who has taken a step of growth in the Lord Jesus Christ can gladly testify that the price has been well worth it.

Mary and Martha

Jesus and his disciples were invited one day to Martha's house for dinner. Permit me to use a little sanctified imagination in explaining this incident. Making a meal for a crowd in those days was a very complex and time-consuming matter. It took time and energy to prepare the breads and vegetables and sweets.

So, when Martha invited Jesus and his friends home, she was willing to sacrifice herself for their comfort. Her sister Mary lived with her, and Martha naturally expected her sister also to help her in preparing the food for the guests. But Mary was nowhere in sight. She looked in the room where the guests were lounging. There, sitting at Jesus' feet, was Mary! Just sitting there! Martha couldn't believe it. She thought: "Wouldn't I like to be in there too, relaxing and hearing Jesus speak? And how can Jesus just let her sit there? He knows I'm in a rush. Why doesn't He make her help?" On and on she fumed as she doubled the speed of her work.

Finally, she was ready to explode. Angrily she marched into the house, her hands sticky with dough and her dress sprinkled with flour. Walking straight up to Jesus she demanded,

> *"Lord, do you not care that my sister has left me to do all the serving alone? Tell her to help me"* (Lk. 10:40).

She must have been totally unprepared for his response. The look of love and compassion in his eyes probably made her want to cry. He said,

> *"Martha, Martha, you are worried and bothered about so many things; but only a few things are necessary, really only one: for Mary has chosen the good part, which shall not be taken away from her"* (v. 41, 42).

Do you hear what Jesus said? Only one thing in life is necessary: communion with him! When I really understood what he was saying, my whole being protested: No, Jesus, that's not true! Lots of things are necessary in the Christian life. There's producing and serving and evangelizing and writing and teaching and caring for the poor. They are all necessary! How can you say they are not?

Probably I was hit so hard by Jesus' words because I was like Martha. I knew if I accepted his words, my whole life would need readjustment. Gradually the Lord began to show me the problem with my thinking. It is true that service, productivity, and evangelism are important, even very important. But they must never become goals in themselves. If they do, we have moved back from relationship to law. Such things are important only so far as they are products of communion.

When I am listening to the Lord, I hear from him the kind and place of service he has created me for; I find fulfilment and success with every effort. And when I follow his leading in evangelism, the catch is so plentiful that the nets almost break. But all of this happens only if the one necessary thing in life—listening to Jesus—has priority. I did not marry my wife so that she would serve me. I married her so that we could be together, enjoy each other's company, and share our lives. What I want most from my wife is not her service or her obedience but her love. Jesus is the Bridegroom of the Church. He is not married to her primarily so that she may serve him, but to share his love.

Paul

Paul was one of the greatest apostles and missionaries that ever lived. He probably was involved in the salvation of more souls than any other apostle. Yet when he expressed the deepest cry of his heart, it was, *"Oh, that I might know him!"* (Phil. 3: 10). Paul said that the thing he wanted most in life was not to win more souls, though he did that; nor to establish more churches, though he did that, too. What he cared about more than anything else was an intimate relationship with Jesus Christ. He wanted to *know him* and be with him and hear from him. Paul longed to love him more and more each day. And as a result of time spent communing with the Lord, Paul went out and changed the world.

We, too, cannot try to change the world and then become intimate with the Lord Jesus Christ once the work is done. All service, all productivity, all evangelism must flow out of communion with him.

The Church

God spoke to humans once again in the New Covenant and offered us a full relationship with him.

When I accepted Jesus as Lord of my life, it is true that I received "eternal life." If I thought very much about what that meant, I assumed it was something like a membership card that Jesus would have given to St. Peter at the pearly gate and thus be admitted into heaven. Eternal life meant I would live forever.

What a surprise when I found out that Jesus had something different in mind:

> *"This is eternal life, that they may know you, the only true God, and Jesus Christ whom you have sent"* (Jn. 17:3).

Eternal life is *knowing* God the Father and his Son. The Greek word for this "knowing," *ginosko*, is a very strong word. It may be defined as being intimately acquainted with someone in a growing, progressive relationship. *Ginosko* is used in the Septuagint translation of such passages as Genesis 4:1, *"Adam knew Eve his wife; and she conceived..."* (NKJV). It involves the most personal, intimate relationship between husband and wife. This, then, is eternal life; to be intimately involved in a growing relationship with the Father and the Son. Eternal life is a relationship!

Knowing God and growing in relationship with the Lord is a matter of grace. The initiative to such a kind of living is from God, since we have completely forfeited all claims in his favour by our sins. What matters supremely is not that I strive to know God, but the fact that he already knows me, a sinner, by making his love known to me. Paul expresses this thought when he writes to the Galatians, *"now that you have come to know God, or rather to be known by God ..."* (Gal. 4:9). The apostle suggests that grace comes first. People knowing God was the consequence of God's taking knowledge of them. We know him imperfectly in contrast to His knowledge of us, 'through and through' as we are. The Bible says:

> *"The Lord said to Moses, '...for you have found favour in my sight and I have known you by name"* (Exo. 33:17).

> *"Before I formed you* [Jeremiah] *in the womb I knew you, and before you were born, I consecrated you; ..."* (Jer. 1:5).

> *"I am the good shepherd, and I know my own and my own know me. ...and I lay down my life for the sheep...my sheep hear my voice, and I know them, ...and they will never perish"* (Jn. 10: 14, 15, 27, 28).

It is a knowledge implying personal affection, providential care, redemption and salvation.

Many people look to heaven primarily as an escape from the cares and trials of this world. That is not what heaven is all about. God gives us eternal life in heaven, so we can continue our intimate relationship with him forever. It would not be heaven without the close communion with our eternal lover that begins in this life and grows sweeter with the passing into eternity. Heaven comes to earth in our relationship with the Father and Son! Heaven can begin for you the day you move from law to love, from rules to relationship—the day you truly begin to *know* God!

Jesus came to offer us eternal life, a return to the garden where our Father is still walking, still loving, still longing for sweet communion with us. J. I. Packer says:

> "What were we made for? To know God. What aim should we set ourselves in life? To know God. What is the 'eternal life' that Jesus gives? Knowledge of God. *'This is the eternal life, that they may know you, the only true God, and Jesus Christ whom you have sent'* (Jn. 17:3). What is the best thing in life, bringing more joy, delight, and contentment, than anything else? Knowledge of God."

> *"Thus, says the Lord, 'Let not a wise man boast of his wisdom, and let not the mighty man boast of his might, let not a rich man boast of his riches; but let him who boasts boast of this, that he understands and knows Me...' declares the Lord'* (Jer. 9:23, 24).

What, of all the states God ever sees man in, gives him most pleasure? Knowledge of himself. *'I desire ...the knowledge of God more than burnt offerings'* says the Lord' (Hos. 6:6)." Hence, Peter exhorts us to *"grow in the grace and knowledge of our Lord and Saviour Jesus Christ"* (2 Pet. 3:18).

Knowing God is a matter of *personal involvement,* in mind, will, and feeling. It is an emotional relationship, as well as an intellectual and volitional one. Knowing God is more than knowing about him. A simple, but true believer in Christ will develop a far deeper acquaintance with his God and Saviour than another more learned person who is content with being theologically correct.

Hebrews 12:18-25 is a word to us, the Church. The writer compared the Israelites' fear at the fiery mountain, where God once offered relationship, to the glory of Mount Zion. In verse 25 He said, *"See to it that you do not refuse him who is speaking."* Once more God is speaking, inviting, wooing. To *"refuse him"* is to perish. Once more he is offering relationship.

Those who disobeyed the voice of God as it was heard in the law were punished accordingly. When privilege is greater, responsibility is also greater. In Christ, God has given his best and final revelation. Those who reject his voice as it now *"speaks from heaven"* in the gospel are more responsible than those who broke the law. *"Escape"* is impossible.

"God, after he spoke long ago to the fathers in the prophets in many portions and in many ways, in these last days has spoken to us in his Son" (Heb. 1:1-2).

He is saying, "Please do not do what the Israelites did. Please do not refuse my voice. Please do not return to the law. Please do not reject Me once more."

We are faced with the same choice. Will we accept the voice and the fire that comes with it? Will we live in relationship and daily conversation with God? Or will we turn away in fear and remain in bondage under the law which can only work death in our lives? Let us not refuse him who is speaking.

His Bride

And I heard something like the voice of a great multitude and like the sound of many waters and like the sound of mighty peals of thunder, saying, "Hallelujah! For the Lord our God, the Almighty, reigns. Let us rejoice and be glad and give the glory to him, for the marriage of the Lamb has come and his bride has made herself ready" (Rev. 19:6, 7).

The climax of history is a wedding! All of creation, all the universe, all of life is building toward the ultimate expression of the Creator's love: the marriage of the Son. And right now, we, the Church, are engaged to be the bride of the Lord. What do engaged couples usually do? They spend lots and lots of time together, sharing their love, sharing their lives, sharing everything.

We are engaged to live in excited relationship with our Lord and Saviour Jesus Christ. His heart is longing to share his ideas and feelings, his dreams and his love with us. Doesn't your heart respond to that love with the same desire? Don't you want to share your whole life with your betrothed?

Our Response

I decided when the Lord revealed these things to me: Love is more important than work. Love is the centre of the universe. I have begun to enjoy life, every single minute, and to share it in love with the Father and those around me. And if no one is around me, I'll just love life, and living, and the beauty of his creation. Love will always be the centre of life for me.

Why don't you stop right here, put this book down and express your love to Jesus? In some way tell or write of your love for him and your gratitude for all the blessings he has given you. Thank him for all the things that he has revealed to you and for his beautiful creation. Just love him for all he means to you.

When you are finished, wait for his reply. He may want to say he loves you too. He may tell you how precious you are to him. He may give you guidance or peace about an area of concern. Whatever he wants to say, give him the chance to say it. He's been waiting for you. Won't you respond?

The first key to clearly discerning God's voice in our hearts is to determine what his voice sounds like. Have you ever thought how pleasant is the voice of God? It is to be compared with the refreshing sound of running water in a pebbly brook – musical, delightfully gentle, and humble.

Our God is a communicating God who longs to make his thoughts and his will known to us. He has given us the *Logos*, the written Word, to teach us the laws that govern life on this earth and show by example the results of keeping or breaking those laws. God also speaks to us through the counsel of spiritual friends and religious leaders. And he uses circumstances to guide us in the way he wants us to go. All of these are vital means through which God communicates his will to man.

There is still another line of communication open to the children of God. There is a knowing, like men and women in the Bible, that *"the word of the Lord came to me."* There is a voice of God that we can hear—not necessarily audibly—but nonetheless clearly.

Chapter 3

Tuning to Insightful Intuition

God's voice in our hearts sounds like a flow of spontaneous thoughts. Therefore, when I tune to God, I tune to insightful intuition.

Many Christians long to have this kind of communication with our Lord. Some of us might have been told, however, that it isn't available to us. We might have been told that "Bible characters" were in some way different and more favoured, that God has chosen not to speak to us by name in this Church Age. By believing this, we have been robbed of the sweet communion for which we were created and redeemed. The deepest longing of our heart is for a relationship with God who made us. He alone, can provide us with love (security), value (self-worth), and purpose (significance) – all of which are essential for a joyful Christian living.

We learn from the book of Genesis how dedicated Abraham was to live in the presence of God and in close relationship with the Lord. The outworking of the Patriarch's habit of walking with God, resting in his revealed will, relying on the Lord, and obeying him even when he commands something odd are examples to follow. Above all we see solid trust in the promise of the Lord, even when he had to wait a quarter of a century, from the age of seventy-five to a hundred, for the birth of his promised heir. We see him utterly devoted to God's will, when he was willing to sacrifice his promised son, the only heir for whose birth he had waited so long. How wisely God had taught him his lesson!

The prophet Elijah was one to whom the word of the Lord came. Yet James 5:17 makes it clear that he had *"a nature like ours."* God doesn't play favourites! I believe that every child of God can experience the same fellowship that Adam and Eve enjoyed in the garden and Moses experienced in the meeting tent. Jesus declared, *"My sheep hear my voice"* (Jn. 10:27). I believe that is true. He is always speaking, and his sheep do hear his voice. Unfortunately, our culture has so affected our minds that we often do not recognize that it is our Shepherd who is speaking. Our civilization has become so rationalistic, humanistic, and scientific that we have left no place for the spiritual to break in on the visible world. But if we quieted our frantic thoughts long enough to hear his words, we would quite certainly hear him. When humanity is the centre of the universe and the source of all knowledge, "I" must be the originator of all my thoughts.

I have found in my own life that a little education, a little training, and a little stepping back from the sophistication of adulthood can make it possible not only to hear and know God's voice, but to carry on a dialogue in intimate communion with him. You may be saying, "But how can I recognize God's voice?" Probably no question plagues today Christians more. For years I searched for the answer. I studied everything I could find in the Bible that indicated how New Testament believers received guidance. I read every book I could find on the voice of God and the gifts of the Holy Spirit. I reasoned that in order to be used by the Spirit in the gifts, particularly the vocal ones, I had to be able to recognize God's voice. Although many wrote about the nature of the gifts, nothing I found clearly taught me how to be used in their operation.

So, I listened, as I have said, for the *"still, small voice of calm,"* but all I heard were regular thoughts running through my mind. In desperation,

I cried, "Where are you, God?" Finally, during a year of searching and studying, the Spirit brought revelation truth to my heart. He showed me that God's voice is sensed as a spontaneous idea appearing in my mind. The key word is *spontaneous.*

The voice of God is Spirit-to-spirit communication, the Holy Spirit speaking directly to my spirit. It is sensed as a spontaneous thought, idea, word, feeling, or vision. Thoughts from my mind, on the other hand, are analytical and cognitive. I reason them out; one logically follows the next. Thoughts from my heart are spontaneous. It is an intuitive process. Now I think you would agree that if this is a true definition of what God's voice sounds like, I have just provided a very simple answer to a very difficult question. Everyone has spontaneous thoughts every day. Are these all God's voice? I am *not* saying that every spontaneous thought is the Holy Spirit speaking to us . I *am* saying that insightful intuition is heart-level communication, and that analysis and reasoning are mind-level communication. Therefore, if I want to tune from my head to my heart, I tune from cognitive, analytical thoughts to the flow of spontaneous thoughts.

When I finally get to my heart, however, I find there are still three "voices" I can hear which need to be distinguished. I can hear those of my own heart, the Holy Spirit's, or Satan's. I still must do some judging and discerning, therefore, but at least I have moved from my head to my heart. That is a major accomplishment for many of us in the world. We will discuss in depth about testing this spontaneous flow later. First, I want to back up the definition I have given you with appropriate Scriptures, and some confirming experiences.

Genesis 28:11-22 gives an example of "a chance encounter" or "an accidental intersecting." Jacob was fleeing to his uncle's house, and he "came upon by chance," a certain place and spent the night there. He was just travelling along and "stumbled upon" this place to spend the night. He was just walking along and there it was. Jacob's whole attitude to life was ungodly and needed drastic changes. It was a divine decision for Jacob to have a vision in such an odd setting. But there it was.

If I were to tell you that prayer or intercession is a chance encounter or an accidental intersecting, you may not agree with me initially. You perhaps may ask me how is prayer or intercession a chance encounter or an accidental intersecting? But let me show you from something you might have probably experienced.

Do you remember a time, perhaps when you were just sitting in your balcony or near a window, just looking at the traffic in the street, when suddenly someone's name popped into your mind and you just knew you were supposed to pray for him? You hadn't been thinking about that person at the time. The thought just "came out of nowhere." But you accepted it as God prompting you to pray. This is intercession. When a "chance" thought intersects our reasoning processes, that "chance" encounter is really a divine encounter. God is speaking quietly and easily into our heart.

This is the voice of God: a chance idea that intersects our mind, not flowing from the normal, meditative   process, but simply appearing in our heart. This is God's voice—an idea from God lighting upon our heart and being registered in our mind as a spontaneous thought.

It was such an exciting revelation to me to realize that I had already heard God speaking to me! Though I had never heard an inner "voice," I had been aware of ideas lighting upon my mind. They had come simply as spontaneous thoughts. This finally taught me what to listen for to hear God's voice. *When I am listening for the Lord's voice, I am listening for spontaneous thoughts.* I have found that if I write out these intuitive thoughts, I am amazed at their wisdom when I re-read them. I am now convinced that I am hearing God's words to me.

God's voice often sounds like a flow of spontaneous thoughts. This is not to say, of course, that this is the only way God can speak to us. Earlier I had listed several other ways to know God's will. When God speaks normally it sounds like a flow of spontaneous thoughts that light upon our mind.

I have discovered certain characteristics of God's interjected thoughts which help me recognize and have confidence they are truly from Him.

They are like my own thoughts, except that I sense them as coming from my heart rather than my brain, in that they are spontaneous, not analytical or cognitive. It has taken a definite and deliberate refocusing for me to turn from living in analysis and logic to living in spontaneity. Now as I am leisurely relaxing, I allow him to speak to me in spontaneous thoughts. I have worked on changing my life so that I am normally tuned in to love and the great lover of my soul. I have found that if I remain tuned to spontaneity when I need to think things through or reason them out, the Lord can better interject wisdom and insight.

God's voice is often light and gentle and easily cut off by any exertion of self. If we interrupt the spontaneous, intuitive flow with our own analytical thoughts or our own will, He will not try to shout above the noise or regain our attention. He will simply be *still* and *wait* until we are again ready to listen.

God's voice will easily come as God speaking in the first person. It is your leap of faith in accepting the words as being from God that will make the difference. Remember, he who comes to God *must come in faith*.

God's voice often has an unusual content, meaning it is better and somewhat different than our own thoughts. It is wiser, more merciful, more discerning, and more concerned with motives. As Jesus so often did while he walked as a man, God may seem to ignore the question asked and address the real heart of the issue.

God's voice often causes a special reaction within us. There is often a sense of excitement, conviction, faith, vibrant life, awe or peace that accompanies receiving God's word. Many times, there is a quickening in our spirit or a sense of sharing a burden with Jesus.

God's spoken word carries with it the fullness of strength to carry it out. The yoke of the Lord is easy, and his burden is light. His will is not to put us under bondage, but to bring us into satisfaction and joy.

Even if he asks a hard thing, he gives the power to do it. If we say yes to him, his grace flows through us to accomplish his will. His Spirit goes out with his word to fulfil his purpose.

Your spiritual senses will be trained as you use them, and as time goes on you will more easily and frequently hear God speaking.

At first, we need to learn to distinguish God's interjected thoughts from the cognitive thoughts that come from our mind. For instance, have you ever been struggling with a difficult problem when all a sudden, the most creative solution you could imagine popped into your mind? What I've come to see is that such spontaneous, creative solutions to difficult problems that just drop into my mind are not mine at all. They are God's. He is speaking them within me. Rather than take credit for them myself, I now give the glory to God.

I have found that almost everyone has had another type of experience also. Have you ever been in the middle of prayer and had some garbage thoughts defile it? Most people have also taken credit for these thoughts, believing they are their own and feeling guilty and embarrassed.

I want to suggest that they are probably not your thoughts at all; it is Satan seeking to break up your prayer time. Again, you shouldn't feel guilty or ashamed; but ignore these garbage thoughts immediately. As we turn our thoughts back to Jesus, we sense an immediate release flowing through our heart and mind.

I have learned to take credit neither for the *spontaneous* good nor evil thoughts that flow within my heart. I give God the credit for the good ones and I give Satan the blame for the evil ones.

Chapter 4

The Power of *Rhema*

In Greek language there are two different words for "Word," *logos* and *rhema*. Dr. Ironside in his Greek lexicon has defined *logos* as "the said Word of God," and *rhema* as "the saying Word of God" or "spoken Word of the Lord." The universe was created by the Word, *logos*, of God. *Logos* is the general Word of God, stretching from Genesis to Revelation. By reading the *logos* from Genesis to Revelation we can receive all the knowledge we need about God and his promises. We may listen to the Word of God and you may study the Bible, but only when the Holy Spirit comes and quickens Scriptures to our heart, burning them in our heart and letting us know that they apply directly to our specific situation, does *logos* become *rhema*. *Logos* does not always become *rhema; b*ut *rhema* is produced out of *logos*. Thus, many scholars define the action of *rhema* as being the Holy Spirit using a few verses of Scripture and quickening it personally to one individual person. Dr. Paul Yonggi Cho defined *rhema* as *"a specific word to a specific person in a specific situation."*

Logos is given to everybody so that they may gain knowledge of God; but *rhema* is not given to everyone. *Rhema* is given to that specific person who is waiting upon the Lord until the Holy Spirit quickens *logos* into *rhema*. If we do not have time to wait upon the Lord, then the Lord can never come and quicken the needed Scripture to our heart and do not receive faith they need for the solutions to their problems. Prophet Isaiah says, *"...Blessed are all those who wait for him* [the Lord]" (Is. 30:18 NKJV).

Before the Lord quickens a Scripture to an individual, He has many things to do. The Lord wants to cleanse our lives and surrendered to him; the Lord will never give promises indiscriminately. As the Lord deals with us , we must take time to wait upon him; confessing your sins and surrendering your life to him. The Scriptural evidence of the power that accompanies God's word spoken by his Spirit into and through us is truly amazing. Let's look at a few examples.

Rhema Releases Productivity

One morning Simon Peter was washing his nets on the shore of Lake Gennesaret. He was tired and discouraged after fishing all night and catching nothing. Caught up in his own thoughts of failure and depression, he hardly noticed the Man preaching nearby or the crowd almost pressing him into the lake in their eagerness to hear His every word.

Suddenly Simon Peter's attention was captured as the Teacher walked over and climbed into his boat and requested that he put out a little way from the land, so he could better speak to the people. Simon Peter did as the Teacher requested. The time seemed to fly by as he sat in the boat, listening to the Teacher. Such words he spoke! Could they really be true? Could there really be a place in the kingdom of God for one such as him? Could Yahweh really love one as rough and loud and impulsive as he?

All too soon the Teacher finished speaking. He turned to Simon Peter and said, *"Put out into the deep water and let down your nets for a catch"* (Lk. 5:4). Brought sharply back to reality, he replied in disgust, *"Master, we worked hard all night and caught nothing."* Then, thinking again of the power of the words he had just heard, he added, *"But I will do so as you say* (rhema), *and let down the nets."* Simon Peter signalled his crew, and they threw the nets over. Suddenly, as if at some unseen signal, fish swarmed into the nets. Soon the nets were full to the breaking point. They frantically called their partners in another boat to come for help. Soon both boats were so full of fish till they began to sink.

What made the difference? Why did they labour fruitlessly for long hours and then catch more than they could handle? The difference was *rhema*. I can do what I think needs to be done, when I think, where I think, and the way I think. I can work hard, exhaust all my energy and resources, and still accomplish very little. When I begin a day, I can look at all the needs clamouring for my attention and wear myself out trying to meet them all. Or, I can start my day in prayer, and receive God's direction as *rhema*, telling me where to devote my time and energy. If I do that, I can walk through my day in peace, free from guilt and hassle, and accomplish far more than I ever could under my own initiative. *Rhema* gives us timing and it gives us location. *Rhema* gives productivity.

Rhema is Life

We have already seen that we must make a choice between living in relationship with Christ and living under interpreted precepts. Since the law was only preparatory (Gal. 3:23-25) and brought nothing to fulfilment (Matt. 5:17), the Spirit gives life. Jesus said, *"It is the Spirit who gives life...the words* [rhema] *that I have spoken to you are spirit and are life"* (Jn. 6:63).

When the Lord Jesus Christ speaks [*rhema*], you can feel the lifting in your spirit, the life flowing through you. The *Logos* can be interpreted as law that can be preached in the power of the Spirit bringing us into freedom and life. The difference is often simply one of emphasis, a lack of clearly proclaiming that the power of the resurrected Christ does the work. If what are preached are rules that must be obeyed to achieve right standing before God, the Word is reduced to law. But when the same Word is opened under the anointing of the Spirit, it shows us the glory of Christ within us and releases us from the power of sin and death.

Rhema Gives Authoritative Teaching

When Jesus taught, the Jews were amazed because he spoke with such authority. Where did he get this power? It was not his own divine right, for Philippians 2 makes it clear that he emptied himself when he became man, laying aside all privileges and powers of Deity. So, what is the secret to the authority of his words? John 14 clearly tells us that he did not speak on his own initiative, but that the Father was abiding in him. The words Jesus spoke were *rhema* to him, *rhema* received as he spent time in the presence of the Father. Because he spoke out of the Father's initiative, his teaching was powerful and authoritative.

The same holds true for believers today. The *rhema* have power to change lives. This is the "anointing," the "divine unction." *Rhema* results in authoritative teaching.

Rhema Results in Fullness of Desire

"If you abide in me, and my words [rhema] *abide in you, ask whatever you wish, and it shall be done for you"* (Jn. 15:7).

If we are living in relationship, hearing the voice of God and obeying it, we will always receive what we ask for. This reminds me of Psalm 37:4,

> "Delight yourself in the Lord; and he will give you the desires of your heart."

The first half of each verse is the key to the second half. If our delight is the Lord, if our greatest pleasure is being with him and pleasing him, then the desires of our heart will be only what give him pleasure. If his *rhema* abides in us, the fire will do its work in us. We will be cleansed and purified of all desires that are not his and what we wish will only be his will. St. Augustine enjoined believers to "love God and do what you please." This was not a license to sin but recognition that if we truly love God, what we please will be to do his will.

Joy in its New Testament sense has to do with the flow of the life-giving sap of the true vine as it flows into the branches, invigorating the growth, producing foliage and fruit which is made into the wine

of gladness. Jesus promises us that if we abide in him as the branches
abide in the vine, then the result will be not only fruit-bearing, but
communicative joy. Jesus said,

> *"These things I have spoken to you so that my joy may be in you, and that
> your joy may be made full"* (Jn. 15:11).

Rhema Brings Faith

Faith is perhaps the most important, most significant result of *rhema*.
Romans 10:17 is a well-known yet little understood verse. *"So, faith
comes from hearing, and hearing by the word* [rhema] *of Christ."* Faith
is the result of divine initiative. Faith is fired in our hearts when we
hear the spoken word of Christ to us.

You have probably experienced it. You were facing a trial or problem.
You wanted to trust God. With your mind you knew his promises and
knew he could keep his word. Yet in your heart you wondered if he
would do it for you. Suddenly, one day as you were reading the Word or
praying or listening to a sermon, a specific word spoke to you and you
knew that God was going to come through for you. Faith was no longer
a mental activity or a spiritual discipline. Faith was alive and vibrant.
No longer was there a striving to believe; you entered the blessed rest
of confidence in your God. *Rhema* resulted in faith.

When you are doubting, and your faith is weak, rather than going
to the *logos* alone, you need to go to prayer and ask the Father to speak
his word into your heart. When he speaks, faith will explode within
you. When you don't know where to go or what to do next, you need
to hear *rhema* from God. To move powerfully in faith, you must move
in response to *rhema*: the witness of the Spirit within you.

God Gave You a Mind...

You may be wondering if I am going to recommend throwing our minds
away since spontaneous heart thought is that part of us through which
the voice of God so often flows. Not at all! God has given us both our

hearts and our minds. We are not to despise or overuse either. They are both gifts from Almighty God, and they both have a place.

In our culture we have essentially idolized the mind and scorned the heart. Many of us need to repent of that idolization and scorning, and to ask God to balance them out in our lives. That is precisely what I have had to do. Repentance provides the foundation for change, and God has the ability and desire to balance each of us.

Let me show you briefly two different approaches to receiving pure revelation from the throne room of God by comparing Luke's method with John's.

St: Luke appears to have been the more analytical one by nature. He tells us how he received his Gospel:

> *"It seemed fitting for me...having investigated everything carefully from the beginning, to write it out for you in consecutive order..."* (Lk. 1:3).

This doesn't sound like an intuitive, heart-functioning person to me. As a matter of fact, it sounds totally analytical. And yet Luke's Gospel is pure revelation.

John used a completely different approach. He seems to have been more the mystic:

> *"I was in the Spirit on the Lord's Day, and I heard behind me a loud voice like the sound of a trumpet, saying 'Write in a book what you see...'"* (Rev. 1:10, 11).

That sounds like an intuitive, visionary approach to receiving revelation! Yet both received and wrote pure revelations that stand to this day.

So, we can see, there are at least a couple of ways to receive revelation from the Holy Spirit. Luke's method for hearing from the Lord will likely appeal to the person who is more analytical by nature. The person who is generally intuitive will probably relate more to John's process.

We may have a hard time accepting and honouring an approach different from our own. We must learn to honour the fact that God grants pure revelation to both. I am most comfortable using Luke's approach. I study things out carefully and then ask the Holy Spirit to put it all together in the way he wants. But I also believe that for me to receive pure revelation I must use more than just my analytical abilities. I must allow intuition and spontaneity to flow into the process also, or else I will only come up with a product of my own analytical reasoning.

If you are overly analytical, God may be calling you to begin developing your intuitive side. If you are very intuitive, he may be calling you to develop your analytical abilities.

Praying with an Idol in Your Heart

Ezekiel 14:4 says: *"Therefore speak to them and say to them. Thus says the Lord God: Every man of the house of Israel who takes his idols* [of self-will and unsubmissiveness] *into his heart and puts the stumbling block of his iniquity* [idols of silver and gold] *before his face, yet comes to the prophet* [to inquire of him], *I the Lord will answer him according to the multitude of his idols"* (Amp. Bible).

When some of idolaters at heart visited the prophet Ezekiel to get counsel from the Lord, the Lord announced that he would answer idolaters directly, not through a prophet. This brings into focus a startling truth concerning an inappropriate method of prayer, which has been practiced by many.

When we come to the Lord in prayer, we are to be a *"living sacrifice."* We are to have laid down our will and be totally abandoned to God's will concerning the issue about which we are praying. If that is not our posture, we are to pray for God to form that posture within us before we begin praying. If we pray about the issue while we still have a definite direction about it in our own heart, that direction of our own interferes with the signals coming from the throne of God and causes us to believe that God is confirming the direction we felt, whether he is or not.

In other words, if I pray about a thing, and the thing is more prominent in my vision or my consciousness than the Lord is, the answer that comes back will be from me, rather than from the Lord. On the other hand, if the Lord is more prominent in my consciousness than my vision of the thing I am praying about, then the answer will come from the Lord and it will be pure revelation, not contaminated with my desires. The principle here is that the intuitive flow comes out of the vision I am holding before my eyes. I am commanded to fix my eyes on Jesus, *"the Author and Finisher of my faith."* If I do, the vision will be pure.

An example of a prophet getting his vision clouded and receiving damaging direction can be found in the story of Balaam in Numbers 22. Balak had sent messengers to Balaam, asking him to come and curse the Israelites. When Balaam sought God about it, God was very clear: *"Do not go with them; you shall not curse the people; for they are blessed"* (v.12).

Balak again sent messengers, more distinguished than before, with the offer that Balak would honour him richly and do whatever he asked if he would only come and curse the Israelites. Apparently gold and riches were on Balaam's mind because he said,

> *"Though Balak was to give me his house full of silver and gold, I could not do anything, either small or great, contrary to the command of the Lord my God"* (v.18).

However, he invited them to stay, saying, *"I will check with the Lord again."*

Since he so desperately wanted the option to receive the honour, gold, and riches, he went again in prayer to the Lord, this time with an idol in his heart. As could be expected, the Lord gave him the answer in view of the idol in his heart. He said, *"...rise up and go with them; but only the word which I speak to you shall you do"* (v.20). However, God was angry with Balaam and sent an angel with a sword to block his path (v.22).

When we pray with an idol in our hearts, we may get an affirmative answer from the Lord, but it will bring us destruction. Therefore, when we pray, we must be certain that our vision is purified and that we see Jesus as one who is much larger than the thing or issue for which we are praying for. Only then will our answer be pure and life-giving.

Logos and *Rhema*

As a concluding note to this chapter I want to mention that Dr. Paul Yonggi Cho has suggested that *rhema*, translated "Word," is used by New Testament writers to describe God's spoken voice within our heart. After careful consideration, I agree with him. If you would like to explore this idea further, the first three appendices may help. Appendix A is "*Logos* and *Rhema* in the Greek New Testament," Appendix B is a list of the seventy uses of *rhema* in the New Testament, and Appendix C is "Understanding the Power of *Rhema*."

From this point on I will refer to God's inner voice as the *rhema* word. This is just one of its uses, but it provides a simple way for us to encapsulate the concept.

It was extremely difficult for me to begin moving out of cognition into the spiritual dimension and intuition. But as I have continued in this walk, the way has become easier and easier. It is almost "first nature" to me now. God has totally refocused my life. He can do the same for you.

Chapter 5

Practicing Quiet Time

KEY #2

I must learn to still my own thoughts and emotions, so I can sense God's flow of thoughts and emotions within me.

So often when we come to the Lord in prayer, we find that all the rush and activity of our life follow us into our prayer closet. All the noise and flurry of everyday life screams for our attention, while pressures and responsibilities call from within. We would like to be able to immediately find sweet communion with our Lord and even after we shut the door of the prayer closet, we are distracted to a great extent. But do not get discouraged.

Take your Bible and a notebook and read a portion from the Bible slowly. Let it soak in your mind and meditate on the verses you read from the Bible. Make a note of anything that comes to you from these verses. Pray then, mentioning any requests or personal petitions you may have. Then relax and listen to see if God has something to say to you. It is far easier to talk than listen; so, don't worry if for some weeks or months nothing comes. Tuning in to God takes time and practice.

Now-a-days the term 'Quiet Time' is regarded by many as being old fashioned, and to our shame the practice of setting time aside to be alone with God is deemed to be unrealistic because life is so busy. But the fact is that those who do not have a 'Quiet Time' are likely to have an unquiet time during the day. Whether or not you use the term 'Quiet Time,' it is vital that you start the day by spending a little time with God. If you do not, then your life will soon lack direction. Therefore, in Scriptures there are so many references to beginning the day closeted with God. Dr. Griffiths has written, "Quietness is not only the opposite of noise. It is the absence of excitement, haste, and consequent confusion." These dissipate strength, while calmness and deliberateness conserve it. The world's mighty people have grown in solitude.

In the early days of the Charismatic renewal, many of its leaders who had been fed on a diet of legalism began to emphasise the joy of knowing Christ's presence through the indwelling Spirit every hour of the day. People often used to say then that they need not have 'Quiet Time' in order to feel God's presence. The danger lies not in emphasising that we are in Christ's presence every hour of the day but the de-emphasis on closeting oneself alone with him in personal prayer and study of his Word. Although most leaders of the Charismatic renewal did not teach or encourage people to dispense with their personal time of devotion with the Lord, many came to believe they could get through the day simply by speaking in tongues.

Nothing must become a substitute for those private and personal moments we spend in prayer and communion with Christ. Our Lord knew and sensed the presence of God with him and in him to a degree we will never fully experience here on this earth, but it is said of him in Scripture that he had two "customs." One custom was to go regularly to the house of God; the other was to pray regularly. And these must be our customs too.

Have you ever gone into your prayer closet with only fifteen minutes to pray and experienced your mind racing, your emotions changing widely? If you have, you have discovered that pressuring yourself to become still is a total waste of time. It's like trying to make yourself go to sleep at night as you toss and turn on your bed. The more pressure you use, the wider awake you are. Similarly, the more we try to force our own busy thoughts and emotions out of our heart and mind, so we can sense God's spontaneous flow within, the more agitation we feel.

On several occasions I have left my prayer closet totally discouraged because I was unable to get beyond my own raging self to the Holy Spirit's gentle inner impressions. I came out after twenty minutes knowing I had not contacted God at all in my spirit. I found this extremely frustrating. When I have so little time for prayer to start with, I am incensed by having to waste time in simply trying to get past myself.

In the following paragraphs I shall share with you an excellent biblical technique that God has designed for us to quickly quiet ourselves in His presence. This is not the end of prayer or a goal in itself; it is, however, the necessary first step so the rest of our prayer time can be spent in dialogue with Almighty God.

Be Still, and Know…
Psalm 46:10 encourages us, *"Be still, and know that I am God"* (NKJV). There is a deep inner knowing in our spirit that each of us can experience when we quiet our flesh and our minds. Even when walking in outer turmoil, we can experience peace.

The New American Standard Bible gives several synonyms or alternate readings for *"be still"* in Psalm 46:10. It may be understood as *"cease striving, relax, or let go."* Each of these phrases gives an excellent description of what takes place inside us when we come to this place of stillness. We must let go of our intense striving and relax into his perfect ability.

Surprisingly many of the believers of the Bible today are so torn on what to focus on; more fear of the Lord, more love, more repentance, and prayer for deliverance, etc? They just don't know how to come to the presence of the righteous God. One of the most important issues in life is fixing our gaze in the right direction. If we look mainly at ourselves, we will be discouraged. If we look only at others, we become distracted. However, if Christ becomes the focus of our attention then the Holy Spirit will help us our hearts are quietened, because we know that the One into whose face, we are gazing has the last word in human affairs. What is more, gazing at him with unveiled faces means that any incipient impure thoughts that may arise are sterilized by his purity. We are all the purer for gazing.

The biblical teaching that we should turn our attention from ourselves to Christ contains a principle that psychologists now accept. They have realized that when we look beyond ourselves to another person we are freed from self-preoccupation – a disease as deadly as cancer. All the cults aim to get you to look within yourself – a healthy thing when done in a balanced way. But endless preoccupation with self leads us to focus on our own state of mind and emotions. There is a law in psychology that says: whatever gets your attention gets you. If Christ gets our attention then we, in turn, get him.

As we engage with Christ in prayer and meditate on his Word, we, to a lesser extent, go through a transformation such as he experienced on the Mount of Transfiguration. The more he enters our lives, the brighter and more beautiful our lives become. Nothing is more glorious or beautiful on this planet than a person in whom the loveliness of Christ is seen.

All of those are needed in greater measures to quietly sit at his feet and to learn of him. We must not be frantic inapproaching him and his presence. As mentioned earlier, simply come and sit in his presence. Draw from him. Be still, relax, cease striving and know that he is God!

How different are our attitudes when called upon to face a crisis? We are more concerned with how we will come out of it than how much God will be glorified. I think it is because we are being brainwashed by a world that is filled with self-interest. Brainwashed Christians need another kind of washing – the washing of the water of the Word (Eph. 5:26).

Be in the receiving mode. One cannot receive when running about frantically in the natural until there is a stopping, and open arms, etc. So, in the spirit, stop! Put out your arms and receive. Do not try to get more fear of the Lord or try to muster it up. The same goes for deeper repentance, etc. Do not go about frantically trying to stir up or force yourself into greater repentance. It is needed in much greater measures and it will come and is coming.

The Greek word for repentance, *"metanoia,"* means "a change of mind." But a change of mind about what? About where life is found? Prior to coming to Christ our minds are shot through with the idea that life depends on such things as self-sufficiency, self-management, ego-building, and so on. The Bible confronts this self-centred approach to living and says that for our lives to work the way God designed them, ego must not be central. In other words, Christ must be central, and the ego revolves around him just as the planets revolve around the sun.

Turn your eyes upon him. Fix your gaze upon him. Focus and set your mind and affection on him and he will do in you all that is needed. Come, rest and receive. Allow him to embrace you and to shower on you over and repeatedly. You cannot learn everything all at once. Do not be so hard on yourself. Receive of him day by day. Little by little, truth by truth, revelation by revelation. Be still and know. It is in stillness that the hearing comes. It is when you are quiet and in a state of rest that you can hear and receive from him and it is through this concentration that the spiritual life is deepened. The great French Christian Blaise Pascal once declared that "Nearly all the ills of life spring from this simple source that we are unable to sit still for long in a quiet room." Be still!

Sitting still can be therapeutic, but what if in the stillness we meet with God? We then receive spiritual therapy. God waits to offer us infinite resources – for the asking and the taking. The Quiet Time is where the soul grows receptive, where prayer becomes "the organ of spiritual touch," where the touch becomes as effective and as healing as the touch of the woman on the hem of Jesus' garment, where peace flows into our turbulence, where love absorbs our resentments, where joy heals our grief, and where we enter into the process of being known. The Quiet Time shuts us in with God, the door closes upon us, and then infinite resources flood into our soul. The door opens, and we move out with an increased awareness of God, ready to face a world that knows so little about him. There is, great benefit in stillness, but when we meet with God in the stillness – ah, what then!

Remove Outer Distractions

But how can we come to this inner stillness? The first step must be removing all outer distractions. In Mark 1:35 we read that Jesus went to a lonely place to pray. The prophet Habakkuk went to a guard post when he wanted to hear from God. And in 1 Kings 19 we find Elijah alone in a mountain cave, frightened and depressed, when the word of the Lord came to him.

I found when I first began seeking inner stillness that I needed to find a quiet place where I could be alone and undisturbed. So, I learned to rise before the rest of my family and allow the quietness of early morning to help bring peace within my spirit. I struggled with this, until the Lord convinced me that I was not indispensable, and life would go on quite well without me.

During the first few weeks of seeking inner stillness, I found that I could only become attuned to intuition first thing in the morning. Since analytical thought had been such a powerful idol in my life, I found I had to carefully avoid becoming involved in analytical thinking before prayer, because I'd then be caught in it for the rest of the day. As I continued, it became easier. You, too, will find that you will cultivate the skill of quieting your heart and mind before the Lord as you practice it.

Get Comfortable!

As I tried to focus my heart and mind on Jesus, I found another distraction: my body. If there was tension or discomfort in any part of my body, I became very conscious of it when I sought to be still.

Our goal in prayer should be to be totally God-conscious, and if our knees ache or feet are tired, our attention may be divided. Hence, each person must choose his own comfortable position and totally relax in body and spirit.

Remove Inner Distractions

Quieting the outside distractions is the easier part of coming to stillness; as I approach quietness, I usually find my mind raging with voices, thoughts, pressures, and tensions that demand my attention. All my unfinished business and my forgotten responsibilities vie for my attention as soon as I become still. I have ignored them, and when they see a chance for recognition, they take it! If I try to push them back down, they only scream louder.

The next voice that often breaks through is our own conscience. If the Lord has spoken to us and we have not yet been obedient, we may hear our conscience wallowing in our guilt? No! If we are going to have fellowship with Jesus, we must not focus on our ugly shell, but on his marvellous grace. So, when I have sinned, I confess my guilt and accept his complete forgiveness. I move beyond myself and my weakness into an awareness of him and his greatness.

We are either going to gaze upon ourselves and our sin and weakness, or upon Christ and His glory and grace. If I have decided to fix my eyes upon him (Heb. 12:2) and see myself "*clothed*" with his righteousness (Gal. 3:27), I then discover myself being drawn into his presence, his glory, and his righteousness. It is so important that we carefully choose our focus. We will either focus on ourselves or on Christ, on our sin or on his righteousness. I have chosen to focus on what the Bible says is true, and I have discovered that I am then quickly ushered into his presence. I encourage each of you to carefully select your focus as you enter prayer. The wrong vision brings death. The right vision gives life.

The goal of being inwardly still is not a total emptying of our mind or a cessation of our thought processes, but rather a refocusing of them.

When all the other voices within us have been dealt with, we must find a way to tune out thinking / reasoning and tune-in intuition.

Refocus on him

The most effective biblical tool for heightening the spiritual sensitivity of most people is music. When Elisha wanted to hear the voice of the Lord, he asked for a minstrel to come and play for him (2 Kings. 3:15). Often when we need to know he is there; we will sing a song of worship and adoration. Thousands of people around the world have been impacted by the simple practice of "soaking" in the Lord's presence, merely being still on the outside and allowing music to carry them into their hearts, where he is waiting.

Paying attention to the song in our heart, especially upon awakening, can be a clue to the message our spirit or the Holy Spirit Who is joined to our spirit wants to give to us, or may be an expression of what our heart feels. Songs of praise and worship can be extremely valuable in focusing our heart and soul on our Lord, especially if we engage the eyes of our heart to see what we are singing . The Sun of Righteousness will rise within us , and faith, hope, love, joy, and the sweet knowledge of his presence will be filled within our heart.

Two other helpful biblical techniques to become still are vision and love. We must look with the eyes of our heart to see in the Spirit a vision of Jesus and we are talking together, and the vision has the power to carry us beyond analytical thought. As we see Jesus with us and we express to him all the love we feel for him, and as our love overflow, we are drawn into the stillness of his presence.

Breath and spirit are indicated by the same word in both Hebrew and Greek. We can use our breath to bring our spirit into stillness. As our breath goes out, we can practice confessing all our sin and guilt. Slowly we may breathe in the cleansing Holy Spirit. As we repeat this exercise, our body and soul come into a peaceful awareness of the presence of the Lord.

The goal in achieving inner stillness is to know deep within ourselves the movement of God.

"Be still and know that I am God." (Ps.. 46:10).

"Rest in the Lord and wait patiently for him" (Ps.. 37:7).

Sometimes this is the hardest for us to do. Waiting is the thing we do least well! But true faith waits, confident that God can do what he has promised (Rom. 4:21). When we really become still, we will sense a shift within us and begin to experience the active flow of the Holy Spirit's feelings, ideas and visions.

Becoming still is not *doing* something; but it is being in touch with the Lord Jesus Christ within. I do not struggle or force myself to be still. It is a letting go, a relaxing, and a ceasing to strive. To be still is to experience Jesus Christ in this moment. He is I AM. To live with the God of now, we must live in this moment. We must not mourn the past or worry about the future—rather we must enjoy Christ in the present moment. We are to let salvation come to this present point in time. We are then sharing that moment with the One we love.

Hindu Religious or Cult Practices?
You might be questioning the similarities between some religious or cult practices, such as yoga, transcendental meditation or Zen, and what I am advocating. Or perhaps you have been taught to fear all inner stillness as a tool of the present age to allow demons access to your mind. It is true that the avenues of approach to the spiritual world are similar. It is true that some cults have spirit-to-spirit encounters. However, they are contacting the evil one and demonic spirits; we have communion with the Holy One. Avenues of approach are not in themselves good or evil. They are merely tools. Remember that Christianity above all religions should be alive with a vibrant relationship with the Holy Spirit.

In later chapters we shall discuss in greater detail on testing and submission to the Word and relationship to the Body of Christ. But for now, we must be clear that Christianity is not simply an intellectual understanding. It is a daily, dynamic, ongoing relationship with the living Lord. Spiritual encounter is God's gift to his people. Satan is the great copy-cat and he has attempted to steal away this precious gift. The demonic religions have offered a counterfeit of the spiritual reality intended for the Church. And should the Church out of fear of the counterfeit reject the reality?

Let us not withdraw from the real just because Satan has made a counterfeit. We certainly must use care and not stand alone when we are dealing with spiritual experiences, but we need not run away from them. God provides us with ample safeguards in His Word and His Church, if we will humbly submit to them. It is time the Church stopped running away when Satan raises his ugly head! The Church must stand up in the authority of Jesus Christ and declare Satan to take his hands off it!

Inner stillness and spiritual encounter are God's gifts to the Church. We were created with an awareness of the spiritual world and a need to be in contact with it. We can never be satisfied with the material world alone. If we do not offer our people, and becoming still, quieting our thoughts and emotions especially our youth, and Holy Spirit a reality for their daily lives, they will seek it elsewhere and be trapped in Satan's lies.

Acknowledge that you are "a longing being" and that your longings can never be fully satisfied except in a deep ongoing relationship with Jesus Christ. If you do not acknowledge this then you are driven to try and meet your longings in other ways. When you do acknowledge your longings, you get in touch with the fact that you are a thirsty yearning being. Focus on that fact; feel the thirst. Our desire to know God and enjoy him depends on how aware we are of a lack in our life. In one sense everyone is thirsty for God, and we know, too, that most will not admit it. Thus, the thirst is masked – masked, but always there. Eugene Peterson says, "Everyone is on the verge of crying out, 'My Lord and my God,' but cry is drowned out by doubts or defiance." Remember it was God who built that thirst for himself into the human soul when he established the human creation.

Don't be satisfied with the mere duties of Christian life. One of the saddest things to see is a believer remaining content with practicing the duties of Christian life and relying on them to bring satisfaction rather than a dynamic and passionate relationship with Jesus Christ. Why is it, I often ask myself, that many Christians I meet have so little passion in their lives? Clearly, they are not in touch with their longings. The only satisfying relationship with God is a passionate one. The Psalmist says:

> "O God, you are my God; I shall seek You earnestly; My soul thirsts for You, my flesh yearns for you ..." (Ps. 63:1).

If we are to go deeper with God, there is a need to understand the importance of *pursuing him with passion.* One of the blights of modern-day Christianity is that so many of Christ's followers are too easily satisfied. They drink from the Fountainhead and seem to be satisfied with what they have received that they have no desire to drink more. Christ most certainly quenches our soul's great thirst, but in quenching it he arouses within us the thirst for more. "To have found God and still to pursue him," said St. Bernard of Clair Vaux, "is the soul's paradox of love." How wonderful it would be today if we are gripped by such an overwhelming desire to know God better, to taste more of him, to feel him at work more powerfully in our souls, to see him as Job did, with our inner eyes, that we turn from this moment and find some quiet spot where we too will pray with Moses, *"... I pray you, show me your glory!"* (Ex. 33:18).

One of the common characteristics we find in the saints and seers of Scripture is the heat of their desire for God. King David is another example. Though he was guilty of two of the vilest of sins – murder and adultery – yet he yearned after God and longed for him with intense spiritual passion. His psalms ring with the cry of the seeker and the glad shout of the finder. But even when he finds him his heart is eager to know more:

"When you said, 'Seek My face,' my heart said to you, 'Your face, O Lord, I shall seek.'" (Ps. 27:8)

"...my soul longs for you, as a parched land" (Ps. 143:6).

The same longing can be seen in the life of the apostle Paul – one of the most outstanding Christians in history. Has anyone known God more intimately than did the great apostle? Yet this is his plea in the letter he wrote to the Philippians: *"that I may know him and the power of his resurrection and the fellowship of his sufferings..."* (Phil. 3:10). But he did know him, yet his plea was that he might know him more.

It is time now to ask ourselves: Are we passionate about Christ? Do we yearn after God? Are we thirsty for God to such a degree that we long after him in the same way that a thirsty *"deer pants for the water brooks?"* (Ps. 42:1). Does he fill and thrill your soul to the exclusion of all else? The thirst for God is there in all of us, but the problem is that we do not sense that thirst or even if we are aware of thirst we are easily satisfied also. We are content with the appetiser and ignore the banquet. Only in a passionate relationship with God will your longings for security, self-worth and significance be met.

If God has placed within us a heart that pants (Hebrew word for 'pant' literally means a desire so intense that it becomes audible) after him, why do we not feel thirstier than we do? What must we do to get in touch with the deep longing for the Lord which our Creator has put at the core of our beings?

The major reason is the stubborn commitment to independence which, due to the Fall, characterises every one of us. We like to feel we are in control of the way our soul's thirst can be slaked. The prophet Jeremiah says:

"My people ... have ... forsaken me, the fountain of living waters, to hew for themselves cisterns, broken cisterns that can hold no waters" (Jer. 2:13).

We see Israel being charged with two evils – forsaking the spring of living water and digging their own cisterns for holding water. Why would Israel do such nonsensical things – turning away from a fresh spring and digging cisterns, *broken* cisterns that could not hold water? Because they liked the feeling, they got from seeking *independently* to find water for their souls. The opposite of independence is dependence. And that is the main prerequisite for experiencing the great thirst that God has put within us. But giving up our independence and trusting God to come through for us is not easy. None of us likes giving up control. When we can learn to give up our independence and enter a life of trust, then the passion for God will not just be experienced in our soul but explode in it.

Although we start off in the Christian life believing we cannot bring about our own satisfaction, and that fullness of life comes from drawing on God's resources, we can, without even realising it, begin to move away from dependence on the Lord to dependence on ourselves.

The self-centred are the self-disrupted. The human personality was designed to have Christ at the centre. The truth is that we were created to function with God at the centre. The ego is meant to revolve around God and his Son Jesus Christ. If we allow self-centredness to govern our life instead of the desire to please God then we will find ourselves in conflict with our own selves , develop all kinds of complexes. We cannot be made into Christ's image unless we reflect his glory. Self-centredness prevents that happening and hinders the process of spiritual transformation.

We give others the impression that we have only the interests of the kingdom at heart, yet deep down we are more interested in what God can do for us than in what we can do for him. Dr. Larry Crabb has written, "For many modern-day Christians our relationship with God is not about knowing him but using him. We always tend to use God to solve our problems rather than using our problems to know more of God." If our dominant motive is to get God to do things for us, and not to know him better, then that can lead to an inner division that will vitiate our spiritual lives.

There are many Christians who have an illusion that if they keep dependence on Christ, material prosperity and thus happiness is assured. They are continually yearning to see always something good. But the trouble is that they want blessing without Blesser, and goodness without God. They want all the benefits of a Christ-filled life, but they do not want the Benefactor.

Does it mean anyway, that when we rely on God to meet the deep needs of our spirit, we will never experience hurt? No, but what it does mean is that though we may be shaken we will not be shattered. Our relationship with God does not insulate us from the feelings of hurt or make us invulnerable to disappointment, but it does uphold us and enable us to go on loving in the same way that we ourselves are loved by Jesus Christ. In times of difficulty BE STILL! Have you not heard His voice saying:

> *"... 'This is the way, walk in it,' whenever you turn to the right or to the left"*
> (Is. 30:21).

He is your Rock, and rocks do not shake. He is your High Tower, and a high tower cannot be flooded. We need mercy, and to him belongs mercy. Do not run hither and thither in panic! Just quietly wait, hushing your soul, as he did the fears of his friends on the eve of Gethsemane and Calvary.

> *"Rest in the Lord and wait patiently for him ..."* (Ps. 37:7).

Chapter 6

Vision in Prayer Lives

A s I pray, I fix the eyes of my heart upon Jesus, seeing in the spirit the dreams and visions of Almighty God.

The third key the Lord opened for us involves the use of vision in our prayer lives. Remember that Habakkuk kept *"watch to see"* what God would speak to him (Hab. 2:1). In some way Habakkuk was using vision as a part of his spiritual encounter with Almighty God. In Habakkuk 1:1 the prophet said, *"The oracle* (burden) *which Habakkuk the prophet saw."* Many of the prophets also spoke of the burden and words that the Lord spoke within their hearts being formed in visions (e.g., Is. 1:1; 2:1; 6:1; 13:1; etc.).

This struck me as an entirely new concept: God uses visions regularly *to speak* his words within our hearts. I had never even considered the use of vision as an important aspect of my communication with God. When I stopped to consider it, I found hundreds of verses from Genesis to Revelation which demonstrated that in every covenant God have chosen to reveal him within human hearts by use of dream and vision.

In Appendix D, references to dream and vision throughout Scripture are listed, and by no means is that list exhaustive. It is recommended that you take a couple of hours sometime and read carefully through these verses to gain for yourself a basic appreciation of the way God uses dream and vision. This will give you the best grounding for the things we are discussing in this chapter.

When we consider the issue of vision theologically and philosophically, we will realize there was no reason not to expect God to continue to speak to his people through dreams and visions, especially because he told us,

> "In the last days...I will pour forth of my Spirit upon all mankind; and your sons and your daughters shall prophesy, and your young men shall see visions, and your old men shall dream dreams" (Acts 2:17).

Dream and vision are inseparably linked with the moving of the Holy Spirit in the last days. In this great latter-day outpouring of the Spirit upon the Church, we can expect that dreams and visions will be restored to God's people.

Oswald Chambers said: "It is easier to serve God without a *vision*, easier to work for God without a call, because then you are not bothered by what God requires; common sense is your guide, veneered over with Christian sentiment. You will be more prosperous and successful, more leisure-hearted, if you never realize the call of God. But if once you receive a commission from Jesus Christ, the memory of what God wants will always come like a goad; you will no longer be able to work for him on the common sense basis."

Many believers struggle, as I initially did, with the concept of vision in their prayer lives. As I said earlier, we live in a culture which idolizes rationalism; to believe that an ongoing visionary encounter with the living God is possible, almost requires a total break with the culture. However, Christians have never been afraid to be different if they are sure they are standing on solid biblical grounds. The Scriptures in Appendix D show the prominence vision has always had in the prayer lives of the saints and offer a biblical perspective on vision in the context of the life of the Church.

Is It Important?

But let us spend some time asking God the importance of using the eyes of the heart to see him and hear his Word. There is no harm in believing God is saying to his Church concerning restoration of the use of spiritual vision in our prayer lives. Therefore, let us explain in this chapter what we mean by vision, various types or levels of vision, a biblical foundation showing the use of vision from Genesis to Revelation, and how to prepare ourselves to receive the divine flow of dream and vision. We will also examine ways of developing the eyes of the heart and how to present them before God to be filled. We will then close by showing how to test vision and give an example of the healing power of vision as used in an encounter with God.

Seeing the Movement of God

When we speak of dream and vision, we are not referring to personal daydreams, but rather to seeing the movement of God in the spirit with the eyes of our heart. Prophets, formerly called seers, were men and women who saw in the spirit the movements of Almighty God (1 Sam. 9:9). There are two worlds and two sets of eyes. Paul prayed that the eyes of the Ephesians' hearts might be enlightened, so that they would know spiritual realities (1:17, 18). If we want to live in the spiritual world, aware of and responsive to the Holy Spirit's actions, then we too must use our spiritual eyes.

Vision can be beneficial in many ways. It can be used in communion with Jesus, as we can visualise the reality of him sitting next to us and speaking words of life. It can be used in ministry to others, as we ask Jesus to show us how he wants to touch someone's need. We can then respond to the vision he gives by speaking it forth, even as Jesus taught us to pray: "Thy kingdom come. Thy will be done, on earth as it is in heaven." The Greek verb in this phrase is in the imperative mood, issuing a command. Likewise, when Jesus looked at sickness, he saw through it to the divine health that is part of the kingdom of heaven, and commanded it, saying "Be healed." And the people were healed.

Types of Visions

There are at least five types of visions. Each category is equally valid. Each must also be tested against the Word of God. The first type is received as a dream or a vision in the night. Paul received such a vision in Acts 16:9. He had been trying to preach the gospel in several cities but had been prohibited by the Holy Spirit. For some reason, he was unable to receive the leading of the Lord through his usual ways. In the night, God gave him a vision of a Macedonian man calling for help, thus guiding Paul in his next step of ministry.

While we are sleeping, our heart (the centre of the human spirit, from which spring emotions, thought, motivations, courage and action) is awake and very capable of receiving messages from the Lord. He may picturesquely and symbolically show us the condition of our spirit, our fears, angers, and hurts. He may reveal to us, often in figurative pictures, situations that need our prayers. The Lord and the believer can even carry on a conversation like Solomon in 1 Kings 3 and Daniel in Daniel 7.

A second kind of vision is received while in a trance. Peter had such an experience in Acts 10:10-16. In this vision, the Lord symbolically told him that the Gentiles were no longer "unclean," and prepared him to minister to Cornelius, the centurion. For many years, this was the only kind of vision we recognized. But as I have come to know more about God's love for me and his desire to have communion with me, I have become convinced that trances are not his first choice. Generally, trance-visions seem to come when he cannot get through to us any other way.

Another form of vision involves seeing outside ourselves with spiritual eyes. For example, in Acts 7:55, 56 Stephen gazed intently into heaven and saw Jesus standing at the right hand of God. He was looking out, but he was seeing with more than physical eyes; he saw with spiritual eyes into the spiritual world.

When I speak of vision in this book, I am not referring to these three kinds of visions: dream, trance, and seeing outside ourselves. There are two other types of vision which are more normative and less spectacular. God desires to be natural with us, though we usually associate his voice with rolling thunder and parting clouds. He wants to speak to us just the way we are. Often such meetings are so ordinary and so natural that we are tempted to disregard them as only products of our own mind. The next two kinds of vision are gentle, simple, and normal.

The fourth type is a spontaneous, unsought inner picture. It is received in the same way as God's voice. Just as we sometimes experience having a person's name light upon our mind and knowing we should pray for him; in the same way we experience seeing a person's face and feeling the call to pray. We might not be in prayer or worship before this type of vision; often it simply appears out of nowhere. The picture is usually light and gentle and is seen within.

The final kind of vision is like the last, except that it is received while seeking the Lord in prayer or worship. As we are before the Lord, we ask him if there is anything, He wants to show us, and we deliberately present the eyes of our heart to him, expecting him to fill them with vision and revelation. This vision is also light and gentle. This type of vision is the primary one to which I will be referring throughout this book.

Daniel the Prophet

Is it right to believe that these gentle, spontaneous visions that simply arise in our heart during prayer are spiritual encounters with God? The Bible clearly teaches that they are. In Daniel 4:13, 14, we read, King Nebuchadnezzar encountered an angel in a vision in his mind:

> "*I was looking* in the visions *in my mind* as I lay on my bed, and behold, an angelic watcher, a holy one, descended from heaven. He shouted out and spoke..." (emphasis added).

Most of us would not assume that an encounter with an angel could take place in a vision in our mind. Yet the teaching of the Bible is very clear.

Consider also Daniel 7:1, 13 and 15. Daniel encountered the Ancient of Days and one like a Son of Man in a vision he had in his mind:

> "In the first year of Belshazzar king of Babylon Daniel **saw a dream and visions in his mind** as he lay on his bed; then he wrote the dream down and related the following summary of it... 'I **kept looking in the night visions,** and behold, with the clouds of heaven one like a Son of Man was coming, and he came up to the Ancient of Days and was presented before Him...As for me, Daniel, my spirit was distressed within me, and the visions in my mind kept alarming me.'" (emphasis added).

We may encounter God the Father, his Son and his angels in visions of our minds as we meditate on the Word of God. These visions can and do come alive and they *are* actual encounters between God and man. In utilizing our visionary capacity, we are presenting the eyes of our hearts before God, asking him to fill them.

A Biblical Foundation

Dreams and visions were an integral part of God's communication with man throughout the Bible. In both Covenants, God has used *rhema* and vision to contact man.

Our capacities to hear and see on a spiritual level are the two primary spiritual senses used to interact with God. In Genesis chapter 12, God spoke to Abram, promising to make him a great nation. This was *rhema*, God's spoken word to him. Abram obeyed that word and went out in obedience to the Lord. Later God returned to Abram with a further word:

> "I will make your descendants as the dust of the earth; so that if anyone can number the dust of the earth, then your descendants can also be numbered... Now look toward the heavens, and count the stars, if you are able to count them...So shall your descendants be" (Gen. 13: 16; 15: 5).

The Lord gave Abram a picture of his *rhema* so that whether he looked up at the sky or down at the ground, he would always be reminded of God's promise to him. The next verse emphasizes the power of vision:

"Then he [Abram] *believed in the Lord; and he reckoned it to him as righteousness"* (Gen. 15:6).

What an amazing statement! The vision crystallized the *rhema* and produced faith in Abram's heart. As a result of vision, Abram's belief moved from his head to his heart.

Balaam was a prophet whose ability to hear from the Lord was so highly respected that even the king of Moab called for his help. Because (at first) Balaam would only speak what he had heard from the Lord, he was unable to curse the Israelites as the king requested. In Numbers 24:2-4 and 15, 16, Balaam spoke of himself as *"the man whose eye is opened...who hears the words of God, who sees the vision of the Almighty."* He also received revelation through *rhema* and vision.

Vision played a major role in the ministry of Jesus as well. In John 5:19, 20 He said,

*"The Son can do nothing of himself, unless it is something, He **sees** the Father doing; for whatever the Father does, these things the Son also does in like manner. For the Father loves the Son and **shows** him all things that he himself is doing..."* (emphases added).

Three chapters later, he again repeated the words, *"I speak the things which I have **seen** with my Father"* (Jn. 8:38). Jesus declared that he could do nothing on his own. All his power and authority came from his Father's initiative. If he saw God laying hands on the sick and healing them, then he laid hands on the sick and they were healed. If he saw God cast out a demon, Jesus spoke to the demon and it left. His actions flowed only out of the movement of God the Father, which *he saw through vision and heard through **rhema.***

We should have purposed in our spirit that we want to live as Jesus did. We should have made a quality decision that we will not live out of what our physical eyes see, but we will respond only to what our spiritual eyes see. *"For the things which are seen are temporal, but the things which are not seen are eternal"* (2 Cor. 4:18). We should believe that God loves us and will show us what he is doing if we will just open our spiritual eyes to see. (We will talk about ways to do this later in the chapter).

Not only did Jesus see vision within himself, He also taught in picture language. Matthew 13:34 says,

> "All these things Jesus spoke to the crowds in parables, and he did not speak to them without a parable."

A parable is an image created with words. It shows us the world through the lens of divine imagination. When Jesus saw a field ready for harvest, it was for him an image of the hearts of people ready to be brought into the kingdom. When he saw vines heavy with fruit, it was for him an image of our fruitfulness if we abide in his life. Jesus taught the crowds by drawing pictures with his words that they might see spiritual reality.

Even more amazingly, Jesus not only saw images and taught in images, but in Colossians 1:15, Paul called him *"the image of the invisible God."* Throughout the old covenant, God sought to reveal himself to his people. He gave them laws and commandments, priests and prophets, and the tabernacle and the temple to reveal aspects of Who he was. Yet the people didn't understand. *We too* don't understand.

How often we have thought of God as a merciless judge meeting out chastisement and punishment for our sins and weaknesses. So, God decided to clear up all the misconceptions and give us a picture of what He had been saying: He sent Jesus. No longer need there be any doubt about what God is really like, for we have the living image who reveals God to us. As we watch the way Jesus moved among men, we see that God is kind and gentle and merciful. The glory of God is revealed in His Son, the image and fullness of God.

It is already noted in another context the close relationship of dreams and visions to the working of the Holy Spirit in Acts 2:17. We are living in a time of mighty outpouring of the Holy Spirit. And, according to Acts 2:17, we should expect that a flow of prophecy, dreams, and visions will come with this outpouring. *Therefore, we should expect vision to be a normal, natural flow within the hearts of believers.*

The centrality of vision in spiritual encounters is also attested to in Revelation 1:10, 11. These are fascinating verses, because they illustrate several of the principles that can lead us into dialoguing with God. John said, *"I was in the Spirit on the Lord's Day, and I heard behind me a loud voice like the sound of a trumpet saying, 'Write in a book what you see....'"*

John was *"in the Spirit"*: that is, he was still, in contact with the Holy Spirit within. He heard a voice: that is *rhema*. He wrote down the revelation. And he saw vision. John even entered the vision, talked with angels, and was part of the activity he saw taking place in the spiritual world.

So, from Genesis to Revelation vision was used to make contact between God and man, crystallize *rhema*, illustrate spiritual truth, and increase faith. I still had a lingering question:

Why did God choose to speak in pictures and parables to teach spiritual truth? In fact, why is the entire Bible a series of stories? Stories leave so much more room for misunderstanding and disagreement. It seems to me that it would have been much more efficient to give us a book of systematic theology. That's what I would have done. I would have laid out all the major doctrines on a nice, neat graph. Then there would be no room for error, misunderstanding, or disagreement.

But God revealed to me that he had a very good reason for writing stories rather than pure theology or graphs: A picture, created with words, moves and stirs the heart. Analysis can only satisfy the mind. And God is most interested in touching our hearts. Therefore, much of what we know of him is revealed to us through a series of images.

The Value of Vision
Dr. Paul Yonggi Cho, the pastor of one of the largest churches, was a strong believer in the power of images. He had stated that the language of the Holy Spirit is dreams and visions, which mean that when the

Holy Spirit wants to speak to him, he will normally, use dreams and visions. His commission from the Lord is to be always "pregnant" with dreams and visions.

Perhaps there is no place where the value of vision can be more readily recognized than in the ability to be creative. God is obviously the most creative Being in the universe. He is the Creator. The ability to create is born in a creative spirit. The Spirit of God brooded over the waters (Gen. 1:2) and he called into being things which had not existed. And behold, the worlds were formed.

You cannot create anything if you do not first have a picture, a vision of it. Long before a skyscraper rises from the ground, there is an architect who envisions it in every detail. When Michelangelo looked at the huge piece of marble, he did not see the rough quarry stone that everyone else saw; he saw within it the beautiful figure of a young man. As he chiselled away, he did not create that figure, but rather released the magnificent statute of David which he had seen within the rock.

God has placed within all men a spirit. That is what distinguishes humankind from the animal kingdom: Human beings have a spirit; animals do not. All of humankind has the capacity to create, to one degree or another, by the spirit within him. But we were designed by God to lend this creative ability of our spirits to the Holy Spirit to fill. We are to ask the Holy Spirit to overlay us, to flow through us and help us yield our will to Almighty God. Rather than creating through any ability of our own, we are the vessels through whom God moves and does his works.

Abraham: The Birth of a Miracle

Abram is a classic example of God bringing a creative miracle through a man's spirit. First, God spoke a word to Abram:

> "Now the Lord said to Abram, 'Go forth from your country, and from your relatives and from your father's house, to the land which I will show you; and I will make you a great nation, and I will bless you, and make your name great; and so you shall be a blessing'" (Gen. 12:1, 2).

Next, God planted a picture in Abram's heart. The Lord came to him in a vision (Gen. 15:1) and showed him the miracle being fulfilled.

"And He [God] took him [Abram] outside and said, 'Now look toward the heavens, and count the stars, if you are able to count them.' And he said to him, 'So shall your descendants be'" (Gen. 15:5).

Conception took place: the purposes of Almighty God were implanted in the heart of a man/woman. A seed was placed in him that, when allowed to germinate and grow, birthed the creative acts and purposes of Almighty God.

It is certainly significant that the spoken word of the Lord within Abram's heart, coupled with God's divine vision, produced a tremendous level of faith in Abram, such faith that even God took special note of it:

"Then he believed in the Lord; and He reckoned it to him as righteousness" (Gen. 15:6).

This is exactly what will happen for each person who communes with God and receives his *rhema* and vision. They will conceive the creative ideas of Almighty God in their spirits which will produce a tremendous level of faith within them. Through such communion with God, we will be changed from a fear-filled pessimist into a faith-filled optimist.

Abram pondered the *rhema* and vision in his heart and *"with respect to the promise of God, he did not waver in unbelief, but grew strong in faith, giving glory to God, and being fully assured that what he had promised, he was able also to perform"* (Rom. 4: 20, 21).

Abram then spoke God's word as he was commanded. God said to him, *"No longer shall your name be called Abram, but your name shall be Abraham; for I will make you the father of a multitude of nations"* (Gen. 17:5).

The name *"Abraham"* means *"father of a multitude,"* so God was asking him to declare what God had promised him every time he spoke his name. Abraham acted upon the word and vision that was spoken within his heart and his wife Sarah bore Isaac, the child of promise (Gen. 21:1-5).

What a wonderful example of how the creative purposes of God can be birthed through our spirits into our physical world!

Every person who begins to dialogue with God with regularity will find a surge of creativity in his spirit such as he has never experienced before. If conversation with God is restored to the Church of Jesus Christ, she will become the most creative force in the world today. Nothing will be able to match it. Creative solutions to the world's difficult problems will be released through the Church, and the world will be healed in a way it has not experienced since the Son of God walked in the land of Palestine.

The humanists have recognized the truth that there is creative power in man's spirit. As Christians, however, we know the full truth: Man's spirit was made to be a womb in which the creative ideas and energies of the Holy Spirit could be planted, incubated, and in the fullness of time, birthed into his world. And we know that any honour and glory that come from our accomplishments belong only to Jesus.

Prepare to Receive

When a person grows to adulthood, he/she throws away all imagination and vision of the young ages and holds back only logical and analytical thinking to successfully deal with the real world. Therefore, when I became convinced of the importance of using the eyes of my heart, it was extremely difficult for me to begin moving in that realm. I found three basic prerequisites I had to fulfil in order to begin receiving communication from God through spiritual vision. Only after discovering the centrality of the eyes of the heart in spiritual encounter was I ready to begin looking in the spirit for the vision of Almighty God.

But after so many years of disuse, my visionary capacity did not naturally and immediately begin receiving images of the spiritual world. Therefore, the second thing I had to do was set aside time to deliberately offer the eyes of my heart to God. I had to wait quietly and expectantly; my inner being completely focused on Jesus. Suddenly there comes an inner awareness and I begin to see the movement of God within.

When I first came to God seeking vision, I had to come in faith believing that he would speak to me through images, vision and inner pictures. Hebrews 11:6 declares that *"he who comes to God must believe that he is and that he is a rewarder of those who seek him"*.

If I don't believe that God wants to communicate with me through visions, then I will not receive revelation from him in that way. If I begin to receive an inner picture and immediately begin questioning whether it is from him, the picture will disappear because doubt has cut off my receptivity. We can communicate with the Lord only by faith.

Developing the Eyes of Our Heart
The Bible speaks of having our spiritual senses strengthened through use. There are several things we can do to strengthen our ability to see in the spirit. Perhaps the easiest and most common way of availing vision for spiritual purposes is to enter a Bible story. Simply picture the action as it takes place. Ask the Holy Spirit to take over in the vision and show you what he wants to speak to you through the story. He will. Watch what he does. Don't just watch as an observer but enter and become part of the action.

God tells us to encourage to use the eyes of our heart as we read the Scriptures (Eph. 1: 18). Don't forget that the Holy Spirit lives within you, and that you can ask him to make the vision come alive with his own life and then let him take you where he wills. God will encounter you during your Bible study with a flow of his divine life. Simply relax as you read. See the scene in your mind's eye and ask the Holy Spirit to take over. You will be surprised at how much vision will begin flowing within you. The Bible says we have not because we ask not (Jn. 16:24; Jas. 4:2b).

Seeing in Prayer
Another time for seeing in the Spirit is during prayer. As we quiet our heart and ask the Lord to show us whatever He wants, we can see Jesus right there with us, listening as we talk to him. Often, we may

see ourselves in a biblical setting, such as walking along a beach or sitting at a well.

Let us not try to paint in detail that do not come naturally. The most important thing is the sense of his presence. He is a being of love—agape love, incomprehensible love. His facial features are unnecessary, even unimportant, to this kind of prayer. His compassion and love, however, are significant. The important thing is that we come to meet with Jesus and then let the Holy Spirit take over.

We should look intently at Jesus in our vision. Let us not struggle or try to force something to appear. We simply look in faith, focusing our attention upon Christ within us. As the Holy Spirit takes over, we will see Jesus begin to move and speak. His words are wisdom and life and his actions are love and peace. It is not that we bring God into touch with our spirit, but we humble ourselves until God is able to convey his mind to us. He is never bound to act in a certain way by our prayers; he does, however, give us revelations and sometimes ask us to speak them forth.

Seeing in Worship
Praise and worship took on new meaning and power when I began seeing what I was singing and allowing the Holy Spirit to control the vision. When I sing about bowing before him, I see myself kneeling at his feet. When I sing about his sacrifice, I see the cross, and watch as he pours out his life for me. When I sing of his Lordship, I see myself joining the angels and multitudes worshiping before the throne. I may set the scene, but the Spirit will take over and show me the vision.

Worship truly becomes a spiritual encounter when we allow the senses of our hearts to become involved! Sincerely speaking *normally* only very few believers use the eyes of their hearts as they worship, and picture the scene they are singing about, allowing the Holy Spirit to take it where he desires. I recommend that the rest of us who are not in that group begin presenting the eyes of our hearts before God as we sing. He generally does not fill what we do not present before him. The prophets were "seers" because they were "lookers."

True worship of God takes place when a person draws near to God *"with a sincere heart in full assurance of faith"* (Heb. 10:22). Archbishop William Temple, the great Anglican theologian, wrote the following important words concerning worship: "Worship is the submission of all our nature to God. It is the quickening of conscience by his holiness, the nourishment of mind with his truth, the purifying of imagination by his beauty, the opening of the heart to love, the surrender of will to his purpose – and all this is gathered up in adoration to the most selfless emotion of which our nature is capable, and therefore the chief remedy for that self-centredness which is the original sin and the source of all actual sin."

We should never forget that in worshipping God we are not demeaned but developed. We are made for worship. Our worship of him completes and perfects us. We perfect our personalities to the degree that we give ourselves to God in worship. In eternity we shall experience full joy because we shall be able to worship him fully. Meanwhile we are tuning our instruments.

The antidote to every human personality problem is worship. Worship means, in the middle of life as it is experienced, that you find some way to be caught up in God's character and purpose so that his will become central.

Seeing in Sleep

My study of dream and vision in Scripture made it clear to me that my dreams are a natural expression of the inner world. Dreams are not simply a mixed-up rehash of the day's events, but rather my heart's symbolic expression of what I am feeling deep within. They provide a natural and readily available avenue for spiritual encounter. When Solomon asked the Lord for wisdom, it was in a dream (1 Kings. 3:5-15). Many of Daniel's prophecies were received in dreams (e.g., Dan. 7:1). We read in the Book of Jeremiah 31:26; *"At this I awoke and looked, and my sleep was pleasant to me."* Scholars of the Bible say that Jer. 30:3 – 31:25 was revealed to Jeremiah in a dream. He awakens at verse 26 quoted above. And Paul's call to minister in Macedonia came as a vision in the night (Acts 16:9, 10).

Having accepted dreams as a valid avenue of spiritual communication, I decided to begin listening to them. When we recognize the value of dreams, they begin to speak to us. For dreams to be useful, we first must remember them. Then we must understand them. Therefore, it is better to record our dreams immediately upon awakening, as Daniel did (Dan. 7:1). We then can ask the Lord to give us the interpretation of our dream. I believe he will do it for you and me, just as he did for Daniel (Dan. 8:15, 16). Dream interpretation is a fascinating subject that we can explore further to deepen our communion with God.

Developing Visionary Capacity

Education of a child is conducted largely through the eye. Any child is moulded by the manners and habits of those he constantly sees. Similarly, one way to understand our visionary capacity is to think of it as a viewing screen projected from three sources, our own intellectual reasoning, prompted by Satan's thoughts, and the divine thoughts from the Holy Spirit.

It is a spiritual principle that whatever is not purposely presented to God is quickly filled by Satan. If we are not taught how to present the eyes of our hearts to the Lord, Satan will take them over without our knowledge. Therefore, we find our imaginations often filled with evil, such as lust, worry, failure, and defeat. We can experience this so often that we may be tempted to curse our imaginations as instruments of the devil.

Satan is more than happy to supply an endless assortment of unhappy possibilities. We must cut off instantly any and all pictures shown on our inner screen on Satan's instinct. We should take every thought captive to the obedience of Christ:

"[Inasmuch as we] *refute arguments and theories and reasonings and every proud and lofty thing that sets itself up against the* [true] *knowledge of God; and we lead every thought and purpose away captive into the obedience of Christ* (the Messiah, the Anointed One)" (2 Cor. 10:5 Amp. Bible).

All men and women's teachings and speculations must be judged in the light of the teachings of the Lord Jesus. Paul is not condemning human reasoning as such but would warn that we must not allow our intellects to be exercised in defiance of the Lord and in disobedience to him. Our ability to see in the Spirit is an incredible gift. Let's rise in the authority of Jesus Christ and reclaim it for His purposes!

We ourselves are operators of the inner screen created by our intellectual thought. We have the power to use it for good or for evil. Looking at any person we can choose the attitude with which we look at him or her. Stroke by stroke, we create our little fantasy to create our little pictures on our inner screen.

We can also use our mind to present the eyes of our heart to the Lord. To do this, we can "prime the pump" by setting the scene, seeing the reality of Jesus present with us, and asking the Holy Spirit to fill the vision with his life. In so doing, we are not trying to prime God, but rather to poise ourselves properly before the Lord, so he can move freely upon us.

Priming the pump in vision prepares us to see what the Spirit will offer. It gets us into a position to receive and draw forth the flow of living water. Our own little image may be stale and impure, but that doesn't prevent the flow that springs up within our soul from being pure and life-giving.

John wrote in Revelation that he looked, saw a door, and heard a voice. Then, *"Immediately I was in the Spirit"* (Rev. 4:2). John wrote it the way he did to teach us something important. Listen to the sequence again. *"I looked and behold, a door...I heard...Immediately I was in the Spirit."*

John had been in the Spirit in chapters 1 to 3, seeing visions and receiving revelation. He must have taken a break at the end of chapter three and afterward wanted to return to the spiritual dimension. At the beginning of chapter four, John primed the pump by *looking*. Then John saw visions and entered the action, dialoguing with angels and heavenly beings.

This kind of revelation is not reserved for special saints! We are all kings and priests. God doesn't grant gifts because we are spiritual but because he loves us. And he has gifted us all with this ability by which we can use to prepare ourselves to receive the vision he wants us to have.

Our part of the thought should be to turn our eyes upon Jesus, look full in his wonderful face, and the things of earth will grow strangely dim, in the light of his glory and grace. Turn and look. Turn away from all but him. Look FULL in his wonderful face. Your looking must be FULL. It must not be the occasional glance. It must not be the odd or rare time when you're desperate. It must be the purposeful and determined turning aside and the gazing and beholding of his splendour and glory. Looking FULL into his face.

This visionary ability on the inner screen is a gift from the Holy Spirit. With his vision He carries us beyond our imagination into the spiritual dimension. In Revelation 4:2, after John had primed the pump by looking, the Holy Spirit took over and showed him visions that went on for chapter after chapter.

Poised Before Almighty God

We should desire earnestly to live as Jesus did, out of the Father's initiative and doing only what he saw his Father doing. However, before we can live that way, we need to learn how to train our insight to see beyond the physical world. It is an enormous step even to believe that such a thing is possible. Once we have grown accustomed to looking expectantly to the Spirit for a vision from the Lord, it appears readily. The simple act of looking in faith opens us up to begin seeing. We must be convinced that the spiritual world exists, whether we see it or not. By becoming such a person attempts himself who can see what is there in the spiritual world, he is learning to bring alive our atrophied visionary capacity and present it to God to be filled. Once our visionary sense has been rejuvenated and presented before Almighty God, He offers us one step to live like Jesus, drawing on the continuous flow of divine vision.

The prophets of Israel simply said, "I looked," and, as they quieted themselves before God, "they saw" (e.g., Dan. 7:2, 9, 13). We can find that when we reclaim the use of our visionary capacity, we, too, can simply quiet ourselves in the Lord's presence, look, and see the visions of Almighty God. You are then a visionary with divine talents simply because you have become an earnest seeker.

If our intuitive and visionary functions have atrophied through lack of use, the process is not as simple as just looking and seeing. Vision must be exercised to restore its vitality. This involves three steps: repenting of sin (the sin of scorning one of God's gifts); asking God to breathe new life into this inner sense of seeing; and developing this sense which God is restoring. This development involves standing in the belief that God will do it, taking the first wobbly steps, and gaining strength.

Through grace we will get to the point of walking with ease, where we are able to allow God to direct our pathway. This is exactly what has happened with vision in the lives of many others. Through the scorn that was heaped upon it and through continuous disuse, our visionary capacity atrophied and died. Therefore, when we begin looking to see the vision God wanted to present to us, we see nothing. We had so scorned our visionary capacity that it was unable to function when called upon to do so.

We must begin the process of restoration by repenting of our contempt for visionary experiences. We must ask God's forgiveness for not honouring and using this gift he has created and given us. We also must repent of idolizing the logic and analytical thinking that had swept over us as well as over our culture. We must covenant to honour and seek his vision as much as we had honoured and sought analytical thought.

Then ask God to breathe upon our visionary capacity and restore it, to bring it back to life and teach us how to allow him to flow through it.

Objections

At this point I want to stop to answer some of the questions you may be asking. First, "Don't you limit God by forcing him to fit into the scene you have set for him to fill?" The answer is, "Absolutely yes!" Of course, God has some freedom as he takes over the scene you have set. He can move it to a certain extent in one direction or another.

However, if your scene is totally removed from the one God wants to show you, you will find that nothing happens. The scene does not come alive; it remains dead. God is not able to move in it. When this happens to us, our response should be to relax and pray, "God, how do You want to reveal Yourself in this situation?" With that, God implants a vision through which he can move.

A second question is, "Well then, why don't you just look for his vision, rather than begin by initiating your own?" As I have said before, that works fine for the naturally intuitive and visionary person. However, those of us with stunted visionary abilities will often need a learning tool to get started. Once accustomed to vision, though, this type of person will be able to discard the learning tool, and simply look and see. "Are you saying that your self-initiated image is a divine vision?" Of course not! My image is my image; God's supernatural vision is his vision. We should never confuse the two. I never say that my "priming of the pump" is God's vision. It is simply my priming the pump. However, when that inner "click" is experienced and the vision moves with a life of its own that flows from the throne of grace, it then is obviously no longer my own. It has become God's. Mine is mine, and God's is God's.

Someone may ask, "Where does the Bible teach that we are to set the scene ourselves, in order for God to begin flowing in vision?" My response is, "Where does the Bible say that we are not to set a scene and ask God to fill it?" I do not think there is a clear teaching on either side, which means we will have to marshal some verses that we could interpret as supporting one of these viewpoints. Another option would be to allow each individual Christian the liberty of working out his own salvation in this area, since there is no clear biblical teaching on the issue.

The closest verses that could conceivably speak against setting a scene are those that speak of avoiding vain imaginations and not setting up any graven images. According to Webster Dictionary, a graven image is "an object of worship carved usually from wood or stone." Obviously, the scene we set in our minds is not carved or worshiped. It serves simply as a steppingstone to the living flow of divine images. Webster defines "vain" as "having no real value; idle, worthless." I do not see a learning tool as something having no real value or being idle and worthless. Learning tools are valuable and have an active place in the learning experience. The fact that the Bible speaks of vain imaginations tells us that there is also an effective use of imagination. I believe that setting a scene for God to fill is one of these effective uses of imagination.

It must be remembered that consciously setting a scene is only a temporary learning tool, needed only by some individuals. The naturally intuitive person will not need this device. He will simply look to see, and the vision will be there. The analytically-oriented person will later put aside this learning tool, once he is able to open himself naturally and normally to vision.

It is possible that if we lived in a more biblical culture, we would not have so many obstacles to overcome. If we normally discussed our dreams at breakfast with our families and sought God's interpretation, as Joseph did, we would find a natural skill built into our lives concerning visionary things. However, who in our lifestyle takes their dreams seriously, and discusses them regularly in a family gathering? Practically no one! If we did, we would be viewed as strange. Is it any wonder that skill in, and openness to, visions are almost totally lacking in our culture?

As a Church, we need to repent for having allowed the rationalism of our time to distort our own perspective of a balanced lifestyle. Some people fear that there may be seeds of Eastern religious thought in some Church teaching today. Did we ever stop to realize that Jesus was not a Westerner, that God did not intend for us to idolize logic and scorn vision?

God is calling us to make Jesus our perfect example, to aspire to walk as he did, to do nothing on our own initiative, but to live as Jesus did, by a constant flow of *rhema* and vision. Will you search until you find the way to that lifestyle and experience? Will you continue until you discover him?

> *"You search and investigate and pore over the Scriptures diligently, because you suppose and trust that you have eternal life through them. And these [very Scriptures] testify about Me! And still you are not willing [but refuse] to come to Me, so that you might have life"* (Jn. 5:39, 40 Amp. Bible).

Lord, we come to you. We repent of allowing our culture to dictate scorn for the visionary capacity which we have created and placed within us. We ask your forgiveness and ask that you restore to our hearts a proper use of dream and vision. Restore our ability to hear and to see. Draw each of us into all that you have for us.

Testing Vision

Many of us have been tempted to fold up our inner screen rather than risk receiving images prompted by Satan. To do so, however, closes the door to one of our most powerful senses for encountering spiritual reality. But the Bible has offered a better idea. Paul exhorted the Church to test all things, reject the evil and hold fast to the good. There are three basic areas that help determine the source of either *rhema* or vision.

The Spirit

First, we need to determine the spirit of the word or picture. Each of the possible sources has distinctive characteristics. If the source is, we, the picture will be born in our mind, rather than our spirit. It will be a picture we ourselves have painted, stroke by stroke—a creation of our own mind.

If the source is Satan, the picture will be an intruding image. It will seem out of place. We should ask ourselves if our mind was empty or idle. The adage about the devil's playground still holds true. If the source of the pictures is God, they will be a living flow coming from our innermost being. We can check to see if our heart was quietly focused on Jesus when the vision came. This method of testing is like that presented and to ask always, "What would Jesus do in this situation?"

Ideas in the Revelation

Another area we may test is the ideas put forth by St. John in his first Epistle:

> *"By this you know the Spirit of God: every spirit that confesses that Jesus Christ has come in the flesh is from God; and every spirit that does not confess Jesus is not from God; ...you are from God, little children, and have overcome them; because greater is he who is in you than he who is in the world"* (1 Jn. 4:2-4).

We do so by examining the content. If the ideas are merely our own, they will be a painting of the things we have learned, an expression of what we have been taking in to our mind and heart. Therefore, if we have been feeding on evil and perversion, what flows out of our will be evil and perverted. If we have been feeding on the Word, the flow of images will be wise, pure and good.

Revelation from Satan will be negative, destructive and pushy. It will be accusative and fearful. It will violate both the nature of God and the Word of God. Perhaps the clearest indicators of satanic influence are ego appeal and a fear of testing. Darkness does not want to come into the light. Reject such ego appeals and any revelation that seeks to be kept hidden.

Constructive thoughts coming out of such a vision lead us toward God, and destructive thoughts are those that lead us away from him. If whatever we feel is hindering our loving involvement with God or with others, then such visions are destructive and needs to be traced to its root. When our feelings turn us towards the Lord in deeper dependence on him and more loving attitudes towards others then the vision is praiseworthy.

Any revelation from God will be open and eager for testing. It will be meek and humble, willing to be submitted to the Body of Christ. Truth seeks truth and is not afraid of the light. Divine revelation will also be instructive, up-building and comforting; we must immediately reject any thought or picture which is not. The Holy Spirit is the Comforter, and His words bring peace. Satan is the accuser, and we will not accept his condemnation.

Of course, the Bible also says that Satan comes as an angel of light. How do we discern him at those times? One way is through allowing *"the peace of Christ* [to] *rule in your hearts"* (Col. 3:15). Perhaps we might have received revelation which seemed good and true but feeling uneasy about it. It just didn't sit quite right. Not that there was anything biblically wrong with the instruction. It just didn't feel right. In a difficult situation like this it is better to take it to our spiritual counsellors, and if it did not win their wholehearted approval, couple these two factors together and decide not to act upon it.

Remember I have said earlier that spiritual revelation comes primarily through *rhema*, vision, and burden. These three need to line up, particularly the burden of peace: a peace that passes all understanding (Phil. 4:7). Satan cannot counterfeit peace. Therefore, make sure that the peace of God rules (or plays the part of the umpire) in your heart.

Examining the Fruit
The final test of revelation is an examination of the fruit it bears (Matt. 7:16). The fruit of our thoughts and pictures will vary, depending on what we have been feeding ourselves. If our heart is full of evil, the fruit will be evil. If our heart is filled with the Word, the fruit will be good.

The fruit of satanic revelation will be fear, bondage, anxiety, and confusion. There will be a feeling of compulsion that we must do something right now. We will be driven to obedience. Our ego is inflated. These result in "Lone Ranger Christians": unsubmitted, rebellious, in and out of fellowship with the Body of Christ. They are easy prey for the devil, and their delusion and deception will increase if they insist on standing alone.

The revelation from the Holy Spirit quickens our faith, instils peace, and brings enlightenment and knowledge. The good fruit of the Holy Spirit will grow as a result of what we have seen and heard. We will increase in humility as we recognize the miracle that the Almighty, all-powerful God has chosen to have fellowship with us. We will be like Moses, who talked with God face to face just as a man speaks to his friend, and yet was the meekest man on all the earth.

As we close this chapter on seeing in the Spirit the dreams and visions of God, let me suggest that you pause, take out a sheet of paper and ask, "God, what do you want to say to me concerning the use of the eyes of my heart? How have I used them? How would you like me to use them? What are your thoughts concerning dream and vision?" Then relax and tune yourself to the spontaneous flow that will begin to bubble up within you. In faith, write down the thoughts that are coming to your mind. When the flow is over, go back and test them. Decide whether you feel they were from God. Share the results of your experiment with someone else. Find out their impressions.

Chapter 7

Biblical Patterns for Approaching God

The tools of becoming still, tuning to spontaneity, and seeing God's visions will bring great release in our communion with the Lord. Through them we can dialogue with him most of the time. However, there are still occasions when we cannot seem to get through to the Lord. I was confused and couldn't understand why this should be so. I knew I should tune my heart to his voice, but no one ever told me where to find the tuning dial! After struggling a long time, the Lord reminded me of the approach he laid out for those who seek his direct presence. This approach is pictured in the Tabernacle of Moses.

The tabernacle is a very important subject in the Bible. There are few complete chapters speaking only about it in the Old Testament. That tells us that the tabernacle is very important to God. It was vital and to be the centre of Israel's life as a representation of God's presence and his plan for them to approach him.

Approach God through the Tabernacle Experience

On Mount Sinai, God gave Moses the design for the tabernacle where the Israelites were to worship God, offer sacrifices, and hear directly from him. Hebrews 8:5 tells us that this tabernacle and the services offered there were a copy, a shadow and example of the heavenly realities. It not only established the way for the Israelites to approach God and hear His voice, but it also demonstrates the way for us.

In the present age very, few biblical scholars believe that the divisions in the tabernacle represent the spirit, soul and body of man. But I believe that the Outer Court of the tabernacle corresponds to man's body, where we receive knowledge mainly through our five senses. To illustrate this, the outer court didn't have a covering on top but was illuminated by natural light, showing that we receive light (knowledge and revelation) through natural means. The Holy Place corresponds to man's soul. It had a roof over it, but inside it was illuminated by oil burning in a lampstand, representing the Holy Spirit revealing truth to our minds. (Oil often symbolizes the ministry of Holy Spirit in the Bible). The Holy of Holies was a totally dark, enclosed tent with no natural or artificial source of light. The only illumination that ever shone in the Holy of Holies was the light of the *Shekinah,* glory of God. When God was present, there was light. If God departed, all was dark. This represents man's spirit, where the glory of God lights our innermost being, giving us direct revelation within our hearts.

Further, theologically the tabernacle speaks of Christ, the Word who became flesh and *"tabernacled"* (dwelt or lived temporarily) among us (Jn. 1:14). It can also be used as picturing God's way of salvation and the subsequent life and ministry of the believer. But although it pictures the way of salvation, it was given to a people who were already in covenant relationship with God. Rather than providing a way of salvation, the tabernacle offered the means by which the people could be cleansed from outward, ritual defilement and thus be able to approach God in worship.

The tabernacle and the services connected with it were copies of things in the heavens (Heb. 8:5; 9:23, 24). This does not mean that there must be a structural or architectural likeness in heaven, but that the tabernacle pictures spiritual realities in heaven.

The tabernacle also illustrates the preparations we need to make if we want to enter God's presence. My study of it, therefore, provided me with the tuning dial I had long searching for. Within the tabernacle there were six pieces of furniture and these instruct us that each represents an aspect of our approach to God.

The Outer Court

The Outer Court was an enclosed open area surrounding the tabernacle proper which housed the Holy Place and the Holy of Holies. In the Outer Court there were two pieces of furniture: the brazen altar and the laver (Exo. 30:28). Enclosing this furniture was a fence of white linen. It received the natural light of the sun and moon.

(a) Brazen Altar: Symbolizing the Cross (Ex. 27:1-8)

The brazen (or bronze) altar was the first thing you faced when you entered the tabernacle. If you wanted to meet with God, you first had to stop at the altar. It was here that the priests offered the animal sacrifices to atone for the sins of the people. These sacrifices were just temporary measures, teaching the people about their sinfulness and the need for blood to be shed for them to be forgiven. The Lord Jesus Christ was delivered to the high priest and the scribes with the fore-knowledge of God to die on the cross. We know from the Scriptures that Christ is the Lamb slain from the foundation of the world. The brazen altar symbolizes the cross, directly inside the gate of salvation. It signifies both our initial commitment to make Jesus the Lord of our lives, and the daily offering of ourselves as living sacrifices, holy and acceptable unto God (Rom. 12:1, 2). Just as he offered himself as a sacrifice for us, Jesus now asks us to offer ourselves for him. Paul said,

> "I have been crucified with Christ [in him I have shared His crucifixion]; it is no longer I who live, but Christ (the Messiah) lives in me; and the life I now live in the body I live by faith in (by adherence to and reliance on and complete trust in) the Son of God, Who loved me and gave himself up for me" (Gal. 2:20 Amp. Bible).

Often, we are tempted to shy away from the brazen altar. We want to avoid it if possible because it is hot! It means death to our flesh. It means laying down what we want and desiring only his will. This must be experienced daily. If we have not laid down our wills, the only voice that will come from our spirits will be our own. We will only hear our heart saying what it wants. It will only be our voice, not the Lord's. We must recognize the lordship of Jesus Christ in our lives if we want to experience true fellowship with him.

The priests sacrificed lambs on this altar to atone for the sins of the people. They believed that a substitute must be sacrificed. Similarly, without washing our blemish in the crimson tide that flows from Calvary there is no entrance to the presence of God. John writes in his gospel (1:29) to *"Behold, the Lamb of God* [Christ] *who takes away the sin of the world!"* We will not be able to truly worship, pray, or serve the Lord until we come to our Saviour. Just as every priest, every Levite had to come to this altar. *"The way of the cross leads home."* If Jesus Christ had not gone by the agony on the cross, we would have no access to God.

Jesus Christ is the *risen* Lamb, who died as substitute to all of us. The sin question must be settled in the Outer Court before entrance can be made into the Holy Place. What a picture this is of the cross of Christ! When seeking the presence of the Lord, we must stop at the brazen altar and perform the proper sacrifice.

(b) Brazen Laver: **Representing God's Word (Ex. 30:17-21)**
The second piece of furniture in the Outer Court was the brazen laver. This was a circular bowl where the priests washed their hands and feet before moving into the Holy Place, but after sacrificing the lambs. The belief was that if they entered the Holy Place without stopping here to cleanse themselves, they would die.

Paul says in Ephesians 5:25, 26 that Jesus cleanses and sanctifies us by the washing of water with the Word. So, the laver signifies our washing ourselves by applying the *Logos* (Word of God, Scripture) to our lives. Defilements of the flesh are washed away when we act in obedience to the clear commands of Scripture.

It is interesting that the brazen laver was made of highly polished brass donated by Hebrew women used for mirrors. In the Outer Court God speaks to us through our natural senses. Our minds are well able to understand the commandments of Christ, and as we obey them our lives are cleansed and become more like our Master. James likened those who read the Word but do not obey it are compared to someone who looks in a mirror and sees that his face is dirty and his hair messed but does nothing to fix himself up, just walking away without making any changes (Jas. 1:23, 24). That is why it is significant that the laver was formed from the mirrors donated by the Israelite women—it represents to us the Word, which reveals the defilements within us. Just as a mirror is useful only if we act on what it reveals, so we must act on the Word of God if it is to be effective in our lives. As we read the Bible, God holds up a mirror to our hearts, showing what we really look like. As we approach God, he wants us to be changed, sanctified, and made holy by applying the cleansing power of his Word to our lives daily. How much serene and acceptable to him it will be if we worship every Sunday after confessing our sins and with a cleansed heart!

The Holy Place

Within the perimeters of the Outer Court stood a beautifully woven tent that housed the Holy Place and the Holy of Holies. Within the Holy Place were three pieces of furniture: the table of showbread, the seven-branched lampstand, and the altar of incense. Inside the Holy Place is the place of worship.

(a) Table of Showbread Symbolizing Our Will (Exo. 25:23-30)

The table of showbread stood to the right as one entered the Holy Place. Twelve small loaves of unleavened bread and utensils made of pure gold were placed on it. Symbolically just as flour is ground fine for the making of bread, so our will is ground fine as we totally commit our way unto the Lord. Eating together, like the priests, represents the fellowship and communion we find within the Body of Christ. God uses our fellowship with other believers as a means of grinding our wills and shaping us into his image. Self and self-will give way to the give-and-take of a committed love relationship between brothers and sisters in the community. Jesus wants our strong self-will destroyed and our hearts committed to his lordship. Only when we have surrendered our "right" of self-determination, and when our desire is truly only to do his will, can we hear his voice with purity of heart. God wants our wills to be set only to obey him when we enter His presence to hear from him.

The priests would come together to eat this bread week by week with wine and this bread speaks of Christ also as the *life-sustainer*. Eternal life is a gift and every believer needs special food to sustain it. Jesus says according to John's gospel,

> *"I am the bread of life; he who comes to Me will not hunger, and he who believes in Me will never thirst* (Jn. 6:35).

Many Christians today are shy of feeding upon their Lord in order to grow. We must feed on Christ crucified, and the atonement made by his death, or we shall die in our sins. Paul says in 2 Corinthians 5:16,

> *"... even though we once did estimate Christ from a human viewpoint and as a man, yet now* [we have such knowledge of him that] *we know him no longer* [in terms of the flesh] (Amp. Bible).

We must feed upon him as risen and living Christ and we are to grow with him in his presence.

(b) Golden Lampstand, representing our illumined mind (Exo. 25:31-39)

The next article of furniture is the ornately crafted seven-branched lampstand stood directly across from the table of showbread, on the left side of the Holy Place (Exo. 25:31-33). It was formed from beaten gold and its flames were fuelled by oil. This lampstand provided the only light for the Holy Place.

The lampstand represents our mind, which is illumined by the Holy Spirit as we study the Word. The beaten gold indicates the cultivation of our minds. As the gold was formed and shaped into the proper design, so our thought patterns are formed under the illumination of the Holy Spirit. He can speak through them, aligning and perfecting them.

Luke's gospel was written in this way. Luke stated, *"Inasmuch as many have undertaken to compile an account of the things accomplished among us…it seemed fitting for me as well, having investigated everything carefully from the beginning, to write it out for you in consecutive order…so that you might know the exact truth about the things you have been taught"* (Lk. 1:1-4). In other words, Luke carefully studied everything he could find about Jesus, analyzed and organized it under the illumination of the Holy Spirit, and wrote down the result of his work. When carefully search, organize material, and analyze Scripture with total dependence upon the Spirit, He breathes into our mind his wisdom and knowledge. The illumination of the Word might have happened to almost every true Christian. While studying the Bible, a verse suddenly seems to stand out, its meaning and application to life crystal clear. In the same way, we can learn to depend on the Spirit's breath in all our thought processes. He can guide our reasoning and help us form godly, wise conclusions. As we submit our minds to Jesus Christ, the oil of the Holy Spirit illumines every thought. Jesus Christ said in John's gospel 14:26,

> "But the Helper, the Holy Spirit, whom the Father will send in My name, he will teach you all things, and bring to your remembrance all that I said to you."

The Holy Spirit reveals to us Jesus Christ as our only Saviour. We must learn to allow intuition and spontaneity to flow into our reasoning processes, thereby allowing our heart and mind to work together, like the seven-branched lampstand.

(c) The Altar of Incense, representing our emotions (Exo. 30:1-10)

The final piece of furniture in the Holy Place was the altar of incense, which stood directly in front of the door to the Holy of Holies where the priest burned an offering of incense morning and evening.

The three faculties of the soul are the mind, will and emotions. The table of showbread illustrates Jesus' lordship over our will. The lampstand represents his lordship over our mind. And the altar of incense stands for the lordship of Jesus over our emotions. The four-square aspect of the altar indicates an emotional life that is perfectly balanced. Such an emotional balance is difficult in the face of all the pressures of life. We often swing from optimism to pessimism, from faith to fear, from joy to despair. There is only one way that our emotional life can be brought to, and remain in, balance. That way is Jesus, and our approach to him is through worship, praise and thanksgiving. Paul told us to give thanks in everything. In every situation, God is worthy of our praise. And through the continual offering of a sacrifice of praise, our emotions will be brought under the control of the Holy Spirit. Only he can bring us to balance.

The incense represents the praise of God's people. The way into the Holy of Holies, the manifest presence of God, is through praise and worship. The psalmist declared that we should enter God's gates with thanksgiving and his courts with praise (Psa. 100:4). Again in Psa. 141:2 he says,

> "May my prayer be counted as incense before You; the lifting up of my hands as the evening offering."

Worship, praise and thanksgiving are necessary parts of our approach to God. Worship lifts us and moves us into the Holy of Holies. Praise and worship are the best way to quiet our hearts and touch Christ within.

The Holy of Holies

A beautiful veil separated the Holy Place from the Holy of Holies. The Ark of the Covenant was the only piece of furniture in this inner room. There was no provision for light in the Holy of Holies. Like our spirits, it was completely dark unless the glorious light of the Lord's Presence filled it.

The Holy of Holies represents our spirits, where we can have direct communion with the Lord. In the Old Covenant, only the high priest was permitted to go through the veil, and only once a year, on the Day of Atonement. When Jesus died on the cross, the veil separating us from God's direct presence (Holy of Holies) and the Altar of Incense was torn from top to bottom, opening the way for each of us to have moment-by-moment fellowship with Almighty God.

The Ark of the Covenant, symbolizing direct revelation of the Spirit into our hearts (Exo. 25:10-22)

This was a chest made of acacia wood overlaid with pure gold. This combination of material may be considered as representing Jesus Christ's majestic deity by the gold and his humanity by the wood. This chest required both gold and wood to maintain the symbolism pointing to Christ as the God-man. Within it were placed the tablets on which the Ten Commandments were written, Aaron's rod that budded, and a jar of manna (Heb. 9:4). The flat top of the Ark was called the Mercy seat. Over it two golden cherubims fashioned of pure gold stood facing each other with their wings stretched out toward the centre as a covering over the Mercy Seat. Moses and Aaron knelt before the Ark and they believed that God spoke to them from the Mercy Seat between the cherubim's. Thus, the Ark provided a *picture* of God's presence for the priests to focus upon as they came to meet with him. This reminds us that out of worship and stillness we enter heart-to-heart communion with God as his glory fills our spirits. It is in the quietness of our hearts that we hear God speak to us.

The manna in the Ark was a reminder of God's supernatural provision. As we wait in the presence of the Lord and receive direct revelation from him within our spirits, supernatural life and strength flow up from deep within, strengthening us to face victoriously the trials of life. His divine life flows through us and out from us to meet the needs of a hurting world.

Aaron's rod that budded was a divine attestation of his God given authority. God's word gives us authority. When we meet face to face with our Father as Moses did, when we hear his Spirit speak to our spirit, and when we speak forth what we have heard, our words ring with divine authority. The Ten Commandments represent the law of God, the standard of holiness needed to meet with him. When we come to God, we come to perfect holiness. But remember what has been placed above the law: The Mercy Seat. Jesus Christ has made atonement for our sins. Through his blood we are cleansed and made pure so that we can have fellowship with the Holy One. We receive access to boldly come before the throne of grace.

The book of Revelation was written out of a Holy of Holies experience. While in the Spirit, John received direct spiritual revelation as visions he then recorded.

In closing the references to the Tabernacle, I want to mention again that there were two altars in the Tabernacle. The brazen altar was where God deals with a sinner. It speaks of the earth and the sin of man. The Altar of Incense speaks of heaven and holiness. The brazen altar speaks of what Christ did for us on earth. The Altar of Incense speaks of what Christ is doing for us in heaven today. It also speaks of our prayers and our part in worship. It speaks of Christ who prays for us. He is the One who truly praises God and prays for us. He is the One who is interceding for us.

We are to learn to worship not at the bloody altar where you go as a sinner. You enter the Holy Place and come to the golden altar. There is no sacrifice there because the sin question was settled outside. The very basis rests upon the fact that, as believers, we are accepted in the Beloved before God. God hears our prayers because of what Christ has done.

We have seen that the Lord can speak to our natural senses through the clear commands of Scripture. As we offer our minds to him, the Holy Spirit can illumine our thoughts, giving us supernatural wisdom and insight. And we can receive direct revelation from the Holy Spirit to our spirits. Each of these experiences is extremely valuable. We do not set aside the Bible because God speaks to us Spirit-to-spirit. If anything, our love for the Word will grow as we spend time with the Lord, and we seek to learn more about our Father and to test His revelation.

There is nothing about having spiritual encounters that makes us better than anyone else. In fact, all kinds of revelation are available to all believers. When the Holy Spirit speaks to our hearts, it says nothing about how spiritual we are, only about how loving and gracious he is.

We need not follow the procedure of the tabernacle every time we come to pray. We can always try to live our life in line with the requirements represented by each piece of furniture. But when we have trouble hearing from the Lord, when our prayers seem to bounce off the ceiling and echo in the room, we need to come to the tabernacle to find out why. We must be prepared to examine ourselves carefully, deliberately, and prayerfully, taking God's Word as our rule and guide. We must do this by seeing ourselves before each piece of furniture and asking the Lord to speak to us through it. We will usually find the reason for the communication breakdown by the time we enter the Holy of Holies. By this wonderful tool, we can tune our heart once again to hear what the Lord wants to say to us.

The tabernacle is a means to help us see the condition of our hearts. We use it to accomplish our goal, which is to live in day-to-day, moment-by-moment fellowship with our Lord and Saviour, Jesus Christ.

Using visions, present yourself before each piece of tabernacle furniture, and ask God to speak to you concerning the experience of it at this time in your life.

1. *Altar*—Am I a living sacrifice?

2. *Laver*—Have I washed myself by applying the Word?

3. *Showbread*—is my will ground fine before God? Am I walking in love and fellowship with the Body of Christ?

4. *Lampstand*—Is God illuminating my mind and granting me revelation as I study the Word?

5. *Incense*—Am I offering a continual sacrifice of praise and thanksgiving before my Lord?

6. *Ark*—Do I stand quietly before His immediate presence and receive His words into my heart?

Be careful to quiet yourself in the Lord's presence so that you get His thoughts rather than your own. You will be able to identify the difference easily. Your thoughts will be very preachy—His will be very loving and gentle. Let His words come to you in the first person. Have a clear vision of yourself kneeling before each piece of furniture, and see Jesus standing there speaking to you. Notice the gentle spontaneous flow that bubbles up from within your heart.

By the New and Living Way

Discovering the place of the Tabernacle experience in our prayer life enables us to tune our heart to hear the Lord much more consistently and through it we can usually discover the reason for any inability we have to break through to dialogue with the Lord Jesus Christ. Still, occasionally we must present ourselves before each piece of furniture, asking Jesus to reveal any failure to live according to the principle represented by it, and find ourselves going all the way into the Holy of Holies without being convicted, yet we may be unable to enter dialogue and fellowship with the Father. As I was pondering Hebrews 10:19-22, I saw how God has provided further fine-tuning to zero-in on His voice. Since discovering and applying this passage to my prayer life, I have been always able to make spirit to-Spirit contact with our Lord.

Hebrews 10:19-22

It is clear from the verse under reference to going *"through the veil"* that the writer was referring to our entering the Holy of Holies. This veil hung within the tent, separating the Holy Place from the Holy of Holies. The Greek text does not include the word *"place"* as used in the New American Standard Version in verse 19. The original simply reads *"the holies."* The writer of Hebrews was discussing the new and living way Jesus has provided for us to come into direct communion and relationship with our Father.

Full Assurance of Faith

The first phrase the Lord directs us to is, *"let us draw near...in full assurance of faith."* Lack of faith is the number one reason why we do not hear the Lord. Sometimes it is hard to believe that God is even present, and we doubt that he cares enough about insignificant us to want to spend time talking with us. Or we are not convinced that it is really the Lord Who is speaking through our spirit. Every time we come to him in doubt, we receive nothing. *"He who comes to God must believe that He is and that He is a rewarder of those who seek him"* (Heb. 11:6). We must believe that the Lord loves us and desires to communicate with us even more than we want to speak to him.

The remedy is to engage in activities that build your faith. You should choose those that are most effective for you. Singing and worshiping in the Spirit nearly always lift our faith level to where we can draw near to God. We may wholeheartedly offer a sacrifice of praise until our entire being is convinced again of His goodness and mercy.

Our level of faith rises when we use vision and see with the eyes of our heart the spiritual reality of Christ with us. The Bible is very clear that, through the working of the Holy Spirit, Christ is present with every believer. We may re-read some Bible promises, especially those referring to God's love and desire to have fellowship with man.

And finally, we sometimes simply take a leap of faith, abandoning ourselves to him who is faithful. We decide to believe with all our heart all that God says. We pour out our heart fully and completely to him. God is always there, waiting to meet with us, speak to us, and share his love with us.

A Clean Conscience

The next phrase the Lord speaks to us is *"let us draw near...having our hearts sprinkled clean from an evil conscience."* Sometimes as we quieted ourselves for prayer, our mind may be filled with the guilt of an unconfessed sin. No matter how we tried to ignore it or go around it, the Lord's voice could not be heard above our conscience. Our mind will wander about from subject to subject, trying to direct our attention to anything but our unconfessed guilt.

It is impossible to approach God with unconfessed, covered-up sin in our lives (1 Jn. 3:21). But if our heart is condemning, we cannot draw near with confidence, except in confession and repentance. As we confess our sin, he is faithful to forgive us. The blood of Jesus Christ washes over us, cleansing us from all unrighteousness. When we repent, we avoid making grand promises of greater obedience in the future. That may be our desire, but we know our weakness and that there is no strength in us to withstand Satan's pressures. If we try to stand alone, our focus will be all wrong, looking to ourselves to perfect our salvation, when Jesus is the only One Who can sanctify us. So, let us recognize that though we are weak, He is strong. Hence the closest thing to a promise that we can make is, by His grace we can seek to walk in holiness before him.

We must stop looking at ourselves and focus instead on Jesus. For us to have an ongoing intimate relationship with Jesus, we must stop focusing on our ugly shell and start focusing on our lovely Lord. If we keep looking at ourselves, we will never get to Christ. But if we look at Jesus, He draws us to himself. By lifting Christ in our thoughts, by recognizing that He is the Author and Perfecter of our faith, by knowing that only through his strength do we stand, we give him freedom to do his will within and through us. His love draws us through the veil to where we can speak with him face to face, as a man talks with his friend.

Washed by Obedience to *Rhema*

The third requirement we must notice is, *"let us draw near...having our body washed with pure water."*

Ephesians 5: 25, 26 tell us that *"Christ also loved the Church and gave himself up for her; so that he might sanctify her, having cleansed her by the washing of water with the word* [rhema]*."*

When God speaks to us in prayer, we must allow it to cleanse us by applying and observing the *rhema*. We have often found in our life that God has nothing more to say to us if we have not obeyed the last word, He gave us. His grace may allow us to continue in communication for a time, but there comes a point when we must either obey or forfeit further communion. *"To obey is better than sacrifice"* (1 Sam. 15:22). God is not interested in how many hours we spend with him if we only hear and do not obey.

A Sincere Heart

Finally, let us come back to the first part of verse 22, *"let us draw near with a sincere heart."* Our hearts must be true when we come to God. There can be no hypocrisy, no deceit, and no lies. We cannot try to hide anything from ourselves or the Lord. This is not usually a big problem for us if we are sincerely straightforward, up-front person. We must say exactly what is on our mind and tend to be quite blunt about it. But there may be time that the Lord shows us the deceptiveness of our heart.

These four things—a sincere heart, fullness of faith, a heart sprinkled clean from an evil conscience and *cleansed by the washing of the word* [rhema] —are the final elements needed to make the way clear for us to have day-to-day, moment-by-moment intimate fellowship with our Lord Jesus Christ.

Keeping Your Heart Pure

The Lord is not the only One Who seeks to inject His spontaneous thoughts into our minds. Just as the Holy One is known as the Comforter, the enemy is known as the Accuser. Satan will try to project into your mind negative thoughts, bitterness, discouragement, and anger. He will accuse you and tell you what a rotten sinner you are, how unworthy you are to enter the presence of a Holy God. He will remind you of your weakness and of sins already confessed. He will try to convince you that there is no forgiveness for one such as you, that the blood is not enough to cover your sins.

Then the liar will begin accusing your family and brothers and sisters in the Body. He'll tell you that they are all hypocrites who just put on a good face to hide their evil hearts. He'll convince you that no one really loves you, that their kindnesses are only setting you up for the day that they will turn on you. He'll make you believe that only you are standing true before the Lord, that you are better than all the rest.

Finally, the deceiver will attack the Lord with his lying words. He'll say that God is not love but anger, not mercy but judgment. He will tell you that God doesn't really care enough about you to want to meet with you. He will point to the injustices and tragedies of this world as proof that God is unconcerned with the affairs of men.

Does any of this sound familiar? Have any of these thoughts appeared uninvited in your mind? It will be such a glorious day of deliverance and victory when we finally realize that the Accuser was the source of these thoughts and, therefore, we do not have to put up with them! By the authority of Jesus Christ, we can reject the words of the enemy and replace them with the peace of the Comforter. We must keep watch over our heart, protecting it from the lies of Satan.

We also must keep watch so that no other person's negative, destructive spirit can be transferred to us. It is so easy to be drawn into bitterness, anger and despair by the conversation of those around us. If possible, avoid people who constantly wallow in sin or hopelessness or criticism. Instead, continue to assemble with other believers who are concerned with how to stimulate one another to love and good deeds (Heb. 10:24, 25). If we must be with those whose spirits tend to bring us down, pray for the Lord to be a shield for us, protecting our spirit from their snares and overwhelming them with the Spirit of Christ. Let us hold fast the confession of our hope without wavering, knowing that He Who promised is faithful (Heb. 10:23).

When the Lord Does Not Speak

It is said repeatedly in the discussion above that the Lord is always speaking and that we will hear him if our hearts are right. But there are at least four exceptions to this statement, four reasons why the Lord will not answer your questions or grant your requests.

As noted earlier, God will not speak if we have not obeyed His last word. King Saul found himself in that situation. He repeatedly disobeyed the Word of the Lord spoken to him through the prophet Samuel. Finally, the Lord had to say to Saul that his disobedience has cost him the throne of Israel and further that he won't be hearing from God anymore. The next time Saul had a problem and went to the Lord for wisdom, *"the Lord did not answer him, either by dreams or by Urim or by prophets"* (1 Sam. 28:6).

When it's none of Your Business!

The Lord will also not speak if you are asking a question He does not want to answer. God does not make himself available to us as our own private fortune-teller. There are many things He does not choose to reveal to us, and if we insist on prying into those areas, we will not only meet silence from the Lord, but we may open ourselves up to deception. The Lord does not open the future for us to see. He will tell us all that are necessary for us to know, and only what is necessary. This is illustrated in the story of the barren woman to whom an angel of the Lord appeared and told her she would bear a son. The angel told her to drink no wine or strong drink or eat any unclean food, because the boy would be a Nazarite to God from the womb and he would begin to deliver Israel from the Philistines.

When the woman told her husband Manoah about the angel's message, Manoah asked the Lord to send the angel back to instruct them in caring for this boy. The Lord allowed the angel to return and Manoah began to ply him with questions: *"What shall be the boy's mode of life and his vocation?"* The angel responded, *"Pay attention to all that I said,"* and repeated the same message he had given the woman the first time he came (Judg. 13:12-14). Manoah was prying where he had no business, seeking to know details about the future he did not need to know. So, God simply ignored the questions and did not give him an answer.

Impure Motives

God will not answer if we are praying with wrong motives (Jas. 4:3). How often do we pray that our lives might be free from pain and pressure? How often do we ask for protection from the consequences of our sin? If an unhappy circumstance enters our life, we immediately pray that it might be removed, without looking for ways that we may grow through our suffering.

> The Bible says that we *"exult in tribulations; knowing that tribulation brings about perseverance; and perseverance, proven character; and proven character, hope"* (Rom. 5:3, 4).

As the fire of the kiln is increased more impurities are burned off, and godly character is established. Therefore, when we encounter pressure, it is not usually wise to immediately pray for its removal. First, we should seek God. Personally, I have found my greatest spiritual growth has come during the times I have experienced the greatest pressure.

Consumed by the commercialism of our age, how many of us covet material blessings far above what we need to sustain our lives? Thinking only of our own comfort and pleasure, we plead for this and claim that. You may perhaps believe that God wants to bless us materially and financially, but surely not so that our fleshly lusts are satisfied. He wants to bless us that we may be a blessing to others. He allows us to be stewards of much if we are wise and compassionate, giving to the needy, the widows, and the orphans, using His resources to extend His kingdom on earth.

God is concerned with eternal values, not temporary appeasements. He is concerned with proven, upright character, holiness and the healing of our souls and spirits far more than in the comfort of our flesh. When our prayers focus on the satisfaction of our flesh, we may not receive the answer we seek. Therefore, when facing pressure or an unhappy situation, we must first seek *rhema*, asking God to show us how to pray. Then, when we pray according to God's will, we can be assured that He will answer.

The Need for Fasting

To fast is to abstain from gratifying any physical appetite. We must admit that fasting has no merit as far as salvation is concerned. But it is of value in promoting self-discipline. It not only cleanses the body of poisonous wastes. Fasting has done wonders when used in combination with prayer and faith. This is a biblical doctrine. Fasting humbles the soul before God (Psa. 35: 13); chastens the soul (Psa. 69: 10); helps to attain power over demons; develops faith; and aids in prayer (Matt. 4:1-11; 17:14-21). If we do not seem to be getting through to God, fasting helps us achieve greater spiritual receptivity. I have always found that God has come through for me, or I have gotten through to him, when I have spent a period in fasting. Many of the most important steps of growth in my life have come through times of fasting.

Isaiah 58 is the greatest chapter of the Bible on fasting. It describes wrong reasons for fasting, the proper motives for it, and the results of fasting correctly. In verses 9 and 11, we are promised, *"Then you will call, and the Lord will answer; you will cry, and He will say, 'Here I am!' … And the Lord will continually guide you."*

Fasting has been a normal part of the prayer life of the Church since its inception. Repeatedly in the book of Acts, Peter, Paul, or the whole Church together is shown fasting. There are many kinds of fasts and partial fasts. A total fast involves abstinence from both food and drink. Such an absolute fast should preferably be no more than three days. A normal fast would be the abstinence from everything but water. A variation of this is to drink fruit juices and other healthful liquids while abstaining from all solid foods. These types of fasts should not continue more than forty days. Partial fasts can also be effective. You can fast every day until a certain time. You can fast one meal a day. Or you can use Daniel's fast of vegetables and water. The Lord will guide you into the right kind of fast. He may lead you into a regular weekly day of fasting. At certain times, He may call you to a special fast of long duration. We are not to come under a law of fasting, but to be responsive to the leading of the Spirit in this special area of prayer.

Please note that individuals with chronic health problems that can be affected by diet, such as diabetes, should fast only under the supervision of a physician.

I Still Can't Hear!

When you have experimented with two-way prayer using the principles found in this book, most of you will find you can effectively dialogue with Almighty God. However, there may still be rare times when we seem to be blocked from hearing His voice. Sometimes we sit quietly eager to hear him and nothing flows. Frustration builds, and we wonder what is wrong with us. Why can't we hear?

There are several things to check in a situation like this. Then you must go deeper, quieting yourself still more, until you touch the depths of your heart and the divine flow is initiated. Go back to the chapter on stillness and learn to quiet yourself until God Almighty takes over. With some practice and experimentation, you will be able to still yourself quickly and easily. As a matter of fact, you will begin to cultivate a lifestyle of inner stillness. You will learn how to stand still before God while you walk among men. This is abiding in Christ.

The Voice and the Fire

A final block I would like to deal with is the issue of fire. God's voice came with fire in Deuteronomy 5. Fire, in the Bible, stands for refining and purifying. A major block to hearing God's voice is the unwillingness of His children to stand in the fire and allow it to do its purifying work, freeing them from bondage to the flesh and releasing them to freedom in the Spirit. The story of the Israelites at the mountain illustrates this. The omnipotent Yahweh had delivered His people! He told Moses what to do and Moses led the Israelites out of bondage, through the sea on dry ground, giving them manna from heaven and water from the rock. Everything was going great! God had provided for all their needs and had required very little in return.

Then they arrived at Mount Sinai (Horeb), and Moses brought them some good news: God was going to come and talk to him and they were invited to listen in on the conversation. The next two days were full of preparations, everyone washing their garments and consecrating themselves, so they would be ready to hear the voice of God.

The promised day finally arrived. The camp was buzzing with anticipation and speculation. Suddenly the ground began to tremble. The mountain was burning with fire. Lightning flashed, and a thick cloud of darkness hung in the air. Moses brought the people closer to meet with God, and they stood trembling at the foot of the mount. Suddenly they turned and ran in terror as the deafening sound of a trumpet gave way to a voice. Fearfully the crowd watched as Moses made his way up, half expecting him to perish at any moment before the awesomeness of Jehovah. Finally, he disappeared into the darkness of the cloud, and they were left to wait.

As the day wore on, probably elders and heads of the tribes kept watch near the base of the mountain. Others returned to their tents and their daily chores. When Moses came down from the mountain, they might have told him that it was a real treat to see God's glory and His greatness, and we even heard His voice. That was all well and good. But, enough is enough! Did you see that fire? If He talks to us anymore, that fire is going to get us! You go back and tell God that we don't want him to talk to us anymore. He can tell you what He wants us to do, and then you can tell us. We promise to do whatever He says. Then we won't have to go near that fire anymore. God's voice is not worth the fire (Deut. 5:24-27). Of course, God heard their words and said, as Moses narrates it in Deut. 5:28-33.

Because the Israelites have refused to hear the voice of Almighty God directly from fire, God told Moses that they must have commandments and statutes and judgments through him. If they won't live in communion, they must live in law.

God has not changed in all the years since that fateful day at Sinai. With the voice of God still comes in the fire of God, the fire that consumes the dross and purifies the gold. If you are longing for the life of communion with God, be prepared for the fire. Determine that for you, the voice is worth the fire! Choose to yield to His hand with whatever purging and cleansing of the flesh He requires.

The Healing Voice

Our relationship we had with the Lord may be affected by the emotional attitudes or mind set-up. Without real love for him, there could be no fellowship, and, like the Israelites in the wilderness, I found myself living under law. I searched the Scriptures many times for principles of Christian living.

> Once the Lord directed me to Micah 6:8, *"He has told you, O man, what is good; and what does the Lord requires of you but to do justice, to love kindness, and to walk humbly with your God?"*

He showed me that He *loves* kindness and *to do* justice. It brings him joy to show kindness, but his holiness requires that He gives justice. All my life I had been just the opposite: I loved justice and did kindness. My approach to every person and situation was first to judge, and maybe, secondarily, to have kindness. He showed me the two aspects of his nature: light and love. God is always righteous judge and showers his loving kindness, divine healing, conviction and comfort. As I looked at him, I learned how unbalanced I was in my whole approach to life. I had focused on the "light" aspects of his nature, living in challenge and requiring infinite precision in righteousness. Now I found him calling me to focus on the "love" aspects: forgiveness, reconciliation and grace.

If we do so, a new spirit will begin to permeate into our life style. Where formerly we have reacted to differences of opinion with confrontation and separation, we will begin to seek peace and reconciliation. Where righteousness according to the letter of the law has been our standard for fellowship, love will become the standard around which we are gathered. Where judgment had always been required for every infraction of the law, we will begin to see kindness flowing from us.

Our newly emerging balance between judgment and kindness will be tested as we begin to walk in communion with God and be aware of the spiritual world around us. Some of our people may not accept this new emphasis and may respond with judgment and confrontation. We will have to try to reconcile our differences, but there may have too many hurts, and too much resentment. During this period of trial in my life I learned though our path leads through the fire, He goes with us every step of the way.

Summary

Jesus Christ has opened the way for us to enter the Holy of Holies by rending the veil and sprinkling us with His blood. He has given us the privilege of direct fellowship with the Father and Son through the Holy Spirit. The way is not burdensome or complicated. Jesus said, *"I am the Way"* (Jn. 14:6). It is Christ Who has done the work. He has shed His blood and applied it to our hearts. He has planted faith within us. He draws us to himself. We simply need to be vessels, willing to receive the finished work of Christ. We need to set our love and attention solely upon him.

In the last few chapters, I presented several concepts to help tune ourselves more precisely to the Lord's voice. Following is a list of summary questions you can use to discern any areas that may prevent you from hearing God speak. Remember, *we do not need* to go through this list every time we come to prayer. But on those rare occasions when we cannot seem to make spiritual contact, this checklist can help us find the reason why and correct it.

The Tabernacle Experience

1. *The altar*: Have I presented myself as a living sacrifice? Am I denying the desires of my flesh and presenting myself to God as an instrument of righteousness?

2. *The laver*: Have I been regularly studying the Bible and obeying the clear commands I have found?

3. *The table of showbread*: Have I been continuing in fellowship with the Body of Christ? Is my self-will being ground fine through close relationships with my brothers and sisters? Is the deepest desire of my heart to do only God's will?

4. *The lampstand*: Have I presented my mind to the Lord to be illumined by the Holy Spirit? Do I study Scripture with my heart tuned to hear His revelation through it? Are all my thoughts and reasoning processes accomplished in a deliberate dependence upon the guidance of the Spirit?

5. *The altar of incense*: Am I continually offering a sacrifice of thanksgiving and praise to the Lord so that my emotions and reactions are under His control? Do I swing from high to low emotionally or is a continual attitude of worship and gratitude bringing me into balance?

6. *The Ark of the Covenant*: Have I learned to walk in His immediate presence and hear His words spoken into my heart?

Fine-tuning

1. Is my heart true and sincere? Am I free from all deception and hypocrisy? Am I being honest before the Lord? Am I harbouring any reservations?

2. Am I coming in faith? Have I made a quality decision to believe all that God says with all my heart?

3. Is my conscience clear? Have I confessed my sin and received the cleansing blood of Christ? Is my confidence in him, that he will sanctify me and present me blameless before the Father?

4. Have I obeyed the *rhema* I have already received?

5. Am I asking questions the Lord does not want to answer? Am I trying to get information I don't need to know?

6. Are my motives, right? Have I asked the Lord how He wants me to pray?

Once again, I want to emphasize that these questions are not the prelude to my every prayer time. They are the exception rather than the rule. Even when we are unable to achieve spiritual encounter, very rarely do we need to go through the entire list of questions. Being aware of potential areas of difficulty, it is usually quite easy to zero-in on the problem. However, positive reactions to each of the questions will surely make it possible for any believer in Christ to have intimate dialogue with the Lord every day, or every time he turns to him.

Chapter 8

How Can I Know for Sure it is God's Voice?

Most of us have been taught to live rationally, according to the dictates of our minds; but I would rather suggest that we must dethrone the mind by recognizing that it is not the organ that receives revelation from God. The heart is the place of Spirit-to-spirit encounter. However, we must never get the idea that as Christians we should throw our minds away. The mind has a very necessary place in the spiritual walk—it is the organ used for testing.

As we try to live out our spiritual dimension, we will make mistakes. The Bible recognizes that fact and accepts it. First Thessalonians 5:21 tells us to *"examine everything carefully; hold fast to that which is good."* We shouldn't jump on what is not good and berate ourselves for our mistakes. Instead we should simply test everything we receive, ignore whatever is not of God, and move on with what is good. To make mistakes is human. The important thing is to learn from those mistakes.

Our goal, as always, is to come to a balance. Most of us tend to operate in extremes. We may look down on those who claim to have mystical experiences. Or, especially if we tend to be somewhat mystical by nature, we may scorn those "intellectual snobs whose religion is all in their head." Neither attitude is proper. God created both the head and the heart. He ordained the functions of each to complement the other. If we try to live our Christian lives depending on either one alone, we will find ourselves going in circles. We need head and heart, the rational and the spiritual aspects of our communion with the Lord.

The number one question we anticipate from our friends after reading this much will be how can we know for sure it is God speaking to us? And my number one answer is to test the revelation by the help of Scripture, for their evaluation.

Factors Affecting the Spirit

One of the primary reasons why we need to test all revelation we receive is that our spirits can be affected by factors other than God. According to 1 Corinthians 6:17, the spirit of a true Christian is joined together with the Holy Spirit. However, this does not preclude other factors from moving upon our spirits and tainting the revelation we receive.

When we are overcome with a great sorrow, our spirits can be affected, and the messages received through them can be misunderstood. There is an example of this in 1 Samuel 1:1-15. Hannah was *"oppressed in spirit"* because she had no son.

Our physical, bodily condition can also influence our spirits. In 1 Samuel 30, David's men came upon a man who had been left for dead by a retreating army. He was very ill and had neither food nor drink for three days. They gave him bread and fruit and water to drink, and *"his spirit revived"* (v.12). We have all experienced the effects of sickness upon our spirits. Doubt and discouragement easily find their way into our hearts when our bodies are weak or filled with pain. We must be particularly cautious about acting upon revelation received when we are physically weak or in pain, until it has been tested when we are physically stronger. This does not, of course, always apply to weakness during a fast.

Satan is also able to affect our hearts. John 13:2 shows that Satan put the idea into Judas' heart to betray Jesus. Often it is difficult for us alone to recognize that we are being led into deception. We need the help of Scriptures to show us the truth.

Finally, we ourselves can influence our spirit. Proverbs 16:32 tells us that *"he who rules his spirit,* [is better] *than he who captures a city."* Our motives must be pure, and our wills aligned with Christ's or the "revelation" we receive will be a dream of our own making.

Testing Revelation

Since so many factors other than the Holy Spirit can influence our spirits and cause impurities in how we hear God, the first thing we must look for in testing any kind of revelation is evidence of other influences. In the chapter on vision, I laid out three specific aspects of revelation that can be tested: the origin, the content and the fruit. Vision and revelation from us, Satan, or God will each have distinctive characteristics. Thoughts from our own spirit are born in contemplation. They are the result of a progressive building of ideas, based on what we have learned. If we have been feeding on what is worldly or evil, that is what will come out of our heart. If we have been guarding our spirit, allowing only what is good and pure and holy to enter, and then the meditations of our spirit will reflect that.

Satan's injected thoughts may come as flashing ideas or images into our mind. They do not fit our train of thought and seem like an intrusion. They are destructive and evil. They bring us into fear or bondage. We may feel pressured or compelled to obey their promptings. They are contrary to both the nature and Spirit of God. They will resist being submitted to the Word or even shared with the Church, often by appealing to our ego.

Revelation from the Holy Spirit is encouraging and comforting. If it involves a conviction of sin, it is specific and instructive, not general or condemning. It has no fear of testing and even encourages it. It is completely in harmony with the nature and the Word of God. *Rhema* quickens our faith and brings peace to our inner man. It is wise. It encourages the development of the fruit of the Spirit in our life.

Every *rhema* and vision we receive should be tested to determine its source. Every revelation should also be compared to the *Logos*, the written Word of God. It is essential that you have a good working knowledge of the Bible if you are going to investigate the spiritual dimension. The Bible is our absolute standard of truth! Any revelation from God will be in perfect agreement with the letter and the spirit of the Word. It will be in keeping with the whole counsel of God on that subject, as revealed throughout the entire Bible. A single verse is insufficient grounds for doctrine or belief. The knowledge of the Bible will provide a solid foundation for our spiritual growth.

The Safety of Relationships

Another vitally important tool for testing revelation is the Body of Christ, the Church. When we belong to a Church, we become part of a believing community and are united as the visible expression of Christ on the earth. There is safety in our relationship to a Bible believing fellowship. And the power and ability to grow are dynamically increased when we are covenanted together with others of like goals.

It is especially helpful to be in an accountability relationship when we are trying to change deeply ingrained habits. An alcoholic rarely can remain dry alone, but with the help of relationships found in Alcoholics Anonymous many are able to succeed.

How often have you read self-help books that promised to reshape your personality and make you a success? You probably tried on your own to apply the teachings, but rarely had long term success. But, if you have studied the same kind of book with a group of others, meeting regularly to share how you've applied it, the results, and your goals for the next week, you likely have experienced a change in your life for the long term. This book is no exception. We believe that you may become very excited about what you read here. You might apply all the principles and suggestions and have wonderful experiences of spiritual encounter. But unless you find another to walk with you on this journey, the excitement will soon disappear, especially when obstacles block the path. This book will then join the host of others collecting dust on your shelves. Growth and change rarely come to those who try to make it on their own. Growth and change happen within relationships.

Understanding the Principle of Authority

In order to properly relate to and respect authority, there are several things we must realize. First and foremost, we must accept the fact that God is responsible for placing all authority over us, according to Rom. 13:1. The psalmist tells us that,

> "Not from the east nor from the west, nor from the desert comes exaltation; but God is the judge; he puts down one and exalts another" (Psa. 75:6, 7).

No one can usurp any authority without God's permission. No one has authority over us except the people God allows to have authority over us.

A question that often arises is what about evil authority? What about people like Hitler? Surely, he wasn't God's minister! Surely, he was a man out of control. The Israelites had their own version of Hitler—Nebuchadnezzar. He swept down upon Judah, bringing death, destruction and terror upon all the land. The people cried out for deliverance from his hand, but a prophet of God named Jeremiah rose up and said, not to resist him; Nebuchadnezzar was God's servant, sent to repay them for their evil ways. He was but God's war-club, a weapon of war in God's hand. (See Jeremiah 25:8-12 and 51:20-23.) But do we really have to obey such evil authorities? The Roman government Paul lived under when he wrote the epistle to the Romans was perverted, sadistic and wicked. Christians were used as torches to light the streets, as bait for hungry lions, and were tormented by the gladiators for the amusement of the people. Yet, to believers living in the very seat of that cruel government, Paul wrote that they were to subject themselves to the governing authorities.

> "Whoever resists authority has opposed the ordinance of God; and they who have opposed will receive condemnation upon themselves...Therefore it is necessary to be in subjection, not only because of wrath, but also for conscience' sake" (Rom. 13:2, 5).

Jesus told His disciples to render to Caesar the things that were Caesar's. Peter exhorted us to submit ourselves *"for the Lord's sake to every human institution"* (1 Pet. 2:13-21).

The second important principle to remember is that God is bigger than any authority. Our confidence should not be in a man, but in God's ability to work through the man. Sometimes we are tempted to protest submitting to another imperfect human. It's easy to say we are submitted to Christ because he is perfect. But why should we open ourselves up to the influence of another person who could be wrong?

The simple answer is that our assurance is in God that he will work through the authorities he has ordained in our life. Proverbs 21:1 says, *"The king's heart is like channels of water in the hand of the Lord; Heturns it wherever Hewishes."* As we confidently place ourselves in the hands of those, He has placed over us, Hewill cause their hearts to be turned according to His will. And even if they try to arrogantly resist the Lord's influence upon their hearts, Hecan cause them to say the opposite of what they planned, so that His will is still accomplished! (See Proverbs 16:1).

All authority is from God. Anyone who has authority over me does so only because the Lord has allowed him to exercise it. The authorities in our lives cannot exist except through the power God has given them. Jesus didn't answer Pilate when Hewas being questioned. Finally, in fear and frustration, Pilate cried,

"You do not speak to me? Do You not know that I have authority to release You, and I have authority to crucify You?" But Jesus replied, *"You would have no authority over Me, unless it had been given you from above"* (Jn. 19:10-11a).

There are not two or three or four authorities in your life. There is but one authority, who is God, exercising His will through men.

When God used nations such as Assyria to chastise His people in the Old Testament, they could have a certain amount of authority over

Israel. But those nations grew arrogant, and soon thought that it was by their own greatness that they had taken Israel captive. So, when they had accomplished the purpose for which they had been ordained, God withdrew their power and punished them. He said, *"Is the axe to boast itself over the one who chops with it?"* (Isa. 10:15). All authority comes from God, and He has authority over all authority. Authorities over us can do only what He allows them to do.

Since God is over all our authorities, Timothy urged us to make *"entreaties and prayers, petitions and thanksgivings, be made on behalf of all"* who are in authority (1 Tim. 2:1, 2). Through our prayers we can lead a quiet and tranquil life in all dignity and godliness.

If we do believe that God is responsible for the authorities in our lives, we can certainly ask him why He has placed them over us. He does not act capriciously or unjustly.

Nebuchadnezzar was given authority to hold Judah captive for seventy years. Jeremiah told the people the reason why this was allowed. For 490 years, Israel had neglected the celebration of the Year of Jubilee. They had stolen seventy years of rest from the land and from the Lord. So, they were forced to pay back that time. There was a reason, not only for the captivity, but also for the precise length of it.

The hard-to-get-along-with characteristics of the authorities over us represent a purpose of God for our lives. We are being moulded into His image; and moulding requires pressures. God is perfecting us, and He will use authorities to do so. As Peter reminded us, if we suffer injustice patiently, we are following in the steps of our Lord.

Disagreeing with authority or spiritual leaders

There are times when we will disagree with our authorities. Perhaps it is simply a difference of opinion, in which there is no clear biblical command to determine the issue. Perhaps we believe the Lord has told us to do something, but our spiritual leaders disagree. What do we do then?

We have a few choices. We can reassert our independence and break away from the relationship, confident that we know God's voice and what is best for us. Or, since we are convinced God works through submission, we can lay down and become a non-person. We can shut off our own minds and lines of communication with the Lord and respond like robots. So often we seem to think that these are our only two choices in an accountability relationship. Either one is not a good suggestion.

God, as always, has a better idea! If we do it His way, we can have disagreement without destruction. We can be submitted, meek persons without becoming mindless, spiritless doormats. In Daniel 1 we find a clear description of the way God guides us in providing creative alternatives which can satisfy both our spiritual leaders and us. Daniel was a young man who was taken into captivity by Nebuchadnezzar. He was chosen for training at the palace for service in the king's court. As such, he was given rich, unclean foods and wine as his daily ration. Daniel had never eaten such things and didn't intend to. There was a great potential for trouble in that situation: Government versus religion. But Daniel was able to resolve the issue with no exchange of hostilities.

The first thing he did was make sure his own heart was purified with tender love. He made certain his conscience was clear, that there were no critical, resistant or condemning attitudes in him. He knew that if he approached the commander with those kinds of feelings the commander would sense them, which would destroy any possibility of relationship. But because Daniel's heart was right, the commander responded with *"favour and compassion"* (Dan. 1:9). Though there was disagreement, there was love and honour between them. If we find that our attitudes have been wrong, if we have felt anger and condemnation toward the authority God has placed over us, we must ask forgiveness of God. A pure heart opens us up for good things to happen.

When Daniel was sure that he had done his part to maintain a good relationship, he sought to discern the basic intention of the one over him. The commander's intention was simple—he wanted to live! If he disobeyed the king's command and the young men suffered as a result, the king would have him executed. But why did the king want the boys to eat such rich foods? Was he trying to defile their religion? Was he deliberately forcing them to choose between obedience to God and man? No! Nebuchadnezzar wanted the boys to be strong and healthy and intelligent. He was giving them the best he had to offer, food from his own table. His basic intention was their well-being.

Many times, when we disagree with someone, we can only see our own point of view. We are blinded by our own wrong attitudes. But when our hearts are pure, we can recognize the motives behind their requests. Often, we are then able to see that they are really looking out for our best interests.

Daniel was faced with an authority who told him to act in disobedience to God's law. He could have risen up in rebellion and simply said, "No! I will not obey!" And he would no doubt have lost his head on the spot. But by keeping his heart full of love, he was able to come up with an alternative that allowed him to obey his God without offending his king. As a result, he rose to a position of authority, where he was able to exercise godly influence in an ungodly land. The solution Daniel suggested was that he and his friends take a ten-day test. During that time, they would abstain from the king's food and eat only vegetables and drink only water. At the end of the trial period, the commander could compare them to the other youths who continued to eat the king's delicacies. Based on what he observed at that time, he could then make his decision.

The commander could accept that. The boys would be in his care for three years. Any damage done in ten days could easily be repaired in three years. So, he agreed to the test, and, of course, Daniel and his friends were in better physical condition than the rest of the young men at the end of the trial period.

In order to come up with such a creative alternative, we must be in touch with the Creator. We must have moved beyond anger to love, so that God's voice is able to clearly be heard in our hearts. When we are faced with a disagreement with our spiritual leaders, we need to prayerfully ask the Lord for an idea that will bring a mutually satisfactory resolution to the problem.

In rare situations, a spiritual leader may force us into the position of Peter and John, who found that they must choose between obeying God and man. Occasionally it is impossible to work out a creative alternative that can satisfy the spiritual leaders' goals without violating our own conscience. If a spiritual leader commands us to do something which is directly contrary to the Word or *rhema* of God to us, if no alternative can satisfy, we must obey God, not man. In such a case we may have to suffer, even though we have done nothing wrong. Better to suffer at the hands of unjust men than to stand at the judgment seat of God. Still we must continue to respond in love and righteousness.

Daniel faced that situation when he was in a position of high authority in the Babylonian government. King Darius was tricked into signing a decree that allowed no prayers to be made to anyone other than the king for a period of thirty days. This time there was no room for compromise, and Daniel went to the lion's den. But God was his strength, and through supernatural deliverance the name of the Lord was glorified (Dan. 6).

It is important, however, that we first make very sure that there is no way to obey both God and His ordained authorities before we resist that authority. Our disobedience must be based on a clear command of Scripture, not our fuzzy personal interpretation. We must remember that if we resist our authority when they are not asking us to disobey God's Word, then we are resisting God himself (Rom. 13:2). God's truth and knowledge and wisdom are too big to be contained in just one person, no matter how great you are! Truth lives in the whole Body of Christ, and we need one another.

Conclusion

The principle of authority should never become a source of bondage in a believer's life. It is a principle that must be applied through the revelation of the Spirit. Authority and submission can be a great blessing, or a great source of pain. Our goal is not to bring anyone under a new law, but to illustrate how great the value of submission to the Body of Christ has been to us.

Chapter 9

More Thoughts on Prayer

"Prayer is a shield to the soul, a sacrifice to God, and a scourge for Satan." – John Bunyan

When You Pray, Forgive

Although in Jesus and through the Holy Spirit we have returned to the fellowship with God for which we are created, we have not yet learned all that the Bible has to teach us about prayer. An investigation of the Scriptures about prayer may reveal to us other insights and principles applicable to our fellowship with the Lord. Many excellent books have been written that cover these various aspects of our prayer life; however, there are certain important principles strongly to be covered here. It is important that we remember the proper place of these principles as we explore them. They are not laws to again bring us into bondage. We should not focus our lives on principles, striving to bring our lives into obedience to them. Our focus should be on Christ, not on bare principles. It is important to thoroughly learn and understand these principles of prayer, but then we must turn our attention to Jesus, trusting him to draw forth whatever we need to know in any situation.

The most important key to answered prayer is forgiveness. Jesus taught His disciples about the power released through prayer (Mk.11). After telling them that they could even move mountains by prayer, Jesus added, *"Whenever you stand praying, forgive, if you have anything against anyone ...*" (v. 25). This command is amazing in its inclusiveness—there are no exceptions allowed. If we want mountain-moving results to our prayers, we must forgive everything we are holding against anyone. Alexander Pope expressed: "To err is human, to forgive is divine." We are to be *"kind to one another, tender-hearted, forgiving each other, just as God in Christ also has forgiven you"* (Eph. 4:32).

When we are living in unforgiveness, we become constricted and closed. Our muscles contract and our jaws tighten. All the functions of our body lose the fluidity and balance needed to operate smoothly. The same thing happens within our spirits. We contract and stiffen, raising our fists in a defensive posture. We effectively prevent the love of God from flowing through us and out to others.

Jesus called His disciples to abide in him, explaining that if we abide in Jesus, we abide in his love (Jn. 15:4, 9). No anger, no bitterness, no critical spirit can be within us if we are abiding in the love of Christ. It is impossible to love more than Christ has loved, for He laid down his life for us. Yet, this is the love we are called to show, a love in which we are willing to lay down our lives, our rights, our all, for our family and friends (Jn. 15:12, 13). This is the love that returns forgiveness for injustice, blessing for cursing, and acceptance for rejection. This love is impossible for man. There is only one who has the power to love in the face of any pain. We cannot grit our teeth and force ourselves to love. We are weak. But the one who is strong, the one who is supremely able to love immeasurably, the one whose name is Love, lives inside of us. It is clear in 1 John 4:12 that if we love one another, no matter what, we have clear proof that God abides in us and that his love is perfected in us, because it is only by his living through us that we will express such love.

If we find ourselves unable to love another person, we don't struggle and strain, promising God, that we will try to love him at another situation. Rather, we may come honestly before him, with no pretext or claim to any strength within ourselves, admit that though we are weak our Lord is strong and loves this person dearly. Pray for exchange of our lack of love for the abundant supply of the love and grace of our Lord. Surely, as we turn our eyes to the reality of Christ within us, love and forgiveness are released, and we will be able to love even our enemies.

Jesus promised that his yoke is easy, and his burden is light. The Lord gave us a beautiful picture of our covenant relationship with him in the Psalms. Our Father tells us, "...*Open your mouth wide and I will fill it*" (Psa. 81:10). Can you see the picture? Imagine a nest of little baby birds. As you peek into the nest all you see are mouths, wide open and waiting to be filled. When they are hungry, mama bird doesn't allow them to try to get food themselves, because they would just fall from the nest and be badly hurt. Instead, she flies about and catches their food. That is our relationship with God. We don't have to flutter about trying to supply our own needs. He is the strong one. He is the provider. Our part is to simply open and receive all He must give us. Forgiveness is only possible by the grace of God. But if we will receive His grace, His ability, love and forgiveness will flow from us.

First John 4:18 declares that there is no fear in love because perfect love casts out fear:

> "There is no fear in love, but perfect love casts out fear, because fear involves punishment, and the one who fears is not perfected in love."

Let us use this verse as a barometer to gauge how completely we are abiding in Christ's love. If we enter a room with fear or judgment, it indicates that our life is out of focus. If we face a situation with fear, we are not abiding in love. Love lifts us out of ourselves, out of our own concerns and needs. Love focuses us on Jesus and others, so that my greatest desire is to minister His love to them.

Anger binds; forgiveness releases. Forgiveness frees both the one who forgives and the one forgiven. And it releases the power of God to work in each one and in situations to bring glory to him. A pure heart, free from anger and bitterness, provides a vessel through which the power of God can be released through prayer.

Wholehearted Prayer

It would be greatly amiss if anyone is left to believe that sitting quietly at a desk is the only way to pray. Sharing love with Jesus is vital, but it is not the totality of our relationship with him. There are times when intense, fervent prayer is called for.

> *"Elijah was a man with a nature like ours, and he prayed earnestly that it would not rain, and it did not rain on the earth for three years and six months"* (Jas. 5:17).

At the end of those three years and six months, he prayed that it would begin to rain again. He crouched down with his face between his knees, seeking God fervently. Six times he sent his servant to look for a cloud, and six times the skies remained clear. So, he continued his earnest petition and the seventh time he looked, there was a small cloud. Elijah knew his prayers had been answered and the two men ran for cover before the storm hit (1 Kings 18:42-45).

The psalmist entreated the Lord's favour with all his heart (Ps. 119:58). All of Judah swore with their whole heart to obey the Lord and sought him earnestly with their whole desire (2 Chron. 15:15). Because of their fervency, the Lord drew back the veil and let them find him.

There is a place for agony in prayer, for compassion, burdens, tears, groanings, and travail. Jesus *"was moved with compassion"* to heal (Matt. 20:34). He *"offered up both prayers and supplications with loud crying and tears"* (Heb. 5: 7). In agony in the Garden of Gethsemane, he prayed *"very fervently and His sweat became like drops of blood, falling down upon the ground."* (Lk. 22:44).

The psalmist called us to *"pour out"* our hearts before God, for he *"is a refuge for us"* (Ps. 62:8). Can you see what he means? Can you visualize the intensity of feeling in one whose heart is poured out before God?

> *"The Lord is near to the broken-hearted and saves those who are crushed in spirit"* (Psa. 34:18).

The Holy Spirit himself makes intercession *"for us with groanings too deep for words"* (Rom. 8:26). God wants us to come honestly and wholeheartedly to him.

Speak to the Mountain

When Jesus cursed the fig tree, his disciples were amazed to see it die within just one day. Seeing their surprise, Jesus told them of the power of prayer, that if they spoke to a mountain in faith, commanding it to be moved into the sea, it would be accomplished (Mk. 11:23). There are times when our prayers should not be addressed to God as petitions, but to circumstances as commands. When Jesus faced the stormy winds and the crashing waves, he did not say, "Oh, Lord, please make this storm stop. Please don't let the wind blow so hard." No! he spoke directly to the problems and said, "Be still!" And they obeyed.

After Moses led the people out of Egypt they were soon in big trouble. In front of them was the Red Sea. To the left and right were mountains. And behind them was an angry army of Egyptians. The people were whining, and Moses was praying. Finally, God said,

> *"Why are you crying out to Me? Tell the sons of Israel to go forward. As for you, lift up your staff and stretch out your hand over the sea and divide it"* (Exo. 14:15, 16).

They didn't need to wait for God to act—He was waiting for them. We have been given authority to rule and reign in this life. We don't always need to ask God to accomplish His will on earth as it is in heaven. That phrase in the Lord's Prayer is not a supplication but a command; not a command to God, but rather to situations to align themselves with the will of God. We have taken our misunderstanding of this phrase and made it the suffix to all our prayers. Because we don't know God's voice, we don't know His will before we pray. Therefore, after presenting our ideas of what He should do in a situation, we tack on the words, "If it be Thy will."

But that is not at all how Jesus was teaching us to pray. The phrase is actually, "Come, Thy kingdom! Be done, Thy will!" We are those who hear God's voice and see His vision. We do nothing out of our own initiative but only what we see the Father doing. We speak only what we have already heard the Father saying. We have seen God's will and God's plan for the situation, and we speak it into existence. Like the dynamic power that brought the worlds into being when there was nothing, the Spirit goes forth with the command and God's will is done! For example, if we are praying for the healing of a broken leg, we should not focus on the limb in a cast and the limitation that brings. Instead, we must look as Jesus did, beyond the sickness to the deeper reality of divine health. We must see the patient running and leaping, praising God. Then we must speak forth, as Jesus did, the kingdom of God, and command the bone to be made whole, just as it was created.

Because of the authority we have received as children of the King, sometimes we must speak to the mountain and see it moved. Then we must hold fast the confession of our hope without wavering, knowing that he Who promised is faithful. God lives in timelessness and sometimes we must wait to see the fulfilment of our declaration. During that time, we must be careful not to give in to doubt but to continue steadfast in our confession.

Pray Until You Praise

Prayer is an acknowledgment of God's all-sufficiency and our utter dependence on him. A need has not really been prayed for until it has been overcome by the power and promises of God, and until you have entered peace.

Philippians 4:6, 7 exhorts us to *"be anxious for nothing, but in everything by prayer and supplication with thanksgiving let your requests be made known to God. And the peace of God, which surpasses all comprehension, shall guard your hearts and your minds in Christ Jesus."*

Notice the progression. We begin with prayer, presenting our requests to the Lord. We then move into supplication, a more intense form of prayer. But how do we move from asking to thanking? How do we move from begging to receiving? Only by taking the time to be still and feel the movement of God. He may show us by vision or tell us by *rhema* how he wants us to pray. He may show us or tell us that the request has been granted. There may be a lifting of the burden or simply a sense of peace in which we relax in the knowledge that He is in control and all will be well. When we know that He has heard and answered, we worship and thank him for his goodness to us.

There may have been times when peace did not come the first day that we pray for a matter—only after several days of earnest supplication we may feel the release in our spirit that told us our prayer was answered. Other times we have only need to pray once and the assurance has come which moved us into thanksgiving and peace. We must let the peace of God rule in our hearts, determining when the matter is settled, and praise can break forth.

Pray When You Need God's Strength

In Psalm 50:15, the Lord encourages us to *"call upon"* him *"in the day of trouble"* and tells us he will *"rescue"* us. The writer of Hebrews called us to *"draw near"* God's throne *"with confidence"* that we might *"receive mercy"* and help in the *"time of need"* (Heb. 4:16). So often we are tempted to do just the opposite. In our time of need, when we have sinned and feel so dirty and so unworthy, we are tempted to run and hide from the face of God. We want to scrub off the dirt and clean ourselves up before we come before the throne. But if we try to do that, we are rejecting the grace of God and relying again upon our own self-righteousness. Only God can make us pure and clean; and he longs to do so. He longs to clothe us in his power and righteousness, but he can only do so if we come to him in our *"time of need."*

When temptation is strong, and we feel that we have no strength to resist, we can call upon God. We do not need to fight Satan with our own power. In fact, we cannot. But the One Who lives within us has already defeated him! When we call upon the Lord, he will deliver us from temptation. The Bible repeatedly reminds us not to try to fight the enemy with our own strength, but rather to put our trust in the Lord. James told us to submit ourselves to God, resisting the devil (Jas.

4:7). We can be assured that he will flee from us. In 2 Corinthians we are reminded that the *"weapons of our warfare are not of the flesh, but divinely powerful"* (2 Cor. 10: 4, 5). With them we can destroy anything raised up against the knowledge of God. We are strong in the Lord and in the power of His might. By putting on the whole armour of God, we can *"stand firm against"* all the *"schemes of the devil"* (Eph. 6:10, 11).

The Movement of God in Prayer

There is a tendency to think of prayer as an activity of the believer. We decide what to pray for, how to pray, and what answer we want. We come to God and present our requests. But such a view represents only part of the true picture of prayer. In Romans 8:26, the Lord reminds us that we do not know how to pray as we should. Our understanding is limited. We tend to see only from our own perspective. Our minds don't always perceive divine purposes. Yet so often we forget our limitations and think we know enough to tell God what to do and how to do it. And if arrogance doesn't motivate us, ignorance does. It takes a revelation from the Lord to make us recognize that our weakness in prayer is perpetual, so that we might learn to be perpetually dependent on the Holy Spirit. Because we do not know how to pray as we should, the Holy Spirit works through us in our weakness. We do not need to hide in our weakness or strive in our weakness. We must learn to rest in dependence upon the Lord to work through our frailty. Because we do not know how to pray, God himself takes over the whole process of prayer. His strength is perfected in our weakness. If we entrust ourselves to him, the entire Godhead will become involved in our prayer life.

God Himself will be the initiator of our prayers. When a need is presented to us, if we will wait quietly before him, the Holy Spirit will form the proper words for us (Eccl. 5:1, 2). If we will still our hearts through worship and contact the Holy Spirit Who dwells within us, he will reveal to us the way we should pray. He may speak a word, give a vision, or allow us to feel his emotions.

When the Holy Spirit has taken hold of us, giving us wisdom

concerning how to pray, we can then speak what He has revealed. If we always pray in the Spirit, our prayers will be inspired, guided, energized and sustained by the Holy Spirit (1 Jn. 5:14, 15). If we pray out of the promptings of the Holy Spirit within us, we know that we are praying according to His will.

Sometimes we feel pressured to pray without first becoming still and tuning in to the voice of the Holy Spirit. This is especially true for us when we are called upon to pray in groups. We feel that we should immediately say something, anything, even if it is not exactly what the Spirit wants to pray for. It takes courage to wait in silence until we sense the movement of God. We must admit that on many such occasions we give in to the pressure and speak out of our own heart. But what is the use of praying if it is only to fill an uncomfortable silence? Surely it is worth the momentary embarrassment to know that God has heard and that He will answer.

The Holy Spirit is not the only person of the Trinity involved in our prayers. Jesus himself is seated at the right hand of the Father, presenting our prayers to him and interceding on our behalf. Prayer is an activity of the Godhead, and we are caught in the flow of Father, Son and Holy Spirit.

Pain of Unanswered Prayer

No depression is greater than that which is caused by what we call "unanswered prayer" – especially when we know that what we are praying for is in line with the divine will. Some of you who are reading this may be in that very situation. Coming to terms with the fact that God delays answering our prayers when we know that what we are praying for is good and right can be real test of our character. To learn how to handle ourselves at such times is not just important, but imperative. The psalmist speaks of the same concern over the silence of God in his verses, Psa. 6:3; 13:1. Such language of impatience and complaint is found frequently in the prayers of Psalms. It expresses the anguish of relief not granted and exhibits the boldness with which the psalmists wrestled with God based on relationship with him and their conviction concerning his righteousness. How strangely silent and inactive God appears to be at times to us. But we often forget to give God the privilege of replying in his own time. The prophet Micah says:

> "But as for me, I will watch expectantly for the Lord; I will wait for the God of my salvation. My God will hear me" (Micah 7:7).

The willingness to wait for God to give us an answer in His own time and in the way, He thinks best is without doubt one of the greatest marks of spiritual maturity. Those who can wait will grow up to be more socially competent, better able to handle stress and less likely to give up under pressure than those who could not wait for an answer from the Creator. Ask yourself now: How good am I at waiting for God's answers to my prayers? The ability to wait says more about your spirituality than almost any other thing.

Again, I remind you of the risks you take when you enter dialogue with God. The light you ask for may reveal more than you wish. It may cause you to tremble within. But I plead with you, when that happens – go on. God provides grace for everything.

> "My grace is sufficient for you, for power is perfected in weakness" (2 Cor. 12:9).

In the words of the old saying, there is needed grace for needed moments. Whenever you need it, it will be there. If you accept the demands God makes and face squarely what the light reveals, the trembling will pass, and you will prove the truth of Isaiah's words; you will find that he will "encourage the exhausted and strengthen the feeble. Say to those with anxious heart, 'Take courage, fear not, behold your God will come....'" (Isa. 35:3, 4). The blessed assurance is that no matter when or why we approach the mercy seat, our Lord's ear is always open to hear our plea. His hand is ready to help. Can you say that prayer is your vital breath, your native air?

What a privilege it is to carry everything to God in prayer! Thomas Brooks would have us remember that "the best and sweetest flowers of Paradise God gives to His people are when they are upon their knees.

Prayer is the gate of heaven." Effectual prayer, however, is that inspired by the Holy Spirit for the ears of God alone, who never fails to hear and answer prayer when it is the natural breath of a redeemed soul. Prayer is the voice of faith.

Chapter 10

The Accuser and the Comforter

Have you ever sought to submit every area of your life to Jesus, hoping for peace, power and serenity, only to discover instead inner thoughts of accusation, condemnation and depression? If so, you have unwittingly been listening to Satan, the "accuser of the brethren."

Jesus is our Wonderful Counsellor Who alone can heal the brokenness of our spirits. Often restoration and healing come through a revelation of divine perspective, the ability to see God's loving rule in our lives and circumstances. In order to maintain this divine perspective, it is necessary that we be able to see the vision of God and hear the voice of God within our hearts.

We have found that communication from the spiritual realm comes to us in the form of spontaneous thoughts or visions which light upon our hearts and minds. We have learned to quiet ourselves and become still that we might know God. We have learned to tune our hearts to receive the spontaneous words and visions from the Spirit. And we have begun to dialogue with God, freeing our minds to receive in faith.

As we begin to move into a greater awareness of the thoughts from the spiritual world, which was spontaneously intersecting our mind, we will become aware that not all spontaneous thoughts were compatible with what we knew to be the character of Christ. Could it be that there were messages from spirits other than the Holy Spirit seeking to fill our mind? What should we do? Some people are tempted to retreat before such a realization. If it is possible to hear from Satan in the same way that we hear from God, wouldn't it be better to simply not listen to anyone rather than run the risk of deception?

While that is one possible response, it is not the course of action which we must choose. We might have struggled too hard and too long to learn to hear God's voice to be willing to let the enemy steal that blessing from us so easily. We must choose instead to become educated, to learn to discern the voice of the Holy Spirit from the voice of the evil one and to stand and fight for the pure voice of the Spirit within us.

Paul exhorted us in the following manner: *"For the weapons of our warfare are not physical* [weapons of flesh and blood], *but they are mighty before God for the overthrow and destruction of strongholds.* [Inasmuch as we] *refute arguments and theories and reasonings and every proud and lofty thing that sets itself up against the* [true] *knowledge of God; and we lead every thought and purpose away captive into the obedience of Christ* (the Messiah, the Anointed One) (2 Cor. 10:4, 5 Amp. Bible).

It is apparent that Paul was aware of the spiritual origin and nature of the thoughts which appear in our minds. He was aware that a battle must be fought, enemies destroyed, prisoners taken, and authority established in our thought processes.

Just because some thoughts enter our minds which are not from the Holy One does not mean we are to stop thinking. Just because a vision lights upon our minds which is impure does not mean we are to shut our spiritual eyes. Rather, we must take charge through the authority of Jesus Christ! Don't surrender without a fight. Destroy the power of the enemy and embrace the power of Christ!

The first step in sorting out the voices that are coming into our consciousness is to become thoroughly acquainted with the character of those who were speaking to us. The words we speak reflect our character. In Hebrew culture and in the Bible, one's name is a capsulization of one's character. When you learned someone's name, you learned a great deal about their life and character. When one's character was changed by God, they often received new names. Thus, Jacob became Israel, Simon became Peter, and Saul became Paul. Therefore, in order to get an understanding of the character of those speaking to us, we must study the names given to Satan and to the Holy Spirit in the Bible. Our life will not be the same thereafter.

The Names and Character of Satan

The Accuser

The essence of Satan's nature is to accuse. The Greek word *diablos*, which is translated "devil," literally means "accuser" or "slanderer." The central work of Satan is to accuse day and night.

In the Book of Revelation, we read, *"And I heard a loud voice in heaven, saying, 'Now the salvation, and the power and the kingdom of our God and the authority of His Christ have come, for the accuser of our brethren has been thrown down, who accuses them before our God day and night.' And they overcame him because of the word of their testimony, and they did not love their life even to death"* (Rev. 12:10, 11).

Notice that salvation, power, the kingdom of God and the authority of Christ come in our lives when we overcome and cast down the accuser.

If the essence of Satan's character is to accuse, whom then does he spend his time accusing? First, as we see here in Revelation, he accuses the brethren to God. In Job 1:9, Satan is accusing Job before God: *"Doth Job fear God for nothing?"* In other words, "Of course Job fears You and serves You, God. Look at all the blessings You have lavished upon him. He only serves You out of selfishness. He doesn't really love *You*, only the things You give him." The accusation of the brethren is not limited to the throne room of God. Every negative analysis, every critical judgment, every accusing thought against another which finds its way into our minds has as its source the "accuser of the brethren."

When we cooperate with his evil purposes and speak forth words of accusation against the brethren, our tongues are *"set on fire by hell"* (Jas. 3:6). When our hearts are filled with demonic wisdom, jealousy, selfish ambition, disorder and every evil thing find a comfortable home

(Jas. 3:15, 16).

Satan also accuses us personally, challenging, criticizing and condemning us in our own eyes. When the Holy Spirit led Jesus into the wilderness, Satan met him there and said, *"If you are the Son of God..."* (Lk. 4:3). Can you hear the accusation in those words? *"If you are really who you say you are...."* He will do the same thing to us: *"If you really are a child of God, why do you act the way you do? If you're so spiritual, why don't you pray more? Dr. Cho prays six hours every day. Why don't you, if you think you're such a great Christian? If you were a good Christian, you would read your Bible more. You wouldn't get mad so often. You wouldn't do this. You would do that."* On and on the accusations mount in our minds until we accept the evaluation of us as valid and give up in despair.

Satan even accuses God to us. Remember, if you will, in the Garden of Eden, Satan (the serpent) said to the woman,

> *"Indeed, has God said, 'You shall not eat from any tree of the garden?' ...For God knows that in the day you eat from it your eyes will be opened, and you will be like God, knowing good and evil'"* (Gen. 3:1, 5).

Can you hear him challenging the motivation of God, accusing God of selfishly trying to keep something good to Himself? Particularly when we are already tending toward depression and self-pity, this is an arrow which easily finds its target in our hearts. "Has God really said that he loves you? If God really loved you, he wouldn't let such terrible things happen to you. If God wanted to, he could stop those people from slandering you like that. If God loved you as much as he loves other people, he'd give you a better job, a nicer house, a happier marriage. God doesn't really love you at all." If we accept these accusations, if we do not challenge their source and their validity, we are on the path to death, as surely as Eve was.

The Father of Lies

"...Whenever he speaks a lie, he speaks from his own nature, for he is a liar, and the father of lies" (Jn. 8:44).

Not only is Satan the originator of the constant stream of accusation that bombards us, his accusations are a mixture of truth and lies. For example, look again at the words of Satan to God about Job (Job 1:9-11). Notice that there is some truth to Satan's words. God had put a hedge around Job and all that he had. God had blessed him abundantly, making him a very, very wealthy man. So far, Satan is telling the truth. Lulled by the accuracy of these words, it is easy to miss the sudden twist, for his next words are a lie. God allowed Satan to touch everything that Job had, yet he did not curse God. Sure, he became depressed. He went so far down he cursed the day he was born. But he did not curse God. That was a lie. Note also that Satan's major thrust was to bring into question the motives and intent of Job's heart. Watch out whenever you find yourself making a negative evaluation of another's motives. You cannot know what motivates another person to speak or act as they do. You cannot judge the intent of another's heart. That is God's territory and only he can rightly discern the heart of man. Do not allow yourself to be a passive recipient of Satan's lying accusations.

Again, remember that much of what Satan says will be true. He is not so foolish as to expect you to accept outright lies. Instead he will mix truth with error in order to make it believable. Begin to look for lies within your own mind. Often, they come in the form of generalized negatives: "I can't do anything right." "I'll never make it." "God doesn't love me because of what I've done." "Nobody loves me." "All people are untrustworthy." Recognize that Satan is attempting to fill your heart to lie (Acts 5:3). Resist and reject every such negative, destructive accusation.

The Adversary and Enemy

"And the enemy...is the devil..." (Matt. 13:39). *"Be of sober spirit, be on the alert. Your adversary, the devil, prowls about like a roaring lion, seeking someone to devour. But resist him, firm in your faith..."* (I Pet. 5:8, 9). *"...He was a murderer from the beginning..."* (Jn. 8:44).

Satan is unabashedly your enemy. He is seeking nothing less than your destruction. Therefore, every destructive, accusing, fear-producing, condemning, guilty, negative thought originally has its source in him. Every idea that leads you down is to be immediately resisted, rejected and replaced with a thought from God.

An "Angel of Light"

Perhaps the most insidious aspect of Satan's accusing work is his ability to *"disguise himself as an angel of light"* (2 Cor. 11:14). While he is injecting thoughts into your mind with the sole intent of bringing you to destruction, he will make you think that those very thoughts are from God. As a result, he will have you walking in constant guilt and condemnation thinking it is God convicting you, while all the time it is Satan seeking to bring you to death. How is such a thing possible? How can we accept the words of the evil one as being from the Holy One? Our enemy is subtle, using even instruments of righteousness for his wicked ends. For example, he will use the Scriptures, the very Word of God, against us. He may try to focus our attention on the laws of God and our total inability to keep them, rather than on the resurrection power of Jesus Christ within us which provides all the overcoming power necessary. He will encourage us to use Scripture to condemn and tear one another down, rather than for edification and encouragement as it is intended (Rom. 15:4). We will find ourselves wielding the Bible as a club to judge and belittle rather than an instrument to bring hope and sanctification.

Satan will also try to confuse conviction and condemnation, effectively crippling our ability to either resist him or receive cleansing by the Spirit. However, we need not be ignorant of his tactics. We can learn to discern the difference, cast down the work of the accuser and bring salvation, power and the kingdom of God into our lives.

- Satanic condemnation promotes a general feeling of despair. It is a vague, over-arching feeling of sinfulness and worthlessness. Holy

Spirit's conviction points to a specific sin. There is a clear recognition of the exact problem being spot-lighted.

- Satan's condemning voice will urge your destruction. He will try to convince you that the only course of action open to a miserable sinner such as yourself is to give up — on God, on others, on yourself, and ultimately, on life. The Holy Spirit, on the other hand, urges you to repent. Yes, you have sinned, but there is cleansing and renewal through the blood of Jesus Christ. He is faithful and just to forgive (1 Jn. 1:9).

- Finally, Satan will tell you that there is no way out. You are hopeless and helpless and there is absolutely nothing you can do. Your life is a dead end. You have failed beyond all restoration. But the Holy Spirit comes with a specific action which you can take.

"He who steals must steal no longer; but rather he must labour, performing with his own hands what is good, so that he will have something to share with one who has need" (Eph. 4:28). *"But now you also, put them all aside: anger, wrath, malice, slander, and abusive speech from your mouth"* (Col. 3:8). *"So, as those who have been chosen of God, holy and beloved, put on a heart of compassion, kindness, humility, gentleness and patience; bearing with one another, and forgiving each other, whoever has a complaint against anyone; just as the Lord forgave you, so also should you."* (Col. 3:12, 13). *"Therefore, laying aside falsehood, speak truth each one of you with his neighbour, for we are members of one another"* (Eph. 4:25).

We are never to argue against the Holy Spirit's conviction. He will not argue back. Instead, our conscience will become seared and our ears dulled to His voice (1 Tim. 4:1, 2). However, we must always actively resist satanic condemnation with the testimony of what the blood of the Lamb has accomplished on our behalf, confessing the word of our testimony.

A Thief

"The thief comes only to steal and kill and destroy; I [Jesus] came that they may have life and have it abundantly" (Jn. 10:10).

Satan is the accuser and source of every evil accusation. He is the liar and the father of lies, mixing truth and error to make us believe the worst about God, others and ourselves. He is a murderer who is always and in every way our enemy. He disguises himself as an *"angel of light"*, trying to confuse us and prevent us from resisting his attacks. And he is a thief who is constantly trying to steal, kill and destroy all that is good in our lives. Whenever our faith, hope and love are being challenged or removed, we know who is ultimately responsible: Satan! But we do not have to let him get away with his evil plans. We can resist him. We can overcome him. And we can cast him down by the power and authority of Jesus Christ Who lives and rules within us.

The Names and Character of the Holy Spirit

Just as Satan comes alongside to resist and destroy you, so the Holy Spirit is called alongside to strengthen you. Just as Satan injects his spontaneous thoughts of destructiveness into your mind, so the Holy Spirit injects spontaneous thoughts of life into your heart. Let us now consider the character and work of the Holy Spirit.

The Comforter

At the very core of Satan's nature is accusation; the essence of the Holy Spirit's nature is to comfort us with words of truth.

> *"...He will give you another Helper* [Comforter], *that He may be with you forever; that is, the Spirit of Truth..."* (Jn. 14:16, 17a).

The words the Spirit speaks will be calming, soothing, consoling. Even when conviction and correction are necessary, they will come to us with gentleness and solace. They will be gracious, and full of compassion and hope. They will lift our hearts and bring a breath of life to our broken spirits.

Before I discourse of Holy Spirit as the *Comforter*, I must make two remarks of the different translations of the word rendered *Comforter*. The Rhemish translation, which you are aware, is adopted by Roman Catholics, has left the word untranslated, and gives it *Paraclete*. This is the original Greek word, and it has some other meanings besides *Comforter*. Sometimes it means the "instructor." Frequently it means "Advocate," but the most common meaning of the word is that which we have here: *"I will send you another Comforter."*

God the Holy Spirit is a very loving *Comforter*. Do you know how much the Holy Spirit loves you? Can you measure the love of the Spirit? Do you know how great the affection of His towards you is?

He loved you when Heforeknew your sin; He loved you with the knowledge of what the aggregate of your wickedness would be; and he does not love you less now. Come to him in all boldness of faith; tell Him you have grieved Him, and hewill forget your wandering, and will receive you again; the kiss of His love shall be bestowed upon you, and the arms of His grace shall embrace you. He is faithful; trust him; hewill never deceive you; trust him, hewill never leave you.

We must all commit ourselves to searching our minds, expelling all negative, accusing thoughts and embracing all thoughts of comfort and consolation. We must become diligent to take every thought captive to the obedience of Christ. We must not let Satan win the battle within our minds, for victory on that front clears the way for control of the very words that we speak and the way that we act.

How specifically can we cast the accuser down from our minds and bring every thought under the authority of Jesus? It is not difficult. It does not take great prayer or faith. What it does require is diligent watchfulness. The moment we become aware of a negative, destructive thought within our minds, we must instantly reject it and replace it with a positive word of truth from the Word and the Spirit. When Satan whispers, "You will fail," the Spirit counters, *"Have faith in God."*

Satan says, "You are inadequate," the Holy Spirit breathes, "You have all adequacies through My power." Satan claims, "You are alone," the Holy Spirit promises, *"I am with you always. I will never leave you nor forsake you."*

You *can* choose whom you will listen to. Even when your faith is low, and your heart cannot say *amen* to the words of the Spirit, hold on to the words of truth. Do not let your emotions determine whose thoughts you will embrace. Hold fast to the word of God and your emotions will eventually be stirred and lifted to praise, comfort and joy.

The Spirit of Truth

We have already touched on the fact that the Holy Spirit speaks only words of truth. While Satan is a liar from the beginning, there is no shadow of error, inaccuracy or deception to be found in the Holy One.

> *"But when He, the Spirit of truth, comes, hewill guide you into all the truth..."* (Jn. 16:13). Truth liberates! Jesus said, *"...the words that I have spoken to you are spirit and are life"* (Jn. 6:63).

Satan tries to bind us with his lies. The Spirit of truth sets us free. Lies destroy us. Truth gives us life.

The Holy Spirit gives enlightening. We cannot make men see the truth, they are sometimes so blind, but when we submit ourselves to the enlightening of the Holy Spirit our eyes are opened. At first, we may see hazily; as the light increases, and our eye is strengthened, we see more and more clearly. What a mercy it is to see Christ, to look unto him, and so to be lightened! By the Spirit, souls see things in their reality; we see the actual truth and perceive what we are. The Spirit of God illuminates every believer, so that he sees still more marvellous things out of God's kingdom.

Notice the words of Jesus as given in St. John's gospel: *"...he*[Holy Spirit] *will teach you all things and bring to your remembrance all that I said to you"* (Jn. 14:26). When we are not under the Holy Spirit's guidance then we tend to fasten on one or two aspects of what Jesus taught and ignore the *"all."* The consequence is an unbalanced form of Christianity with an overemphasis on some things and an under-emphasis on others. Therefore, in many churches there are Christians who are controversial; they must be controversial to justify their imbalance. Christians who are under the control of the Spirit are not controversial but creative.

When Jesus said, he *"will teach you all things,"* he did not mean, as some have taken it, that the Holy Spirit would provide us with an encyclopaedic knowledge of all matters relating to heaven, earth and hell. The *"all things"* relates to all that we need to know in order to live an effective life for Jesus here on the earth – *"all things"* pertaining to godliness.

John Stott suggests that in one sense we may say the teaching ministry of Jesus had proved a failure. That sounds rather negative but listen to his argument. Many times, Jesus had urged His disciples to humble themselves like a little child, but did they take His words to heart? No, they were proud, arrogant, and conceited right to the end of His time with them. He told them also that they ought to love one another, but John, who appears to have been one of the most loving of the disciples, wanted on one occasion to call fire down from heaven on the Samaritans who were resistant to our Lord spending the night amongst them (Lk. 9:54). Then we read: *"he [Jesus] turned and rebuked them"* (Lk. 9:55). He rebuked them because of their unspiritual attitude.

Take the case of Simon Peter; he was brash, impulsive, blustering, and at times loud mouthed. Yet when you read Peter's first letter you cannot help but notice how the man has been changed. He writes so much about submission and obedience and holiness that at first, we wonder if this is the same Peter that we read about in the Gospels.

John it seems, carried the nickname "Son of Thunder" (Mk. 3:17) right up to the time when Christ left them, but his letters are full of that most excellent of qualities – divine love. What brought about the difference in Peter and John? It can only have been the work of the Holy

Spirit in their lives who gave them a deeper understanding of what Jesus had taught. Clearly the Holy Spirit is a teacher par excellence.

The Holy Spirit within us is for guidance. He is given to lead us into all truth. Truth is like a vast grotto, and the Holy Spirit brings torches, and shows us all the splendour of the roof; and since the passage seems intricate, he knows the way, and he leads us into the deep things of God. He opens to us one truth after another, by his light and by, his guidance, and thus we are taught of the Lord.

As we read God's Word prayerfully, spend time listening to God speak directly to us, and abide in his presence, he speaks through the effortless, spontaneous flow within. We must choose to incubate his words of truth that they might bear the peaceable fruit of righteousness in our lives (Jas. 3:18). We must be diligent to guard our minds that only thoughts of comfort and truth be allowed to remain unchallenged. Consider the chart following in one of the pages below. Covenant within your heart that the moment you become aware of a Satanic lie within your mind, such as those in column one, you will instantly reject it, cast it down and replace it with the eternal Word of Truth, as seen in column two.

The Convincer
The Holy Spirit is always seeking to comfort us by lighting words of truth upon our minds. This peaceful, gracious nature infuses every aspect of his work in our lives, even when he must speak to us concerning our sin.

> "And he, when he comes, will convict the world concerning sin, righteousness and judgment" (Jn. 16:8).

The word "convict" would be better translated "convince." The concept of conviction usually has a negative connotation in our minds. However, when the Holy Spirit points out sin in our lives, He does so in a totally positive manner. He gently calls us upward to greater righteousness rather than driving us down with guilt and condemnation. He positively draws us to change our minds and our actions through his love and grace.

St: Paul writes to Colossians, *"...in whom* [Christ] *are hidden all the treasures of wisdom and knowledge"* (Col. 2:3).

The point he has been making is that no essential truths are withheld from anyone who belongs to Christ. *"All"* – notice the *"all"* – *"all the treasures of wisdom and knowledge"* are hidden in him. But notice also that it is *"hidden"* truth. That means Holy Spirit conceals as well as reveals.

"The unfolding revelation of Christ," says one writer, "puts a surprise around every corner, makes life pop with novelty and discovery, and makes life well worth the living." The Christian life is dynamic, not static. The more you know, the more you know you don't know, and what you know sets you on fire to know more. The more we know of Christ the more we want to know, and this discovery will go on for ever. We will never go beyond him.

Satan runs roughshod over your personality, wanting only to dominate and destroy you. The Holy Spirit is always gentle, entreating you to set aside sin, to put on righteousness and to recognize righteous judgment. He is the *"Spirit of Life,"* setting you free from sin and death (Rom. 8:2). Satan drives; the Holy Spirit draws. Satan demands, the Holy Spirit entreats.

The Edifier

The comforting words of truth which convince us of sin and righteousness will always result in our edification. If we are obedient to his words, we will never leave the presence of God without being built up within our spirits. *"One who prophesies speaks to men for edification..."* (1 Cor. 14:3).

When the Comforter speaks to his Church through prophecy, his first order of business is to edify or build up. Even when pointing to sin and error, the element of instruction and hope will always result in the listener being encouraged and strengthened. According to the judgment of the Law, we deserve to be destroyed. According to the grace of Christ, we have eternal life. We may be approached, by others and within our own minds, in two ways: (1) with the Law, followed by judgment, or (2) with grace and mercy, through the blood and righteousness of Jesus Christ. We must be diligent to accept only those words which minister grace, life and edification. Further, we must be careful to *speak* only those words which encourage, build up and ignite hope. We have become ministers of reconciliation, not messengers of doom and destruction.

How do you react when you have sinned? Are you able to receive the grace and mercy Christ offers when you repent? Are you able to get back up when you fall and move on in the Spirit? Or must you wallow about in your guilt for a time, bemoaning your sinful condition, mentally flogging yourself for failing yet again?

Satan's Thoughts: Negative, Destructive	God's Thoughts: Positive, Up building
I can't...	I can do all things through him who strengthens me (Phil. 4:13).
I lack...	My God will supply all your needs according to His riches in glory in Christ Jesus (Phil. 4:19).
I fear...	God has not given us a spirit of timidity, but of power and love and discipline (2 Tim. 1:7).
I don't have faith...	...God has allotted to each a measure of faith (Rom. 12:3).
I am weak...	The Lord is the defence of my life (Psa. 27:1).
Satan has really got me...	Greater is He who is in you than who is in the world (1 Jn. 4:4).
I am defeated...	But thanks be to God, who always leads us in triumph in Christ (2 Cor. 2:14).
I do not know what to do...	Christ Jesus, who became to us wisdom from God (1 Cor. 1:30).
I expect to get sick occasionally...	By His scourging we are healed (Isa. 53:5). He [Jesus] himself took our infirmities and carried away our diseases (Matt. 8:17).
I am so worried and frustrated...	Casting all your anxiety on him, because He cares for you (1 Pet. 5:7).

| I am in bondage... | Where the Spirit of the Lord is, there is liberty (2 Cor. 3:17). |
| I feel so condemned... | There is now no condemnation for those who are in Christ Jesus (Rom. 8:1). |

The Exhorter/Teacher

"But one who prophesies speaks to men for edification and exhortation and consolation" (1 Cor. 14:3*)*. *"...he* [The Comforter] will teach you all things"* (Jn. 14:26).

"Exhort" is another one of those words which has taken on a different connotation than that intended by the author and translator. Some seem to think that exhortation is the time to "let another have it," often more closely resembling the work of the accuser than the work of the Comforter. The literal definition of exhortation (*parakaleo* in the Greek) is "to call a person to the side to encourage some course of conduct, always looking to the future." Notice how close it is to *parakletos,* which is translated *"Comforter."* Exhortation is thus distinctive in three ways: (1) we call a person to the side. We do not generally correct a person in public. We wait until we can speak in private, if possible. (2) We are encouraging to some course of conduct. We are not simply reciting his errors. Most of us are all too aware of our sin and failure. We do not need another pointing them out to us. What we need is assistance in breaking free from our bondage; specific constructive suggestions that will help us live the life of godliness we aspire to. (3) Exhortation always looks toward the future. We do not wallow around in the past.

A perfect example of proper exhortation is Jesus' response to the woman taken in adultery (Jn. 8:3-11). According to the law, she was guilty and worthy of death. But Jesus went beyond the law and offered mercy, grace and pardon. He spoke one simple sentence to her: *"I do not condemn you, either. Go. From now on sin no more"* (Jn. 8:11). He didn't lecture, moralize or sermonize, as we would be tempted to do. Instead, in those few words he offered pardon, acceptance and encouragement toward wholeness. Again, there was no need to point out her sin. It was ever before her. In the same way, the kiss of love, coupled with the word of exhortation, can often bring healing to our broken lives. And, if we are willing, we can be used by the Spirit to bring wholeness to others in the same way.

If we believe that the Lord wants us to exhort another, we must remember that all exhortation is to be done lovingly (1 Cor. 13), gently (Gal. 6:1), patiently (I Thess. 5:14), with great mercy (2 Cor. 1:3b) and with a desire to comfort (2 Cor. 1:3c).

> We must *"let no unwholesome word proceed from* [our] *mouth, but only such a word as is good for edification, according to the need of the moment, that it may give grace to those who hear. Do not grieve the Holy Spirit of God"* (Eph. 4:29, 30a).

Summary

In summary, let's look at a Psalm of Asaph, Psalm 73. It is a rather long chapter, so the text is not included here in full, but encourages us to read the entire psalm, not just the verses indicated below. Asaph begins:

> *"Surely God is good to Israel, to those who are pure in heart! But as for me, my feet came close to stumbling; my steps had almost slipped. For I was envious of the arrogant, as I saw the prosperity of the wicked...."* (vv. 1-3)

Asaph begins with a pure heart but suddenly he loses his divine perspective, focuses his eyes on the lifestyle of the arrogant and wicked, and his heart is contaminated. Instead of seeing God, he sees men. Instead of listening to truth, he accepts the lies of the enemy. As we read verses 4 through 15, it is clear that "the father of lies" is at work in his mind. There are some facts given:

> *"Pride is their necklace; the garment of violence covers them...the imaginations of their heart run riot. They mock...."* (vv.6-8)

It is all true. However, mixed in with these facts are some lies, which Asaph is accepting as truth:

> *"There are no pains in their death...They are not in trouble as other men, nor are they plagued like mankind."* (vv.4-5)

Not true! From the outside, to the envious eye, it may appear that they are leading a charmed life, but it simply is not so. Asaph is reasoning outside of the presence of the Holy Spirit, and when we do that, we quickly reason ourselves into a hole in the ground.

However, Asaph is wise enough not to remain in that condition. He knows where to go to find truth. He knows that in order to restore his pure heart, he must regain divine perspective.

Finally, in verse 17, he begins the process of restoration: *"Until I came into the sanctuary of God..."* In the following verses, we read his perspective in the presence of God, the response of God to his complaint and unspoken question. First, God shows him the truth about the wicked.

> *"They are destroyed in a moment! They are utterly swept away by sudden terrors!"* (v.19)

In a few words, or perhaps a picture, God brings the light of truth into the darkness of Satan's lies and they are undone. Next God shows Asaph the truth about himself.

> *"When my heart was embittered...I was senseless and ignorant; I was like a beast before you."* (vv.21-22)

When we think and reason outside of his presence, when we accept lies as truth, we are as senseless as a wild beast.

> *"Nevertheless, I am continually with you; you have taken hold of my right hand. With your counsel you will guide me, and afterward receive me to glory."* (vv.23-24)

Though Asaph was deceived, though he sinned and lost sight of his God, yet he was not forsaken. When he saw his own sin, superimposed upon it he saw the mercy and grace of his God. No wonder the chapter closes with worship!

When we see God and his truth is revealed within, our hearts are purified, communion is restored, and joy breaks forth like the morning.

This is the same process we must go through. When we lose divine perspective, when we cannot see God's hand and our minds are clouded by the mixture of truth and error, we too must come into the sanctuary of God. We too must come into his presence, pour out our doubts, angers and fears, and allow him to speak in response. Only through his voice and his vision can we be made whole.

Response

As we have read this chapter, are we aware of Satan's work in our minds? Have we begun to see more clearly the difference between the voice of the accuser and the Comforter? Have we recognized generalized negatives and outright lies from the enemy which were accepting and incubating? Have we seen God at work in our life and circumstances?

We must take some time right now to come into the sanctuary of God. Quieten our heart, tune to the spontaneous voice and vision of Jesus and look to God in earnest prayer with our questions, doubts and fears. Then make sure we listen for his response and look for his vision. Record in your memory what you see and hear. Rejoice in the goodness of God!

Chapter 11

Incubating only Christ and Striving to Grow Spiritually

Have you ever noticed that you can be going happily on your way, enjoying life, praising God, content just to be alive, when suddenly, within minutes or even seconds, anger or depression explode within you and all your joy is as naught? How can such a dramatic change of spirit take place so quickly? What causes it to happen? Is there anything we can do to prevent it, or at least reverse its results?

As we became more aware of the words of the accuser and Comforter within us, we became more aware of such sudden "mood swings," and they bother us.

Divine Revelation of their Source and Deliverance

The Bible everywhere teaches that we can control what we think. It is useless to adopt a defeatist attitude, saying that we simply cannot help it when our minds are filled with unwelcome thoughts. The fact of the matter is that we can help it. The secret lies in positive thinking. A person cannot entertain evil thoughts and thoughts about the Lord Jesus Christ at the same time. If, then, an evil thought should come to him, he should immediately get rid of it by meditating on the Person and works of Christ. The more enlightened psychologists and psychiatrists of the day have come to agree with the apostle Paul on this matter. They stress the dangers of negative thinking.

The human mind will always set itself on something and Paul wished to be quite sure that the Philippians would set their minds on the right things. This is something of utmost importance, because it is a law of life that, if a man thinks of something often enough, he will come to a stage when he cannot stop thinking about it. His thoughts will be quite literally in a groove out of which he cannot jerk them. It is, therefore, of the first importance that a man should set his thoughts upon the fine things and Paul makes a list of them in Philippians 4:8.

You do not have to look very closely to find the Lord Jesus Christ in this verse. Everything that is *true, honourable, right, pure, lovely, of good repute, excellence, and worthy of praise* is found in him. If we are diligent to fill senses of our spirits continuously and only with our Lord Jesus Christ, we will be able to live in the reality of the verse given above.

In the previous verse, Paul had assured the true believers that God would garrison their hearts and thoughts in Christ Jesus. But Paul reminds them that they too have a responsibility in the matter. God does not garrison the thought-life of a man who does not want it to be kept pure.

Herein exists freedom, joy and the abundant life which is promised to us as children of God! What are the spiritual senses which are the fountainhead of creativity within man? It is through spiritual senses that realities are birthed into the physical world. These senses are always functioning, always at some stage of the incubation process. They can be filled by either the Holy Spirit or Satan, working both life and hope in our lives or death and despair.

Just as there are three stages in the birth of a child, so there are three stages in the birthing of spiritual realities into our dimension.

Conception

- Occurs when the inner ear *hears* a word from either the Holy Spirit or Satan, and

- The inner eye *sees* a vision from the Holy Spirit or Satan.

Incubation

- As the inner mind *ponders* the word and vision,

- The inner will be set and we begin to *speak* out of that which fills our hearts, and

- Our inner emotions are stirred causing us to *act* upon the word and vision.

Birth

- In the fullness of time, the spiritual reality becomes physical reality.

Whether we are aware of it or not, our hearts are constantly in the process of creating and bringing forth into the third dimension that which was conceived in the spiritual realm. Therefore, it is imperative that we present the eyes and ears of our hearts only to Christ to be filled by him that the peaceable fruit of righteousness may be born through us. Jesus said,

> *"The eye is the lamp of your body; when your eye is clear, your whole body is also full of light; but when it is bad, your whole body also is full of darkness..."*
> (Lk. 11:34-36).

The eyes of our heart are one of the most powerful tools for good and evil which God has created within us. The focus of our inner eyes provides the most powerful dynamic of our lives. We are told to fix *"our eyes on Jesus, the author and perfecter of our faith"* (Heb. 12:2). Only by focusing our inner eyes on Jesus can our eyes be clear and our whole body be full of light. If we do not deliberately offer them to Christ to be filled with his divine light, they will automatically be filled by Satan bringing the darkness of lust, fear, failure and inadequacy to our whole bodies. Once we have heard God's word and seen his vision, we must incubate it within our spirits, allowing our inner mind, inner will and inner emotions to become saturated with it. We thus become pregnant with the purposes of God and carriers of his sovereign power in the world. Our inner mind ponders only God's thoughts, never the doubts and negativism of Satan.

We choose with our inner will to speak forth with faith that which God has spoken. As our inner emotions are charged with the vision of God, they motivate us to move out and act in faith upon God's glorious promises, expecting a miracle. In the fullness of God's timing, not ours, he will bring forth his promise, giving glory to his name. To make sure we are not eligible to receive any of the glory, he will wait until we have stopped trying to bring his promises into being in our own strength. When it is totally evident to all that it cannot be done in the natural, he will do it supernaturally.

Abraham, the Father of Faith

Abraham is a classic example of this experience. In Genesis 12:2, God spoke a *rhema* word into Abram's heart, *"I will make you a great nation."* What a glorious promise! What a positive, edifying, joyful word! As you hear God's voice, you, too, will find that God's words are glorious, positive, edifying and joyful. He will promise to do great things through you, too. Satan will try to steal these words of truth with his accusations, "God can't use you. Look who you are." But the Spirit breathes back into our condemned and discouraged hearts, "I will use you. Look at Who I AM!"

Eleven years later, Abram had another visit from the Lord. This time, God showed him the stars of the sky and the sands of the seashore in a vision. *"So, shall your descendants be,"* he said. Here stands Abram, 86 years old and childless. How does he respond to such an amazing promise? *"Then he believed in the Lord...."* Abram must have believed the *rhema* word which came to him so many years before because he acted in obedience to it. However, the faith that came as a result of vision was so deep and powerful that it was worthy of comment in the Word. Such is the power of vision. It solidifies the promise, giving substance to that which cannot be seen in the natural. Having received both word and vision, Abram filled his inner mind with only thoughts of faith.

"...In hope against hope he believed...without becoming weak in faith, he contemplated his own body, now as good as dead...yet, with respect to the

promise of God, he did not waver in unbelief but grew strong in faith, giving glory to God, and being fully assured that what God had promised, he was able to perform..." (Rom. 4:17-22).

Though years went by without seeing the physical manifestation of the promise of God, Abram did not falter in faith but filled the mind of his heart with the words and vision he had received from the Lord.

Thirteen more years passed without the birth of a child. Finally, God appeared again with a command to Abram,

"...Your name shall be Abraham, for I will make you the father of a multitude of nations" (Gen. 17:5).

Abraham had been pondering the word and vision of God for twenty-four years. He had conceived, he had incubated, and he was pregnant with the promises of God! Many-a-time when we confess words of faith, we sound foolish to the unbelieving world and are often mocked and criticized as a result. If this happens when the seed is small and has not yet been firmly established, it is easy to abort the vision and abandon the word.

God also gave Abraham the command of circumcision when he was 99 years old (Gen. 17:10-24). No mention had been made about conditions of the covenant up to this point. However, Abraham's inner emotions were so attuned to the Spirit that he was moved to immediate obedience.

"In the very same day Abraham was circumcised..." (Gen. 17:26).

Notice that the Lord continued to give Abraham instructions concerning his preparation for the miracle during the incubation stage.

Finally, after twenty-five years of waiting, there came forth the creative power of God and Isaac was born. However, that is not the whole story. During the time of waiting, Abraham made one mistake: *"Abram listened to the voice of Sarai"* (Gen. 16:2). It was understandable. A long time had passed since the promise had come. So, Abraham forgot the voice of God for a moment and listened instead to earthly wisdom. The next time God came to speak to him, he proudly pointed to the results of his efforts and said, *"...Oh that Ishmael might live before You!" But God said, 'No...'"* (Gen. 17:18, 19). Our efforts cannot achieve God's goals. If we try to make it happen, our effort becomes a hindrance and the vision remains unfulfilled. Only when our efforts are exhausted and all-natural hope is gone can God supernaturally move, fulfil his promise and bring glory to himself.

Our Conviction of God's Trustworthiness

Unless we have a strong conviction that God is entirely trustworthy and perfect in character, we will not desire a deep and ongoing relationship with him. Do you realize that the reason for the distance between God and the first human couple in the Garden of Eden was doubt about God's goodness? Doubt about God soon leads to dislike of God, and dislike of God soon leads to disobedience.

Since the Fall, every child born into this world has within its nature a basic distrust of God. Paul puts it like this:

> *"The mind set on the flesh is hostile toward God; ..."* (Rom. 8:7).

The word *hostile* can be translated, "of an enemy, or unfriendly, or opposed." No one trusts someone they regard as an enemy. Distance between humankind and God arose when the first human couple doubted his goodness. Closeness between human beings and God comes when we have confidence in his goodness. If we do not have complete confidence in him, we will not desire a close relationship with him.

How do we develop trust in the goodness of God when so much that happening in the world seems to contradict it? Reality is grim – innocent children are abused, starved, massacred – and countless other forms of atrocity are carried out around the world daily. We must not blind our eyes to these facts and pretend they are untrue because they appear to contradict the concept of God's goodness. Pretence must never be our refuge. When we face life honestly and allow ourselves to be jolted by what we see, then and only then, are we ready for God to speak.

The book of Job, as you know, records the story of a godly man who underwent some of the bitterest experiences it is possible to meet with in this life. It was when he faced his hardships, recognized how he really felt and admitted it that God came to him and answered him (Job 38:1 – 41:34). We must never be afraid of admitting that what we see around us does not match up with what we know about the character of God. We must face difficult issues for it is only when we do so that we are ready to hear God speak. If we refuse to face reality, then our souls are not alerted to hear his voice. We fear that we might hear something to make us even more uncertain of God, and thus prefer to take refuge in illusion.

When Job faced the reality of his situation and how he really felt then he was ready for God to speak. But notice God did not give any answers to Job's questions. He gave himself. Job had an encounter with God that more than satisfied him. He could live without answers when he knew that God was there.

Oswald Chambers states: "Life is more tragic than orderly." Chambers knew that unless Christians are willing to grapple with this truth and accept it, they will be led down the road of illusion.

The Fall has turned this fair universe of God's into a shamble, and though much about the world is still beautiful, accidents, calamities, and suffering prevail. And these will continue until the time when God brings all things to a conclusion. Life will go on being more "tragic than orderly" until Christ returns and finalises his plan for this fallen planet. This is reality – and the sooner we face it the better. True faith is not built upon illusion but upon reality.

Response
It is important that you give God a chance to apply the truths you are taught to your own life. If you hope to be counselled by God, you must meet with him, talk to him and listen to him. Go to a quiet place where he can reveal himself to you. What dreams has he given to you? Have you given up on your dreams? Do you continue to ponder them in your

heart? Are you speaking them forth as God directs? Are you listening and obedient to every word the Lord is speaking to you, preparing the way for its fulfilment? Are you resting from your works and allowing God to work through you?

> "*Fixing our eyes on Jesus, the author and perfecter of our faith.*" (Heb. 12:2).
> "*I am the Alpha and the Omega, the first and the last, the beginning and the end*" (Rev. 22:13).

Striving to Grow

Every Christian has two things necessary to thrive – the inner urge to develop and the spiritual resources to help us grow, which has been made available to us through Jesus Christ. If we fail to grow, then it is not because God has withheld what we need to grow. The fault lies with us. The Living Bible paraphrase of Rom. 8:29 reads thus:

> "For from the very beginning God decided that those who come to Him – and all along he knew who would – should become like his Son..."

God is so excited about Jesus that he wants to make everyone like him – not in appearance, of course, but in character. Since this is God's clearly stated intention if we do not strive then the fault is certainly not God's but ours. We have either stifled the urge within us or not availed ourselves of the grace as said in the epistle to Ephesians 4:7;

> "But to each one of us grace was given according to the measure of Christ's gift."

Even if we are compelled to live in an environment which is hostile to our spiritual growth, God in his foresight and love has graciously provided us with the resources which will enable us to grow, and nothing can prevent those resources becoming ours except our own unbelief or unwillingness to draw upon them. God has supplied everything for our spiritual growth. Alongside our disabilities stand his abilities. Our task is to exchange what is ours for what is his.

Chapter 12

Seeing God in the Past

"*Blessed are the pure in heart, for they shall see God.*" (Matt. 5:8). But what about those times when we were blind to see God? What about those horrible experiences in our past which so traumatized us that we are still affected by them today? What about the times that were so awful, we were afraid that God wasn't there? How can our heart be cleansed and healed of the wounds we received even before we intimately knew Christ?

Only our Wonderful Counsellor Who lives outside of time can be with us simultaneously in the present and the past. Christ is the eternal I AM. He is never "I was" nor "I will be," but only "I AM," forever in the now of time. He exists beyond time; it has no power to limit him. It is just as easy for him to be present at a moment in your past as it is for him to be present right here and now. Indeed, He *was* present in our past at the same time as he is present in our now and in our future. He is everywhere and always here. He is the God of the here and now, and every moment of time is to him, at every moment, the here and now. These concepts are too big for our minds to comprehend but they are nonetheless true.

Because they are true, because Christ is omnipresent and lives in timelessness, He can minister total healing to every hurt of our past.

This experience is called by various names: inner healing, healing of memories, deep healing, or healing of the soul. The name doesn't matter, except as a way of capsulizing several truths of Scripture. Essentially, deep hurts of the past are healed through forgiveness and allowing Christ to walk through the scene with healing love. There are several things inner healing is not:

1.   It is not *you* drumming up hurt to be healed. We do not scour our memories and dredge up every negative experience we can find. It is *Christ* gently bringing to our consciousness an experience that he wants to touch.

2.   Inner healing is not you manufacturing a new scene. New Age teaching has a form of inner healing in which one replaces in his memory the words or actions which hurt him with ones of love and kindness. Such a restructuring of the past is never the work of the Holy Spirit because it is built on lies, and he can never lie. Instead, true inner healing occurs when we *see Christ* moving freely within the scene as it happened.

3.   Inner healing is not a list of formulae, even though we may tend to present it that way. Inner healing, like all counselling by God, is a living encounter with a living God.

Many excellent books have been written on inner healing, especially in recent years. Certainly, it is not attempted to say all that should be said on the subject in one short chapter. Instead an overview of the process as illustrated in the ministry of Jesus in the Gospel of John is given briefly.

The story begins on the night before Jesus' crucifixion. Peter, strong, dynamic, and impetuous, had tried to defend his best Friend. Wielding a sword as the soldiers attempted to take Jesus away, he had managed to cut off one man's ear. But instead of receiving commendation and gratitude, Jesus had rebuked him and restored the ear. Now Jesus was on trial before the high priest and there seemed to be nothing Peter could do. He waited in the courtyard for some word, not wanting to be too far from his Master. As he sat with the others in the courtyard, warming himself by a charcoal fire, a servant girl announced, *"You, too, were with Jesus the Galilean."* Fearfully he denied the fact and moved away from the girl. Before long, another servant repeated the charge and again Peter denied that he even knew Jesus. Finally, a bystander claimed, *"The way you talk gives you away. You must be one of His followers."* Immediately Peter changed the way he talked and began to curse and swear, saying, *"I do not know the man!"* As the cock announced the arrival of a new day, Peter went out and wept bitterly. No other time in Scripture does it speak of Peter weeping. Clearly this was a deeply wounding event in his life. In fact, as a result, he turned his back on his call to ministry and returned to his former employment.

Few days passed. Jesus appeared to many of is disciples in many places. He even went to the shore of the Sea of Galilee where a big burly fisherman was trying to put the past behind him and get on with his life. Just as the day was breaking, Jesus appeared to him and his friends who were fishing together. He prepared them a breakfast of fish and bread over a charcoal fire. After they had eaten, Jesus began to question Peter,

> *"Simon, son of John, do you love Me...?"* Peter replied, *"Yes, Lord, you know that I love You."* Jesus responded, *"Tend My lambs."*

Again, Jesus asked him the same question, Peter gave the same reply and Jesus responded in a similar way. And again, a third time, the conversation was repeated. What was the point of this whole encounter? Jesus was ministering inner healing to the deep wounds Peter had experienced as a result of his three-fold denial of Christ. Notice the correlation of the following chart:

The Inner Healing Process

	The Step Taken	A Biblical Example
		Peter: Lk. 22:54-62/Jn. 21:2-17
1.	Using vision, go back and re-enter the hurt	Charcoal fire
		Twilight
		Three-fold confession
2.	Using vision, bring Jesus into the scene	"Jesus stood on the beach…"
3.	Using vision, let Jesus move freely healing the hurt with His loving presence.	Jesus' statements of affirming love:
		"Tend My lambs; Shepherd My sheep; Tend My sheep"

Let's discuss each step of the inner healing process and see how it was applied to Peter.

(1) Using vision, go back and re-enter the hurt

It is important that you see the scene and feel at least a small portion of the emotions you felt at the time. Don't become so involved in the emotions that you are again unable to see Christ there. If the experience was too emotional and traumatizing, Jesus may choose to take you to a scene soon after the event instead. However, the use of vision is essential. Notice how Jesus re-set the scene of Peter's pain for him: It happened just as day was breaking. It happened beside a charcoal fire. (These two passages – John 18:18 and 21:9 – are the only times a charcoal fire is mentioned in the New Testament). And it involved a three-fold confession.

(2) Using vision, invite Jesus to reveal himself in the scene

Healing only takes place when we are touched by Jesus. He was there when the painful event took place. We may think, "It was too awful! He couldn't possibly have been there." Yet the Psalmist David says, "…

if I make my bed in Sheol, behold, you are there" (Ps. 139:8). There is no place and no experience so bad that he is driven from our side. We are simply asking our eyes to be opened that we might see what he was doing and what he wanted to do if we had allowed him to. In John 21:4, *"Jesus stood on the beach...."* He came to Peter and entered the scene of his failure and pain.

(3)   Using vision, let Jesus move freely, and healing the hurt with his loving presence

Again, we must know, we are not manufacturing false visions. Jesus was there in our painful experiences. It was only our blindness or overwhelming emotions which hid him from our sight. He was working and moving, even though we could not sense his presence. Now, as our eyes are open, we see Christ and are healed. We must hesitate to even offer suggestions about what we might see him doing, for he is so creative that the possibilities are limitless. We should quite confidently say that he probably won't do what we expect him to do. From this detached distance, we can say, "He might do this or say that." But such theories do not bring healing to our souls. Only experiencing the living Christ can set us free.

There are many truths to be found in Jesus' conversation with Peter, but we will zero in on just one. What was Jesus' response to Peter's confessions of love? *"Tend My lambs; Shepherd My sheep; Feed My sheep."* In other words, Jesus was saying, "I forgive you, Peter. I accept you and I want you to carry on with the ministry which I have given you. You are totally restored." Couldn't Jesus have simply shaken Peter's hand and said, "I forgive you, Peter. Carry on."? Why go to all the trouble of re-setting the scene of his pain? Because *spirit-level emotions do not respond to cognitive facts.* The spirit speaks the language of pictures and only through vision can the spirit be touched and healed.

Summary

Through the ministry of Jesus which we call inner healing, we can see Christ even during painful experiences of our past. As we offer the eyes of our heart to him, asking him to reveal his presence and work in these events, he will often call upon us to forgive those who were responsible for our pain. Not that we in any way condone their words or actions, but through forgiveness, we are set free to receive forgiveness and healing from God. Those who wounded us are also set free by our forgiveness to be touched by the healing power of the Spirit of Christ.

Response

Inner healing can happen in many ways. Often it happens at the altar when we pour out our hurt and anger before the Lord. He gives us revelation and divine perspective and we come away healed and restored. He responds with love and grace and, again, divine perspective is restored. Much inner healing takes place "naturally" (supernaturally) as a result of our growth in the Lord. Increase in knowledge and understanding and a deeper experience in him produce healing. Inner healing can also take place as one or two individuals pray with us. This is especially effective when we run into roadblocks which prevent us from letting Christ complete the work.

If you have become aware of a need for inner healing in your life, first you go to the Lord directly. Remember to use vision throughout the experience. If you are unable to find release on your own in this way, you should go to someone who has an established prayer ministry of inner healing; someone whom you know has a respected reputation. Our Wonderful Counsellor wants to set you free from all the angers, hurts, disappointments, bitterness, fear and failure of the past which bind you and rob you of your joy in him. When you see him during every experience of your life, your heart will be healed.

Chapter 13

From Fear to Faith

Probably the most paralyzing emotion which can overwhelm us is fear. No other emotion can so effectively negate our faith, stifle our joy, disrupt our peace and manacle our walk with the Lord. Fear is such a pervasive emotion in our society that many centres have been established all over the nation for the sole purpose of helping individuals overcome, or at least learn to live with, their fears. Many different methods are used to bring release from the bondage. In this chapter, we will examine only one: moving from fear to faith by hearing a *rhema* word from God.

> *"There is no fear in love; but perfect love casts out fear..."* (1 Jn. 4:18).

Jesus came to heal us of our fear. Fear is the result of the incubation of Satan's mendacious evaluation of life. Faith is the result of the incubation of the Lord's perspective which is full of grace and truth.

Fear is not simply a psychological problem. Its root is in satanic *rhema*, which makes it a spiritual problem. The Bible says:

> *"The weapons of our warfare are not of the flesh, but divinely powerful for the destruction of fortresses. We are destroying speculations and every lofty thing raised up against the knowledge of God, and we are taking every thought captive to the obedience of Christ"* (2 Cor. 10:4, 5).

Paul clearly teaches that our thought processes are, to a large extent, of a spiritual nature. Therefore, when our minds receive a negative thought which lures us into the pattern of fear, we are involved in a spiritual warfare which can only be won by spiritual means. Fear is destroyed by replacing Satan's *rhemas* with God's.

What is it that we fear and worry about? Studies have indicated that as many as 90% of our worries are unjustified, either because they involve things that will never happen, things in the past that can't be changed through worry, or petty, unimportant things which do not warrant the effort. If you will examine your own worries, you will probably find this is true for you as well. Therefore, most of your worrying is a waste of time and energy and is in fact time spent building the kingdom of darkness. Remember that worry is a form of incubation and eventually that which grows within us must be delivered into the physical world in some form.

However, even the 10% of our worries which might be considered legitimate causes for concern should not bring negativism and fear into our hearts and minds. If these issues are indeed important items that should be considered, how should they be handled, if not with worry?

"Be anxious for nothing but in everything by prayer and supplication with thanksgiving let your requests be made known to God" (Phil. 4:6).

Here then is the solution to fear and worry prayer plus supplication plus thanksgiving equals freedom. Perhaps you have heard that formula before. Perhaps you have even tried it and found it an empty, meaningless ritual. You are right; it is empty and meaningless, *unless* during your prayer, you contact the Wonderful Counsellor and hear His words of *rhema* to you on the subject. Mechanical formulae do not heal spiritual wounds. Academic exercises do not set the spirit free from its bondage to lies. Only a living encounter with the living Christ can transform your heart of fear to a heart of faith.

Therefore, the steps to moving from fear to faith are actually:

1. With prayer and supplication, make your needs known to the Lord. Pour out all the needs, concerns and worries which are holding your mind captive.

2. Quiet yourself in the presence of God.

3. Receive revelation from God. Hear his words and see his vision of life.

4. Respond with worship and thanksgiving. You won't need to be reminded to do this. It will be the automatic response of your heart to the healing presence of Christ.

Let us examine a biblical example of this process. Psalm 61 is a psalm of David which begins with a heart of fear and ends in worship.

> "Hear my cry, O God; Give heed to my prayer. From the end of the earth I call to You when my heart is faint; Lead me to the rock that is higher than I…Let me dwell in Your tent forever; Let me take refuge in the shelter of Your wings" (v. 1-4).

David is crying out to the Lord for shelter and defence. His heart is fainting with fear. He feels he is far from God, even to the end of the earth, yet he knows that God has been his protection in times past. So, he comes before the Lord and pours out his feelings and his request. At the end of verse four, we see a Hebrew word, *Selah*. The New American Standard Bible indicates that this means "a pause, a crescendo, or a musical interlude." When David had finished expressing all his negative feelings to the Lord, he stopped talking and quieted himself in the Lord's presence while music continued to play to help him remain still. This is the place we so often miss the power of prayer. How quick we are to run into the sanctuary, blubber out our prayers and run away again. No wonder our prayer times become empty, dry rituals. We have missed their purpose entirely. Prayer is not to be a monologue, but a dialogue, two people sharing back and forth, conversing about the things on both of their hearts. If we are going to be healed and delivered of our fear, we must not only express our feelings to the Lord, but we must then stop talking and give him a chance to respond. The change in David's heart as a result of this quiet musical interlude is strikingly clear in the rest of the psalm.

*"For You **have** heard my vows, O God; You **have** given me the inheritance of those who fear Your name. You **will** prolong the king's life; his years **will** be as many generations. he **will** abide before God forever..."* (vv. 5-7, emphases added).

There is clearly a new sense of confidence in David's spirit. These are strong declarations of faith based on the revelation of God within his heart. No more is he bound by fear but now he fairly leaps with faith.

It is no wonder that the psalm ends with praise, worship and obedience. When we have heard from the Lord and he has replaced our fear with faith, no one will need to exhort us to praise. No one will be able to keep us from it! Again, let us remember that this is not an academic process. You can't talk yourself out of fear intellectually, because it is not mental but spiritual at its roots. Faith must well up from within you as a result of encounter with Jesus Christ in order to be set free from fear.

In using this process, it is important to remember that we are not attempting to drive out the darkness of fear. We cannot force the darkness from our minds by our own efforts any more than we can push the darkness from a room with our hands. Instead, we are bringing light into the dark place and instantly the darkness flees. Neither are we trying to empty our minds of fear. An empty mind is never the goal of the Spirit of God. In fact, we do not focus on the fear at all. Perhaps you have found that the more you focus on something, the greater it looms within your mind, even if your focus is on trying to avoid it. For example, if you are dieting, you may try not to think about ice creams and sweet items. The more you think about not thinking about them, the bigger the desire for them grows within you. Temptation and sin cannot be conquered by direct attack. Instead, we overcome by replacement. Instead of focusing on ice creams and other sweet items, see yourself slim, healthy and full of vitality. Instead of focusing on emptying your mind of fear, fill up your mind with faith. Hold on to that *rhema* word and vision you have received from Christ. Let it roll around and around in your mind and heart. Meditate on it day and night. Incubate his truth until it is birthed into your existence.

Finally, we are not *coming against* the fear. Even though it is something evil which we are attacking, still a negative stance is always destructive. Instead, we are *coming unto* God in a positive action that he might speak life to our souls.

How can God speak words of *rhema* which will bring us peace? There are many ways. He may speak through the illumined Word (Eph. 1:17, 18). As we meditate on the Scriptures, his message may suddenly leap off the page and into our hearts. He may also speak with "a still small voice of calm" in the spontaneous thoughts and impressions which come as we are quiet before him (1 Kings 19:12, 13).

God has promised to speak to us through dreams and visions (Num. 12:6; Acts 2:17). In our culture, dreams have been dismissed as simply yesterday's leftover lasagne, and visions as the escape attempts of an unstable mind. But that is not God's view. He has promised that he would give wisdom and knowledge to his children through dreams and visions, if we will but have ears to hear and eyes to see. The language of the spirit is pictures, and the spirit can be touched most profoundly through the images that come to us from the Lord. The *rhema* of God may come to us in the form of our conscience which either accuses or excuses us:

> *"...their consciences* (sense of right and wrong) *also bear witness; and their* [moral] *decisions* (their arguments of reason, their condemning or approving thoughts) *will accuse or perhaps defend and excuse* [them]*"* (Rom. 2:15 Amp. Bible).

And God will speak to us through his creation, revealing truth to replace the error we have believed.

> *"For ever since the creation of the world his invisible nature and attributes, that is, his eternal power and divinity, have been made intelligible and*

clearly discernible in and through the things that have been made (His handiworks) ..." (Rom. 1:20 Amp. Bible).

Elijah: From Faith to Fear to Faith

The story of Elijah's triumph over the prophets of Baal and subsequent depression is very familiar to us. But let's examine it once more and notice the *process* at work in Elijah's life which produced such profound "mood swings." In 1 Kings 18:1-46, we read the story of Elijah's triumph over prophets of a false god because he heard God's voice and obeyed it. What a marvellous day that was! He called down fire from heaven, killed 350 false prophets, prayed earnestly and ended a three-year drought, and outran a chariot for twenty miles. I would call that a successful day of ministry! He certainly was "God's man of the hour full of faith and power!" However, it is easy to forget that this was also a very draining day, spiritually, emotionally and physically. Therefore, he was a prime candidate for depression.

It is good for us to realize that following our moments of greatest spiritual victory, we are most vulnerable to Satan's attacks of fear, discouragement and depression, as well. Satan never misses such an opportunity. In this case, he had a willing helper in the form of the wicked queen Jezebel (1 Kings 19:1ff.). She sent word to Elijah: I vow that I will have you killed within the next 24 hours. Here was a word from Satan dropped into Elijah's mind. He had a choice. He could quiet his heart before the Lord and hear the Lord's response to the threat. Or he could do what he did do receive the negative word, be filled with fear and run for his life. It is understandable. He had just been through a fierce spiritual battle. He was exhausted. He did not seem to have the strength to engage the enemy again. But Satan fights dirty, attacking us when we are least prepared. So, Elijah allowed the evil word to sink into his heart, and he began to incubate it.

His actions and words came under the control of the incubated evil word. In verses 3 & 4 we see him running into the wilderness, separating himself from those who would care for him, throwing himself down under a tree and wishing for death. *"It is enough; now O Lord, take my life."* "I've had it. I'm no good and I just want to die." No matter how greatly we are used by God, it only takes a moment to receive an evil word from Satan and fall into depression.

But, praise God, we don't have to stay there! If we will receive it, our Father is waiting to restore us to faith. The first step in Elijah's healing was sleep. Sometimes, the most spiritual thing we can do is go to bed. If your mind and spirit are exhausted, don't stay up all night wrestling with the devil. Leave him in the Lord's hands and get some sleep. He will be much easier to defeat in the morning. The second step to restoration was to eat. There is a time when God calls us to fasting. Indeed, Elijah will go the next forty days without food. But right now, when his body and soul are weakened by spiritual battle, the Lord sends an angel with food and encouragement to eat and rebuild his strength.

Somewhat refreshed by the food and rest, Elijah now knows what he must do. *"So, he arose…and went…to Horeb, the mountain of the Lord."* At least his mind had cleared enough that he knew he had to hear from God. In verses eight through fourteen, his Father God gently and lovingly restores divine perspective and renews his heart of faith. *"What are you doing here, Elijah?"* Of course, God knew what he was doing there. But He wanted Elijah to express the fears that were strangling his spirit.

> *"I have been very zealous for the Lord, the God of hosts; for the sons of Israel have forsaken your covenant, torn down your altars and killed your prophets with the sword. And I alone am left; and they seek my life, to take it away"* (v. 14).

Can you see the mixture of truth and error? Obviously, Elijah has been listening to the voice of the liar. Before he is fully restored, he must accept the truth in place of these lies.

What did God say to Elijah in his "still small voice of calm"? Did he rebuke him for his lack of faith? Did he condemn him for his weakness? Did he criticize him for listening to the enemy's voice? No, not at all. In

verses 15 through 19 God responds to Elijah's fearful confession with
the word, "*Go....*" God did not even mention the events of the last few
days. Instead, he looked to the future and re-commissioned Elijah into
ministry. He gave him authority to anoint kings. He instructed him to
anoint another prophet to be with him and carry on his ministry. And
finally, he spoke the truth to counter the lie Elijah had been incubating,

> "*Yet I will leave seven thousand in Israel, all the knees which have not bowed
> to Baal, and every mouth which hath not kissed him*" (v.18).

Completely restored to a spirit of faith, Elijah went from the mountain
of the Lord to carry on with the ministry God had called him to.

Summary

Jesus is the Counsellor who can destroy the debilitating fear which
consumes us and ignite again the faith we need to live a life of victory.
We must have a living experience with him in which we take our fear
before God in prayer. Then we must quiet ourselves to listen to his
response and allow his words of truth to destroy the lie of the enemy.
As a result, we will be free to praise and worship him, rejoicing in his
victory which we have received.

Response

Are there areas of fear in your life? To help you discern them, write down
all the endings to the question "What if...?" you have asked yourself
recently. When you have laid all your fears before Jesus, quiet yourself
in His presence and receive the mind of Christ on each situation. Listen
what he says and shows you. Unite faith with his words and enter rest
(Heb. 4).

Chapter 14

From Guilt to Hope

According to Dr. Paul Yonggi Cho, fear, guilt and anger are three of the great sins of the flesh. They are also three of the most physically destructive emotions we can entertain. They have been found to be contributing factors in a wide range of sickness and disease. Now that we understand how the process of conception and incubation result finally in delivery, it is clear to us how the incubation of Satan's destructive words and visions must have as its fruit sickness and death. However, our confidence is in the knowledge that the process also works for good, and the incubation of holy words and visions brings forth life, health and righteousness. In the last chapter we learned how to overcome fear through hearing the voice of God. In this chapter we will examine the driving power of guilt and how it can be replaced by the drawing power of hope.

Just as there is true conviction of the Holy Spirit and false satanic condemnation, there is corresponding true guilt and false guilt. When we sin, God convicts us, and we feel true guilt. This must be dealt with through confession and cleansing.

However, when Satan tries to immobilize with false guilt, no amount of repentance can set us free. False guilt must be dealt with in a totally different way.

We should never act out of the motivation of guilt or rationality. Instead, we should only act on the impulse of love and *rhema*. That is a revolutionizing idea. But most of us often rarely did anything except out of guilt or because we reasoned that it was the right thing to do. Generally, we are not able to conceive of any other way to live. If guilt or reasoning did not motivate us, what would? And if the guilt that was motivating us wasn't right, what was wrong with it?

True Guilt

We all know that there is a place for true guilt in our life. When we sin, we feel guilty because we are guilty. How are we to handle this true guilt? How do we deal with the guilt of our sins and shortcomings? There are three essential revelation truths which must be firmly fixed in our minds and hearts in order to deal with true guilt:

1. *We must know our frame*

David declared, *"Just as a father has compassion on his children, so the Lord has compassion on those who fear him. For he himself knows our frame; he is mindful that we are but dust"* (Ps. 103:13, 14).

Do we know that about ourselves? Are we mindful that we are but frail dust? Or do we have a vision of ourselves as something better than that? Do we see ourselves as strong as steel, supposedly able to withstand all the fiery darts of the enemy in our own strength? We must recognize that we will always be weak in our relationship and He will always be the strong one. When we think we are strong, we are at our weakest because we will trust in our own strength to be righteous and we must surely fail.

When Jesus was hailed as *"Good Teacher"* He replied, *"Why do you call Me good? No one is good except God alone"* (Mk. 10:18). Even Jesus, the perfect Godman would not accept the title of *"good"* for himself. Are we deluded into believing that *we* can become good? It is only because of his righteousness that we become holy and clean.

2. We must know the righteousness that is by faith

We have *"hearts sprinkled clean from an evil conscience"* (Heb. 10:22). Only through faith in the blood of Jesus can our hearts be cleansed. Jesus himself has become to us righteousness and sanctification, because we are in him:

"But it is from him that you have your life in Christ Jesus, whom God made our wisdom from God, [revealed to us a knowledge of the divine plan of salvation previously hidden, manifesting itself as] *our Righteousness* [thus making us upright and putting us in right standing with God], *and our Consecration* [making us pure and holy], *and our Redemption* [providing our ransom from eternal penalty for sin]*"* (1 Cor.1:30 Amp. Bible).

We can never be free from the guilt of our sins if we do not accept the forgiveness and regeneration that comes to us by faith in the blood of Jesus.

We must see ourselves as God sees us, wearing a spotless robe of righteousness, *"clothed with Christ,"* coming boldly before *"the throne of grace"* in time of need (Gal. 3:27; Heb. 4:16). This is the movie which must be continually played on the screen of our mind: we are only dust, but we are fused to glory. We are clothed in a white robe of righteousness because of what Christ has done for us. By His grace and power, we can live righteous before our God.

3. We must know the power that works within.

The power to become righteous is not resident in our flesh, but it is available to us because of the One Who indwells us and fuses his strength to us.

"I can do all things through him [Christ] *who strengthens me"* (Phil. 4:13).

We can be strengthened with power through his Spirit in the inner man according to the power that works within us.

"He would grant you, according to the riches of His glory, to be strengthened with power through his Spirit in the inner man.... To him who can do far more abundantly beyond all that we ask or think, according to the power that works within us" (Eph. 3:16, 20).

When these truths become revelation knowledge to us by the power of the Holy Spirit, true guilt will no longer be a problem to us. If we sin, we recognize our weakness, but we do not accept our sinful condition as true spiritual reality. We acknowledge our guilt, repenting earnestly, and accept the righteousness that comes to us through faith in the blood of Jesus. Because God has forgiven us, we can forgive ourselves.

We can pick ourselves up, even from the most shameful descent into sin, repent, receive forgiveness and go on, trusting in the power of the Spirit that works within us to keep us from falling again. We can receive the vision of truth from the Word of God that when he cleanses us from sin, we are truly clean and clothed in glorious white robes of righteousness.

False Guilt

True guilt comes as a result of the convicting power of the Holy Spirit, spot-lighting sin in our lives. It is specific, it urges our repentance, and it instructs us in positive actions to avoid missing the mark in the future.

Where then does false guilt come from? Ultimately, it finds its root in the *accuser of the brethren.* Unfortunately, it often finds its way into our minds through the well-intentioned words of our Christian preachers and friends. As we earnestly attempt to grow in our spiritual life, many voices call for our attention and demand our time, talents and money. The special speaker at church declares, "I pray six hours every day." The evangelist asserts, "I witness to everyone I meet and have led at least one person to the Lord every day for the last three years."

The teacher exhorts, "You should read through the Bible every year." The church leader urges, "Whenever the church doors are open, you should be here. Also, you must attend a home cell group to be personally ministered to and Bible school for your personal growth. And we really need Sunday school teachers, youth workers, and volunteers in every department of the church."

You start having chest pains from the stress of trying to meet the expectations of your church, and your doctor advises, "Get at least eight hours of sleep and exercise 45 minutes a day." On top of all these responsibilities, you must hold down a *very* good job in order to not only meet the needs of your own family but tithe to the church, and give to the building fund, special ministries, and every other plea for money that crosses your doorstep! Where does it all end? How can you possibly live without guilt for having failed to do something important? No matter how good you are, you are never good enough to satisfy all the voices that clamour for your attention. Is there a way to be free?

Praise God, there is a way! When a multitude of voices scream for our attention, we must close our ears to them and listen only to the one Voice. We must discover what God's expectations are for our lives. We must know exactly what God wants us to be doing this year, this month, this week, this day and this hour. We do not live out of the expectations of other people, but only out of the commission of Christ to us personally.

Paul declared, *"When they measure themselves with themselves and compare themselves with one another, they are without understanding and behave unwisely"* (2 Cor. 10:12b Amp. Bible).

Comparing ourselves to each other can only result in confusion and frustration. We are never to compare ourselves with another person. We must only judge ourselves based on what God has called us to do.

In order to determine God's expectations for us, we must discern his gifts and callings upon our life. If you aren't sure what gifts he has deposited within you, ask yourself the following questions:

1. What are the deep desires God has placed within my heart? What do I feel a burden for?

2.   What are the areas and ministries in which I am effective?

3.   In what areas does the Body of Christ confirm my effectiveness?

If we only think we are great teachers, we probably do not have the gift of teaching. However, if our students regularly express appreciation for the way the Lord has used our teaching to change their lives, there are little doubt about our gift and calling.

We all face the tendency to force others to fit into our mould. We must resist the temptation of "gift projection," in which we expect all Christians to feel the same burdens we feel, support the causes we support and exercise the same gifts we do, in the same way. This gift projection is the tool Satan uses to bring false guilt and condemnation on so many Christians. We are part of a many-membered body, everyone having a unique and important ministry. If each member will do what God has called him to do and let everyone else do what God has called them to do, God's purposes will be accomplished on this earth.

Once we know what gifts God has placed within us, we still need revelation as to the way he wants that gift used. For example, many people in the Body have the gift of teaching, but it is expressed in different ways. Some are called to teach children and some adults. Some teach publicly in large groups, others privately in one-to-one encounters. Some teach verbally, others through writing books. You must seek the Lord for the specific task he has for you at this time in your life.

When the Lord tells you what his priorities are for your life, he will usually place a vision in your heart of the results of your accomplishing his goals for you. As you keep that vision before the eyes of your heart, hope will spring up within your spirit. This hope becomes the new motivation for action to replace the guilt under which we previously lived. Instead of being driven by guilt, we are now drawn by hope.

Hope

Biblically speaking, hope is "a confident expectation of good." It is the mental frame of mind we have because of our faith in the presence and power of God. Although hope involves the mind, it is not merely wishful thinking.

Hope is part of the armour of God which we are to put on in order to stand against the attacks of the enemy.

"...having put on the breastplate of faith and love, and as a helmet, the hope of salvation" (1 Thess. 5:8).

The helmet of hope is the protection God has provided for our head, our mind and our thoughts. As we look faithfully at the vision God has placed in our hearts, hope bubbles up and becomes the defence our minds need in spiritual warfare.

Hope is the by-product of being with Christ. Ephesians 2:12 says that to be separate from Christ is to be with *"no hope and without God in the world."* When we forget to bring Christ into our considerations and calculations, we are without hope. When we do not see Christ in our life and circumstances, we have no hope. But when we are united to Christ, when we see him working all things after the counsel of his will, when we see him ruling and reigning in our life, hope is the stimulus that keeps us going.

What kept Jesus on the cross? Amid horrendous pain, when for a moment it seemed even His Father turned his back on him, what motivation was strong enough to enable him to fulfil the call of God upon his life? It was love that took him to the cross, but it was hope that made him stay.

"For the joy set before him [he] *endured the cross, despising the shame"* (Heb. 12:2).

Jesus had a clear vision of what God planned to accomplish through his life and death. When every other motivation lost its power over him, hope in the vision of joyfully bringing you and me with him into glory guarded his mind and kept him true to his call.

When we close our ears to the multitude of voices around us and open our inner ears to only the voice of Jesus, we will find ourselves moving forward with a singleness of mind and purpose which we have not experienced before. God's *rhema* will free us from the tyranny of the urgent as we act only in obedience to his leading.

But what about all the things we turn our back on and leave undone? The accuser will do his best to bring worry and guilt back upon us regarding those things. When he tries to ensnare you with these thoughts, remind him that you are no longer a slave to his tricks. No longer are you a puppet on his string, jerked back and forth by every crying need. You are about your Father's business. You are doing what God designed you to do and that is all you can be concerned about.

As Jesus hung on the cross He said, *"It is finished"* (Jn. 19:30). There were still many souls to be saved. There were still many sick to be healed, oppressed to be delivered and hungry to be fed. How could he possibly think anything was finished? Only because Jesus knew why God had sent him to earth could He leave in peace. The work God had given him to do was done.

Summary

Guilt is a powerful motivating force in many people's lives. If we are to break free, we must learn to distinguish between true and false guilt and deal with each properly. True guilt is a result of the conviction of the Holy Spirit. Our only response must be to agree with the Lord, repent of our sin, receive the righteousness of God through faith and appropriate His power to overcome in the future.

False guilt comes as a result of allowing the accuser to gain a foothold in our minds. Freedom from such guilt comes as we reject the demands of the enemy and listen only to the voice of Jesus. He will give us focus, direction and vision for our lives.

From this vision, hope will spring up within, guarding our minds from future attacks of Satan.

Response

Determine in your heart that you will no longer be a slave to the overwhelming demands that are made on your life, your time, your talents and your money. Instead, ask the Lord what he wants your current focus to be, what he wants you to be doing and what he does not want you to be doing. Examine your heart to see if there are any areas of your life in which you do not have a "confident expectation of good." If there are, take them to Jesus and record the *rhema* and vision he gives, so that you are no longer *"without hope and without Christ."*

Chapter 15

From Anger to Love

Is there anyone in your life who causes your blood pressure to go up, just by hearing their name? Is there someone who can start your stomach churning with anger or resentment, just by walking into the room? Are there events in your past that you rehearse repeatedly in your mind, keeping your anger and bitterness alive? When you hear the words "anger" and "forgive," is there any name that comes immediately to your mind?

How easy it is to fall into the lifestyle of incubating anger and unforgiveness! When someone hurts us, or deprives us of our rights, or treats us unfairly, it is easy to become obsessed with the negative emotions that rise within us. But what is the effect on us when we are angry? Our muscles contract, we become tense in every part of our bodies, we are vulnerable to pain and sickness, and our spirits are strangled, prevented from drawing deeply upon the Spirit of Life. We become a slave not only to the emotions which control us, but to the one with whom we are angry as well. Because we perceive their actions as the cause of our condition, we are in bondage to them.

Anger and unforgiveness are among the most common needs which drive people to medical doctors and professional counsellors. Is it possible for us to find release and healing from these crippling emotions at the feet of our Counsellor Jesus? Not only is it possible, it is his deep desire to minister the Spirit of Love to you that can set you free — freer than you have ever been in your life.

Understanding Anger

Anger is not a sin. The Bible does not command us not to be angry. Rather, it exhorts, *"Be angry, and yet do not sin..."* (Eph. 4:26). The anger is not the problem. Our response to the anger we feel is the problem. How we deal with our anger determines whether we sin or have victory.

If anger is not a sin, what is it? Bill Gothard has given the following definition: "Anger is an inner alarm system revealing personal rights which we have either not given to God or have taken back from him." Let's examine this definition carefully.

"Anger is an inner alarm system...." Anger lets us know there is a problem within us. It warns us that the security system of our spirits has been breached in some way. It alerts us to the need to shore up our defences against sin in some area of our lives. The first response must be to find out what triggered the alarm, and then neutralize the enemy which is attempting to steal our peace.

"Anger...reveals personal rights which we have either not given to God or have taken back from him." We have been born with certain rights. Our constitution includes among these "inalienable rights" life, liberty and the pursuit of happiness.

As Christians, we might include other "rights" which have been given to us as children of God — perhaps the right to joy, health, prosperity, answered prayers, whatever your doctrine defines as the rights of the covenant of salvation. We live in a society that is obsessed with protecting its rights and demanding more. Our law-court system is overwhelmed with individuals and groups suing other individuals and groups for depriving them of what they perceive to be their rights. Even the Church has been infected with the spirit which demands its due from God.

How far this can be perceived from the example of our Lord. In Philippians 2:5-8 we see a totally different approach to life. Jesus had a right to be worshipped as God because he is God! Jesus had a right to be treated with respect for he is the Lord of the Universe. He had a right to exercise all power and authority over every created thing, because he is the Creator. He had a right to life, because he is the Giver of Life. He had a right to a fair trial, since he is the Righteous Judge. He had a right to receive justice, for he is Just.

Yet how did he view his rights? He *did not regard* [them] *a thing to be grasped.* He did not demand his rights but instead *"emptied himself"* of everyone. Rather than clenching his hands to hang on to his rights, he opened his hands and let them be nailed to a cross.

"Have this attitude in yourselves which was also in Christ Jesus."

God wants us to yield all our personal rights and possessions, every blessing that we think we deserve, to him, and let him decide when he will return them to us. We may believe we have a "right" to a good reputation. God says, "Give your reputation to me." We think we have a right to plan our time and live under an orderly schedule. God says, "Let me be the Lord of your time." We believe we have a right to personal dignity. God says, "Trust yourself to me." Herein is lordship. Are we willing to give God everything, our children, our marriage, our future, our health, friends, business, money? Do we really believe that he loves us and is willing and able to work all things out for our good? Can we totally trust him to take care of everything that is important to us without placing conditions or offering suggestions about how he should handle it?

If we have emptied ourselves of everything, as Christ did, there will be no place for anger. We become angry when we believe that one of our rights has been violated. Think about it for a moment. What was the last thing you became angry about? Was it unfair treatment at work? Why did that make you angry? Because you have a *right* to be treated fairly and with dignity. Why do you become angry when your children misbehave? Because you have a *right* to respect and obedience and a peaceful home and a good reputation as a parent. Why do you become angry when your possessions are damaged? Because they belong to you, you bought them with money you worked hard to earn, they are your responsibility, and you have a right to enjoy them.

You are angry and upset at someone who has injured you in some way or another. Your Christian conscience, guided by the Word of God, tells you that you ought to acknowledge the anger and put it away by handling the right to take vengeance over to God (Rom. 12:19).

But there is something within you that resists that idea – your carnal nature. So, a conflict ensues. You are caught between your natural desire for revenge and your sanctified conscience which tells you to take another way. It is at this point that the rationalisation of desire begins. Since it feels good to harbour the thoughts of revenge you begin to think of reasons for your anger to justify the maintenance of that feeling. You might even persuade yourself that you can help the Lord out by being his instrument for vengeance! But it is an evil desire – an argument of sin.

Now, in the court of your soul at such a moment another voice is quietly speaking – pleading the truth and inviting you to take a different view, a more spiritual one. How much easier it would be for us to go our own way and to sin were it not for the ministry of the blessed *Paraclete* in our hearts.

The Holy Spirit seeks not only to plead through words but through our non-verbal communication also. By non-verbal communication I mean the things we convey through our actions. The indwelling of the Holy Spirit should make it apparent that we have forgiven the other person. The indwelling of the Holy Spirit gives us a face-lift that makes us appear redeemed, an inner assurance that makes us feel redeemed and reinforces every part of our personality so that we act in a way that shows we are redeemed. It is the Spirit who makes the convinced convincing. May every one of us who names the Name of Christ be worthy of that Name!

Therefore, let us accept that anger is a warning system that alerts us to any rights or possessions we have either not entrusted to the Lord's care, or have taken back from him. If we sense anger welling up within us, our response should be to examine our hearts, under the illumination of the Spirit, to determine what "right" has been violated. When we give that right back to him, our anger will end.

To remain free of anger, we must
1. **Yield the right to God (Phil. 2:5-8).**

2. **Realize that God will test His rights (Gen. 22:1-14).**

Usually a time of consecration is followed by a time of testing, not to humble us through our failures but to demonstrate the marvellous power we have released by giving the Lord free reign in our lives.

3. **Respond to the loss of rights with a godly attitude.**

We do not become doormats with no character who welcome every loss or put down. We do not become passive masochists. We become worshipers, glorying in the power of God to handle all that we cannot and work it for our good.

> "...The Lord gave, and the Lord has taken away, blessed be the name of the Lord" (Job 1:21b).

Once again, we must realize that legalistic adherence to this formula will never produce life, only death. If we, by our own efforts, force ourselves to crush our anger and ritualistically turn our rights back over to the Lord, we will become spirit-less, character-less, religious robots. That is not what God wants from us. He wants us joyful, exuberant, and bubbling with life and vitality! What He wants only comes through encounter with Christ.

The Emmaus road experience is the only path to true freedom. Let's adjust our "formula" for healing once again. When we feel anger rising within us, we must:

1. *Immediately turn to Jesus and tell him how we feel* (**Lk. 24:13-24**).

Remember, we want to talk it over with Jesus, not our neighbour. We can carry on a conversation with another person in which we each express our angers and frustrations and accomplish nothing except greater anger and frustration. Only if someone brings in the wisdom of Christ is it beneficial to share your negative emotions with another.

2. **After we have emptied our hearts of all the destructive feelings, we must** *quiet ourselves and listen to the Lord's response* (**Lk. 24:25-30**).

Sometimes he will illumine Scripture to our hearts. Sometimes he will speak through another believer. Sometimes he will speak directly. He will show us the gift he wants to give us through the bad experience. Perhaps we will grow in character, or poise, or godliness, or faith, or perseverance because of what happened, if we allow the Lord to use it for our good. He does not condone the sinful behaviour which caused us pain, but he does promise that through it, we can become more like him.

3. **We must** *unite his words with faith and take on Christ's reaction* (**Lk. 24:31-35**).

Complete healing and forgiveness come only when we receive the working of God in the pain and accept the gift, He wants to give us through it.

Understanding Love

We have noticed that some people are more prone to anger than others. Some people seem to find it quite easy to look with compassion and forgiveness upon those who wound them. For them, seeing God at work even in painful situations and receiving the gift from them is no problem. For others, anger never seems far from the surface and is likely to break out at the slightest provocation. People like this often have a hard time accepting that the guilty person who wronged us deserves to be forgiven.

We might have come across Christians who try to justify their anger by saying that it was not really anger; but it was "righteous indignation" over the sins of others! When a so-called brother stepped from the narrow path of righteousness and brought shame on the name of Christ through sin, holy indignation should move us to correct such an offender. We must not forget that truth, knowledge of right and wrong, is the centre of Christianity. We should firmly believe that doctrinal purity and unswerving adherence to a strict moral code are the proofs of Christianity and the basis of our fellowship with others.

Thankfully, the Lord is both Light and Love. Both words reveal one aspect of his character. But what do these words mean? How is the character of Light revealed in God, and how does he demonstrate love? Consider the following chart.

God Is:

Light	and	Love
Rightness		Compassion
Judgement		Forgiveness
Challenge		Reconciliation
Confrontation		Healing
Division		Unity
Hatred of Sin		Love of Sinner
Condemnation		Comfort
Justice		Mercy
Infinite Precision		Matchless Grace

The character traits and activities of both columns are found in God. Very often our thoughts are centred primarily around column one. We enter every situation prepared to judge the rightness of the people and theology, challenge and confront anything we find to be out of line, separate ourselves from anything and anyone questionable, and insist on infinite precision to the law and demand justice for all transgressors. This attitude had been fed by most of the churches, as well as the teaching of our spiritual leaders even. We all believe it is godly. And, to a certain extent, it is true also. God exhibits all those same traits. However, our life often lacked the balancing character of the "Love" column. Let us look to Bible what the Lord says in Micah 6:8,

> "He has told you, O man, what is good; and what does the Lord require of you
> but to do justice and to love kindness, and to walk humbly with your God?"

God *loves* to show kindness, but only *does* justice because righteousness demands it. Most of us are just the opposite: We love justice and only did kindness if we felt it was deserved. We loved what God did and did what God loved. No wonder my life was so unfulfilling.

Although God is Light which must stand against darkness, his greatest joy is to show love. Although sin must be challenged, he offers reconciliation to him and to one another.

To him, unity is more important than doctrinal purity. For someone like us, who had always aspired to truth above all else, it was a life-changing revelation to discover that truth is a person, and that person is love.

John wrote his gospel that those who read might believe and have eternal life (Jn. 20:31). He wrote his first epistle to those *"who believe in the name of the Son of God, so that you may know that you have eternal life"* (1 Jn. 5:13). This letter offers proofs of salvation by which we may judge ourselves and others. They are summarized in 1 John 3:23,

> "This is his commandment, that we believe in the name of his Son Jesus Christ,
> and love one another, just as he commanded us."

Two simple tests: Who is Jesus? And love one another. The only doctrinal truth that must be intact is that Jesus Christ is the eternal Son of God. All other theological theories and beliefs are not legitimate cause for division. If you have accepted the cleansing work of Jesus on the cross, you belong to my family, and I love you.

Recognizing and accepting God's evaluation of the imbalance in our life was only the first step to change. Although we are commanded to love, the power is not resident in our flesh to do so. We must repent of our sin (even an over-emphasis on holiness can be sin if we miss the mark of perfect, *agape* love), turn away from our old ways, receive his forgiveness, and accept his grace and power to change. If we read and re-read the Gospels through several times, looking especially at the way Jesus loved people and study the Psalms, focusing on the amazing love which permeates every word and every act Jesus ever did, the Holy Spirit will be able to re-shape our heart to be more like his. Our judgmental, fractured heart will be healed, and we will become an instrument of reconciliation and blessing in his hand. What a freedom! What a joy!

Summary

Anger is an indication that there are areas of our lives which we have not completely placed under the lordship of Jesus Christ. When we sense anger rising within us, we must come before the Lord, listen to his voice and act in obedience to it. We must learn to process all our emotions before God, giving him the opportunity to reveal himself at work in our lives.

God is love and he is light. He loves to show mercy and compassion on his children. Every word he speaks and every deed he does is bathed in non-performance-oriented love. Because he is also righteous, he requires holiness and justice, but all his judgments are tempered with mercy. As we abide in his presence, spend time communing with him, watch him at work in the spiritual world always working all things out for our good, our hearts will be moulded into his likeness. We will begin to love mercy. We will look on every situation as an opportunity to show compassion and express to someone the overwhelming love that fills our hearts.

Response

Is there anyone against whom you are harbouring anger? Is there someone who hurt you so deeply that you have been unable to forgive them? Has the Lord been speaking to your heart about rights which you have not yet yielded to him? Express whatever is on your heart to the Lord, and then give him a chance to respond. Perhaps he will lead you into an inner healing experience, as described in Chapter Twelve. Perhaps he will show you the gift he wants to bestow upon you through this experience. If you allow him the opportunity, he will show you the situation from his perspective. Unite his word with faith and be healed.

> *"Be subject...as unto the Lord"* (Eph. 5:22). *"...just as Christ also loved"* (Eph. 5:25). *"...obey your parents in the Lord"* (Eph. 6:1). *"...bring them up in the discipline and instruction of the Lord"* (Eph. 6:4). Employees be obedient, *"... in the sincerity of your heart, as to Christ"* (Eph. 6:5).

Employers treat your employees right in the sight of the Lord (Eph. 6: 9). If you give a cup of cold water to the thirsty, you are doing it for the Lord. If you give food to the hungry, you are doing it for him. If you visit the sick or the prisoner, you are ministering to Christ (Matt. 25:31-46).

If our eyes are open, he is everywhere, and everything we do is done for him.

"Whatever you do, do your work heartily, as for the Lord, rather than for men; knowing that from the Lord you will receive the reward of the inheritance. It is the Lord Christ whom you serve" (Col. 3:23, 24).

Chapter 16

From Inferiority to Identity

Do you ever feel like the demands upon you are just too great and you simply haven't the strength to meet them? Do the responsibilities you face threaten to overwhelm you and send you plunging into despair? As you look at the people around you who are facing similar challenges, do they seem better equipped and more capable than you? Do you exhaust yourself trying to accomplish all that is expected of you each day without ever quite reaching the bottom of the pile? Have you ever felt inadequate, insecure, or inferior?

Surely you have struggled with such feelings from time to time. May be for you it's just an occasional problem. Or perhaps it is such a pervasive problem that it cripples you emotionally, preventing you from even making the attempt to achieve the desires of your heart. Does Jesus care when we are in the grips of these devastating emotions? Is he willing and able to lift us from their clinging grasp and give us the security and sense of wholeness and adequacy we so desperately need? Praise his name; he is not only willing to do so; he has been praying that you would find your identity in him since he walked upon this earth as a man. Even on the night before he died, though he knew he was facing torture both in the flesh and the spirit, you were on his heart and he prayed earnestly that you would accept your unity with him, which alone can set you free from inadequacy and inferiority (Jn. 17:21, 23).

The Causes of Inferiority

You know how inferiority and self-rejection feel. You have held yourself up in comparison to others and found yourself lacking. You have tried to cover your inadequacies by giving over-attention to your clothes or awkwardly trying to hide those things about yourself which you cannot accept. You have experienced the floating bitterness which can be expressed toward almost anyone but is really directed toward yourself and God, who made you the way you are. Perhaps you have over-compensated for your weaknesses with perfectionism. Probably your tongue has been silenced and your brain frozen in shyness by the belief that since you can't accept yourself, no one else would want to know you either.

Where do such destructive feelings and actions come from? Of course, ultimately, they are the works of Satan in our lives. But how is he able to so completely deceive us that we turn against ourselves? Again, the answer is the same as we have seen in the other sin areas we have considered. When we take our eyes away from Jesus and fix them on ourselves, others or Satan's hateful delusions, we will always have an inappropriate self-image. Only as we fix our eyes on Jesus can we clearly see ourselves.

Cause #1: Wrong Comparisons

One of the major causes of an inaccurate self-image is comparing us with others.

> *"When they measure themselves with themselves and compare themselves with one another, they are without understanding and behave unwisely"* (2 Cor. 10:12b Amp. Bible).

We may compare our physical appearance — height, weight, hair, skin, and perceived conformity to a mythical ideal. We may compare our spirituality — amount of time spent in prayer, Bible verses memorized, and people won to the Lord. Or we might compare our gifts — academic ability, musical talent, or any of the multitude of ways in which God gifts us. Comparing ourselves with others will always result in a wrong attitude. If we compare ourselves only with those over whom we feel excel, we will develop an attitude of superiority. If we compare ourselves with those whom we feel are better than us in any way, we feel inferior. How then can we judge ourselves? If we are not to compare ourselves to others, how will we know if we are performing adequately and being successful? In a society which has no absolute standards, we have nothing to compare, ourselves to except each other and we have indeed become *"without understanding."* Even in school, we are graded not according to our own ability but in comparison to the others in the class. No wonder school has such a destructive effect on so many children. How then shall we know when we have succeeded?

> *"For* [it is] *not* [the man] *who praises and commends himself who is approved and accepted, but* [it is the person] *whom the Lord accredits and commends"* (2 Cor. 10:18 Amp. Bible).

Positive identity comes when we compare ourselves to the Lord's expectations for our lives. He created each of us with unique physical characteristics, intellectual abilities and spiritual gifts. He has special tasks for each of us to do during our lives and he has fashioned us to be perfectly suited to accomplish them. He does not judge us based on the gifts he has given to anyone but us.

> *"...From everyone who has been given much, much will be required..."* (Lk. 12:48).

If we allow him to show us ourselves exactly as he sees us, we will be amazed and echo the words of the Psalmist,

> *"I will give thanks to you, for I am fearfully and wonderfully made; Wonderful are your works, and my soul knows it very well"* (Ps. 139:14).

The Lord judges us based on his perfect knowledge of us. Remember the parable of the talents (Matt. 25:14-30). The master gave to each of the servants because of his ability. The first two servants, who had received five and two talents respectively, through the wise use of the talents returned five and two more. To the first servant, who had earned five more, the master said,

"Well done, good and faithful slave. You were faithful with a few things; I
will put you in charge of many things; enter into the joy of your master."

The second servant only increased the master's wealth by two talents.
How did the master respond? Did he ask why he had not also earned five
talents, as had the other slave? Did he criticize him for not performing
as well as another? Not at all. Instead, he spoke the very same words
of blessing to the one who earned two as to the one who earned five.

The Lord knows our abilities and expects nothing more nor less
than our very best.

What about the areas of our lives that are clear weaknesses? How
can we have a positive self-image in the face of our inabilities and
defects? Paul says:

"And He has said to me, 'My grace is enough for you, for power is perfected in
weakness.' Most gladly, therefore, I will rather boast about my weaknesses, so
that the power of Christ may dwell in me. Therefore, I am well content with
weaknesses...for when I am weak, then I am strong" (2 Cor. 12:9, 10).

When we offer our weaknesses to Christ to be filled with his strength,
our areas of weakness become our areas of greatest strength. There is no
need for shame or embarrassment or dissatisfaction with our inabilities,
because they are the very vehicle through which Christ can be most
gloriously manifested in our lives.

"But God has chosen the foolish things of the world to shame the wise, and
God has chosen the weak things of the world to shame the things which are
strong...that no man may boast before God...that, just as it is written, 'Let him
who boasts, boast in the Lord'" (1 Cor. 1:27, 29, 31).

What about our areas of strength? How shall we view them? First, we
are expected to use all our abilities to their fullest.

As we exercise our talents in the service of the Lord, they are
stretched and increased. Just as the servant in the parable mentioned
above received five talents, used them to develop five more and as a

result was given an additional one, so we can use our talents to develop more and increase our giftedness.

Second, we are to use our strengths to bless those who are weak. Rather than becoming boastful and lording over those who do not have the same gifts as we, we must yield our gifts to them to cover their weaknesses and give them strength. This attitude should pervade every area of our lives, from home and family to church and business. God has placed us together that our united strengths will overcome our united weaknesses and as a single entity, in his strength, we will be able to handle anything.

Cause #2: Not Understanding or Appropriating Biblical

Principles

You were created in the image of Almighty God. You are so important to him that he was willing to allow his only Son to die a terrible death in order to bring you back into fellowship with him. The very God, Creator of the universe, knows you and calls you by name. The Bible has much to say on the dignity of man and why he wants you to have a positive self-image. Genesis chapters 1 and 2 clearly teach that we were created to be kings and queens and to rule. God designed us to be his regents upon this earth, to reign out of a position of submission to his supreme authority. Deep within us is a hunger to be honoured as the royalty which we are. As we are joined in covenant to God through salvation, we are once again restored to our position as kings and priests and this driving appetite for esteem is satisfied:

> "You are a chosen race, a royal priesthood, a holy nation, a people for God's own possession, so that you may proclaim the excellencies of him who has called you out of darkness into his marvellous light" (1 Pet. 2:9).

When we attempt to attain honour or power or position through any means besides submission to the King of kings, we are doomed to sin and failure.

This truth, probably, cannot heal you or deliver you from deep inferiority. Only a revelation of the Spirit to your heart as you meet Jesus face-to-face can heal your soul. These concepts provide a foundation of truth from which the Lord can draw out *rhema* to meet your need. Only an encounter with the living God can give you life.

One cannot be whole by living in *principles* of truth, no matter how good these principles are. The religious people of Jesus' day searched the Scriptures. Jesus says,

> *"You search the Scriptures because you think that in them you have eternal life; it is these that testify about e; and you are unwilling to come to me so that you may have life"* (Jn. 5:39, 40).

Eternal life is knowing God, being totally intimate with him.

"And this is eternal life: [it means] *to know* (to perceive, recognize, become acquainted with, and understand) *you, the only true and real God, and* [likewise] *to know him, Jesus* [as the] *Christ* (the Anointed One, the Messiah), *whom you have sent* (Jn. 17:3 Amp. Bible). It is experiencing the same reality of inner union with God that Jesus had.

How can we turn our knowledge *about* God into knowledge *of* God? J. I. Packer says the rule for doing this is demanding, but simple. "It is that we turn each truth that we learn *about* God into matter for meditation *before* God, leading to prayer and praise to God....Its effect is ever to humble us, as we contemplate God's greatness and glory, and our own littleness and sinfulness, and to encourage and reassure us – comfort us, in the old, strong, Bible sense of the world – as we contemplate the unsearchable riches of the divine mercy displayed in the Lord Jesus Christ." What is the best thing in life, bringing more joy, delight, and contentment, than anything else? Knowledge of God.

> *"Thus says the Lord, 'Let not a wise man boast of his wisdom, and let not the mighty man boast of his might, let not a rich man boast of his riches; but let him who boasts boast of this, that he understands and knows me, that I am the Lord who exercises lovingkindness, justice and righteousness on earth; for I delight in these things,' declares the Lord."* (Jer. 9:23, 24).

Cause #3: Living on the Surface

Finally, a good self-image occurs whenever we experience our inner union with Jesus Christ. The Bible says, *"to live is Christ,"* and that *"Christ, who is our life"* (Phil. 1:21; Col. 3:4). Repeatedly in the New Testament we find this beautiful union spoken of.

> *"I have been crucified with Christ; and it is no longer I who live, but Christ lives in me; and the life which I now live in the flesh I live by faith in the Son of God, who loved me and gave himself up for me"* (Gal. 2:20).

It is the experience of inner union that heals my inferiority, insecurity and sense of inadequacy and allows me to experience my identity with Christ.

It is so easy to lose sight of that union and return to living on the surface of my life. I feel hollow within, and because the "I" is no longer the "Christ-I" but myself, I face the issues of life alone. My self-image is destroyed; I feel fractured, torn apart, stretched out.

Probably there are times when we all feel this way. From the moment we awake in the morning, we can entrust ourselves and our activities to the guidance of the Spirit. When we enter our office and see the abundance of tasks calling for our time and attention, we can quiet ourselves before the Lord, asking him what *he* wants us to do that day. We can confess once more that we no longer live but Christ is now our life. We can confidently trust him to face the issues of our life and move through us to make the right decisions. He will show us where to begin and give his grace that we may be productive in accomplishing what is required of us. Sometimes he will direct us to something that wasn't even on our list of priorities. But if we are willing to trust his wisdom, we can go through the day in peace, knowing that we are doing the Lord's will in the Lord's strength, and he will take care of the consequences.

Then when interruptions come, we can welcome them as from the Lord. If we abide in him, there will be peace and joy not only in our heart, but in the lives of those we touch.

Our unity with Christ is an eternal fact if we are born again. *But the person who is united to the Lord becomes one spirit with him"* (1 Cor. 6:17 Amp. Bible). Nothing can separate us from him. It is not that we are living apart from him; it is only our perception which is faulty. Therefore, when we recognize that we have begun to operate out of a false independence, we do not waste time berating ourselves but quickly repent and return to the truth in our heart. It is necessary that we all know the best ways to help us move from surface illusions to true inner reality. For some, heartfelt praise, worship, and for others, it may be reading the Word is the most effective avenues. Discover the things you can do which make you aware of the Lord's presence within you and use them whenever you need to return to living out of that union.

Paul says to believers in Colossae: *"If you have been raised up with Christ, keep seeking the things above, where Christ is, seated at the right hand of God"* (Col. 3:1).

One of the purposes of Paul in this letter is to show that Christ is pre-eminent – first and foremost in everything – and that the life of every Christian should reflect that priority. Eugene Peterson paraphrases Paul's words in this way: "So if you are serious about living this new resurrection life with Christ, act like it. Pursue the things over which Christ presides." Because we are rooted in him, alive in him, hidden in him, and complete in him then we must live for him.

'Living for Him' is the theme that Paul embarks upon as he begins the part of this epistle, and the way in which he delineates that theme is in terms of 'relationships.' It has been said that 'the chief business of every Christian is to maintain his relationship with Christ.' If this relationship is not kept intact then it is impossible for other relationships to succeed.

The injunction to set our hearts on things above is because we have been raised with him. Think what that means we have been granted a relationship with Christ, who is at God's right hand. This relationship we are to pursue by holding fast to Christ, who is the centre and source of all our joy. A Christian is someone who in a sense lives in two places at once: in their earthly place of residence and in Christ. The question we must ask ourselves is this: Where are we most at home?

Our relationship with Christ shapes every other relationship – our acquaintanceships, our friendships, our working relationships, our marriages, and everything. So important is to grasp this truth that Paul continues with this theme in Colossians 3:3 also. He says: *"For you have died and your life is hidden with Christ in God."*

Do not go through life looking down or just looking at the things in front of you, he is saying: "Look up and see what is going on around Christ. That's where the action is. See things from his perspective" (Eugene Peterson, *The Message*).

It has been said that the Christian faith, unlike some other world religions, has no geographical centre. Judaism focuses on Jerusalem, and Islam on Mecca. The Christian faith, however, focuses on heaven where Christ is seated at the right hand of God. Without being 'other worldly' and ignoring our responsibilities here on earth, we seek the things that are beyond the earth. We have died in Christ and now we enjoy a new life – a life that is hidden with Christ in God. Why hidden? Well, the union that exists between Christ and his people is hidden from the eyes of the men and women of this world. Though they see us going about our tasks they are unaware that the strength by which we live and the power by which we practise our faith is drawn from another world. But true believers can only enjoy and draw this life as they daily reach up through the avenue of prayer and avail themselves of the resources that are hidden with Christ in God.

Summary

Inferiority is a problem that pervades our society. There are many causes of this sense of not quite measuring up: wrongly comparing ourselves to other people, not knowing or applying some basic biblical truths about self-esteem and living without an awareness of our unity with Christ. The development of an accurate self-image comes out of time spent in the Lord's presence. He will teach us about ourselves, helping us to recognize and use our strengths to serve him and others, and offer our weaknesses to him to be filled that he might be glorified. He will take the truths of Scripture and make them revelation knowledge which can transform our hearts. And he will gently lead us into an ever more consistent life of abiding in the knowledge of our union with him.

Response

How big is problem of inferiority, insecurity and inadequacy in your life? As you read through the chapter, did the Spirit show you the contributing factors to your poor self-image? If not, ask him to show you now. Then quiet yourself and receive the revelation which he wants to give you that can heal your aching heart.

Chapter 17

From Depression to Joy

I am sure you know "what it is like:" the sadness, hopelessness, anxiety, and hostility, the "weeps," the loss of appetite, the apathy and erratic sleep behaviour. What can have such overwhelming control over our lives? We call it depression, and I dare say that every single person has faced it at some point in his life. A good percentage of people will be so crippled by its heaviness that they will seek professional help. An even greater percentage will trudge wearily through life, accepting the blackness that clouds their heart as normal and inescapable.

Is there a way out of this web of despair? Is it possible to *do* something which can hasten a return of the sunlight in our souls? Is there a reason for hope?

Depression Defined

Depression may be defined as "giving in to the pressures of life while letting go of our faith in God." Depression is the direct result of listening to the wrong voices and focusing on the wrong vision. When we listen to the lies of the accuser and stop our ears to the comfort and wisdom of the Spirit of God, we have started down the road of depression. When we fix our eyes on the circumstances around us, how they are affecting us and how we will attempt to handle them, while ignoring the promises and purposes of God in our life, we have set our face toward the darkness of despondency. There are a few people who very rarely feel the cold touch of depression. Most people experience mild or even serious depression occasionally throughout their lives. Others constantly live under the black cloud of severe depression that swallows up every joy, leaving only an empty void in its place.

But regardless of the level of depression you face, *"the Lord is near to the broken-hearted and saves those who are crushed in spirit"* (Psa. 34:18). The Lord has promised a way out for you!

Catalysts and Surface Causes of Depression

The most common surface causes of depression are life's trying circumstances; unconfessed sin or guilt; religiosity; sickness or physical malfunction; poor care of the body; and lack of personal discipline.

Often, if we are asked why we are feeling depressed, we will point to one of these: "My life is so hard. I think I'm coming down with the sickness. I didn't get enough sleep last night." It appears that our unhappiness and depression spring from these sources.

However, I would like to suggest that these are not *causes* but merely *catalysts* which precipitate the manifestation of depression. In other words, it is not the difficulty, which is facing, that is causing us to be depressed. If that were true, everyone in the same circumstances would respond in the same way. This is simply not true. While many people do indeed sink into depression while during stressful events, other people are able to respond positively and rise above their trials to new levels of faith and character. Therefore, we must look deeper to find the true source of the depressive response.

Moving one step closer to the core of the problem, underlying the negative apparent causes of depression, there is a layer called "self-pity." This is the underlying root manifestation for most depression people face. "My life is so miserable. I don't feel well. I can't seem to get control of my life. Life is so unfair." Wrong thoughts and attitudes permeate our mind and spirit so that when sickness, trials or uncontrollable circumstances enter our lives, they immediately plunge us into the dark abyss

But how do we become so full of self-pity? Very simply, by losing our divine focus. Instead of focusing on God and his purposes, we focus on ourselves and the lying words of Satan. Rather than fixing our eyes on Jesus, we look only at the unhappiness of our situation. Rather than quieting our hearts to hear "the still small voice of calm" of the Spirit within, we thrash about in surface reaction. The cure, then, to most of the depression we face is in hearing the voice of God and seeing the vision of God. But let us examine each of the surface causes or catalysts more carefully to see how this principle applies to each.

Life's Trying Circumstances

Not everyone reacts to the trials of life in the same way. Some see only the pressure, feel only the pain, and hear only the destroyer's voice. These respond with anger, bitterness and depression. Others respond as James and Paul commanded (Jas. 1:2; Rom. 5:3-5).

How can we possibly be expected to not only accept trials without complaint, but leap for joy when tribulation and sorrow are upon us? There is only one way. We must be convinced that the, *"Most High is the Ruler over the realm of humankind"* and that He always *"causes all things to work together for* [our] *good"* (Dan. 4:17; Rom. 8:28). We must have not only a theological conviction of his great love for man, but an experiential knowledge of His tender mercy toward us as individuals. We must hear His voice promising that through this tragedy, He will bring good.

It is easy for us to believe that holy, just men can be used by God to achieve his purposes. After all, they seek his will and move in obedience to it. It is more difficult to accept that the hateful, jealous acts of spiteful men can have any place in the plan of God for our lives. Surely wicked men acting out of their selfish initiative are beyond the redemptive power of the Lord. Yet it is not so.

God promised Joseph that he would rule over his entire family, even his parents. But soon afterward he was sold into slavery while on an errand for his father, thrown into prison for not succumbing to immorality, and forgotten by those whom he helped. It must have been hard for Joseph to believe that God's hand was upon him. There must have been times on that auction block and in that dark prison cell when he was tempted to doubt God's promise to him and give in to anger and depression. But the Bible indicates that he kept his heart pure. He didn't curl into a ball in the corner, nursing his self-pity with a rehearsal of the injustices heaped upon him, though surely if anyone had a right, it was he. Nor did he lash out in anger at the ones who held him under their control. Always his spirit was so pure that he gained favour even among his captors and owners. Always he conducted himself with such dignity that he was given authority over his peers.

How was he able to withstand such hardship and tribulation? Because always before the eyes of his heart were the vision God had given him in his youth, strengthening his faith and giving him hope. So firmly was that vision planted in his heart that he was able to receive those who wronged him with love and forgiveness, affirming that though they meant evil against him, God meant it for good (Gen. 50:20).

The apostle Paul experienced great suffering during his Christian life. He was stoned, beaten, imprisoned, and mocked. He was *"afflicted in every way, but not crushed; perplexed, but not despairing; persecuted, but not forsaken; struck down, but not destroyed"* (2 Cor. 4:8, 9). Why was he able to rise above all these trials and write, even from a prison cell, *"Rejoice in the Lord always; and again, I will say, rejoice!"* (Phil. 4:4)? Why did he not despair? Because he knew in his heart that all that was happening to him was for a purpose, that all his suffering was having a positive result (2 Cor. 4:15). The vision God had given him was to be a messenger of the good news of Christ to the Gentiles. That was his only goal in life, and the trials that came upon him were instruments in accomplishing that goal. God was using his suffering to work grace into the lives of others (2 Cor. 4:17, 18). Compared with the wondrous joy of spending eternity with those whom he had won to Christ, the suffering he experienced seemed but momentary and light. When he sat in that dirty prison, wounded and bleeding from the beating he had received, he did not even think about the material, physical world and his own pain. Rather, he kept his gaze fixed on the eternal truth which is not seen with earthly eyes but only through a revelation of the Spirit, the eternal salvation of souls.

God has promised that the afflictions which come upon us will produce an eternal weight of glory, a lovely imperishable jewel. But that promise is conditional. The full purposes of God in our hearts will only be accomplished *"while we look not at the things which are seen, but at the things which are not seen."* We must take our eyes off the pain and focus them on the glory. We must look beyond the means and see the end. The sorrows of our life are only temporary, even though they may last for months or even years. Compared with eternity, they are but momentary.

In those times of pressure, during life's trying circumstances, we *need* revelation. We must ask the Lord what He is doing through this. We must have a vision which can carry us through to the other side. If we will listen for the voice of God, look for his vision, and hang on to what we receive, we need not be crushed with despair, but we can be overcomers, full of joy and the grace of God.

Unconfessed Sin

The knowledge that we have unconfessed sin in our lives, that we stand guilty before a holy God, can bring us into depression also. David spoke for all of us when he said,

> *"For my iniquities are gone over my head; as a heavy burden they weigh too much for me"* (Psa. 38:4).

Unconfessed sin brings with its heaviness, depression and bodily sickness. Why do we take so long to repent? Do we deceive ourselves into believing that indulging the flesh can give us lasting pleasure? Don't we realize that the flesh is never satisfied, but is an insatiable craving whose strength only increases with indulgence? Are we too proud to acknowledge our weakness before God and man?

Covenant within yourself that no longer will anything stand in the way of a clean conscience before the Lord. Commit yourself to daily and instant confession of every sin the Holy Spirit convinces you of. Wholeheartedly repent and receive the cleansing of the blood of Jesus. Be restored to the joy of your salvation.

If confession of all known sins still leaves you with depressive guilt, study again the chapter on the accuser and the Comforter. Make sure that you are not accepting false condemnation from the enemy who is trying to paralyze you with depression. Then walk in the joy of a purified heart!

Religiosity

Here we have come to the catalyst for the depression which may lead us to a struggle for a longer time. In our devoutness, before we could have had established a communion with God, we might have lived under an intense list of Christian rules which we believed were expected of us. We might have earnestly studied the Word and recorded every command and principle we found. We set out each day with that list before us, doing our best to conform to its standards. Whole areas of our life were cut off and discarded, bringing death to our personality and creativity. For example, living the Christian life was a serious undertaking and there was no time to play or have fun. Emotions were expressions of the soul, not the spirit (or so we might have believed then), and therefore they were denied and quenched. Each day became a dreary striving to achieve approval from ourselves and God. And each day might have thus become a disappointing failure as we fell short of the mark. Depression became a constant enemy.

Our Christianity would have been reduced to a religion same as other worldly ones. Like the Galatians, though we have received Christ through faith, we may be attempting to live for him in our own strength (Gal. 3:2-3). Religion and Christianity are diametrically opposed to one another. Religion is a set of established rules; Christianity is a relationship. Religion stifles creativity; Christianity increases and releases the creativity of the Creator through us. Religion brings heaviness to our spirits as we view the great task and our inability to accomplish it; Christianity brings lightness to our hearts as we accept the strength of God to do his will. Religion is hard work; Christianity is rest and play, for we have ceased from our own labours (Heb. 4). Religion expresses itself in perfectionism, where we try our best to do what is right; Christianity is expressed in excellence, where we allow God's best to flow out through us. Religion breeds depression; Christianity produces joy.

How can we break free from the bondage of religiosity? When we learn to hear God's voice, we will discover Someone very different from the picture we had established in our mind. We can hear words of love and forgiveness and acceptance. Most importantly, we will find Someone inside of us who was not only able to keep the Laws of God in his own earthly life, but He who wanted to keep them through us! We will discover that we can draw upon the flow of grace that was living inside of us to overcome any temptation that came my way.

If you are bound by the legalism of religion and walking in depression, you can be free. Make contact with the Holy One living inside of you. Listen to his words of truth. Look at his vision of glory. Look up and rejoice!

Lack of Personal Discipline

Often, we overlook this possibility in our search for a cause for our depression. Especially if it is our normal way of living, we may not recognize that there is another, better way. If we do not have clear, divinely generated goals for our life, we will find ourselves slipping into depression. We don't know where we are, where we are going or if we are on the right path to get there. We may be on a road going nowhere and perhaps we want to get off.

It is imperative that we must know what God wants us to do each day. This is especially important for the self-employed, the unemployed or the homemaker. God may direct us to the obvious tasks before us, but if we are commissioned to them by God, we work under a sense of divine purpose and the most mundane task becomes meaningful. This is not to say that we must have a big prayer meeting before we can do anything. Generally, if we are living in obedience to Christ and our heart is fixed to serve only him, the spontaneous flow of thoughts and urgings are from the Lord. The point is to learn to be sensitive and responsive to the spontaneous voice of God, not controlled by the evidence that our physical eyes see.

Indecisiveness can also bring depression. We are faced with an important decision. For weeks we waver back and forth between the alternatives. Finally, under pressure, we make our choice, then spend the next few weeks wondering if our decision was wise. Our energy is drained, and our spirits become depressed. Isn't there a better way?

When we must make an important decision, our first step is research. We read whatever we can find on the subject. We seek out people of God who are trained and experienced in the area under consideration and receive their counsel. When we are confident that we have all the data available, we bring it all into the presence of the Lord, through earnest prayer request and receive the leading of the Spirit of God. Finally, when we are satisfied that we have done all that God requires of us, we make our decision and act upon it. We should not allow ourselves to second guess, even if the results are not what we anticipated. We must simply entrust ourselves to the One Who has been leading us and Who is able to work all things out for our good, even if we make a mistake. That sounds like quite a time-consuming project. What about decisions that must be made quickly? Then, we simply trust the Spirit Who lives within us to give us wisdom for the need of the moment. There is always time to quiet the outward tensions and sense "the still small voice of calm" of God within.

Follow his leading to the best of your ability. Again, don't allow yourself to second guess. Even if you make a mistake, your God is big enough to somehow turn it to accomplish his will for your good. Trust him.

Poor Care of the Body

Poor diet, exercise and sleep habits can all contribute to depression. There are some foods that bring sluggishness to body and spirit. Overeating results in becoming overweight which contributes to poor self-image which breeds depression.

We need a vision of ourselves eating only to the glory of God and developing the healthy body God intended us to have (1 Cor. 10:31).

Studies have shown that people suffering from depression will break free from its bondage twice as fast if they are exercising. Find out what kind of exercise routine the Lord has designed for you and draw upon his strength to carry it out. As your body responds, so will your spirit and the light of joy will begin to break through the clouds of depression.

Sickness/Physical Malfunction

Physical illness and disease can become the catalysts that plunge us into depression. There are several reasons this is so. Our bodily conditions have a direct effect on our spiritual condition. When physical sickness afflicts us, it is easy to fall prey to spiritual weaknesses of doubt, fear and depression. One way that physical illness can precipitate depression is through a lowering of our energy levels. When everything we do seems to require more effort than we must give, discouragement can set in. If our prayers for healing are not answered in the way we hoped, doubt can lead to despair. Particularly, long-term and recurring pain and suffering are fertile soil for the seeds of depression.

Chemical imbalances can also cause bouts of depression. Our emotions are closely tied to the chemical, endocrine and hormonal systems of our bodies. One reason exercise is so effective in fighting depression is that it releases chemicals into our bodies which promote a feeling of well-being. If you can pinpoint the causes of these imbalances and recognize that they are temporary, it can help you survive until you see daylight again. Don't make any rash decisions and avoid conflict if possible. Read a book and go to bed early. Chances are good that when you awaken, the cloud will have passed, and you will once again be able to rejoice in the goodness of God.

There are some people who suffer on-going depression because of chemical malfunctioning or glandular disorders. However, if you have examined your life carefully under the illumination of the Spirit and are totally convinced that you are listening only to the voice of God and seeing the vision of God, and yet depression holds you in its grip, you should consider the possibility of a physical cause. Earnestly seek God for healing, and if the healing tarries, receive the assistance of health care professionals to control the imbalance until the Lord corrects it. The abundant life is a life of joy, and God wants *you* to experience it!

Learning to Pray When You are Depressed

Psalm 31 provides an excellent format for prayer for the depressed person. Although we will not write out the entire chapter here, we encourage you to read it through in your Bible. At the time of its writing, David appears to have been facing several of the catalysts we have discussed. The circumstances of his life were trying, the weight of his sin was upon him and there are allusions to bodily illness. But despite all these negative conditions of his life, notice how he begins his psalm:

> "In You, O Lord, I have taken refuge; let me never be ashamed; in Your righteousness deliver me. Incline Your ear to me, rescue me quickly; be to me a rock of strength, a stronghold to save me. For You are my rock and my fortress; For Your name's sake You will lead me and guide me...You are my strength...."

David does not immediately begin his prayer with a recitation of his complaints. Instead, he turns his eyes upon the Lord, focuses his attention on his goodness and blessings, quieting himself before his presence. He gets his priorities right. He declares forth his confidence in and commitment to his God. He establishes proper focus right from the beginning.

In verse 6 he begins to allude to his problems, and finally, in verse 9, he begins to present his sorrow and need to the Lord.

"...I am in distress; my eye is wasted away from grief, my soul and my body also. For my life is spent with sorrow, and my years with sighing; my strength has failed because of my iniquity, and my body has wasted away....."

His life was not going at all well. Enemies were seeking his life. Friends pretended they didn't know him. His name was slandered through the land. The guilt of his sin weighed upon him and his body was sick and in pain. Once he was in the presence of God, he felt a freedom to express all his fears, angers, hurts and sorrows. But he didn't stop there. If our prayers are merely a rehearsal of our problems, there is no life in them, only further death.

Once David had poured out all his problems before the Lord, he reaffirmed his trust in God to deliver him from them.

"But as for me, I trust in You, O Lord...My times are in Your hand; deliver me from the hand of my enemies, and from those who persecute me...Let me not be put to shame...Let the lying lips be mute...."

From verses 14 through 18, David tells the Lord how he would like him to handle the situation, always emphasizing that the Lord is in control and well able to deliver.

Finally, in verses 19 through 24, David concludes his prayer with praise, faith, love and hope.

"How great is Your goodness, which you have stored up for those who fear you, which you have wrought for those who take refuge in You...Blessed be the Lord, for he has made marvellous his lovingkindness to me in a besieged city...."

Only when we have touched God can the trials of our life be turned to cause for praise and rejoicing. Only when we have heard his words of comfort and wisdom, only when we have seen his vision of the joy set before us, can we come up out of the pit of depression into the sunshine of his glory.

Summary

The root cause of most depression is self-pity, which is a direct result of losing our divine focus and failing to see God. There are many catalysts which can contribute to our foray into the "sloughs of despond." Among the most common are life's trying circumstances, unconfessed sin, religiosity, lack of personal discipline, poor care of the body and sickness or physical malfunction. Every one of these causes can be overcome by returning to our divine focus by quieting ourselves, listening to the voice of God, seeing the vision of God and acting in obedience to it.

Response

Is depression ever a problem in your life? How persistent a problem is it? Are you able to see that you have lost divine focus at those times? Are you currently suffering in depression? Were you able to recognize the catalysts that plunged you into this darkness? Are you willing to come to Jesus, quiet yourself in his presence and allow to speak words of faith and hope and wisdom, restoring you to divine perspective? Do you want to see God in your life and circumstances? Do it now and enter the joy of your Lord.

Chapter 18

Victory through Death and Resurrection

Are there areas of sin in your life against which you have battled for a long time without finding consistent victory? Do the words "consecration," "holiness," and "self-denial" brings a sense of guilt and doom into your heart? Have you tried to present your body as a living sacrifice, only to have it crawl back off the altar? Do you ever wonder if the Christian message of freedom from sin is an empty promise with no hope of fulfilment? Does your heart echo the words of the Apostle Paul?

> *"Wretched man that I am! Who will set me free from the body of this death?*
> *"Thanks be to God through Jesus Christ our Lord! ..."* (Rom. 7:24, 25).

There is a way of deliverance! The promises of the Word are always true. Freedom from sin and a life of holiness are available to the child of God. But there is only one way to find it. Standing tall in the centre of the Gospel, overshadowing every other doctrine and dogma, there is a cross. The death of Jesus, the holy, blameless Son of God, on the cross, satisfied forever the debt of our guilt and delivered us from eternal death. It is the only possible way.

Firmly believe that we were with him that day. We were crucified with Christ (Gal. 2:20). Again, according to St: Paul's writing to Colossians we have died, and our life is hidden with Christ in God (Col. 3:3). When we made Jesus Lord of our lives, philosophically, our decision was made. Positionally, it was done. Yet there remains this warring within our flesh.

"The good that I wish, I do not do; but I practice the very evil that I do not want" (Rom. 7:19).

If I am dead, why do I act so very much alive?

There remains a personal cross which we must take up daily (Lk. 9:23). We must learn to consider ourselves to be dead to sin, but alive to God in Christ Jesus (Rom. 6:11). This is so important, for while death on the cross to all our selfish desires is an absolute necessity, it is not the final goal. Death is only a doorway, a means to an end. The goal of Christianity is that we may live in resurrection life, both now and throughout eternity. We have the glorious hope of the resurrection of our physical bodies to strengthen us through the terror of death and uphold us through the sorrow of mourning. In the same way, we have the hope of resurrection life in our spirits to sustain us through the death of our old self, our body of sin (Rom. 6:6; 8-13).

That we died with Christ on the cross is an absolute reality. Our responsibility in dying daily is to remember this truth, reckon or consider it to be so, and call it forth in our life. When we investigate the Word of God, we no longer should see the law standing in judgment over us. Instead, we should see Jesus fulfilling the law both in his own earthly life and out through us. We do not attempt to keep the law through crucifying our own flesh, but we stand upon the fact that we have already been crucified.

We do not war against the sinful passions which rise within us to tempt us to evil. Instead we turn our eyes from the fleshly desire and contemplate the reality that we are clothed with Christ, that the fullness of his life indwells us, that sin has no more power over us, and we are free to live a holy life.

"And all of us, as with unveiled face, [because we] continued to behold [in the Word of God] as in a mirror the glory of the Lord, are constantly being transfigured into his very own image in ever increasing splendour and from one degree of glory to another; [for this comes] from the Lord [Who is] the Spirit" (2 Cor. 3:18 Amp. Bible).

If we set our mind on our sinful flesh and the apparent power that sin has over us, we will become frustrated and discouraged. But if we set our mind on the Spirit and his resurrection power flowing through us, strengthening us to conquer any foe, we experience *life and peace.*

"For the mind set on the flesh is death, but the mind set on the Spirit is life and peace" (Rom. 8:6).

How can these theological ideas be put into practice in our everyday life? When temptation strikes, how can we reckon ourselves dead to sin but alive to Christ? For example, suppose a friend whom we trusted betrays our confidence. Our initial, instant reaction is hurt, which will express itself in anger and an urge to retaliate. This is our old self in reaction. So far, we have not moved into sin; we are just strongly tempted. At this point, we will not open our mouth or act in any way, because we know that if we do, we will sin since we will be acting out of ourselves.

Instead, we must turn our thoughts inward, to Christ Who lives within us. We will call to mind the fact that we are dead to personal responses. Though they may tempt us, they have no power over us to cause us to obey them. We will focus on Christ, who is our life, praying, "Lord, I feel hurt and angry. I have no power to forgive. But Lord, you are an eternal wellspring of love within me. You forgave even during deepest agony. Be to me now all that I need. Fill me with Your love, Your forgiveness, Your understanding and Your compassion. Consume with Your grace all that would revolt against me." Remembering the instruction given by Paul to Philippians, *"Your attitude should be the kind that was shown us by Jesus Christ"* (2:5, Living Bible), the great black scientist, George Washington Carver's says: "I will never let another man ruin my life by making me hate him." As a believer in Jesus Christ he would not allow evil to conquer him.

Sometimes gradually and sometimes instantly, there will come a release from the hurt and anger and a welling up within of the Spirit of Christ. When all our fleshly responses have been swallowed up in

Jesus, we can respond to our friend with the character of Christ. Then we can become minister of reconciliation and messenger of peace.

We can go through this process in seconds, minutes, hours, months or even years. If we choose to nurse our wounds or cling to our fleshly responses to temptation, we will never move beyond our selfish reactions. If we focus on the temptation and its apparent power over us, trying to battle the flesh with the flesh, we will live in defeat. But if we will quiet ourselves in God's presence, express our need and weakness to him, and allow him to respond with words of grace and visions of victory, we will overcome. Our automatic and spontaneous reaction to all of life must be to move quickly through each stage of death and resurrection. Our goal of life is to live always in the final stage, standing peacefully within Jesus while walking through life. There are three different perspectives we can have as a Christian.

We can focus our eyes on *self, who is alive,* which is essentially living as a non-Christian. When temptation rises before us, we give in without a fight. Perhaps we have a false understanding of sin and believe that the immediate response of our flesh is an act of sin, and therefore, since we have already failed, we may as well complete the action. However, sin does not occur until we act upon the reaction of self. If we live with this perspective, we will live in self-effort, hurt, anger, retaliation, and self-will. We will experience anxieties, fears and extreme emotional ups and downs.

A second place we may focus our eyes is on *self, who is dead.* We will try to push the darkness of sin out of our life through our own efforts. We will become a religious zombie, reacting neither from ourselves nor from Christ. We will become lifeless, boring and very religious. There will be neither spark nor personality, and there will be no place for fun, excitement, or joyous activity. Our life will be centred on nothing but religious activities.

Obviously, I am not recommending either of the above perspectives. Instead, I have a different focus, one of *Christ living within me.* Though I recognize that I am crucified, and the old self is dead, I also acknowledge that I have been raised up with Christ and now is alive with resurrection power.

When we see an area of darkness in our life, we drive it out by turning on the light, by bringing the presence of Christ into it. As a result, we begin to flow with the life of Jesus. We become loving, caring, and full of faith, kind, wise and free. Because we are healed of our hurts, we can be used to heal the hurts of others. The character of Christ becomes manifest in us by the fruit of the Spirit. The power of Christ becomes manifest by the gifts of the Spirit.

Crucifying the desires of the flesh is not easy, nor is it fun. Let no one imagine that a life of sanctification and holiness can be entered lightly. There will be pain and suffering. But if we will endure the cross, we will find a joyful release and freedom from bondage such as we have never experienced. Martin Luther in his own words makes suffering the very definition of a Christian, *"Christianus quasi crucianus"* meaning, "Christians, as if (the word meant) crucified ones." Jesus came to earth for the express purpose of dying on the cross. Before he began his ministry, he fasted for 40 days and overcame the temptation to find an easier way to fulfil his purpose. During his years of ministry, he was lauded as Messiah and King and offered the opportunity to sidestep the cross and establish his kingdom another way. Every temptation had to be overcome one by one, as repeatedly Jesus affirmed, *"Lord, not My will but Yours."*

Finally, on the night before his death, there came the hour of greatest struggle. He knew what lay ahead. He knew the price that had to be paid. There in Gethsemane, Jesus agonized in prayer until the flesh was overcome by the Spirit, and once again He affirmed, *"Not My will but Yours."*

Jesus did not wait until they threw him down upon the cross to make his decision. He did not wait until the thorns pierced his brow to surrender his will. The battle was won in Gethsemane. Because he had prevailed in prayer, he was able to endure the cross.

We must also come to Gethsemane. Though we have made our decision early on to follow him, we must repeatedly affirm our resolve in every aspect of our lives. Again, and again, we must get alone with God and pray until our spirit overcomes our flesh and we can say, *"Not my will but yours."* A saint of a few centuries ago prayed: "Each day and every day I surrender myself utterly and in all things to Divine Providence ... like a little child in the bosom of his good and tender-hearted mother, to want everything and yet to want nothing – everything that God wills, nothing that he does not will." Then, when we face the cross and the fleshly desires must die, the battle will already have been won.

What happens at Gethsemane? We have our vision restored and our focus clarified. Often, we come to prayer, knowing that we want to obey God and deeply desiring to do so, yet blinded by the desires of our flesh. As those desires loom so large before us, we may become focused on them and all that we are being asked to give up. Or we may see only the suffering that we expect to endure in order to become free. We may become so focused on the cross that we can no longer see the resurrection purposes of God beyond it. In Gethsemane, the Spirit will gently turn our focus outside of ourselves. He will show us the life of holiness flowing in resurrection power that will be ours. He will enable us to become like Jesus, *"who for the joy set before him endured the cross"* (Heb. 12:2). Because of Gethsemane, we will be able to look beyond the cross to the resurrection.

Summary

"Truly, truly, I say to you, unless a grain of wheat falls into the earth and dies, it remains alone; but if it dies, it bears much fruit. he who loves his life loses it; and he who hates his life in this world shall keep it to life eternal" (Jn. 12:24, 25).

Death and resurrection are the keys to abundant life. If we cling to our life, demanding our rights and enjoying our sin, we shall lose it. But if we will give up our life, surrendering our rights and clinging only to Christ, we shall experience resurrection life. The fruit of righteousness will begin to grow, and we will become a haven of peace in a weary world.

Response

Is the Spirit speaking to your heart about an area of your life which must be crucified? Will you find your Gethsemane, your place of prayer where you can pray through to victory? Will you listen to "the still small voice of calm" of the Spirit within you, giving you wisdom, understanding and grace? Will you receive the vision Jesus wants to instil within you of a life of holiness and purity? Will you cling only to his words and focus only on his vision, allowing them to lead you through death, into resurrection life?

Chapter 19

Seeing God in All

"*Blessed are the pure in heart, for they shall see God.*" I tried to determine what a pure heart is, and what it is not. I suggested that a pure heart is one that is free from sin, fear, guilt, anger, inferiority, depression, and crippling effects of past traumas. A pure heart is full of faith, hope, love and joy. Those who have a pure heart live in an awareness of their identity with Christ, which gives them victory over sin. Purity of heart comes only by the working of the Spirit of God. While the counsel of wise brothers and sisters can be used as an instrument of correction and healing, it is only the Spirit that can circumcise the heart and make it pure.

Communion with God through quieting ourselves, listening to His voice, and looking to see his vision is a very effective way to have living encounter with Christ. As we turn aside from all the other voices that would demand our attention, as we reject every vision of fear, failure and sin, as we focus only on our living Lord and Saviour, we will touch Jesus, and in touching, be made whole.

For most of us, attaining a pure heart has been a struggle. For some, it has meant letting go of angers and resentments that have given definition to their lives for years. For others, it has meant learning to say no to the multitude of demands which are made on their lives so that they may say yes only to Christ. For still others, it has meant time in Gethsemane, gaining the strength to endure the cross that they might live in resurrection victory over sin. For everyone, it has meant a restoration of divine focus, a renewal of our ability to see God and hear his voice in our hearts.

Now that we have come so far, how can we maintain a pure heart? How can we live free from the bondages that have held us in the past? Jesus said that *the pure in heart shall see God.* We may believe that the inverse is also true: that those who see God shall have a pure heart. Therefore, we may suggest the key to maintaining a pure heart is *seeing God everywhere.* When we worship, it is easy to have a pure heart. We don't mean when we just sing; but rather we mean when we touch the heart of God in worship. When we worship, we focus on the Lord and while we look, we become a reflection of him. The problem comes when we turn from worship and look at people, events and the world around us. How quickly we lose our sense of his presence and power! Therefore, we must learn to see God everywhere we look.

We can see God as central to all matter because *"in him all things hold together"* (Col. 1:17). We could also say: "Out of him all things fly apart – they go to pieces." One commentator explains it like this: "everything in him [Jesus] is centripetal; everything outside of him is centrifugal." Everything in Christ is bound together in perfect harmony, not simply by power but by love. On one occasion our Lord said: *"He who is not with me is against me; and he who does not gather with me scatters"* (Matt. 12:30). Everything outside of Christ scatters.

We can see him in all circumstances, for it is he *"who works all things after the counsel of his will"* (Eph. 1:11). We see Christ as the centre of all our spiritual attainments, because,

> *"by his doing you are in Christ Jesus, who became to us wisdom from God, and righteousness and sanctification and redemption"* (I Cor. 1:30).

We should see him as central to our life, our movement and our existence, for *"in him we live and move and exist"* (Acts 17:28). We can see God everywhere, because he is everywhere.

"Where can I go from your Spirit? Or where can I flee from your presence? If I ascend to heaven, you are there; If I make my bed in Sheol, behold, you are there. If I take the wings of the dawn, If I dwell in the remotest part of the sea, even there your hand will lead me, and your right hand will lay hold of me" (Ps. 139:7-10).

David had learned that even in the most horrible situation, even in hell itself, God was present and visible of faith. And because God is everywhere and knows all things and has all power, his hand can lead us individually and his right hand can hold us, no matter what earthly circumstances are.

The prophet Habakkuk spoke of a glorious day when the whole world would see as David did:

"For the earth will be filled with the knowledge of the glory of the Lord, as the waters cover the sea" (Hab. 2:14).

Notice, he did not say that a day was coming when the glory of the Lord would cover the earth. Indeed, that day is now here and has always been here since creation. Rather, it was recognition of that glory, knowledge of it, and an ability to see the glory that would cover the earth. When man fell, he lost his ability to see spiritual reality. When we are born again, we regain that ability, if we will but receive it. Therefore, our prayer must always be, *"Open my eyes, that I may behold..."* (Psa. 119:18).

God Revealed in his Creation

"For since the creation of the world his invisible attributes, his eternal power and divine nature, have been clearly seen, being understood through what has been made, so that they are without excuse" (Rom. 1:20).

There is so much of God that can be seen in what he has created. If our eyes are open, we will learn divine truths through the four seasons, through the rain and the sunshine, through the birds and the animals. We will become better acquainted with our dearest friend through seeing him in his handiwork. There are many marvellous Scriptures that tell of God's presence in nature the passage given in the Book of

Job is one of such examples (Job 37:2-13). What a demonstration of his eternal power!

Jesus takes us to nature to give us a picture of his Father's divine nature in the Gospel of St. Matthew 6:26-32. As we see the lovingkindness and tender mercy God bestows on the most apparently unimportant creature in his world, we learn more about his unending love and care for us. As we see him, our faith grows, and our hearts are healed. When David wanted to describe the invisible attributes of his God, he also turned to nature to find the right words (Psa. 36:5-9).

Only the immensity of his creation could begin to compare to the enormity of God's character. Let our prayer continually be, "Open my eyes, Lord, that I might see you in Your wondrous creation."

God Revealed in Spiritual Growth

Most of the non-believers firmly believe that they are in control of their life, making their own decisions, doing what they wanted. Though this was not true, for they were really under the authority of *"the prince of the power of air"*, they were deceived into believing that they were the one in charge.

Few of the believers also carry that myth over into their new life. Because we are followers of Christ, we must obey him and live a godly life, still in our own strength. This may even take us to many years of frustration and failure to learn that natural man can never live a supernatural life. It is only through the power of the Spirit that works within us that the Christian life is possible. If we forget that we have died, and Christ is now the source of our life, we will become wrapped up again in our efforts to keep the Law and lose the pure heart we have received.

Not that we no longer strive to be righteous, but now our striving is not according to our own power, but *"according to his power, which mightily works within"* us, making us *"complete in Christ"* (Col. 1:28, 29). Therefore, when we are called upon to keep his commandments, we can take a step back into ourselves and call forth the only One Who is truly able to do so. For example, apostle John reminds us that *"if we love one another, God abides in us, and his love is perfected in us"* (1 Jn. 4:12). We are not able to love one another through our own strength. If we are going to love, it will only be because of the love of *"God which abides"* within us. If there is an area of spiritual growth which you are struggling to attain, come and yield your struggles to the One Who is able and has already won the war. Recognize that you are but a branch, grafted into the Vine, supported and sustained by the life of Another.

"I [Jesus] am the vine, you are the branches; he who abides in Me and I in him, he bears much fruit, for apart from Me you can do nothing" (Jn. 15:5).

Ask him to open your eyes that you might see his hand at work in your life, conforming you into his image.

God Revealed in Everyday Work and Service

If only we could always be involved in worship and ministry, how easy it would be to see Christ then! If we believe that, then we are believing another lie of Satan, that there is a division in life between the secular and the sacred. In Christ, there is no division. All of life becomes an act of worship for those who see God in all.

> *"Whatever you do in word or deed, do all in the name of the Lord Jesus..."* (Col. 3:17).

You are to do everything as representing him; you are to do it in his name, in his stead, and in his Spirit. We are the only Bible some people will read. Whether at home, on the job or in church, everything we do is to be done unto the Lord.

> *"Wives be subject to your own husbands, as to the Lord"* (Eph. 5:22). *"Husbands love your wives, just as Christ also loved the Church..."* (Eph. 5:25). *"Children obey your parents in the Lord, for it is right"* (Eph. 6:1). *"Fathers... bring them up in the discipline and instruction of the Lord"* (Eph. 6:4). *"Slaves be obedient to those who are your masters...in the sincerity of your heart, as to Christ"* (Eph. 6:5). *"And masters, do the same things to them, and give up*

threatening, knowing that both their Master and yours is in heaven, and there
is no partiality with him" (Eph. 6:9).

If you give a cup of cold water to the thirsty, you are doing it unto the
Lord. If you give food to the hungry, you are doing it for him. If you
visit the sick or the prisoner, you are ministering to Christ (Matt. 25:
31-46). If our eyes are open, He is everywhere, and everything we do
is done unto him.

"Whatever you do, do your work heartily, as for the Lord, rather than for men,
knowing that from the Lord you will receive the reward of the inheritance. It
is the Lord Christ whom you serve" (Col. 3:23, 24).

Let us pray that our eyes may be opened that we might see God in
every facet of our lives, that every word we speak and everything we
do may be an act of worship to our Lord.

God Revealed in the Circumstances of Life

Is it possible for man to comprehend the fact that God has given man
free will, and at the same time, he is to work all things after the counsel
of his will? Such a dichotomy of truth is beyond our ability to grasp.
Thank God that he does not require complete understanding or even
perfect theology, but only steadfast faith!

"...God causes all things to work together for good to those who love God, to
those who are called according to his purpose" (Rom. 8:28). *"We have...been*
predestined according to his purpose who works all things after the counsel of
his will" (Eph. 1:11).

We must have our eyes opened to the movement of the hand of God
in every circumstance that surrounds us.

But you may wonder, what about evil authorities and rulers? Surely
God does not place them in positions of power!

"For not from the east, nor from the west, nor from the desert comes exaltation;
but God is the Judge; He puts down one and exalts another" (Psa. 75:6, 7).

But what about the unrighteous judgements of rulers and people in authority? What if they give rulings which are contrary to what God wants?

> *"The king's heart is like channels of water in the hand of the Lord; He turns it wherever He wishes"* (Prov. 21:1).

Because we know that our God is bigger than any other ruler, we can confidently submit to every authority in our life. Through prayer, we have influence over every king, judge and employer. If we earnestly pray that God will guide their words and judgments, we can rest in whatever decisions they make, knowing that their hearts have been turned by the Lord. Of course, if we have failed in our responsibility of earnest prayer and supplication for all in authority, God may allow ungodly rulers and poor judgements to be made so that we will be corrected and called back to our dependency on him.

> *"I [Paul] urge that entreaties and prayers, petitions and thanksgivings, be made on behalf of all men, for kings and all who are in authority, so that we may lead a tranquil and quiet life in all godliness and dignity"* (1 Tim. 2:1, 2).

How easy it is to believe God is sovereign during the times of joy and peace! How hard it seems to accept that He is in control during sorrow and misfortune. But only by doing so can we maintain a pure heart and not be overcome with fear, doubt and anger. But try to understand clearly what the prophet Isaiah says in 45:5-7. Not only must we see the hand of God in every circumstance of life, we must also hear the voice of God that we may know how we are to respond. Just because God has allowed a calamity to come into our lives does not mean that we are to passively accept the evil. There is a time to submit and a time to overcome. Only the voice and vision of God can give us guidance that we may know our proper response.

The people of Judah had been living in rebellion for many years. Again, and again the word of the Lord came through his prophets that they must repent or suffer destruction. Yet they would not obey. Finally, the day came when God's righteous judgement had to be satisfied. He spoke through his prophet Jeremiah 25:8, 9. Because of your sin, said Jeremiah, this judgement is upon you. Therefore, submit to the power of the enemy, for he is acting as a servant of God for your discipline. When the time of judgement is passed, the Lord will turn and judge Nebuchadnezzar for being such a willing vessel for your destruction and you shall be restored. But for now, this is your discipline from the hand of the Lord. Therefore, submit. But that does not mean we are always to stand powerless before the enemies of God.

The prophet Elisha was in a similar situation to the people of Judah (2 Kings 6:14-23). He was also surrounded by an enemy bent on his destruction. Yet he did not submit. Because he was a prophet, he knew that God's plan for him was not submission but authority. Though there were only two in his house, himself and his servant, he said, "...*Those who are with us are more than those who are with them*" (v. 16). His eyes were opened that he could see the armies of God and he spoke words of faith. The chariots of angels stood ready to consume his enemies, but they were under the authority of the servant of God. Therefore, when Elisha said, "...*Strike this people with blindness, I pray...*" (v. 18), the Lord moved in response to his prayer, and Elisha was the victor. There is a time to submit and a time to conquer. We will only know for sure how we are to respond if we can see what God is doing in the situation and hear his words of guidance.

Moving from Spiritual Confusion to Confidence

Prophet Habakkuk begins his prophecy by confessing his confusion as to why God allows evil to continue, he ends it by affirming that he has gained complete and utter confidence in the ways of God. How was the prophet able to move from the place of confusion to the place of confidence?

> Habakkuk began his ministry by asking God a pointed question: "*How long, O Lord, will I call for help, and you will not hear?*" (Hab. 1:2)

Like many other prophets, he was perplexed by the continuance of evil. He could not understand why God did not intervene to restrain the godless nations around him. The Almighty's apparent slowness in dealing with this issue caused him a great deal of confusion and concern. All prophets of the Old Testament speak God's word to us, but Habakkuk also speaks our word to God. Eugene Peterson says of him, "He gives voice to our bewilderment, articulates our puzzled attempts to make sense of things, and faces God with our disappointment with God." This is a major spiritual issue which requires great honesty to confess that one is spiritually confused.

The very first thing we must do whenever we are confused by God's seeming non-intervention in human affairs is to admit our confusion than dishonestly pretend to confusion does not exist. Bring all your questions, doubts and feelings to God and talk directly to him about them. Some regard Habakkuk's direct questioning of God as impertinent, but I do not see it in that way. Habakkuk did what everyone should do when they fail to comprehend the ways of God – he talked openly to him about it:

> *"Why do You make me see iniquity, and cause me to look on wickedness?"*
> (Hab. 1:3).

So, whenever you feel confused about the state of the world do not be too eager to enter a dialogue with other people. First enter a dialogue with God.

> *"Let us draw near with confidence to the throne of grace, so that we may receive mercy and find grace to help in time of need"* (Heb. 4:16).

If we would learn to bring our doubts, our fears and our confusion to God and talk to him about these matters in believing prayer then there might be fewer unresolved problems in the Church. When we talk to God about our problems then we are showing him and providing to ourselves that the roots of our dependence are in him.

As soon as Habakkuk had finished speaking and was ready to listen, God started answering him – but not in the way that he expected. First, God tells him that despite all appearances to the contrary, he is not inactive:

*"I [God] am doing something in your days – you would not believe if you
were told"* (Hab. 1:5).

We begin to see now a reason for the silence: Habakkuk had not been
ready to receive the answer he was praying for. It is obvious that God
was not doing what the prophet imagined – standing back and allowing
things to proceed unchecked. He had already put into operation his
plans and purposes, but in a way that Habakkuk would find unbelievable
and unacceptable.

When God announced that he was about to see the brutal Chaldeans
to punish his people Habakkuk was utterly taken aback.

*"I [God] am raising up the Chaldeans, that fierce and impetuous people who
march throughout the earth to seize dwelling places which are not theirs"*
(Hab. 1:6).

The Chaldeans are synonymous with the newly resurgent Babylonians.
The apostate nation of Judah is to be punished by an invasion of the
Babylonians. Now the prophet was more confused than ever. First,
God took an exceptionally long time to answer him, and when He
did, the answer He gave was more difficult to receive than the silence.
Can we begin to see now that one of the reasons why we go through
times of spiritual confusion and frustration is because although we
are big enough to ask the questions, we are not always big enough to
understand the answers? What is the point of God unfolding to us his
plans and purposes when He knows that we cannot understand them
or are unwilling to do so? Our inability or unwillingness to accept God's
purposes and see things from his point of view precludes us from being
informed of them.

As nature has its secrets, so has its God. Until he reveals them to us,
we can but trust his wisdom and his love. In one of his great sermons,
C. H. Spurgeon said, "Let me not strive to understand the infinite, but
spend my strength in love. What I cannot gain by intellect I can possess
by affection, and I let that suffice me. I cannot penetrate the heart of the

sea, but I can enjoy the healthful breezes which sweep over its bosom, and I can sail on its blue waves with propitious winds."

Isaiah, too, knew something of this. He pleaded with God to give him insight and understanding on the political situation of his day so that he might comprehend what was hidden from others. He prayed for divine illumination in order that his gaze might pierce the future and he might speak forth a prophetic word to his people. And God gave him light! His prayer was answered! The darkness turned to twilight. When he knew, he almost wished he did not know. The light glimmered all around him, but pain of revelation made him wish that he was back in the darkness of ignorance once again. What did he see?

"My mind reels, horror overwhelms me; the twilight I longed for has been turned for me into trembling" (Isa. 21:4).

He saw the people he loved broken by the force of the enemy. He saw their homes and cities shattered by the most ruthless of foes.

Having seen how Habakkuk and Isaiah experienced the pain of answered prayer, we should clearly submit:

"As the heavens are higher than the earth, so are My ways higher than your ways and My thoughts than your thoughts" (Isa. 55:9).

God's thoughts are not only higher than ours – sometimes they are also diametrically opposite to ours. If you accept the demands God makes and face squarely what the light reveals, the trembling will pass, and you will prove the truth of Isaiah's words; you will find that He will *"strengthen the weak hands and make firm the feeble and tottering knees. Say to those who are of a fearful and hasty heart, 'Be strong, fear not! Behold, your God will come...'"* (Isa. 35: 3, 4 Amp. Bible).

Always it is such a comfort to know that God is in control, especially during the dark hours of our lives. The most difficult times of my life so far have been times of transition, when God was moving me into the next phase of my life. The first time it happened, I didn't know what was happening. Every stable force in my life just seemed to disintegrate.

Because I did not recognize the voice of God in my heart, I fell into doubt, anger and despair. Being a man of action, I looked around for a new position. Every option seemed closed to me except one. Because I could find no other choice, I pursued the only course open to me. I thought I was moving simply out of logic and necessity. Only later was I able to see the hand of God guiding and keeping me, even when I had no faith and the way seemed dark and aimless. What a blessing it was for me to realize that even though I had not seen it, God was still in control.

The next transition came in my life after I had learned to hear God's voice and see his vision. Again, all the circumstances seemed negative. Sometimes I would become depressed and think that other people were controlling my life and my future. But when I listened to the Lord through dialogue prayers, He assured me that He was in command of the situation and nothing could happen to me that He did not allow or ordain. He showed me when to speak and when to be silent, when to act and when to be still, when to submit and when to take authority. Though I cannot say I came through that time without any doubts or failures, I was more victorious than I had been the time before.

Right now, I am again going through a time of change. It is certainly the guidance of God that has me writing this book during this time. Every day I have an opportunity to put into practice what I am recommending to you. I know that it works because it is working in my life day by day. I am doing better this time, I think. I have a greater confidence in the sovereignty of God than I have had in the past. When I seem to be treated unfairly, I have an assurance that no one can prevent God's will from being accomplished in my life except me. If I purpose in my spirit to do only his will and I keep my heart pure of anger and bitterness, he will turn hearts and circumstances to bring about his best for me. I am confident that no one has authority over me unless it has been given them from above (Jn. 19:11). Because I hold before me a vision of what God has planned for me, and that vision carries me through the times of distress.

Whatever you are going through now, God is still in control. Ask him to open your eyes that you might see his hand of love upon you. Open your ears that you might hear his words of truth.

Summary

"His name shall be called Wonderful Counsellor!" When our hearts are wounded, our spirits crushed, our minds clouded by doubt and despair, we have a Friend who loves us and offers us hope. If we will be still, listen, and look, he will speak words of healing and peace and give visions of joy and hope. When divine perspective is restored our hearts shall be pure, for we shall see God everywhere.

Chapter 20

Living Tuned to the Lord

"*If we live in the Spirit, let us also walk in the Spirit*" (Gal. 5:25). God is the great "I AM" (Ex. 3:14). He always lives in the present moment; not the future or the past, but the *now*. We, too, must learn to live in the now and not constantly be looking forward and backward, but simply sharing this moment with Jesus. He does not want us to set aside a special time for a special spiritual activity that we call "sensing our spirits." Instead, he wants us to go on with all the necessary activities of life, doing them with him and for him as acts of love to him. Whether it is washing clothes, showering, eating, working in a factory, reading, preaching a sermon, or counselling—each of these activities can be done either as love gifts to Jesus, or simply endeavours we perform. Each of these can be done with an inner ear and eye turned to him, or totally caught up in ourselves and the activity.

> "*Whatever you do, do your work heartily, as for the Lord, rather than for men*" (Col. 3:23).

Therefore, God is not so much calling us to do a different "spiritual" activity, as He is calling us to make our "regular, normal" activities "spiritual" by doing them "for" and "in" him.

Abhishiktananda, the Belgian Benedictine monk, out of his many years of Christian life in India, writes concerning what he calls the Holy Presence:

"God is always present to us. There is no time and no place in our daily life or occupations in which God is not present to us; there are not even certain times or occupations in which God is more present to us or less present to us. God is always the same, the Almighty, the Infinite, the Eternal...Everywhere and always he is, he is himself in his fullness; there is no sense in which he can be more 'here' or less 'there' since he is indivisible. In truth, it is to himself alone that God is ever present... he enjoys for ever the unspeakable bliss of his presence to himself, the presence of the Father to the Son and of the Son to the Father, and the mutual Presence of both to the Holy Spirit. This mystery is revealed to us by Jesus himself, out of his experience as Son of God (Jn. 14:10, 11, 16; 15:10, 26; 16:13, 14; 17:5, 22-24).

Creation is simply the communication of this presence, this mysterious life of God in himself. Everything that exists, every being that lives and thinks, does so by sharing in his being, his divine life and self-awareness. It is from and through this very presence of God to himself that all creatures exist, that living creatures are born and grow, that man is aware of himself, and finally becomes an individual being, endowed with personal call and vocation for time and eternity."

What a release! I am not required to add another activity to my already busy schedule, but rather to find eternal rest in the activities I am already doing:

> "So there remains a Sabbath rest for the people of God. For the one who has entered his rest has himself also rested from his works, as God did from his. Therefore, let us be diligent to enter that rest, so that no one will fall, through following the same example of disobedience" (Heb. 4:9-11).

The believer ceases his efforts to gain salvation by his own works and rests in the finished work of Christ on the cross. As I enter God, I flow from eternity and will return to eternity, so I live in timelessness (eternity) and therefore at perfect peace. As I do various activities in him, he makes them so much easier and simpler. I lose my anxious pushing, my fretting, my striving, my doubts and worries, my self-centeredness, and in some cases, he totally adjusts, removes or replaces the activities.

The Lord is calling us to stand in communion with him while we walk among men. We must learn this way of living. To form the habit of awareness of God continually takes diligence to apply, but soon is continued because of the inward excitement experienced by his love and presence. It begins with much prayer in our hearts. Your contact with people will be a loving contact, bringing the mystery of God's presence in you to others, simply by your being there. Your being there makes Christ more present. Your goal is simply to live in union with God. It is reached by a thousand little steps of removing areas of self-dependence, one after another, and having your heart opened through the healing power of his love.

We approach God with the absolute simplicity of a child. We are convinced of God not by our studies and reasoning and elaborate meditations, but because we are experiencing him in our hearts, as he gives feeling, revelation, faith and life. This entire manual, having helped guide us into our spirits more fully, has now become a speck of nothing in eternity, because we have found the one who fills our hearts, and who is all and in all. Our lives are in abiding in him, not in abiding in the concepts of this manual. So, all of life only finds meaning as it is experienced in him, because he is Life and outside of him there is nothing.

After Abraham had received the greatest treasure that God had promised him (a son), he was asked to give it back to God. So often after receiving a promised treasure from God, we would cling to the treasure rather than our God. As God asked for the treasure back from Abraham, Abraham was driven back to clinging only to a faithful God, and *"he considered that God is able to raise men even from the dead"* (Heb. 11:19). And so, too, we may treasure revelations of truth from this biblical meditation, but God calls us to live in a daily communion with him, out of which come revelations for the present day.

As we live in direct contact with the Divine Lover of this universe, we ourselves are transformed by his love. We become tender and gentle, comprehending the goodness of all God has made, and our tenderness and gentleness are expressed toward all his creation: ourselves, others, and all things. We have become mirrors reflecting his glory. We have learned to live in our hearts, encountering God there, rather than living in our minds, and only thinking of him. We have found simply him.

Embracing the Cross!

One of the biggest hindrances to the life of living out of the voice of God is not the time it takes, but rather the lack of willingness to embrace the cross when it is placed before us (Matt. 16:24). The way of Christ is the way of the cross, and over and over our commitments to the cross are tested as God works death and resurrection in another area of our lives. Jesus committed himself to the way of the cross while in the wilderness, and yet had to struggle desperately in Gethsemane as He embraced it. That which impedes our spiritual growth is our unwillingness to go to Gethsemane and agonize in prayer until the flesh is overcome by the Spirit. How was Jesus able to accept the horror of the cross? Hebrews 12:2 tells us that *"for the joy set before him, he endured the cross."* Jesus kept before himself the reason and the reward for his suffering. He saw Abraham and David and the other Old Testament saints released from paradise and worshipping before the throne. He saw you and me enjoying the sweet fellowship of his Spirit. And for that joy, he endured the cross. The same is true for us. The vision that carries us through the cross is the vision of resurrection life on the other side. We must cling to God, and that vision, if we are going to be able to endure the cross set before us.

You cannot endure the cross if you are simply clinging to the cross. It is the hope we have of God's resurrection life that flows on the other side that we cling to as we endure the cross. Much can be endured if one lives in hope and faith. The vision of the beyond is what gives hope and faith to our hearts. Therefore, whenever God places the cross in front of you and asks to remove something from your life, don't spend time battling; simply come to God and cling to God, receiving your all from him. This is the only way you can successfully embrace the cross in your life.

Embrace the cross in all its aspects. Do not let anything stand between you and your life of abiding rest. He is the true Life-giver within our inner beings. And once we have found him there, we know that nothing in this world is comparable to him (Phil. 3:7-11; 1 Pet. 5:10, 11).

Let me share with you the following notes from *The   Practice of the Presence of God* by Brother Lawrence, a 16th-century monk who served in the kitchen of a monastery.

1.   All bodily mortifications are useless unless they serve to arrive at the union with God by love. The shortest way to God is continual exercise of love and doing all things for his sake.

2.   The love of God is the end of all one's actions.

3.   Establish yourself in God's presence by continually conversing with him.

4.   When failing to practice his presence, acknowledge sinfulness and return in greater trust to God (without whipping yourself).

5.   Live in the present, realizing God's present grace. Do not be anxious for tomorrow.

6. He sensed himself more united to God in outward employments (kitchen duties) than in times of prayer.

7.   Many do not advance in Christ because they do penances and other exercises while neglecting the love of God, which is the *end*.

8.   The only thing necessary to approach God is a heart resolutely determined to apply itself to nothing but him, to love him only.

9.   The greater perfection a soul aspires after, the more dependent it is upon divine grace.

The day dawns—the Morning Star arises in our hearts

Prayerfully meditate on 2 Pet. 1:19, *"So we have the prophetic word made more sure, to which you do well to pay attention as to a lamp shining in a dark place, until the day dawns and the morning star arises in your hearts."*

This verse picturesquely describes what happens in our hearts over and over. Our hearts can become a *"dark place."* Did you ever look inside at your heart, and say "Eek, how ugly, black and disgusting? All I see is sin and selfishness within. All I see is my own evil within. My heart feels lonely, empty, forsaken, and black." Then at other times, you look inside, and you see Christ shining in all his glory. You're bursting with love, joy, peace. You feel radiant, light, like you can handle the whole world, because such overcoming life is flowing from the Christ within.

Well, in 2 Pet. 1:19, Peter is describing going from the first state to the second, allowing *"a lamp to shine in a dark place, until the day dawns and the morning star arises in our hearts."* Our dark hearts are made full of light because Jesus has come and filled our darkness with his light, and it's just like the dawning of the day within us. Like the sun arising upon the earth and flooding it with light, so Jesus has arisen upon our hearts, flooding us with his light. Oh, how we need this experience over and over. We need it at the beginning of each new day. We need it during the day when we've lost it for one reason or another. This experience, we find, must be constantly repeated in our lives.

And what causes Christ, the Morning Star, to arise in our hearts? Paying attention to *"the prophetic word"* (the illumined Logos, rhema, and vision). As we turn our attention to what Jesus is speaking and doing within our hearts that in turn centres us upon Jesus, the Morning Star. So, as we turn our attention to Jesus Christ, we find that He arises within our hearts.

For example, I discover that I am feeling like my heart is dark and empty and full of sin. To heal this problem, I begin by recalling that

Christ lives within, so I centre down, perhaps through music. I sing over and over a Scripture song that speaks of him. I look to see him. I become still. I cease striving. I come back to my position in him. I reject extraneous thoughts along the way of doubt, negativity or defeat. I hear Christ speak in my heart. He reminds me of his indwelling glory; I feast on it, allowing it to fill my inner mind, will and emotions. I speak it forth. I become full and begin to overflow with Christ's manifest presence. I step forth in life responding to the fullness of Christ's manifest presence which has been restored within. His being has filled my inner being. My inner being has transformed my outer being. The Morning Star has arisen in my heart, giving life to me and the world around me.

Oh, how glorious is the dawning of Christ within our hearts! The hurt, emptiness, loneliness and weakness are replaced by his healing, fullness, friendship and strength. And these are just the tip of the iceberg. He grows and grows within us becoming more and more precious and fulfilling with every passing day. In each step of growth, I find an additional way God wants to manifest himself within me and I allow him to do that, until he becomes my all, my life, my breath, my hope. All of life becomes reduced to Jesus Who is all and in all. The writer of Proverbs describes this path of the righteous as *"the light of dawn that shines brighter and brighter until the full day"* (Prov. 4:18). It is such a glorious path! It is so different from the path of the world. They strive to accomplish, while the Christian strives to enter rest so that God can accomplish. The world strives to learn. The Christian meditates prayerfully waiting upon God for his revelation of truth, knowledge, wisdom and righteousness. The world strives for security in things and accomplishments. The Christian finds security only in Jesus, the solid Rock on Whom he stands, and in being sheltered under the wings of the Almighty God.

Yes, the way of the world is utterly opposed to the way of faith in the power of the indwelling Lord Jesus Christ. Let us not be deceived into thinking that Christian growth is growth in simply *learning* about God. It goes beyond that to *experiencing* God in all his life-giving encounters.

Therefore, we must know how to encounter him. We must know how to have spirit-to-Spirit communion, and we must have it. Without avenues of direct encounter with God, He cannot begin to become to us what he desires. Therefore, we must train ourselves in coming to him and truly encountering him in faith, awareness, and communion, because apart from this we will miss much of God's choicest blessings.

So now, life is reduced to Jesus, and simply abiding in him and allowing him to be our all. In that, all pride is broken. We have found that we are nothing that he is everything, and we walk in glorious humility, branches grafted into a vine, alive only because of the life we receive from him (Jn. 15:4, 5).

Now where does this growth occur, if not simply through meditation on the Bible? Well, it starts there, and biblical meditation must never in any way be discouraged, but after we have paid attention to the prophetic word, God takes us on the hard streets of life to mould these truths into us on the anvil of testing and tribulation. In the time of testing, the Bible moves from our heads to our hearts. In the time of tribulation, we find ourselves clinging to "the Head," and finding in Him those things He promised would be there.

And so true spiritual growth is accomplished. The day dawns, the Morning Star, Jesus Christ, arises in our hearts, having become to us all that we need.

Chapter 21

Joy and Pain of Suffering

Does it seem strange to include a chapter on pain of suffering in a book on joyful living? From the outset, I was persuaded that it is impossible to write about joy without awareness of sorrow, pain, and suffering. And this is not only because of honesty and integrity – for life is a mingling of joy and sorrows – but because I am able to affirm the primacy of joy. Joy is basic, and to drink of the springs of humanity is to drink of the springs of joy. And joy continues, flowing as the river of God throughout our lives, and ultimately into the ocean of God's eternal love. Pain of suffering is not last word, for joy converts the enemy of even death into our sister who is welcomed after the long pilgrimage of earthly life.

Now lest it be thought that I am not taking sickness and death seriously. Let me say that there is a sense in which death is the enemy – though an enemy which will itself be destroyed. St: Paul says to Corinthians:

"The last enemy that will be abolished is death" (1 Cor. 15:26).

Though suffering is often more obvious among the bereaved than the patient, nevertheless, there have been times of great sadness and distress with dying people especially among those who have taken no thought of preparation for the journey we must all make. I affirm all the joy and rejoicing spoken of earlier in the first paragraph of this chapter, but the other side of the coin is the acceptance of grief and pain in the loss of a loved one for whom one should and must grieve, as Jesus grieved and wept at the grave of Lazarus. Grief repressed gives rise to dangerous symptoms for the person concerned and for all around.

I am also aware that it is not only the facts of personal and family grief or even bereavement that face us here, but the awareness of wider grief, cruelty, suffering, torture and bloodshed presented before our eyes and to our hearts daily via the mass media, from all parts of the world. What are we to make of it all – how can we talk of joy in the face of such accumulated suffering – and can anything make up for such carnage, torture and violence? Here I wish to remind you to believe that there is strong reason to listen to the words of St: Paul when he says:

> "For I consider that the sufferings of this present time are not worthy to be compared with the glory that is to be revealed to us" (Rom. 8:18).

But we cannot help feeling that Paul did not know what we know, after the holocaust, either of the depth of man's inhumanity to man, nor the breadth of the extent of horrific and refined cruelty in our contemporary world. I believe that he realised, more than we do, the depths to which man can sink, though he could not have known the universal practical application of such suffering that we can and do inflict upon each other in these days.

All such violence cruelty, warfare and bloodshed are death-dealing, and Christians must take it seriously, showing themselves to be people of reconciliation and compassion in a violent world. They must work by life and word for disarmament and peace, even if it means losing their material possessions, standard of living, and life itself. Easy words, but such is the crisis and challenge today, for whatever position one holds regarding nuclear weapons and disarmament, it must cause any heart touched with love of Christ to sorrow and weep for the sins of the world.

In the face of all this, endeavouring to take grief and suffering seriously, and looking into the face of death, how can there be room for joy? Can Christian theology and experience make any sense of the sad reality of the absurdity of human life and the apparent meaningless of our existence in the world today?

The answer to these questions lies in the wholeness of the Christian tradition. It draws not only upon the revelation of God in Scripture, but in the living and continuous experience of the people of God down through the ages, including our own days. We have already learned about the experiences of Christians under persecution and torture, have heard the song of the martyrs and witnessed the triumph of the suffering Church under pain of death. Christians of this calibre would say that if there was no world to come, if this life was the only one, and if there was no judgement and justice and no consummation of love in the life to come – even then there would be no life to be lived but the Christian life, and no death to die but a Christian death. For in life and death the promise of Christ's love and presence is validated to those who launch out into the deep waters of daring faith.

True believers do not lead Christian lives or die martyrs' deaths in order to deserve, earn or merit eternal life. If our lives are to be lived in the experience of forgiveness and compassion, then whether that results in productive fruitfulness or in persecution and death, that is still the way to live. True Christian does not love Christ for fear of hell or for hope of heaven, but just because of love. And if that love ends in death, then so be it – but love he will!

Let's be quite clear. The Christian hope is the living reality of Christ's forgiveness, compassion and presence here and now. And all such compassion must be channelled toward the alleviation of human suffering and the promotion of forgiveness, reconciliation and peace among people and nations. So even if suffering and death is the end, there is still abundant purpose and meaning in life – and in death. Better to die in love and compassion possessing nothing and devoid of power, than to die having amassed wealth, territory, power and reputation, if one's hands are stained with blood.

But having said all that, it is impossible for me to think that Christian life and the experience of God's love is limited to this life. St. Paul says in a tremendous chapter on death and resurrection:

> *"If we who are* [abiding] *in Christ have hope only in this life and that is all, then we are of all people most miserable and to be pitied"* (1 Cor. 15:19 Amp. Bible).

Then he goes on to speak of the risen life of Jesus and of our life in him. The fact is that the whole Christian tradition down through the ages has affirmed life and love in Christ for today – and for ever. Once eternal life is brought into the saving and forgiving love of Christ, the river of such love flows on into eternity, and into the blessedness of a dimension in God which sorrow and sighing shall be no more, tears shall be wiped from every eye. Then we shall gaze upon the face of God in glory and be joined to him by the Spirit of love.

Indeed, a true Christian may suffer more than the unbeliever, and lose everything in the world – but it does sustain the suffering believer with inward peace and joy, even in humiliation, and suffering.

> *"...In the world you have tribulation,"* said Jesus on the eve of his torture and crucifixion, *"but take courage; I have overcome the world"* (Jn. 16:33).

Who was He to offer such comfort, when He was taken, beaten, tortured and crucified to death? But that's the very point – "God was in Christ, reconciling the world to himself." It was Love himself upon the cross for us, suffering *with* the world, dying *for* the world, but rising in power, glory and joy, in order that He might reconcile all people to the Father in ultimate joy at the last.

And there is, above all, the increasing awareness of fellowship and loving union with Christ, being made more and more into his image, and anticipating the vision, glory and transfiguration of union in the mystery of God. St. Paul was joyful in Christ, even in his prison cell, believing it to be part of his ministry and witness, but his yearning indicates the anticipated joy that welled up in his heart. He writes to Church in Philippi:

"This is in keeping with my own eager desire and persistent expectation and hope, that I shall not disgrace myself nor be put to shame in anything; but that with the utmost freedom of speech and unfailing courage, now as always heretofore, Christ [the Messiah] *will be magnified and get glory and praise in this body of mine and be boldly exalted in my person, whether through* (by) *life or through* (by) *death. For me to live is Christ* [his life in me], *and to die is gain* [the gain of the glory of eternity]. *If, however, it is to be life in the flesh and I am to live on here, that means fruitful service for me; so, I can say nothing as to my personal preference* [I cannot choose]. *But I am hard pressed between the two. My yearning desire is to depart* (to be free of this world, to set forth) *and be with Christ, for that is far, far better; but to remain in my body is more needful and essential for your sake."* (Phil. 1:20-24 Amp. Bible).

The psalmist gives his living hope in Psa. 73:24. Along with the psalmist our firm belief must be, when we reach the end of our earthly pilgrimage our loving Guide directs us to the presence of the Almighty to behold his glory. In the New Testament the Holy Spirit is often referred to as our infallible Guide and He has promised to be our guide even to the end.

As we await our translation, we must surrender to him to be guided how and where He pleases, and we must trust him to direct our steps correctly through the encircling gloom. We must take no step without his order and aid, if we would experience the full joy of being received by him the moment, we find ourselves in his immediate presence. This brings us to the borders of a consideration of Eternal Joy.

Eternal Joy comes in the Morning

The theme of joy through intimate relationship with the Lord has carried us up to the borderlands of consummation, seeking to trace the joy of God in every department of our human lives. We have found joy in all forms of creativity and intellectual experiences and rejoiced in the vitality of communicative joy both in personal and corporate life.

Since eternal life is a present possession for the true believer, then we are already recipients of the grace of God. We know the joy of forgiveness and reconciliation, and powers of the new birth into the kingdom of God. By the indwelling of the Holy Spirit we have a foretaste and pledge of future glory, and in close communion with our Lord Jesus Christ in prayer life and worship, we enter, even now, into actual experience of relationship with the living God.

The empty tomb is not a matter for speculation but for celebration, and the fact that Jesus was no longer in the tomb means not only that he is *existentially* present within the heart, but that he will end the present historical process at his coming in glory. He will initiate the Kingdom of God in *eschatological* destruction and transfiguration putting an end to evil and death. The stories of the transfiguration and the resurrection are the basis for our hope, reflected in one of the loveliest promises of the New Testament contained in the Epistle to the Philippians:

> *"Our citizenship is in heaven, from which also we eagerly wait for a Saviour, the Lord Jesus Christ; who will transform the body of our humble state into conformity with the body of his glory, by the exertion of the power that He has even to subject all things to himself"* (Phil. 3: 20, 21).

Where has all these led us? To the heart of biblical religion! We have been brought to the point where David's prayer in Psalm 16 may become our own:

> *"Preserve me, O God, for I take refuge in You. I said to the Lord, 'You are my Lord; I have no good besides You'* (vv.1, 2). *The Lord is the portion of my inheritance and my cup; You support my lot* (v.5). *I will bless the Lord who has counselled me; ...* (v.7). *I have set the Lord continually before me; because He is at my right hand, I will not be shaken* (v.8). *Therefore, my heart is glad ...* (v.9). *You will make known to me the path of life; in Your presence is fullness of joy; in Your right hand there are pleasures forever"* (v.11).

Then one may say with Habakkuk in the face of economic ruin, or any other deprivation:

> *"Though the fig tree should not blossom and there be no fruit on the vines, though the yield of the olive should fail and the fields produce no food, though the flock should be cut off from the fold and there be no cattle in the stalls, yet I will exult in the Lord, I will rejoice in the God of my salvation. The Lord God is my strength..."* (Hab. 3:17, 18, 19f).

Happy the man who can say these things and mean them!

I believe that the theme of joy in the presence of the Lord has been the golden thread throughout creation, redemption and consummation. The fullness of such joy is not yet. We have the foretaste, pledge, promise, hope, but the fullness yet awaits us. The anticipation of joy in the presence of the Lord forever gives me joy in the present moment. My ecstasies and despairs in this mortal state are all bound up in such anticipation, and the restlessness of heart which I now experience is akin to the present and impatient attitude of the lover who awaits coming of the Beloved.

In this poor world we live in the darkness before dawn. We are assured that though our weeping may endure for a night, joy comes in the morning, and already the wide sky is heavy with anticipation and expectant longing, so that the last words of the Bible are entirely appropriate.

> *"He who ... testifies to these things says, yes* (it is true). [Surely] *I am coming quickly* (swiftly, speedily). *Amen* (so let it be)! *Yes, come, Lord Jesus! The grace* (blessing and favour) *of the Lord Jesus Christ* (the Messiah) *be with all the saints* (God's holy people, those set apart for God, to be, as it were, exclusively his). *Amen.* (so, let it be)!" (Amp. Bible)

We have examined a lot in this book on how to have fullness of joy in our lives. Now I would like you to get alone with God in prayer and ask him to form for you a comprehension of what communion with the Lord and counselled by the Lord entails for you in your life, and what specific things He would say to you. Meditate prayerfully, with your eyes turned to Jesus and your ears tuned to the intuitive impressions of your heart. Then you will get what He wants to say to you rather than simply the thoughts of your mind. May God grant his revelation unto you.

"GLORIA IN EXCELSIS DEO"

Appendix

Appendix A

Logos and Rhema in the Greek New Testament

Very few biblical scholars are of the opinion that there is distinction between *"logos"* and *"rhema,"* the two Greek words translated "word" in the New Testament. They say that *rhema* is fellowship with the Holy Spirit. It is the spoken word of God in our hearts. The idea seemed right that we live out of our fellowship with the Holy Spirit, the voice of God within our hearts. But to our dismay in many concordances there is nothing to substantiate this distinction and there appeared to be much overlap between *logos* and *rhema*.

But while studying through the seventy verses where *rhema* is used in the New Testament (see Appendix B), we will be shocked to discover that in each of these references, *rhema* seems to refer to a spoken word, never the written word. *The Dictionary of New Testament Theology* defines *logos* as, "Collect, count, say, intellectual, rational, reasonable, spiritual." *Rhema* is, "That which is stated intentionally; a word, an utterance, a matter, event, case." *Vine's Expository Dictionary of New Testament Words* defines *logos* as "The expression of thought. Not the mere name of an object (a) as embodying a conception or ideal; (b) a saying or a statement." *Rhema*, "Denotes that which is spoken; what is uttered in speech or writing."

According to Strong's # 3056, *logos* (log-oss): A transmission of thought, communication, a word of explanation, an utterance, discourse, divine revelation, talk, statement, instruction, an oracle, divine promise, divine doctrine, divine declaration. Jesus is the living *logos* (Jn. 1:1); the Bible is the written *logos* (Heb. 4:12); and the Holy Spirit utters the spoken *logos* (1 Cor. 2:13).

But the explanation given to the Greek word, *rhema* (hray-mah) according to Strong's # 4487 is as follows: That which is said or spoken, an utterance, in contrast to *logos,* which is the expression of a thought, a message, and a discourse. *Logos* is the message; *rhema* is the communication of the message. In reference to the Bible, *logos* is the Bible in its entirety; *rhema* is a verse from the Bible. The meaning of *rhema* in distinction to *logos* is illustrated in Eph. 6:17, where the reference is not to the Scripture as a whole, but to that portion which the believer wields as a sword in the time of need.

The distinctions between *logos* and *rhema*, according to the *Dictionary of New Testament Theology* are, "Whereas *logos* can often designate the Christian proclamation as a whole in the New Testament, *rhema* usually relates to individual words and utterances: man has to render account for every unjust *rhema* (Matt. 12:36); Jesus answered Pilate without a single *rhema* (Matt. 27:14); the heavenly ones speak unutterable *rhemas* (2 Cor. 12:4)." The significance of *rhema* (as distinct from *logos*), according to *Vine's Expository Dictionary of New Testament Words*, "is exemplified in the injunction to take the sword of the Spirit, which is the Word (*rhema*) of God (Eph. 6:17); here the reference is not to the whole Bible as such, but to the individual Scripture which the Spirit brings to our remembrance for use in time of need, a prerequisite being the regular storing of the mind with Scripture."

Coupling these definitions with my own personal insight received by examining every use of *rhema* in the New Testament, I suggest that the voice of God we are hearing within our heart is *rhema*.

John the Baptist said that Jesus spoke the word (*rhema*) of God. Jesus declared, *"...I speak these things as the Father taught me...the things which I have seen with* [or in the presence of] *My Father"* (Jn. 8:28, 38). When Jesus spoke *rhema* words, He cut through the surface and touched the spirit, the very heart of men.

Appendix B

The Seventy Uses of Rhema *in the New Testament*

Rhema is translated "word" in the following fifty-four passages:

Matt. 4:4	John 6:63	Acts 10:22	Eph. 5:26
Matt. 12:36	John 6:68	Acts 10:37	Eph. 6:17
Matt. 27:14	John 8:20	Acts 10:44	Heb. 1:3
Mark 14:72	John 8:47	Acts 11:14	Heb. 6:5
Luke 1:38	John 10:21	Acts 11:16	Heb. 11:3
Luke 2:29	John 12:47	Acts 13:42	Heb. 12:19
Luke 3:2	John 12:48	Acts 16:38	1 Pet. 1:25 (2)
Luke 4:4	John 14:10	Acts 26:25	2 Pet. 3:2
Luke 5:5	John 15:7	Acts 28:25	Jude 17
Luke 20:26	John 17:8	Rom. 10:8 (2)	
Luke 24:8	Acts 2:14	Rom. 10:17	Rev. 17:17
Luke 24:11	Acts 5:20	Rom. 10:18	
John 3:34	Acts 6:11	2 Cor. 12:4	
John 5:47	Acts 6:13	2 Cor. 13:1	

Rhema is translated "statement/saying" in the following eight passages:

Mark 9:32	Luke 2:17	Luke 2:51	Luke 9:45 (2)
Luke 1:65	Luke 2:50	Luke 7:1	Luke 18:34

Rhema is translated "thing" in the following three passages:

Luke 2:15   Luke 2:19   Acts 5:32

Additional Verses:

Matthew 5:11 — "... shall say all manner of evil [lit., every evil *rhema*] against you falsely...."

Luke 1:37 — "With God nothing [lit., not any *rhema*] shall be impossible."

Appendix C

Understanding the Power of **Rhema,** *"The Spoken Word"*

Kinds of *Rhema* and Biblical Examples

Most life-giving:

"... *The words* [rhema] *that I say to you I do not speak on My own initiative, but the Father abiding in me does his works*" (Jn. 14:10).

"*The words* [rhema] *which you gave me I have given to them...*" (Jn. 17: 8).

(See also Lk. 1: 38; 5: 5; Jn. 5: 19, 20, 30; 8: 26, 28, 38; 3: 34; 6: 63; Acts 10: 13; 2 Cor. 2: 4; Eph. 6: 17; and Heb. 11:3; 12:19.)

Possibly life-giving: I speak the written Word of God.

"*Go, stand and continue to speak to the people in the temple the whole message* [rhema] *of this life*" (Acts 5:20).

Neutral: I speak out of myself.

"*By the mouth of two or three witnesses every fact* [rhema] *may be confirmed*" (Matt. 18:16).

Somewhat destructive: I speak the generalized word of Satan, which I have heard in the past.

"*Every careless word* [rhema] *that people speak, they shall give an accounting for it in the day of judgment*" (Matt. 12:36).

Most destructive: I speak what Satan is currently speaking within.

"We have heard him speak blasphemous words [rhema] against...God" (Acts 6:11).

"The tongue is a fire...set on fire by hell" (Jas. 3:6).

Our Goal

To produce the maximum amount of life by saying only what the Father is currently speaking within us, through our fellowship with the Spirit (Jn. 14:10, 16).

Appendix D

How God Uses Vision and Image

The best approach to discovering what God has to say on an issue is to gather all the Scripture from Genesis to Revelation on that subject and then meditate on them for a time, asking the Holy Spirit to speak to you. While compiling these, only indicative selected verses are given below.

While asking the Lord to grant you a spirit of revelation (Eph. 1:17, 18) meditate on these verses, allowing God to reveal to you how He desires to use dream and vision in your life. Following are some questions you may want to explore:

1. What is God's desired use of dream and vision in my life?

a. Does God speak through them?

b. How common should this experience be?

c. Does Satan speak through dream and vision?

d. How do I test dream and vision?

e. Is there anything I am to do to promote the flow of divine   vision within me?

2. Does God use images as part of his encounter with us?

a. If so, how is image to be used properly?

b.   What is the negative use of image?

3.   Can we be trained in the use of the eyes of our hearts?

Mandates

Num. 12:6 *"He said, 'Hear now my words: If there is a prophet among you, I, the Lord, shall make myself known to him in a vision. I shall speak with him in a dream.'"*

Psa. 89:19 *"Once you spoke in vision to your godly ones, and said, 'I have given help to one who is mighty; I have exalted one chosen from the people.'"*

Hos. 12:10 *"I have also spoken to the prophets, and I gave numerous visions, and through the prophets I gave parables."*

Joel 2:28 *"It will come out after this that I will pour out my Spirit on all mankind; and your sons and daughters will prophesy, your old men will dream dreams, your young men will see visions."*

Acts 2:17 *"And it shall be in the last days, God says, that I will pour forth of my Spirit on all humankind; and your sons and your daughters shall prophesy, and your young men shall see visions, and your old men shall dream dreams."*

John 5:19, 20 *"Therefore Jesus answered and was saying to them, 'Truly, truly, I say to you, the Son can do nothing of himself, unless it is something, He sees the Father doing; for whatever the Father does, these things the Son also does in like manner. For the Father loves the Son and shows him all things that he himself is doing; and the Father will show him greater works than these, so that you will marvel.'"*

John 8:38 *"I speak the things which I have seen with my Father; ..."*

Opened Eyes

There is a place and a need to have the eyes of our hearts opened by the Spirit, so we can see the vision of God. The Scriptures clearly state that not everyone has opened eyes. We must recognize this lack and need and seek God that he would open the eyes of our hearts.

Gen. 21:19 *"Then God opened her eyes and she saw a well of water; and she went and filled the skin with water and gave the lad a drink."*

Num. 22:31 *"Then the Lord opened the eyes of Balaam, and he saw the angel of the Lord standing in the way with his drawn sword in his hand; and he bowed all the way to the ground."*

Num. 24:2-4 *"And Balaam lifted up his eyes and saw Israel camping tribe by tribe; and the Spirit of God came upon him. He took up his discourse and said, 'The oracle of Balaam the son of Beor, and the oracle of the man whose eye is opened; the oracle of him who hears the words of God, who sees the vision of the Almighty, falling down, yet having his eyes uncovered'"*

Num. 24:16 *"The oracle of him who hears the words of God and knows the knowledge of the Highest, who sees the visions of the Almighty, falling down, yet having his eyes uncovered."*

1 Sam. 3:9, 10 *"And Eli said to Samuel, 'Go lie down, and it shall be if he calls you, that you shall say, Speak, Lord, for your servant is listening.' …Then the Lord came and stood and called as at other times, 'Samuel! Samuel!' And Samuel said, 'Speak, for your servant is listening.'"*

2 Kings 6:17 *"Then Elisha prayed and said, 'O Lord, I pray, open his eyes that he may see.' And the Lord opened the servant's eyes and he saw; and behold, the mountain was full of horses and chariots of fire all around Elisha."*

Psa. 119:18 *"Open my eyes, that I may behold wonderful things from Your law."*

Isa. 42:20 *"You have seen many things, but you do not observe them; your ears are open, but none hears."*

Isa. 44:18 *"They do not know, nor do they understand, for he has smeared over their eyes so that they cannot see and their hearts so that they cannot comprehend."*

Jer. 5:21 *"Now hear this, O foolish and senseless people, who have eyes but do not see; who have ears but do not hear."*

Mark 8:18 *"Having eyes, do you not see? And having ears, do you not hear?"*

John 12:40 *"He has blinded their eyes and he hardened their heart, so that they would not see with their eyes and perceive with their heart and be converted and I heal them."*

Acts 28:27 *"For the heart of this people has become dull, and with their ears they scarcely hear, and they have closed their eyes; otherwise they might see with their eyes, and hear with their ears, and understand with their heart and return, and I would heal them."*

Rom. 11:8 *"God gave them a spirit of stupor, eyes to see not and ears to hear not, down to this very day."*

Rom. 11:10 *"Let their eyes be darkened to see not and bend their backs forever."*

2 Cor. 4:18 *"While we look not at the things which are seen, but at the things which are not seen; for the things which are seen are temporal, but the things which are not seen are eternal."*

Looking to See

Scripture places great emphasis on lifting our eyes and looking to see.

Exo. 3:2-6 *"The angel of the Lord appeared to him in blazing fire from the midst of a bush; and he looked, and behold, the bush was burning with fire, yet the bush was not consumed. So, Moses said, 'I must turn aside now and see this marvellous sight, why the bush is not burned up.' When the Lord saw that he turned aside to look, God called to him from the midst of the bush and said, 'Moses, Moses!' and he said, 'Here I am.' Then*

He said, 'Do not come near here; remove your sandals from your feet, for the place on which you are standing is holy ground.' He said also, 'I am the God of your father, the God of Abraham, the God of Isaac, and the God of Jacob.' Then Moses hid his face, for he was afraid to look at God.

Exo. 16:9, 10 "Then Moses said to Aaron, 'Say to all the congregation of the sons of Israel, come near before the Lord, for He has heard your grumblings.' It came about as Aaron spoke to the whole congregation of the sons of Israel, that they looked toward the wilderness, and behold, the glory of the Lord appeared in the cloud."

Josh. 5:13-15 "Now it came about when Joshua was by Jericho, that he lifted up his eyes and looked, and behold, a man was standing opposite him with his sword drawn in his hand, and Joshua went to him and said to him, 'Are you for us or for our adversaries?' He said, 'No; rather I indeed come now as captain of the host of the Lord.' And Joshua fell on his face to the earth, and bowed down, and said to him, 'What has my lord to say to his servant?' The captain of the Lord's host said to Joshua, 'Remove your sandals from your feet, for the place where you are standing is holy.' And Joshua did so."

1 Chron. 21:16 "Then David lifted up his eyes and saw the angel of the Lord standing between earth and heaven, with his drawn sword in his hand stretched out over Jerusalem. Then David and the elders, covered with sackcloth, fell on their faces."

Psa. 141:8 "For my eyes are toward You, O God, the Lord; in You I take refuge; do not leave me defenceless.

Isa. 8:17 "And I will wait for the Lord who is hiding his face from the house of Jacob; I will even look eagerly for Him."

Isa. 17:7 "In that day man will have regard for his Maker and his eyes will look to the Holy One of Israel."

Ezek. 8:4 "And behold, the glory of the God of Israel was there, like the appearance which I saw in the plain.

Ezek. 44:4, 5 *"...And I looked, and behold, the glory of the Lord filled the house of the Lord, and I fell on my face. The Lord said to me, 'Son of man, mark well, see with your eyes and hear with your ears all that I say to you concerning all the statues of the house of the Lord and concerning all its laws; and mark well the entrance of the house, with all exits of the sanctuary."*

Dan. 10:5-16 *"I lifted up my eyes, and looked, and behold, there was a certain man dressed in linen, whose waist was girded with a belt of pure gold of Uphaz. ...So I was left alone and saw this great vision; ...But I heard the sound of his words; ...Then behold, a hand touched me ...He said to me, 'O Daniel, man of high esteem, understand the words that am about to tell you and stand upright, for I have now been sent to you.' ...Do not be afraid, Daniel, ...When he had spoken to me according to these words, I turned my face toward the ground and became speechless. And behold, one who resembled a human being was touching my lips; ...'O my lord, as a result of the vision anguish has come upon me, and I have retained no strength."*

Zech. 4:2 *"He said to me, 'What do you see?' And I said, I see, and behold, a lampstand all of gold, with its bowl on top of it, and its seven lamps on it with seven spouts belonging to each of the lamps, which are on top of it."*

Acts 7:55 *"But being full of the Holy Spirit, he gazed intently into heaven and saw the glory of God, and Jesus standing at the right hand of God."*

Rev. 4:1 *"After these things I looked, and behold, a door standing open in heaven, and the first voice which I had heard, like the sound of a trumpet speaking with me, said, 'Come up here, and I will show you what must take place after these things.'"*

Rev. 6:8 *"I looked, and behold, an ashen horse; and he who sat on it had the name Death; and Hades was following with him. Authority was given to them over a fourth of the earth, to kill with sword, and with famine and with pestilence and by the wild beasts of the earth."*

Rev. 14:1 "*Then I looked, and behold, the Lamb was standing on Mount Zion, and with Him one hundred and forty-four thousand, having his name and the name of his Father written on their foreheads.*"

Rev. 14:14 "*Then I looked, and behold, a white cloud, and sitting on the cloud was one like a son of man, having a golden crown on his head and a sharp sickle in his hand.*"

Rev. 15:5 "*After these things I looked, and the temple of the tabernacle of testimony in heaven was opened.*"

"**He leads us on** by paths we did not know;

Upward He leads us, though our steps be slow,

Though oft we faint and falter on the way,

Though storms and darkness oft obscure the day;

Yet when the clouds are gone,

We know **He leads us on.**

He leads us on through all the unquiet years;

Past all our dreamland hopes, and doubts and fears,

He guides our steps, through all the tangled maze

Of losses, sorrows, and o'er clouded days;

We know his will is done;

And still **he leads us on.**"

www.ingramcontent.com/pod-product-compliance
Lightning Source LLC
Chambersburg PA
CBHW031144050726
47495CB00018B/837